ENDLING

ALSO BY MARIA REVA

Good Citizens Need Not Fear

ENDLING

Maria Reva

virago

VIRAGO

First published in the United States in 2025 by Doubleday,
a division of Penguin Random House LLC
First published in Great Britain in 2025 by Virago Press

1 3 5 7 9 10 8 6 4 2

A CIP catalogue record for this book
is available from the British Library.

Hardback ISBN 978-0-349-01271-1
Trade paperback ISBN 978-0-349-01272-8

Printed and bound in Great Britain by Clays Ltd, Elcograf S.p.A

Papers used by Virago are from well-managed forests
and other responsible sources.

Virago Press
An imprint of
Little, Brown Book Group
Carmelite House
50 Victoria Embankment
London EC4Y 0DZ

The authorised representative
in the EEA is
Hachette Ireland
8 Castlecourt Centre
Dublin 15, D15 XTP3, Ireland
(email: info@hbgi.ie)

An Hachette UK Company
www.hachette.co.uk

www.virago.co.uk

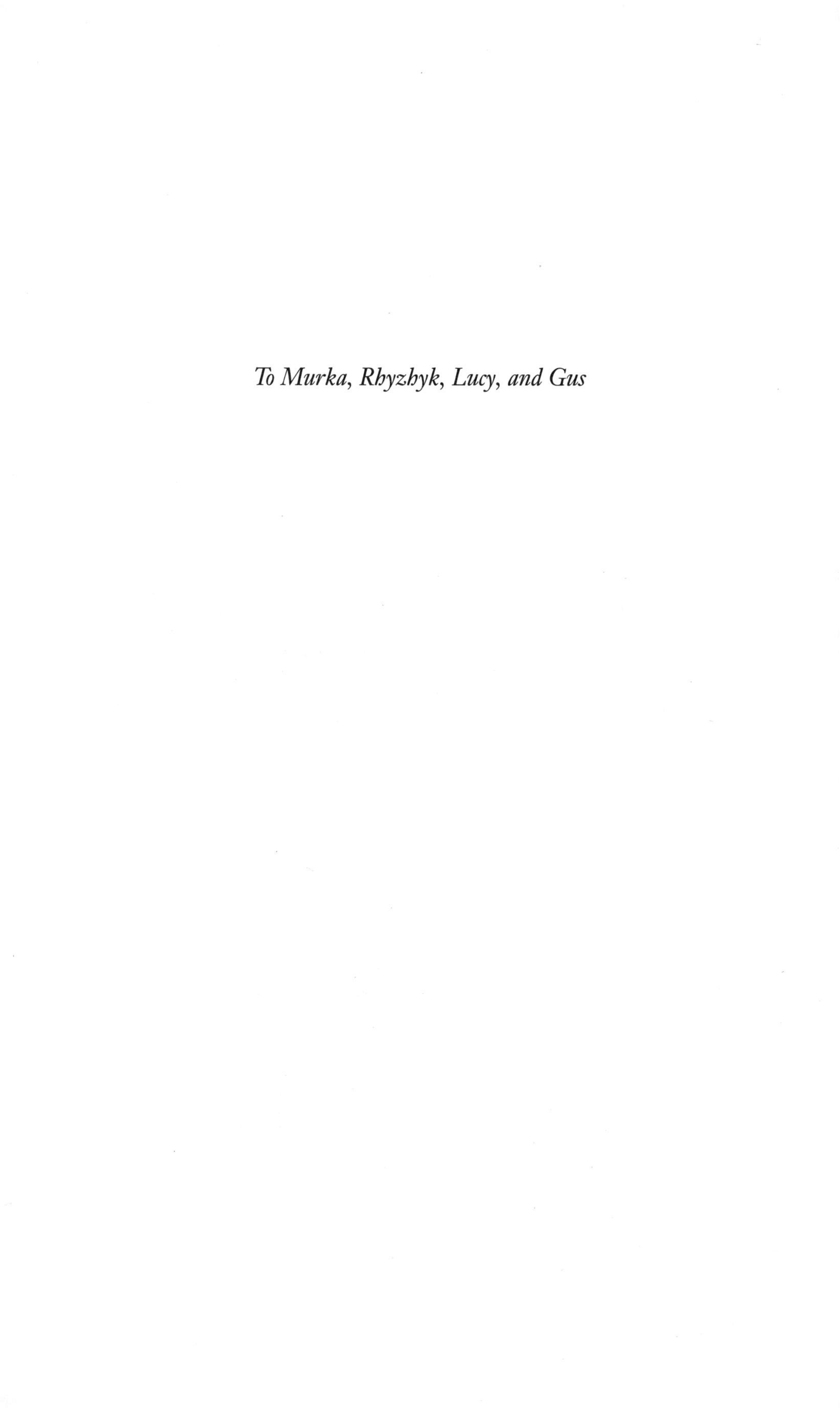

To Murka, Rhyzhyk, Lucy, and Gus

People don’t live history, they live their lives. History is a catastrophe that passes over them.

—Chus Pato

I’d rather go down in flames, quite frankly, than have a nice little book. I’d rather go down screaming in flames. You can quote me on that.

—Zsuzsi Gartner

PROLOGUE

IN THE CITIES, buildings still stood whole. Some new or freshly renovated, some worse for wear but functional, complete with floors, walls, ceilings. When a hand turned on a tap, water poured from it. A flick of a switch, and light flooded a room. The parks also lay whole, grass stretched uninterrupted. Residents lived and residents died, in balance. Animals too lived and died in balance, mostly inside the buildings; those who roamed the streets in search of their owners were few. Beyond the cities, fields. Yellow and brown, pockmarked by farmhouses, sliced by trenches for irrigation. Beyond the fields, sky. A sturdy, solid blue, like a freshly painted ceiling. Not much fell from it yet, the occasional bird. Once, a fragment of comet, catching the breaths of those who witnessed in terror the flash of light—but when it was over, they clapped at the miracle.

PART I

1

ANASTASIA, THE GIRL called herself. Achingly young—too young, thought Yeva, to be taking part in the romance tours. Yeva would be getting talked at by some bachelor, and from across the banquet room or yacht deck she'd notice the girl watching her intently, round blank face trained on her like a telescope dish. That face, normally flat and deadened, as if the girl had long ago checked out, twitched, tried to wink, send a signal to Yeva, now that the girl's handler had loosened her clutches. *Help.* Maybe the girl was being trafficked, who knew. Once, the girl followed her to the parking lot and watched as Yeva got into her trailer. She was probably longing to get in, too, be whisked away somewhere safe before her "interpreter" caught up with her, quick and officious, and yanked her away by the elbow.

Rumor had it the girl was into God. Of course she was, sad thing. The religious ones made the perfect victims, used to bowing under threat from above. In the past Yeva would have risen to the rescue, but she was done caring. All those earthly worries she used to have—mollusk conservation, romantic prospects, the Russian tanks amassing at the border and how no one believed anything would come of it except Yeva, who according to her family was always crying wolf and blowing everything out of proportion, prattling on about the collapse of this ecosystem or that, ruining all the fun, ruining, on behalf of barely there river turtles, the marriage agency's balloon release over the Dnipro—blah blah blah. None of it mattered anymore. Even Yeva was tired of Yeva.

How Yeva became involved with the romance tours: a blue-eyed blonde had approached her at a gas station as she was refueling her mobile lab. The woman had seemingly materialized out of nowhere. This was on the dusty outskirts of some backwater town after another expedition (a success: two gastropod survivors found). As Yeva watched the numbers tick up on the diesel pump gauge, her tank taking forever to fill, the woman chatted on about the weather. Then she told Yeva about an "opportunity" to get free headshots.

When Yeva asked what in hell she'd need headshots for, the stranger seemed taken aback, like Yeva had just turned down a free lottery ticket. She recovered quickly. "Pardon me, I hope you don't mind my saying so," the woman said in a low secretive voice (which surely was part of her script, too), "I just thought you might be an aspiring model."

Had Yeva's family sent the woman, in their latest matchmaking scheme? Had they stooped as low as that, plotting to send portraits of her to any viable suitor?

When the fuel pump clicked off, Yeva tore her credit card from its slot (the payment authorized, she saw with relief) and began her usual maintenance check of the mobile lab. Some idiot had graffitied FREE CANDY on the expanse of white on the trailer's side. Yeva swore under her breath, continued the check. Kneeling by the front wheel, she had already forgotten the woman when a chirping voice asked from above, "Nice RV. Are you on holiday?"

Yeva saw the way the high-heeled stranger peered at the piles of clothes strewn over the bench seat of the driver's cabin, the crumpled-up sleeping bag, the slimy yellowed mouth retainer on the dash. The woman's face sank with pity over Yeva's itinerant life.

The woman told her about a party at the hotel in town that night. Did she want to come?

Yeva climbed into the driver's seat, about to slam the door on the stranger.

"Free entry for the ladies. There's a thousand-dollar raffle." The woman emphasized, "USD."

That Saturday night was the first time Yeva had ever won anything. She'd stayed through the entire party, waiting for the winner to be announced at 2:00 a.m., tipping back free rosé at an empty corner table as more blue-eyed blondes in tight club dresses and stilettos wriggled around her to the thumping music. The hotel: self-consciously second-tier, the faded carpet patterned with crowns and the letters VIP. The wine tasted like acid reflux; back in that golden time, Yeva was still full of hope and cared what alcohol tasted like. There were a few men there, foreigners dressed like they'd just come from a ball game, accompanied by interpreters. Some of them tried to yell words at Yeva over the crackling loudspeakers beside her. Their interpreters gestured, urging Yeva to follow them to a quieter place: Photo booth? Outside? Anywhere but beside these earsplitting speakers? Yeva stayed in her spot, ignoring whatever this was—an afterparty of diplomats? A corporate retreat?—eyes on her phone in case of an alarm from her lab, until at last the hall went silent and a matronly woman in a powder-blue pantsuit stood at a tippy lectern, introduced herself by an ancient-sounding name, Efrosinia, and began rattling off the raffle numbers.

Before the romance tours, Yeva had relied on government and NGO grants, which had dwindled in recent years. Who wants to fund the research on functionally extinct species? People like Yeva are never the stars of environmental summits and galas, prattling on and on about yet another battle lost, yet another species gone down the chute. Donors only want to fund winners.

That evening, holding the raffle money in her hands, for the first time in her life Yeva felt like a winner. Later she suspected that the raffle was rigged in favor of newcomers to pull them into more of these weird parties, but winning felt good at the time. And one thousand USD got her far: a new multi-stage filtration and misting system, specialized full-spectrum lighting with automated dimming, a sanitization chamber for soil (secondhand, but still good), more realistic terrarium landscaping that included live moss.

Soon Yeva started going on dates with the foreigners. The work—though she'd never admit it to the whiny interpreters—was easy. She quickly understood that the marriage agency didn't expect her to actually marry any of the men it carted in from the West. Sure, a few women really were there to find love—"Needles," they were unofficially called. But then there was everyone else, the shining golden hay, just there to populate the parties, show up for a date or two, keep the bride-to-bachelor ratio high. Yeva didn't mind being the agency's shimmering bait, her headshot plastered all over their website. Let these men come here to look for their Needles in the hay. The hunt must be part of the thrill, she figured, what kept some men coming back tour after tour. Meanwhile, women like Yeva—nicknamed "Brides"—could also return tour after tour and, without bending any rules, make decent money. In fact, the agency endorsed the practice: any gifts ordered by bachelors through the agency—gym membership, cooking class, customizable charm bracelet—could be redeemed by the brides for cash from the agency offices. And most reliably, the hourly interpreter fee had to be split with brides after each date (this, with a great condescending sigh from the interpreters, as if they were being charitable, as if they were doing all the work). Even if the brides spoke English, which Yeva and many others did, the bachelors were not allowed to converse with the brides without these middle-women present. Translation apps on phones were also no-nos. What's less romantic than a lady and gentleman on a date, eyes glued to their phones? Translation apps drained transnational love of its mystique, Efrosinia and her assistants lamented. Yeva had heard of brides who went further than receiving and redeeming gifts, who outright scammed the men through kickbacks with overpriced restaurants, or through fake medical procedures they said they needed to fund, but in Yeva's estimation this wasn't worth the effort or the risk. She did fine just by showing up, date after date, racking up hours like in any other job.

Soon Yeva had refurbished her entire lab. New decontamination bath for foods introduced to the trailer, a backup generator, a solar panel for the summer months, upgraded software for alerting her phone whenever humidity, temperature, light levels rose or fell outside tolerance. She traveled around the country looking for survivors, knowing that when she ran low on funds she could dip into one of the many cities and towns that were part of the romance tours and top up. No more paperwork that ate into fieldwork, no more waiting for measly grants while species slipped through her fingers like sand.

(She should have been more careful, she knew. Should have waited to raise enough funds to establish a captive rearing lab with a dedicated staff, a stationary haven for gastropod populations while she conducted evacuations. She should have endured the slow grind of bureaucracy: applying for grants, collaborating with university labs, playing politics, and tiptoeing around the egos of the older researchers, many of whom still ascribed to an outdated Soviet-era taxonomy that didn't even recognize some of the most endangered species as distinct. If only there had been time. But she'd had to go rogue, haul the lab with her.)

The greatest challenge for Yeva during her dates with the bachelors: her phone. The constant pinging, the alarms, drove the interpreters crazy and drew side-eyes from the administrators during socials, but Yeva told herself that the interruptions made her look desirable to the men. Like she had a rich social life, countless friends pulling her in all directions, suitors knocking. She wanted to believe this herself. Whenever she had to run out in the middle of a date to adjust humidity levels in the lab or open another air vent, she'd invent an excuse. A work call from some normal job a normal person would have. A cousin in need of relationship advice. A baby—her own! (This last being the nuclear option: a way to end not only that evening's date but the possibility of future ones.) Never would the bachelors suspect what she was leaving them for: the bottomless needs of 276 snails.

Snails! There'd been a time when she would tell anyone who'd listen how amazing these creatures were.

How the many gastropod species have evolved to live anywhere on the planet, from deserts to deep ocean trenches. How they have gills to live in water, or have lungs to live on land—some, like the apple snail, possess one of each, to withstand both monsoons and droughts.

How some species can survive extreme temperatures, unsuitable for human life, with their highly reflective shells and the insulating properties of their spirals. How they can create a mucus seal between shell aperture and rock to minimize water evaporation, and can stay dormant for years before rains wake them up.

How a snail can possess both male and female parts and reproduce solo.

How the giant tritons can grow to up to a foot and a half, while some types of dot snails can fit through the eye of a needle.

How they represented, for the Mesoamericans, joy and rebirth, the shape of their shells the circle of life.

How some can crawl upside down along the surface of water, grabbing onto ripples of their own slime, or make rafts out of bubbles.

How some resemble medieval knights—shells reinforced with iron, soft flesh armored in thick metal plates—as they edge along toxic hydrothermal vents.

And yet, what did it matter now?

So what if every hour, another native Hawaiian snail perished at the jaws of the invasive wolfsnail?

So what if the tiny jelly-mantled Glutinous snail, once one of the most widespread snails in Europe, had been all but wiped out?

So what if every fifty-three hours, one of the most diverse animal groups on the planet lost yet another of its species?

Snails weren't furry or cute. They weren't interactive with humans.

Snails weren't pandas—those oversize bumbling toddlers that sucked up national conservation budgets—or any of the other charismatic megafauna, like orcas or gorillas. Snails weren't huggy koala bears, which in reality were vicious and riddled with chlamydia. Nor were snails otters, which looked like plush toys made for mascots by aquariums, despite the fact that they lured dogs from beaches to drown and rape them.

A crunch under the boot. A speck to flick off a lettuce leaf. Not much better than slugs. The genus name *gastropod* woefully uninspiring: stomach-foot. Dumb and slow. The woodland ones Yeva had been trying to save were not even colorful.

Snails were just that—snails.

On grant applications, before she self-funded through romance tours, Yeva wrote about the calcium cycle and the terrestrial mollusk's pivotal role in regulating it. About turkeys that, during egg gestation, deliberately sought out snails like vitamin pills. About the role of gastropods in deadwood decomposition. How, due to their low mobility and sensitivity to environmental changes, gastropods served as barometers of a biome's health. Birds and insects can fly, unwittingly lay eggs in outlying areas where their offspring can't survive, but snails stay in place. It's the snails that tell you which ravine to save, which patch of forest lies at the core of their own species alongside many others.

But that's not why Yeva loved them, not really. Snails could've been useless, purely ornamental, and she'd still have scoured every leaf and grass blade for them. She could spend hours watching them in their terrariums, hours while her own mind slowed, slowed, emptied. When she lifted her eyes, the world seemed separate from her, a movie in comical fast motion, something she could turn off.

During Yeva's first year working the romance tours, when bachelors asked about her day job and she was in a rare mood to divulge, she'd frame what she did as a rescue mission. She was plucking endangered snails from their shrinking habitats and reviving their populations in captivity. One day, she'd reintroduce them into ecologically protected zones (of which there were few, but Rome wasn't built in a day). She toured all around the country, including the self-proclaimed People's Republics of Donetsk and Luhansk, where the war puttered on. She evacuated survivors even if she didn't have room for them. (She had vowed never to repeat one of her early mistakes: once, she'd chosen not to rescue the dozen *Annilika severus* from their ravine at the base of the Carpathians, but by the time she came back for them, new terrarium at the ready, the ravine had been filled by a mudslide. She never saw another *A. severus* snail again.) And she witnessed just enough miracles to blind her with hope: two rare *Tordionus bazilikae* on an onion stalk sticking out of a dumpster, when she wasn't looking for them. Another time, a cluster of newborns at the edge of a military range. These early successes had to be signs—she was destined for this rescue mission. She and her charges would outpace environmental destruction. It wasn't impossible, after all. She'd steer her Noah's Ark to every nook and cranny of the country, no leaf unturned.

"A dangerous thing, early success," a bachelor told her during one date, describing his own investment ventures. A jackpot in his early twenties had led him to believe in his own so-called instincts until he hit financial ruin. But Yeva was hardly listening. Her interpreter had long ago wilted into her martini, and Yeva's eyes were glued to the terrarium cam on her phone (agency rules be damned). Two *Pacillum dulcis*, the only known surviving members of their kind, had been circling each other for the past six hours in courtship, and at last, one had stabbed the other with its calcareous dart. The other counterstabbed with its own dart. Any moment now, they would finally copulate. Within two weeks their population might balloon to fifty. Yeva would need more supplies.

Yeva needed to keep going on dates.

Sometimes, to the wrath of the interpreters and boredom of the bachelors, she felt inspired to talk about the minutiae of her work, the metrics she had to keep steady.

Once, a bachelor asked over dinner, "Ever tried eating them? Escargot?"

Yeva almost bit through her tongue.

A year into the romance tours, after the mobile lab was fully refurbished, Yeva had a little money to spare. She hired a teenager she'd spied graffitiing a bridge to paint a logo on the side of the vehicle: a green cross (like a red cross of an ambulance) and below it, two hands cupping a clump of dirt with a two-leaved sprout. The hands were cliché, she knew. They screamed environmental. Who, in real life, held dirt and a sprout in their hands like that? Any individual or nonprofit claiming the thinnest allegiance with the planet used that stupid picture. But she hadn't been able to think of an alternative. What was she going to ask the teenager to paint instead—a snail? She'd been ridiculed enough, by old lab mates at the university with loftier pursuits, by her family, who considered her homeless, by the internet at large (well, not personally, but she couldn't help but take it as such).

The internet ridicule had started with a question by Grass-Toucher89 on an online English-language forum: *What do you call a snail expert?*

The upvoted answers:

I thought this was the beginning of a joke.
A little disappointed it isn't.
Same here!
A Frenchman?
It's Steve, but his full name is Steven.
Here's a better question: What do you call a radio show about snails? A gastropodcast!
So-nailed it.

Of course Yeva had to get in there, give these clowns her five cents, slip in a comment about the term "gastropodologist"—how it was the most accurate but only the sticklers adopted it, while most experts preferred the broader term "malacologist" despite its inclusion of mollusks without backbones (clams, octopi, et cetera); "malacologist" was also the term endorsed by the Estuarine Mollusk Alliance, who, in their annual Musseling in on Biodiversity conference, pledged to be more inclusive of land snails. To which MadamePeanutButter responded: *This is fucking adorable*—which enraged her further, powering her five-hundred-word counter on the history of the (now outdated) term "helicologist" (*Helix* being a predominant genus for shelled land snail), concluding with the statement that, really, snail experts were a pacifist crew and you could call them many names, just not "conchologist," amateurs who collected shells on beaches in white linen pants and formed drum circles and disturbed the peace (and the calcium cycle). Yeva's comment kept being upvoted, overtaking all others—and that was when she began to suspect they were still making fun of her.

After that, she had the logo of the hands cradling a sprout painted on the side of her lab. From the outside, not a whiff of the malacological.

Begrudgingly, she also had a collapsible outdoor shower installed at the back of the lab after a diva interpreter refused to work with her, claiming she stank. Yeva justified the expense as an investment in more bachelor dates, which meant more money for snailing.

Two hundred and seventy-six specimens. Thirteen species, six of which were already considered extinct in the wild. Those were the numbers at the height of the mission. To think back on those numbers now! To remember what it felt like, to see populations stabilizing instead of shrinking! To shed the sad, humdrum mantle of eclipsazoologist!

(Eclipsazoology: the study of extinct animals, with "eclipse" originally meaning abandonment or downfall. Now that's what you call a snail expert, she wanted to add to the online fray—her last word—but held herself back.)

(*Eclipsazoology: not a widely accepted term*, some smart-ass would surely comment. *What you mean is paleontology*. But the latter connoted ancient life, fossils, mass extinction events humans had nothing to do with.)

Her lofty long-ago conservation mission made her laugh now. Her new mission was whittled down to a simple checklist:

1. Earn one more paycheck
2. Procure one canister of hydrogen cyanide and a wedding dress for burial
3. Climb into trailer, never wake up

It was a conservationist in Hawaii, extinction capital of the world, who'd helped her set up her lab. She'd reached out to him online after reading a profile in a malacological journal describing how he'd built a mobile rearing lab for three hundred native snail species. The article boasted double-page spreads of his charges—arresting glossy shells, their designs like blown-glass Christmas ornaments, so much better suited for public sympathy than Yeva's drab grayish specimens. There was a clear villain to the story: the invasive rosy wolfsnail—originally introduced by the Hawaii Department of Agriculture to control another previously introduced invasive snail—which followed native snails' slime and yanked them out of their shells with its jagged jaws. Yeva had marveled at the conservationist's tireless efforts, the decades he'd spent caring for his charges in his trailer, the exclosures he'd designed: patches of forest protected by special walls (too slippery for lizards and chameleons, too deep for rats to burrow, and at their tops, to ward off the final contenders, rosy wolfsnails, a spiny copper mesh and electric charge.)

Yeva and the conservationist texted back and forth for years. In English peppered with Latin (why not also resurrect a dead language while they were at it?), they shared data and snail care tips. Though they'd never admit to having favorites, two snails dominated their exchange: His, an eighteen-year-old *Achatinella spirita* named Jonah, a school tour celebrity who not only survived being eaten by a rat (he had the telltale gashes on his shell) but was found, in poetic justice, atop the carcasses of two rosy wolfsnails that had tried to eat each other; hers, a tree snail, preternaturally social, whose scraggly conical shell spiraled to the left instead of the right, rendering breeding impossible with 99 percent of his species. To an already decimated population Lefty was, biologically speaking, useless. She loved him all the more.

From the usual pings of her phone, which she couldn't turn off even when she slept, the conservationist's texts were a reprieve. A warm rock to lie on. The one soul, across hemispheres, who took her mission seriously but could also rib her about it. They joked about their monk-like lives, inseparable from their trailers as snails from their shells. They would die in those trailers, and the snails would crawl over their faces, but would not eat their faces, as cats might. Instead, the snails' rejuvenative slime would imbue their corpses with a youthful glow.

But their efforts would be worth it, they reminded each other. Some of the populations grew under their care and, even if it took decades, would surely draw back from the brink of extinction. There were signs that Hawaii's rosy wolfsnail population had peaked, was now cannibalizing itself. Ditto for humanity, the conservationist said. His and Yeva's charges would prevail. They'd adapt to ever-scorching climes, droughts, floods. They just needed time to do so in peace, without people around. Snails were, by definition, slow.

Yet for some species, it was too late. Sometimes the population numbers were too small to begin with (Yeva would return to the sites of their evacuations every quarter, scour every leaf and twig, looking for more survivors without success). Or Yeva and the conservationist couldn't crack the exact metrics necessary to replicate native habitats. Or they did crack the code and their charges slithered around their tanks happily but refused to mate.

Sometimes the texts contained no words, only numbers:

00:01
04:13
17:45

Or, if it happened during a four-hour sleeping shift:

23:00–03:00

A time stamp. More precisely, a death stamp. The moment a species vanished.

This was also the moment when Yeva and the conservationist needed each other most. For comfort, for reassurance that, despite setbacks, their labs still offered the snails a higher chance of survival than the wild. They needed each other to bear witness, because the rest of the world didn't. The news might get published in a niche journal or website, but most of the time media outlets ignored these humble victims of the Earth's sixth mass extinction. Meanwhile, Najin and Fatu, the last northern white rhinos (mother and daughter), were the belles of the extinction ball. They lived round the clock under the protection of armed guards. Tourists visited from all over the world to pet them, then cry in their cars. When the rhinos passed gas together, *The New York Times* called it "the rarest symphony in the world."

Yeva remembered the first time she'd had to record an extinction time stamp. It wasn't always easy to tell if snails were dead; they'd often seal themselves in their shells with mucus as though for hibernation, then shrink away inside, leaving the world quietly. The weightless shells, exit still barred, taunted her like a disappearing act, a last magic trick. This first endling, though, announced the *Gula mirabilus* extinction with a loud thunk when it fell from its terrarium wall. Not an abnormal occurrence in itself, the falling: snails fell from their surfaces surprisingly often. But Yeva had sensed something was off and tried to reattach the endling. It wouldn't hold. She stroked its buttery yellow underside, willing it to retract into its shell. This species had been known for their loud chewing. On windless nights, when Yeva lay awake feeling crushed by the weight of her work, their raspy gnawing calmed her. She imagined herself surrounded by an entire forest of these vigorous eaters. One day, she told herself on those nights, surely she would be.

She did not know how long she'd sat cradling the limp little body in her palm, paralyzed by an indescribable feeling, as if she was swelling and shrinking at the same time. A twinge of awe, to be the one to witness an evolutionary branch millions of years in refinement be snipped off; a twinge of power, to have played a hand in it just by having been born human. But mostly, she felt tiny and dumb and powerless.

A year later, Yeva was driving to Polesia when she received another time stamp—not for one of the conservationist's endlings, but for one of his colleagues', out in Alaska. She pulled over to the side of the road as soon as she saw the digits flash on her phone. The endling had been a polar peeper frog with oversize childlike eyes, named Tutan—Tlingit for "hope." On the eve of his death, Tutan had sung for the first time in years, calling for a mate that did not exist. The conservationist forwarded Yeva a recording.

"Do you hear him?" he texted.

Yeva thought she could pick out the occasional chirp from the scratchy recording. "Loud and clear," she lied. She felt a small pang of resentment: the endling's last moments on Earth, and it pined over not getting laid. Of course, this was normal. If anything, endlings should pine all the louder for the sake of their species. Yeva was the abnormal one.

"Isn't Tutan's song beautiful?" he texted.

At least gastropods yearned in silence, Yeva thought but did not say.

("Wouldn't it be more humane to put them out of their misery?" a notary from Illinois once asked during a date, when Yeva made the mistake, again, of discussing her work. His words were the cruelest she'd ever heard. Finish the endlings off, just because they couldn't fuck? The conservationist never would have said such a thing. He seemed the only one who understood what they were doing, didn't see it as pointless. Or maybe he did, but he kept at the task anyway.)

The conservationist was typing, ellipses bouncing on her phone screen. Yeva rummaged around in her glove box for a pack of cigarettes, lit one, took a long drag. She shouldn't, she knew. She had to keep herself healthy, but each death stamp hit her harder and harder in those days. Populations were slipping. She glanced again at the screen.

"Te amo," he'd typed, in Latin.

At first, Yeva thought he'd made a mistake. Or perhaps she misunderstood this dead language? But it was such a simple phrase, loud and clear.

He video-called her immediately. A rarity, given the expense, the data charges. She picked up. From twelve thousand kilometers away, from remote Hawaiian forests to deep Ukraine, his smile met hers. His raven-black hair, his neat goatee. His very existence was a miracle, Yeva knew. His great-grandmother had been a so-called picture bride from Japan, matched by family to an Osakan tradesman in Kauai. But when she'd stepped off the ship into the dockside wedding ceremony that awaited her, when she'd seen how much older her about-to-be husband really was, she'd stepped right back onto the ship and locked herself in a crew room. It was the husband's younger, stylish cousin who enticed her off the ship, and so she'd stayed and married him instead.

The conservationist's kind, puffy-eyed face said, "I want to come meet you."

No, no, no. They needed to backtrack. "Nice to meet you, too," she babbled, pretending not to understand.

"I mean I want to visit you. *Meet* you. In the flesh."

In the flesh. The phrase made her wince. She forced a laugh, hoping he'd made a joke, but he kept talking, making plans. He confessed that he'd been thinking this through for months. It was risky, but he could do it. He'd been training an intern who could hold down the fort at the lab. He couldn't be away long, of course, only a couple of days—he'd be hopping on the plane and hopping right back on the return flight the next day, and he'd be horribly jet-lagged in addition to the usual sleep deprivation from the nightly lab alarms, but they'd finally meet face-to-face. Wouldn't that be nice?

It would. Yet she mumbled something about bad reception, hung up. That was the last time she responded to his texts and time stamps. She willed herself to forget his name.

Later, Yeva told herself she'd cut things off with the conservationist because she didn't want him to leave his wards—she wasn't going to be responsible for a mass extinction event in Hawaii—but deep inside, she knew there was another reason. She'd imagined their future together, and it didn't head anywhere good. She'd greet him at the airport. They'd run at each other, collide in a desperate embrace, a moment of pure bliss. They'd talk long into the night reaching into each other's souls, which should be enough, but somehow never was for anyone but her. Inevitably, with anyone she'd ever loved, the equation never changed:

I have genitals.
You have genitals.
Let's mash them together.

Once, before the romance tours, on the eve of Yeva's thirtieth birthday, her mother had sat her down, plied her with tea and fat-free chocolate babka, taken a deep breath, and announced she knew what Yeva was. "One of the lesbians."

This was okay, mother informed daughter, because lesbians, too, could have children. In fact, they could almost lead normal lives so long as they kept their heads down, stayed in the big cities, abstained from the rainbow parades, didn't proselytize.

Before this, her mother had given Yeva special vitamins. A vaginal dilator. Offered to pay for hormone tests. Made every effort to answer the question: Why wasn't Yeva out there, coupling? Yeva, the beauty of the family, her mother always said. Somewhere under the cargo pants and vests and pilled fleece sweaters, under the clutter of pockets and zippers and clasps and the "fieldwork" baubles that clattered from them: a lady. Legs, hips, waist, bust, everything where it should be and in just the right amounts. And that hair! (Inherited from her mother, who else?) Normally Yeva kept her waves balled up at her nape, strangled with a telephone cord tie, but they possessed an unseemly power when let loose. During her visits to her parents' home between expeditions, after spending hours collapsed in the bathtub, then on the chaise longue on the ground-level balcony, wrapped in a short robe, her freshly washed mane would rise from her shoulders, thick, black, and glistening as tar. It would stun passersby, who'd press their faces against the glazed glass of the balcony barrier.

Yeva, who never had so much as a boyfriend. Yeva, whose beautiful eggs promised beautiful children but were shriveling with each passing day.

She sighed, set down her teacup. She had chocolate smeared across her chin, which her mother kept herself from wiping off with her thumb. "I'm not gay."

"It's okay," her mother insisted. After all the effort to make herself accepting, here was her daughter, not accepting that the mother was accepting. "I've already talked to your father. He needs time."

Yeva's words came slowly. "You know how there are some people out there, people who . . ."

Her mother didn't like where this was going.

Yeva tried again. "People who like both men and women."

Her mother closed her eyes. She was trying, trying her hardest to expand her mind to fit such people. There was even a word for them. She didn't understand them herself, but with time could grow to tolerate them, if these were her daughter's people. Friends, at least—her daughter had so few. In fact—here the mother's heart leapt—maybe this was actually good news. She'd gotten her daughter all wrong. Maybe, if Yeva liked both men and women, she was out there having double the sex of a normal person but felt so bad about it she didn't tell her mother—that was why she'd been so secretive. And double sex (yes, let's assume whatever it was women did together counted as sex) was still better than no sex. Even this, she could grow to accept.

"I'm the opposite," Yeva said. "I like neither."

Her mother's eyes snapped open. "Neither what?"

"Men nor women."

Her mother threw her head back and laughed, but Yeva kept a straight face. Steadying her breath, her mother licked her thumb and wiped that smear off her daughter's chin, the gesture automatic. Yeva scrunched her face and drew away, just as she'd done as a child.

"That's impossible," her mother assured her.

Yeva said nothing.

"My dear, you just haven't found the right one."

"Oh, I have." A strange smile spread across Yeva's face. "I've found the right none." She broke into a hollow laugh.

Was it all one big joke? Yeva's years ticking by? The grandparents, uncles, aunts, cousins pestering her, the mother, with questions? If only Yeva had been born ugly—no one asked Cousin

Leeda why *she* was still single. No, her daughter had to look like this.

It wasn't natural, someone like Yeva, all alone.

Whatever was wrong with her daughter, whatever she wasn't saying, it was even worse than her mother had thought.

06:58
12:15
23:01

The time stamps kept coming, long after Yeva had stopped responding to the conservationist's calls and texts. And they were the hardest to ignore.

10:00–14:00

She wondered if the conservationist was making up the time stamps to try to get her to respond—could that many species really be disappearing so quickly?—but she never took the bait. Still, she felt terrible. Yet another person who'd turned away from his plight. She wanted to ask, which endling was it this time? Surely not Jonah, whom she'd grown partial to herself, who despite his old age seemed so spritely in the videos? She hated imagining the conservationist in his trailer all by himself, stowing another tiny body in the death cabinet. She yearned to reach out to him and—what, exactly?

Yeva had "dated" before. Her mother may not have known it, Yeva herself may not have known it, not right away, but there were witnesses who could attest to this fact.

There was that soft-spoken boy in high school who claimed she'd already been his girlfriend for three months by the time he introduced her as such to his parents. "We've *held hands*, Yeva," he'd said, incredulous at her surprise. "We've *kissed*."

That freckled girl in first year of university, who'd wait for her after class to make out behind the crab apple bushes. But the girl insisted she was only doing it as practice before she met a man, and how could Yeva not help out a friend?

And when Yeva was twenty-one, puttering around her grandparents' dacha between summer semesters, there'd been that boy who trailed her through the swamps. He was willowy and mostly wore green, and so tended to blend in with the scenery. When she loaded herself in her grandparents' canoe, he'd already be sitting up front. When she shoveled fresh cedar chips into the outhouse, he'd hang around passing bucketfuls, like he had nothing better to do. She didn't mind him tailing her, even enjoyed it, and soon they spent most of their hot humid days together. One night, as she scratched away at the many mosquito bites spotting her arms and legs, the boy himself sat still as a gryphon. He was immune to mosquitoes, he told her. He offered to cure her itchiness once and for all. He knew a trick. The trick was to take off all your clothes and lie in the swamps, let the insects take you for a night.

"That sounds like hell," she said.

"After you heal up, you won't feel another bite."

Soon afterward, there they were, naked in the fields, every insect of the swamps upon her, and he too was upon her, pumping away. She'd given him the signal, a hand on his moonlit thigh, thinking this was as good a time as any to finally dispense with her virginity. And most important, to distract from the mewling in her ears, the pinpricks all over her body. His penis stung her at first, before a drab numbness took over. So this is it, she thought. What all the fuss is about, what all the women's magazines gossip about in the grocery store aisles.

As he panted above her, gasping for God, she waited for something to happen. For a chasm to open within her, yielding new wisdom, a new state of being, a key to the human condition.

"Oh, honey," a classmate consoled her, when the new semester began. "That's just the first time. It gets better, I promise."

It didn't.

How she tried! Once, while high. On a moving train. In a public park. With different orifices. Using pheromone creams.

The definition of insanity is doing the same thing over and over and expecting different results, Einstein might have said. (But probably didn't. It was one of the many unverifiable quotes men at bars loved to throw at her when they found out she was studying to be a *scientist*, to show they knew a thing or two about science, too.) But she did feel like she was going insane, enduring trial after trial, reconfiguring sex this way and that with the same result. Or nonresult. If, at the very least, the act repulsed her, repulsion was still a feeling, something she could work with, massage over and over in her hands until it warmed and mellowed, like plasticine, into desire.

For a while, she blamed the mosquito "trick." The willowy boy had been right—after that night in the swamps, when her welts healed, her skin never reacted to mosquitoes again—but something else must have happened to her that night, some side effect of the mosquito trick. Maybe, just as her body was cracking open, transcending from virginity to that other state—that grown-up state, where one engages in regular intercourse and even enjoys it, like flossing teeth or buffing shoes—all that insect spit flooded her blood, numbed her like a shot of pentobarbital. Maybe, that night fundamentally broke her.

Of course, this was a ridiculous theory. Yet every time her mother tried to set her up with neighbors' sons, or an aunt slipped her a viciously pink vibrator, or an uncle offered to introduce her to a nice friend of a friend who also happened to be a therapist—when each intervention failed to stir anything in her, Yeva remembered that night.

Her mother's theory: The Internet was to blame. The Internet overwhelmed young people with dating choices. The original Yeva, biblical Eve, had no such choice. God put her in front of the fact of Adam, and that was that.

"Didn't she cheat on him with the snake?"

"But it wasn't with the snake that she created all of humanity."

"Have you seen humanity lately?"

"My daughter, ever the sunbeam."

"Take a bite of the apple yourself, watch the news once in a while."

By the time she had reached her third year of doing the romance tours, the way in which Yeva spoke of her work changed. She wasn't running a rescue mission for gastropods after all. She was finding fewer and fewer survivors, and the populations she'd previously evacuated had dwindled in their terraria. She wished she could shake the answer out of her charges, find out what precisely they needed, how she could help them. Even her *Achatina terrestrium*, which could self-reproduce, wasn't budging, as if waiting for the real deal of copulation, another slimy body against its own.

"It's not your fault," she imagined the conservationist saying. His low, dry voice, which still lulled her mind in dark moments. "We all perish, eventually."

Now, when a bachelor asked about her job, she told him she was running a hospice. They'd all nod sympathetically, change the subject.

In Yeva's fifth year of the romance tours, two tragedies occurred in her trailer, both Yeva's fault.

The first was a contaminated lettuce leaf. Or so she suspected, afterward. The fungal carnage was quick: populations halved in a matter of days. Hardest hit were the more social species, the ones who'd held the greatest chance of recovery. (Mercifully, Lefty was spared, though of course his species still had no chance.) Each of the remaining 147 snails had to be quarantined in a separate jar, an impossible feat in her cramped trailer. Yeva sped to her parents' apartment in Kharkiv, parked her trailer outside, enlisted every available canning jar in their building. She barely slept, checking on each snail for signs of infection. Meanwhile, her parents nagged at her.

Mother: "So this is how you've been spending your time? Collecting garden snails?"

Father: "Anya's niece collected june bugs in matchboxes, but *she* grew out of it."

What came first, a nosy neighbor wanted to know: Yeva not having a life, or Yeva living in a trailer? Did her nomadism keep her from meeting someone, or was it a convenient excuse not to try?

Yeva could've slept on the foldout in her childhood room. Instead, she opted for sleeping in the trailer, her one true home, where she could sip ethanol straight from the vial to knock herself out for a few hours at a time. It was the only way she could sleep.

What came first, she would wonder later: the sipping, or the slipups in the lab? When, a few weeks later, the software controlling misting levels bugged out, could Yeva have prevented it? Her phone must have lit up with alarms, but she'd slept through them all. When she came to that afternoon, head throbbing, a terrarium had been flooded. Its entire population of five adults and two hatchlings lay inert on the bottom, unattached to any surface. She'd taken care of the adults for four years before they'd finally begun to breed. She tried not to think of this as she placed the lost species in a jar of formaldehyde and stowed it in the chilled death cabinet—research protocol for all casualties, to figure out what went wrong, as though the culprit weren't obvious here.

Yeva never got over this loss.

She resumed her cross-country expeditions, but not for very long. More populations dwindled. More branches of evolution dried up. Yeva stopped trusting herself with the endlings. The smallest mistake could mean extinction, another time stamp to record in her journals. If she hadn't plucked members of a species from their bush, she tortured herself, they'd still be out there, alive.

"Don't be so sure. That bush could have burned in a wildfire," the conservationist might have consoled her, if she hadn't cut him off. She couldn't remember his face anymore, but she wanted his voice again, for that voice to curl around her like snail shells curl around their soft, vulnerable bodies. Soon he'd go silent in her mind, too. No more dreams, hauntings.

For the past two years, after she'd stopped speaking to him, Yeva had traveled around the country with a reverse mission: instead of collecting snails, she restituted them. Sometimes their homes would still be there—the exact bush or tree still tagged with its bright blue ribbon; sometimes a swath of empty land greeted her, cleared for construction or burned down by a wildfire or, if in the East, cratered by shelling. She'd find a new spot close by, release the snails, and hope for the best, telling herself that her charges would fare better without her. As her trailer emptied of life, she drank more. Since she wasn't accountable to anyone anymore, who was going to stop her?

Now, if a bachelor asked about what she did for a living, she'd answer, voice cracking: "I kill snails. Or, used to."

They'd nod in approval. "Pest control. Good line of work."

2

MAY YOU FIND the One," the moonfaced girl greeted Yeva. The girl's eyes darted around the hotel parking lot, no doubt waiting for her "interpreter" to find her. It was the second time she'd approached Yeva.

"May you find the One," Yeva greeted back, automatically. She was in the middle of hooking up some newly bought hydrogen cyanide to the lab's exterior hatch. There were simpler ways to go—she didn't have to fill an entire trailer with noxious gas—but in her last act, why not allow herself a bit of flair? A bit of poetry? She'd die the way she'd lived, inside her trailer, her shell, like all those snails who'd died—were still dying, all around the world—curled inside theirs.

"I need a favor," the girl said.

Of course she did. In her heavy makeup the girl looked even younger up close, like a child playing dress-up.

"That trailer of yours," the girl began.

"I don't have a trailer."

The girl pointed right behind Yeva, eyeing her as if Yeva were drunk, which admittedly she was, but only a little.

"That there is a mobile lab," Yeva corrected. Yeva did call it a trailer herself, but the kid hadn't earned the informality.

"How many people fit into it?"

Three hundred snails, Yeva wanted to say, though that was pushing capacity. But people? "I have no idea. Why?"

The girl didn't answer. She was surveying the lab with her dark-penciled eyes, like she was seeing through the metal walls, like she'd already arrived at the answer to her own question and it satisfied her. "Ever rent it out for a day or two?"

"Why would I do that?"

"Vacation."

A lie, and an insulting one at that. Yeva felt herself straighten, sober up. "My lab wasn't made for joyrides. You'd need a special license." She spoke of the dangerous potential of the chemicals inside, the sensitivity of its software systems, how the lab was worth hundreds of thousands of dollars, how it was flammable in the wrong hands.

The girl finally blinked. "Flammable. Like, more so than a standard vehicle?"

Standard vehicle? What kind of child talked like that?

"Is that handler of yours putting you up to this?"

"My what?"

"The one who *interprets* for you."

"Sol? That's just my sister."

Her own sister. The situation was worse than Yeva had thought. It was tragic, really, the trafficked girl now trafficking others. Yeva checked into her depths, probed herself for any ounce of caring left. None. A relief. "I'm not helping you smuggle other women across borders."

The girl tipped her head sideways in confusion, then laughed. Or imitated a person laughing, poorly. "Is that what you think I'm doing?"

"Why don't you enlighten me, then."

She was silent a moment. "If I tell you, you'd be implicated."

"I'm already implicated."

The girl began walking away.

"I'm phoning the hotline," Yeva called after her, despite herself.

The girl came back. "Please don't phone the hotline."

"It may seem impossible now," Yeva said, willing herself, for once in her life, to shut up, "but there's a way out." At least, that was what the administrators promised in their wooden tones at every induction session. They were mandated to disclose help hotlines to participants in case anyone saw suspicious activity, any bride in danger.

The girl sighed. Scrunched up her face in thought. She was so new at all this. And so thin. It occurred to Yeva that the girl had been getting thinner every tour. "It's the bachelors. That's who I'm taking. A full hundred."

This, certainly, Yeva hadn't been expecting. She asked, slowly, "And where is it you're taking them?"

"A romantic getaway."

"This is through the agency?"

"Doesn't matter. It would only be for a night or two." She added, "You'd get the trailer back. Just don't tell anyone. It's very exclusive, hush hush." Yeva caught Efrosinia's gossipy lilt in the girl's voice, like the girl was trying to mimic her, and this made Yeva feel all the more queasy. She had heard of this kind of thing—a bachelor lured into a secluded spot by his date (an empty park, or his date's supposed apartment), getting mugged by waiting thugs. But one hundred bachelors, all at once? Maybe the girl was in graver trouble than Yeva had thought, the pawn of an extensive crime ring. She really should call the hotline, but did she want to get pulled into yet another petty earthly worry, when she was so close to leaving it all behind?

Yeva shut the hatch over the gas canister. "Tell your handlers my lab isn't for rent."

"I told you, I have no handlers." The girl raised her chin. "I answer to no one, not even my mother. Do you know who my mother is?" This sounded like a threat. The girl seemed on the verge of naming this supposedly scary, infamous mother, then held herself back. She sighed. "Thank you for your consideration."

"No need to thank me. Zero consideration." Yeva smiled.

Before turning to go the girl smiled in response, as if she were seeing through Yeva now, too.

3

THREE DAYS EARLIER, before Nastia knew Yeva would be useful to her, Nastia had stood in silence among the other brides-to-be in the hotel banquet hall, waiting for the men. It was Valentine's Day. The agency had advertised the ten-day itinerary as Extra Lux, promised Double the Romance, but the tour began the way it always did. The men's induction session, held on the hotel's rooftop solarium, was running late. The leather of two hundred stilettos creaked as the women shifted their weight. Above Nastia, a French wire chandelier swayed lightly, as if from an underground tremor or an approaching mob. She steadied her breath, watched the chandelier's plastic candles flicker in unison.

Valentine's Day. The day she'd been waiting for for the past eight months, but not because of any romance. Today was the day by which her mother had promised to return to her and her sister, Sol. Their mother had disappeared eight months ago, just as Nastia was finishing her last year of high school, saying she needed to lie low for a bit, what with the outstanding charges against her and her certainty that the secret police from Yanukovych's days in power still followed her. She didn't explain why she'd chosen Valentine's Day as the deadline for her return, but she didn't need to. It was exactly Iolanta Cherno's style to plot her splashy reentry into the public eye with an anti-marriage-industry stunt on the day of romance, a day when couples placidly kissed on the Lovers' Bridge in Mariinskyi Park and latched to its rails stainless-steel locks embossed with their names and promises such as *Always Forever.*

The woman beside Nastia fidgeted with the big heart-shaped sticker on her chest, peeled off the pointy tip. Tampering with the sticker was a Big No-No, Efrosinia always warned—doing so risked compromising the custom scannable code below your name. This woman standing next to Nastia, with her tight curls and overrouged cheeks, must be new. When she leaned toward Nastia, perfectly lined lips about to part, Nastia stepped away. The agency discouraged the women from speaking to one another, sororizing. The more frosty to each other, the more they appeared to be in competition, the better, and Nastia had to look like she was playing by their rules.

Nastia's own sticker read *Anastasia B.* The last initial stood for a fake name. She couldn't use her real name and risk being banned from the tours because of an association with her mother, but that wasn't the only reason. A fake name made Nastia feel as though this was all just playacting, like she could break character at any moment, drop out of the game.

She'd been adamant about keeping her first name, though. When the bachelors heard the name Anastasia, they thought about Russian royalty—about the Duchesse who'd vanished by the time the White Army reached her family, having either been murdered or escaped. A Disney movie about her, and at least five women who'd cropped up in the West years after the disappearance, claiming to be her—the name meant "resurrection," after all. The fact that Nastia wasn't Russian didn't matter: to the bachelors, close enough. A Ukrainian was basically a knockoff Russian, the online bachelor forums said. And most important, while being exotic and enigmatic, the name was still easy to pronounce.

If the brides absolutely had to address each other, they were to adhere to the names on their heart stickers. No nicknames or pet names among brides who already knew each other outside the tours. No Nastia for Anastasia, Khrystyna for Ekaterina, Ksyusha for Oksana. No Manya, Mariyka, Marusia, Masha, Mashuta, Mashunya, Mashulya, Mashenka, Manyunya for Maria. The way a Slavic name can bend and fold in countless forms was, Efrosinia warned during the women's induction session, deeply confusing to the Westerner. "So, stick to the stickers."

"What about the interpreters?" Nastia had asked months ago, during her first tour.

"What about them?"

"They didn't get stickers." She regretted saying this immediately.

Nastia felt a gentle hand on her arm. "Don't worry about their names," the fellow bride whispered. Her long, shimmery eyelashes looked like a butterfly about to take flight. "Just pretend they aren't there."

The women's induction session, earlier that evening, had been held in a windowless conference room. By now Nastia could recite Efrosinia's speech herself. The administrator, matronly in her lavender pantsuit, would always begin by reeducating the participants about international dating, saying how mainstream media and society at large didn't understand these women's decision to make a radical lifestyle change. How terms like "mail-order bride" and "bride buyers" were outdated, sexist. "Romeo Meets Yulia is a modern company," Efrosinia lectured. "A boutique matchmaker. One of the world's greatest love stories made into reality. We believe in reaching across public prejudice in the name of love and destiny."

They were to call the men "bachelors."

Themselves: "brides-in-waiting" or, more affirmingly, "brides."

But mostly, the agency simply referred to them as "girls." That's what some of them still were—baby-cheeked, blinking in bewilderment under the banquet room lights at Efrosinia and her assistants, who fussed over them. A few wore floor-length high school graduation gowns, their modest pearl earrings probably gifts from their mothers or (now ex-) boyfriends. Nastia herself figured among the youngest participants—just six months over the minimum age of eighteen—but already felt decades deep into the industry's murky depths.

"Think of us as the fairy godmother you've always wished you had," Efrosinia would say, referring to her agency. "In just seven days, each and every one of you could meet your Romeo and embark on a new life." She'd scan the conference room magnanimously, her gray eyes sweeping in every bride, even the rare few in their forties or with children at home or who were not quite height-weight proportional.

Occasionally, her gaze would linger on Nastia. By now, Efrosinia didn't seem surprised to see her back, tour after tour. Efrosinia had stopped assuring her that she would find someone soon, that every pot has its lid. Nastia wondered which she was supposed to be: the pot or the lid. If the pot, Nastia imagined herself hollow and filled with light, the lid sliding over her like an eclipse, everything going dark. She preferred to imagine herself as the lid, the one doing the eclipsing.

The marriage agencies Nastia and her sister had registered with at first, before Romeo Meets Yulia, had been nicer. The bachelors more soft-spoken, the hotels fancier, with vaulted ballrooms and iron historical plaques written in English, the workers in these places power-washing engine oil off driveways and smiling at Nastia placidly, as if she were a paying guest. But she preferred Romeo Meets Yulia, with its worn veneer of respectability. Every time she pulled on a tight dress, participated in icebreaker games like Capture the Skirt Hem, every time she let a bachelor thumb an eyelash off her cheek (planted there by Sol) and tell her to make a wish, she wished for one thing only: that her mother could see Nastia now, what she'd turned into, and that her blood would turn cold.

What had Nastia looked like before the tours? She could hardly remember. Maybe it pained her to reminisce about that lost version of herself, like recalling a dead sister.

A bowl cut, rat-brown hair—she remembered that.

A paunch?

Thighs that must have rubbed together, her old jeans threadbare in those spots. If she once had muscles on her arms, no one would guess it now: they'd long since withered away without a trace.

It was the mundane things that Nastia missed most about her former self: climbing stairs without getting winded, standing up without getting a head rush. Now, the most impressive things Nastia found about her new body—her Anastasia body—were its half-valiant attempts to keep itself alive: how Anastasia's hand would reach for a chicken skewer without Nastia noticing it; how, as Nastia pressed a napkin to her mouth to spit out a half-chewed cheeseball, Anastasia had already swallowed three.

On the rare occasions she happened to see classmates from school—they'd moved on to bigger, better things, studying in grand lecture halls across Ukraine and abroad—they told her she looked tired, haggard. They asked if she was coming down with something.

Even the other brides sometimes remarked on her wraithlike look. "Hyperthyroidism?" one of the brides had asked her during the previous tour, jealous.

Now, at last, the banquet room doors swung open.

But no mother appeared, not yet.

No storm of angry women, her mother at the helm, wearing flower wreaths and trailing silk ribbons, ripping off their clothes to reveal naked skin marked with black block-letter slogans like war paint: UKRAINE IS NOT A BROTHEL. SEXPATS GO HOME. And before they were dragged off by security, screaming girlishly, the moment would come, the one Nastia had fantasized about hundreds of times: Iolanta Cherno's eyes landing on her daughter. Newly pretty Nastia, new long blond hair, the kind of girl she would have recruited to her protest troupe, the kind of girl who looked good naked, who was made for sexy press photos. Except, of course, that Nastia was on the other side now, the wrong one, the side of the marriage industry.

From behind the banquet room doors, just like every other time, the bachelors filed in.

Was Nastia disappointed? Relieved?

It was only noon, after all. Another twelve hours left in the day, and an infinite number of ways her mother could reappear. The TV monitors could switch to breaking news about her, or all at once cellphone screens might brighten, begin to ring like sirens.

Nastia willed herself to focus on the men. There were around fifty, half the usual number. Over the last month, foreigners had been draining out of Ukraine, urged to do so by their governments in light of the supposedly larger threat, the Russian buildup at the border. As a result, this romance tour promising Double the Romance was half-price.

Most of the men had opted for suits and ties, but there were a few outliers in jeans and button-ups. Unlike the brides, who mostly looked cast from the same mold—measurements of 36-24-36, as listed on their online profiles, long, thin fawn limbs (the women the agency took in to appear "body diverse" and appeal to "eclectic tastes" were rare)—the men's shapes varied. Scrawny, round, muscled, top-heavy as bulldogs. Many silver-haired, or bald, their freshly shaved heads glistening under the lights like waxed fruit. As they chatted among themselves, Nastia saw the men cast glances across the room. No doubt they had bonded on the charter bus that took them from town to town. Sol had told Nastia that the bachelors who already knew each other for years called themselves "veteran brothers," reminisced about previous tours as though they were military ones. Nastia could tell they were nervous, even the confident ones. Sweat slid down necks into stiff collars, seeped from underarms. Nastia had heard of men who drained their savings accounts to be here, took out loans or monthly financing plans. Their one shot at happiness, their investment, and only ten days to see a return. The TV monitors on the walls boasted wedding and honeymoon photos of past couples, proving that it was indeed possible.

Yet no one approached. The no-man's-land between brides and bachelors held.

At any moment, a side door would open for the interpreters, Sol among them. Nastia imagined these women idling behind the door, delaying their entrance as long as they could to keep the brides and bachelors waiting, to show how lost the hopefuls would be without them. It wasn't that the brides knew no English—Nastia had met many who did—but they were discouraged from addressing the bachelors directly. "The English language is full of land mines," Efrosinia always warned. "The simplest question or request cloaked in layer upon layer of an elusive kind of grammar which they call politeness. Modal verbs, deliberate vagueness, an avoidance of the present tense, the imperative practically taboo. Naturally blunt and low-voiced, the inexperienced Slavic woman trying to speak English is like a horse in a mouse maze."

Sol had told Nastia that the other interpreters looked down on the brides. The interpreters had worked hard to learn English, they'd dreamed of the English countryside, had imagined walking the mossy cobblestones they'd seen on the covers of grammar textbooks. Many had their sights set on working for the UN, the EU, WHO, the IMF, the NGOs. And yet here they were in the same banquet room, breathing in the same musk of cleaning solution and sour milk as these brides, who only had to swish their hips and click their heels to have the world promised to them.

When the side door opened, the interpreters entered. They formed the smallest group, around fifteen in number, and were on average older than the brides. Many were graduate students, but it wasn't uncommon to see women well on in years, retired English teachers. Unlike the brides, this group wore no stickers or identifiers, their utilitarian smocks blending into the gray of the carpet. Lubricants of courtship, Efrosinia called them. "You're never supposed to notice the oil that makes the parts move."

The interpreters did hold a power, Nastia knew. Their tongues could transform a dud into a star, but if you rubbed them the wrong way, they could just as easily do the opposite.

Sol wasn't hard to spot among the drab gray, white-blond stubble on her head shimmering under the banquet hall's lights. She'd had it shaved before the first tour, had given her carefully tended waist-length curls to a hairdresser who'd chemically straightened and then glued them to Nastia's roots. Sol was older than Nastia by two years, but nobody would guess. Most people wouldn't even guess they were related. Small, curveless, shorn, Sol could pass for a boy belonging to one of the interpreters, dragged along while his mother worked.

"Ready?" Sol whispered when she reached Nastia.

With the brides, bachelors, and interpreters present, with the waiters now milling around with trays of skewered fruits, a few pioneers began their slow approach. Gazes flitted over Nastia, but the men kept away at first. This is normal, Efrosinia had advised. The bachelors might be overwhelmed, confused by all the beauty in front of them. They don't know where to start. Give their eyes time to adjust to the light. A tip from Efrosinia: Add one flaw to your outfit. A conversation starter, something a stranger would feel compelled to fix. A linden leaf stuck to your coiffure, a flipped-up tag.

While the other interpreters milled around, ready to be swept into budding conversations, Sol stood by Nastia's side. The sisters waited.

It didn't take long for a warm, moist hand to slide the fallen silk strap of her dress back onto her shoulder. Before Nastia turned around to face their first bachelor, Sol reminded her to smile.

At every induction session, the agency's founder would call in from her home office across the ocean, in Canada. She lived just outside Vancouver, in a city that was not a suburb of Vancouver. It was a proper city, she'd insist, the former capital of British Columbia that had lost its status over a hundred years ago to another city in a ploy to keep the Americans from invading.

The founder's face, blown up to twice its size on the monitor, would fill the basement conference room, take in the fresh batch of brides perched on rows of plastic chairs. The sun that had set over the Kyiv hotel not long ago would illuminate her face. Above her was a ceiling of wooden planks, as though she were calling from a sauna or a yacht cabin. The planks looked vaguely Scandinavian, expensive.

"May you find the One," she'd greet the brides, beaming, as if she'd invented them. "I'm Maria, but you can call me Masha," she'd insist every time, the no-pet-name rule her own to break.

The insulation of her house, the rumor went, was made of recycled bridal catalogs from the pre-internet days. How old was she? Thirties? Forties? Impossible to tell—the camera filters made everything soft and airbrushed, and she might well have been Botoxed.

The founder's speech always began the same way. She told her story about how, not so long ago, Masha was just like any other Ukrainian girl, lost and lonely. She alluded to a few bad experiences with local boys—"No, I wouldn't call them men"—and had all but given up on love. At the time she'd been an organist, had filled the emptiness inside her practicing for hours and hours at her church, to mostly vacant pews. Her hands and feet would run wild over the many keyboards, clutch at the cracked porcelain stops. On one such day, when she resurfaced from yet another Czerny fugue, she saw a handsome gentleman sitting in the front pew. She did not know how long he'd been sitting there. His eyes were closed, like he was praying. When he opened them, he looked at Masha like no man ever had before, like his prayers had finally been answered. They didn't speak a word of each other's language, but her music told him all he needed to know. They married within a few months. And here was Masha now, founder of her own company, writing romance novels on the side. "The agency is in your hands," she told the brides.

But like any adventure, the process of marrying a foreigner had its hurdles, Masha warned. The brides would have to contend with resistance (jealousy) from family and friends. Naysayers aplenty would spring up. "It's easy for outsiders to criticize, but what are they doing to better themselves? My brides are the ones who are actually seizing life, looking for more."

My brides. These were the words Nastia's mother had used, too. My brides to fight for, my brides to save—as if she'd married each and every one herself. What was her mother saving them from? Sure, she fought the industry, its men, but beyond that? She was saving them from themselves.

"Back in my time, international dating was like setting out into a stormy sea," Masha went on. What a luxury it would have been to have an interpreter by her side. How she'd wished she had a team of experts guiding her every step of the way, ironing out not just linguistic errors but cultural faux pas. To be able to confer with an on-site psychologist or relationship counselor, to be referred to an immigration attorney. That's why she'd founded Romeo Meets Yulia: so that future brides wouldn't have to sail forth blind like she had.

Nastia recalled the stories: The bride who'd thought all of America looked like New York and ended up hanging herself from a rafter at her new husband's hog farm. The bride whose husband forbade her from leaving the house for months while she was between health insurance plans. The bride who kept getting sicker and sicker, kept getting medical procedures and surgeries, until she discovered that her organs were being harvested.

"Those are literally wives' tales," Nastia had told her mother, during one of their fights. To Nastia, the agencies had never seemed so bad, and couldn't women do whatever they wanted with their lives? Wasn't that exactly what Komod, her mother's protest troupe, was always fighting for?

In response, her mother had reminded Nastia of the worst cases, the ones that made the news or became subjects of true crime documentaries. Susana Remerata, who had left her fiancé after ten days and was shot three times in a courthouse as she waited for her divorce proceeding. Head, chest, pregnant belly. And then there was Anastasia King—always Anastasia King, as if the name alone ended all argument—strangled and hidden under a dirty mattress at a Seattle dump two years before Nastia's birth. Sometimes Nastia wondered if she'd been named after that Anastasia—her mother's attempt to rewrite the woman's ending.

On the monitor, Masha would blow her new brides a kiss.

"When my husband's friends meet me and see how happy we are together, they ask if I have a sister," she said. "And you know what I tell them? Not just one sister, not just two. I have millions of sisters." Then her hand would reach toward her computer, as though to stretch through the screen and across the ocean and take each and every bride by the hand—and the transmission would end, the video go black, and she would be gone.

The first man to fix Nastia's dress strap introduced himself as Mark from Arizona. Sixties, purplish bags under his eyes, a residue of black dye at the hairline. Nastia knew Sol approved: the more concerned a bachelor was with his own mortality, the more he needed Anastasia. The man's gaze flitted over her nude-colored dress, patterned with inky fingerprints. When he wished her a Happy Valentine's Day, Nastia's eyes again turned to the TV screen that hung along the banquet room's walls, the one streaming the day's news. Nothing about traffic disruptions, bridge closures, flash mobs crashing the day of romance. Instead, a map of Ukraine, its easternmost edge pulsing red. The Russians were transferring mobile hospitals and supplies of blood to the border now—further proof that these weren't simply training exercises? But that threat seemed far away, unimaginable—the day of the invasion predicted by American counterintelligence kept getting pushed back, like an ill-fated wedding—while her mother's imminent arrival felt concrete, inevitable.

A smiling hotel concierge lifted a remote control and flipped the screen to a different channel, an ad for the upcoming Eurovision contest.

Nastia turned back to Mark from Arizona. After the standard chitchat—what Anastasia did for a living (part-time med student, part-time bikini model), what Anastasia liked to do for fun (learn new recipes, polish pans), what Anastasia's family would think of her dating a foreigner (they'd only be so delighted)—the man pulled out his phone to scan her sticker. The agency app made a loud whoosh, like an arrow hitting its target ("At least you know he isn't just taking a snap of your chest," Sol had conceded the first time they'd heard the sound.) This granted him access to Anastasia's dating profile, where he could schedule a date.

After he bade Nastia goodbye, she flicked her dress strap back down.

The next bachelor, Alvin from Denver, heavily sideburned, introduced himself as a charter bus driver. He looked nervous at first, eyes downcast, but Sol's soft voice drew his gaze up. So disarming, that boyish little face, Nastia thought. To a bachelor drowning in a sea of sirens, here was a weedy island, a place to catch his breath. But Sol soon steered Nastia away. "Widower," she whispered. "A dead wife is a saint wife. Even Anastasia won't compare."

The third bachelor who approached, pinch-lipped and smelling of laundry detergent, left without scanning Nastia's sticker. Sol told her that he hadn't taken well to her joke about one of the fingerprints on Nastia's dress matching his own. "Says he doesn't touch until marriage." Sol's eyes trailed him as he walked off. "I'd defile him myself. Too bad I'm just a lowly translator." She pulled a long cartoonish face.

"I'd gladly swap. Teach me English," Nastia joked.

"As soon as you teach me Pretty."

They both knew the switch was impossible. Their roles were set, unbridgeable. The only English Nastia knew came from the protest slogans of Komod—words hurled violently, words that scraped vocal cords to a rasp by the end of the day. She couldn't muster a desire to learn more. It was Sol who did all the talking—she had studied the language at the university, a supposedly softer version, found in Jane Austen or Emily Brontë novels—yet the bachelors paid her little attention. Sol was not *not* pretty, although Nastia seemed to be the only person who thought so. Nastia found her sister striking. Sol had jagged features, a pointy nose and chin, a face that looked like it had been chiseled by a zealous sculptor. From this sparkled two eyes bright as lacquered walnut.

The bigger problem for Nastia was that even if she did trudge through studying English, learned to speak for herself, she still couldn't be Anastasia on her own.

The problem was her face. Not the way it looked—with the right makeup, Nastia never had trouble getting accepted for the tours—but what it was capable of. Despite researching the warm Ukrainian female temperament these bachelors were expecting to find, she could do only so much to meet that expectation. She had witnessed her own shortcomings on tour after tour, catching sight of herself in the wall mirrors of the banquet room: her smile never reached her eyes, she couldn't cock a brow, couldn't wink. Once, a bride trained as a dermatologist had asked Nastia about what she assumed were years of Botox, wishing her own clients had been as proactive in their younger age. Efrosinia sometimes lamented that Nastia's problem was one for all Slavic girls—that they could seem expressionless, reserved. She was always telling the brides to be "open" like the Westerners, to "smile, smile, smile" as if they were onstage, in a musical. But Nastia suspected that the problem with her own face ran deeper than cultural difference, and was immutable. Plus, she hated musicals.

Whatever Nastia lacked in expression, Sol made up for with words. Nastia could say anything in Ukrainian, she could recite a nursery rhyme or the ingredients of her last meal or how she wished she could cut off circulation to her feet so that they'd stop screaming in their high-heeled shoes, and Sol would spin her words into something wholly new. Sol would relate a funny yet touching story from Anastasia's childhood or reveal supposedly local wisdom like "A man is only as old as the youngest woman he's been with." The bachelors would chuckle, lean in for more. Sometimes Sol wouldn't bother with translation, giving Nastia stage directions: "Look sad. His mother died of something degenerative." "Play coy. He made a joke he thought was funny." Sol was more ventriloquist than interpreter. She brought Nastia to life as Anastasia.

During their first tour together, Nastia had been surprised how well her melding with Sol worked, how readily the bachelors bought in. In fact, the more inert Nastia made herself, the better. The bachelors superimposed Sol's personality onto Nastia's face, and voilà: Anastasia. Dream woman. They'd be seduced by Anastasia, who, unbeknownst to them, tariffed through overpriced taxi rides and dinners, through kickbacks with restaurants who charged inflated prices, through jewelry pawned off the next day. The bachelors chalked up the three-, four-, five-figure bills to the local currency anyway. Just the weakling hryvnia, ever falling in value. The Easter-colored bills flew out of their wallets like play money.

Sometimes, people on the street would shoot knowing glances at Nastia. Ah, it's *that* kind of date. They'd spot the age difference, the telltale interpreter as third wheel. When the smiling foreigner opened his wallet, bystanders would often look at Nastia with judgment, disgust. It was women like Nastia who smeared the name of Ukrainians, the name of all women.

Nastia didn't care—she, too, once used to judge the brides—but what got under her skin was the occasional look of pity, as if Nastia was someone to be led away, a wool blanket thrown over her shoulders, and plied with soup. Once, at a restaurant, while her date and Sol were fussing over his declined credit card at the cash register, Nastia heard a whisper beside her. "Do you do okay?"

Startled, Nastia turned to the woman sitting at the table beside her. German, judging by the accent. Dowdy cardigan, anthropological meal of borscht and varenyky. She felt the woman's gaze boring into her, past the glossy platinum hair and layers of makeup, like she was trying to guess how old Nastia really was, virtually unwrapping her bandage dress in search of something floppy and boneless inside. The woman had slipped a card into Nastia's palm listing human trafficking helplines.

Nastia had smirked at the do-gooder, at the handful of Ukrainian words this woman had diligently learned. Did she carry a stack of these cards around with her, ready to rescue the natives? "Yes, I *do okay*," Nastia said, mimicking the woman's accent. She dunked the card, like a slice of bread, into the woman's borscht.

The woman drew back, face red.

If only the woman knew that there was only one person who had the power to drag Nastia away from all this—by the wrist, by the ear—make it *hurt*, why not. The only person this was all for, the only person this was all against.

Their mother had insisted that Nastia and Sol call her Iolanta—to dispel archaic notions of bloodline and hierarchy, she said. But Nastia had always wondered if there was one word that embarrassed her in front of the other Komod girls, who were younger and unencumbered: Mother. What a letdown it must have been, after all the other words the press called her: Pioneer. Performance artist. Crazy. Sextremist.

One online article about Iolanta, which cited "a close source," suggested that her (very public) vendetta against the bridal agencies was fueled by having been rejected from theater school, similar to the way Hitler had unleashed his anger on the world after being rejected by art school. It was a matter of stymied self-expression, the article theorized. After Iolanta's theater dream was quashed, she'd briefly turned to bookkeeping as a job, and one of her clients had been an international marriage agency. One day she'd flipped through their fat, glossy catalog of eligible women. These were the days when such catalogs landed on the doorsteps of Western subscribers, men who'd tick the boxes of the brides they wanted to send letters to, and the agency would translate their letters to Russian or Ukrainian and field them for a steep fee. Iolanta had flipped and flipped, until she discovered her own photo. Not just any photo, but one of the headshots she'd used when applying to theater school: against an azure background, wearing her best white silk blouse with blooming sleeves and big silver buttons shaped like anchors, she'd gazed into the camera like it held her bright future. She'd saved up for months to pay for the hairstyling, makeup, studio space. The photographer must've sold the headshot to the agency, and they'd used it to bulk up their catalog. Iolanta Cherno was incensed. How long had her photo been circulating like this, under a fake profile? Not only was she not an actor but here was her past self, her radiant destined-for-the-stage self, haunting mail-order catalogs, being sold off alongside other women like a doorknob or wallpaper pattern or pack of socks. She fought with the agency over the photo, tried to get it taken out of circulation. The administrators didn't budge. What was the agency going to do, issue a worldwide recall of their catalog? Reprint an entire catalog before the season was up, just for one photo? Was the agency swimming in money? They were multiplying love, not profits. (False, Iolanta knew from their accounting books: they did swim in money.) Anyway, what was so bad about being in their coveted catalog? Many women could only dream of such an opportunity, the administrators told Iolanta.

Was this story true? Maybe, maybe not. Nastia could hardly imagine her mother in a normal job like bookkeeping, but then again, that too could have been an act, part of the shapeshifting.

("Give me a name, any name," Iolanta would say to Nastia and Sol as she got ready for her protests. It was their little game. She always needed to know her stage name. She'd lean into the toothpaste-speckled bathroom mirror, reshape her eyes using eyeliner, sculpt her cheekbones with shimmering blushes. "If you're nobody you can't be somebody unless you're somebody else," she'd say, supposedly quoting Marilyn Monroe.)

To Nastia and Sol, their mother had always described her past in blurry terms, something she'd cast off. She'd had a mother in academia. A father in the military, who'd doused her daily in ice water to harden her up. Sometime in her early twenties there must've been a man who'd fathered Nastia and Sol, but she never spoke of him. It was as if her children had been immaculately conceived.

Whenever the thought crept up on Nastia that Iolanta had cast her daughters off just as she'd shed her past, she pushed it away. She knew that by now word must have passed through Komod to Iolanta about Nastia's betrayal (Sol's, too—but joining the tours had been Nastia's idea). At its height, the core group of Komod had been a carefully chosen six- to eight-girl band size—but Iolanta had always alluded to a larger shadow network spanning borders and genders, countless ears to the ground.

Shame or guilt—these were emotions Iolanta was immune to. But anger? Anger would bring her back.

Whatever the origin of her mother's vendetta against the agencies, Nastia did understand it. She'd often seen the buses, the gleaming double-deckers with tinted windows that passed for private school groups or foreign delegations or business partners visiting for a textile exhibition. Throughout her childhood, Nastia had squinted up at these charters, trying in vain to see through the glossy black windows, to decipher how many pairs of eyes were peering back at her and her mother, prospecting. Some buses whispered their purpose in small silk-ribbon lettering:

Glass Slipper Tours
Night Knights
Maiden Voyage
Cupid's Conquest
Dream Catchers

Her mother had taught her to spot those who'd arrived by such buses. Dressed either too formally—a suit and tie, freshly polished shoes that avoided every pothole and loose cobblestone—or in all-season cargo shorts and baseball caps. Some long-limbed girl draped over their arm, barely able to walk in her stilettos. Keeping close by, a matronly schoolteacher or a reedy university student translating the stilted conversation. Kyiv was the new Berlin, her mother told Nastia, and everyone, including the sex tourists, was flocking in while it was cheap. This was no secret: in a presidential speech, Yanukovich had invited fans to Kyiv for the Euro Football tournament and promised that it was the time of year when local women began to undress, while a Dutch company ran ads for an at-home beer tap that promised worried wives to "Keep Him Home" instead of being tempted by Ukraine.

And then there were the weddings.

In park pavilions, on cathedral steps. In chestnut groves, or at the stainless-steel feet of the Motherland Monument. On the wooden bridge in Mariinskyi Park, sagging under countless lovers' padlocks. August swelter or January freeze—no matter. As a child, Nastia couldn't always tell which weddings were curated by a marriage agency and which weren't. The white dresses and black tuxedos looked the same, as though handed down from one couple to the next, but her mother had claimed she could always spot the difference. Just look at the way he looks at her, she'd say. That's not love, but something else entirely.

Before registering for her first tour, Nastia had studied the agency websites, pored over the kinds of women promised to Westerners. She looked at how she was supposed to act. She hit a translation button on her browser and the sites blinked from English to Ukrainian, like a cryptogram decoding.

Behold! the sites screamed. The phenomenon of the Ukraine Woman! Well groomed with the legs of the antelope and eyes of the feline. The Ukraine Woman keeps her hair long and body narrow, however she has a master's degree and plays musical instruments! A former American president and owner of Miss Universe pageant confirmed: Ukraine is always well represented in the contestant demographic.

But what is the science of the Ukraine female phenotype? Why can't Western Woman—entitled and overweight and overvalued by mainstream media—keep up? According to endocrinological investigations, the Slavic Female enjoys more estrogen in the blood. She can't help love being female and show off being female, unlike Western counterpart, who actually wants to be male. Western Frankenmonster still expects males to be chivalrous while refusing to be maiden in return.

If not endocrinological, the secret of the Ukraine Woman could be edaphological! Ukraine's soil. Ukrainians have special name for their soil, chornozem. Chornozem has long been famous, black and fertile with loam and humus. Wars have waged over chornozem. Envisage fields of rippling gold wheat and melons bursting at the mosquito's touch—Ukraine Woman is birthed of that same soil. Chornozem, bless you! Ukraine not only is a breadbasket, but a bride basket also.

In addition to edaphological, the secret of the Ukraine Woman may be genetical. Invasions and wars led to fruity intermixing. Slant eyes and thin waist from Genghis Khan. Mysticism and fine fashion from the Tatars. Pragmatism and hair plaits from the Poles. Flammable spirit from the Balkans, et cetera.

Inside the Ukraine Woman, the races melt together and you get best of everything! Like a buffet.

More precisely, like your second plate at buffet. The carefully curated plate after that first plate, which you had packed mostly with duds.

That first plate is a good analogy for Western Women. You approached them with a warm spirit and wide-open tray but you left hungry.

Another benefit of the Ukraine Woman: She will not turn away from your advance. She will not bite. This, due to her hospitable interior, as rich and deep and loamful as chornozem. Her spiritual nature has survived seventy years of Communist repression followed by chaos of capitalist freefall. Her eyes—blue or chestnut but can be green—speak of the trials of a struggling country, but they can laugh with the indomitability of her people. Ukraine is not yet dead, its anthem pines, and this is indeed factual. She has matured among dire political and economical climate and has learned to kindle warmth within self. She is a small but firm flame in the tundra.

The Ukraine Woman is only so happy to make you feel her flame, too!

Unlike Western Woman, Ukraine Woman isn't spoiled by male attention! The local men are too busy dying from drink or the war in Donbas or industrial accidents or locating abroad to find career. In some regions of Ukraine, for every 10 women there are only 2.5 men.

Imagine an entire country of beautiful *and* lonely women!

An impossible combination, yet it is here.

This is where you, Western Man, enter.

Your compatriots who are less enlightened pay thousands to financial planners, plastic surgeons, and fitness trainers to look more attractive to the Western Woman, who will not notice anyway. But you are daring and think outside the box. All you must do is board that plane. Within less than twenty-four hours, when your foot graces chornozem, you are richer, younger, and more handsome. You are the man you always knew you were.

"See what they're saying about the brides, about us all, every woman?" Nastia's mother would yell, waving her phone screen in Nastia's face.

As she had grown older, Nastia had wanted to point out that this was still better than what onlookers, both men and women, yelled at Komod during their topless protests in Kyiv. *Feminazis. Whores. You bring shame on our country.* Insults that had made Komod scream all the louder.

One stunt Nastia remembered well had taken place at the Vatican. Iolanta had crashed the St. Peter's Square Nativity scene on Christmas Day, the words GOD IS A WOMAN painted across her bare chest. (Nastia's Christmas present that year: the tight little Jesus fist Iolanta had managed to break off, as a trophy, before the police dragged her away.)

Another protest, when Nastia was eight and Sol ten, had taken place in Minsk. Iolanta had said she would be gone for two days, but it was weeks before she came home, after she and two other Komod members had been abducted by the Belarus KGB, taken to a forest, stripped naked, had diesel poured over their bodies, been threatened with a match and told never to return.

"You won't, though, right? You won't go back?" Nastia had asked. She swore her mother's skin still smelled like diesel and wouldn't let Iolanta use the gas stove for a week, following her from room to room in case she tried to light a cigarette or a candle. Or simply vanished again.

Iolanta had kissed Nastia's head but promised nothing, revealed no plans for future trips, as if Nastia and Sol were leak risks.

Back then, Nastia had forgiven their mother's absences. Komod was making headlines all over the world. Their mother was fighting for a greater good, a better future for all girls. And Nastia and Sol were never alone—there was a rotation of young women through the tiny apartment on the city's outskirts, Turkish coffee bubbling on the stove. Many were university students Iolanta had recruited from campus. One was a dancer at a club frequented mostly by foreigners; Nastia remembered her stretching herself into impossible contortions in the kitchen doorway. Another was a runaway who'd spent her adolescence sequestered in a series of churches, painting icons before running away again. Wherever they came from, they had the same look: thin, blond, light-skinned, chin held high. The ones who couldn't stand proud in front of the cameras never made it far in Komod.

When she was little, Nastia wasn't hung up on the nudity she saw all around her. In the summers, she herself ran wild on Dnipro's beaches among countless other unclothed children. A body was just a body. Often, it was Nastia or Sol who painted slogans onto the goose-fleshed skin of Komod protesters, in brutal black brushstrokes. A child's handwriting, the women agreed, possessed a raw, untampered violence.

Nastia was nine when she got her period. Freakishly early, she'd thought. While Sol still didn't bleed and stayed curveless, Nastia's chest began to bud. It was as if her body was speeding ahead to join the rebellion, revolting against Nastia herself. All she wanted to do then was to cover herself up in as many layers as possible. At school, the boys in older grades had taken to snapping her new bra in the hallways, the sting like a lashing. They asked when she was going to start stripping like her famous mother. And the way Iolanta looked at Nastia did change—as if Nastia's body suddenly held the same potential as her own, as if all this time Iolanta had been growing her daughter as an extension of herself, her newest weapon.

There was a loud thunk, the sound of an arrow hitting its target.

Nastia blinked, her mind dragged back to the hotel banquet hall. Before her, a bachelor smiled into heavy jowls, chatted away as he scrolled through the photos on her dating profile. Was it hers, or another girl's? The agency's studio shots all looked the same if you blurred your eyes. Geometric foam blocks or fainting couches or movie-set kitchens. Backs arched, mouths slightly open; perched on a narrow banister overlooking a Kyiv vista, or collapsed on a shag rug, or in the fetal position with head on knees, wide orphan eyes.

The hall's tables had been pushed to the back and sides, and the room throbbed with techno. This was the most tolerable part of the evening for Nastia, when she got to pretend she didn't hear the bachelors over the music and Sol could take charge completely, filling in Anastasia's story as if Nastia weren't there.

She slipped away to the ladies' room. It was there, among the candy bowls of tampons and Tiffany-blue fainting couches and mirrors with stage lights, that the brides engaged in the forbidden. They passed long-suppressed gas, adjusted padded bras, patched up ragged feet, doled out skin tape. They sororized.

Nastia sat on the toilet listening to the others, fingerprint dress collapsed around her ankles. She kicked off her heels and felt the static of blood rushing back into her toes. Today, the discussion focused on laser taste bud removal. How much it cost, whether it worked for weight loss.

"I just worry the taste buds would keep growing back, like leg hair, you know?" the bride who had begun this discussion was saying. Through the crack between the stall door and its frame, Nastia watched the woman gloss her lips. She recognized this bride from a previous tour, remembered how the bachelors had been surprised that a Ukrainian woman named Svitlana could be black. Her very existence blew their minds, as if she lived in two dimensions at once.

"Might take a few treatments to really get rid of them," Nastia's stall neighbor suggested, on the topic of taste buds.

"You think I have that kind of money? Might as well take an iron and scald my tongue myself."

"You'd still have your sense of smell, though," said the bride with fishtail braids, perched on the counter beside her, smoking. She exhaled into the exhaust fan on the wall above her. "Isn't smell a part of taste?"

One bride said you could bypass the mouth altogether—her trick was to smell her favorite foods instead of eating them, since they were basically the same thing. Another recommended a medical diet designed for obese patients who needed to slim down before surgery. Another said she'd bought probiotic pills from some baba at the bazaar which turned out to be tapeworm eggs, but the worms worked so well, she never got them treated. Now she could eat for two, or fifteen, the bride boasted, and still keep losing weight.

Svitlana asked the bride with the fishtail braids for a cigarette. "Might just stick to good old nicotine for now."

Nastia liked these bathroom confessionals. They were nothing like the online "clean eating" videos she'd seen, where light-soaked Western women called water loading "hyperhydration," starvation "fasting," breakfast a "societal construct," and dinner something to "transcend." At least these brides were honest about the violence they were committing. They reminded Nastia of people she'd read about who got away with a crime but turned themselves in anyway, just to tell someone how they did it, recount the details of the mutilation.

Efrosinia liked to remind the brides how lucky they were to have so much control over their looks. Women could make themselves taller with high heels, emphasize cheekbones with the right contouring, make their eyes and lips look bigger. A man, on the other hand, could hardly cheat the genetic lottery. He had to accept the hand he'd been dealt.

Nastia flushed, took her time washing her hands in one of the lavender-colored sinks.

The redheaded woman two sinks away, who'd been powdering away the freckles on her nose, now turned to Nastia. "So what do you do?"

The bathroom crowd grew quiet, listening. Nastia knew the woman wasn't asking about her job. Every time the question of her trade secret came up she felt herself fill with pride, a sugary sense of camaraderie: the bride considered Nastia disfigured enough to ask. Nastia had become one of them.

Most times, she made up a vague lie, how she'd turned to God. A knowing hum would pass among the brides, a communal nod, as if Nastia had said a code word for some illegal skinny drug or an underground bariatric surgeon. But today was the day her mother would return, and Nastia would never see these brides again, so she thought, to hell with it. She'd be honest.

"I ran out of money for food."

An awkward silence filled the bathroom. Then the other brides continued their primping with a renewed zest.

But this wasn't the full truth, not really. After the money Iolanta had left behind dwindled, Nastia and Sol could've gone to the Krishna temple for the lentil lunches or subsisted on instant noodles, but by then Nastia had lost her appetite. A hunger strike, of sorts. That's how she stayed thin.

And to look thinner still, there was the shapewear. Thick, punishing, flesh colored. The first time Nastia wrangled it over her hips as Sol watched, wincing, she thought of the nature documentaries her mother had liked to watch, the extended segment of a python trying to swallow a whole antelope. Both animals looked on the brink of death. The python could split any moment, and the antelope kept struggling, but the more it struggled, the farther the flesh tube climbed. When, at last, the garment closed in around her middle, the effect was immediate: whatever was left of that middle—maybe the organs themselves—squeezed into her chest and hips, sculpting the "Kardashian waist" the glossy packaging had promised. A modern corset, binding women, setting them back decades.

"It's perfect." Nastia had beamed at herself in her mother's armoire mirror. She could speak if she took quick shallow breaths.

At first, Sol had refused to join the tours herself even as an interpreter, on principle, but eventually the question of money was irrefutable. Their mother had been gone five months by this time. The amount of money she'd left behind had been laughable—how had she expected them to get by? The romance tours felt familiar, the way one can know an enemy more intimately than a friend. And then there was the guaranteed hourly interpreter fee, to be split with the brides, and the gifts bachelors could buy through the agency, which the brides could exchange for cash. And didn't Sol want to practice her English? Be able to afford her next tuition bill? She'd been studying Victorian literature and spent her evenings watching TV shows set in England, where straight-backed ladies in long dresses sipped tea in mahogany drawing rooms and plotted advantageous marriages. In the end, Sol had agreed to join the tours on a few conditions: that she would interpret for Nastia and Nastia only; and that if any of the bachelors so much as touched Nastia, Sol would pull the plug. The most important condition, the most obvious, was left unspoken: Nastia would marry no one, board no plane.

"Try smiling," Sol had said when Nastia first put on the shapewear.

The garment seemed to grow tighter with each breath, but Nastia shaped her mouth in a smile.

"That's more of a grimace. Relax that face." Sol demonstrated by puckering her mouth and then yawning it open.

Nastia tried again.

Sol said, "How about we leave the smiling to me?"

The next day, when she was in line at the registration table for their first romance tour, Nastia glanced at herself in one of the lobby's floor-to-ceiling mirrors. The final addition that morning: Anastasia's glossy white-blond mane. The ends brushed the small of her back like a gentle hand, like she was always being ushered somewhere. A "glacial waterfall," one bachelor would later call it. "Sheet metal in the sun," said another. Nastia saw her reflection move forward without her. It took her a queasy moment to realize that she'd been looking at another blonde in line who was wearing a dress of the same color. When it was Nastia's turn in front of Efrosinia, the woman barely looked at her as she waved her through.

The rest of Valentine's Day passed uneventfully. Dress strap flipped down, flipped back up by nervous hands. The divorcé who only wanted his next wife to be "nice and happy." The Alaskan who collected wolfdogs and asked how much she weighed, and would she be willing to wrestle the beasts to the ground and bite their ears as an occasional but vital show of domination. The retiree in his seventies who offered a doctor's note certifying tip-top health. The accountant who showed photos of the bonsai rhododendron he'd choked and molded with wires over the past twenty-three years, who invited Nastia back to his hotel room at the first lull in conversation. Another bachelor showed photos of his vintage Jaguar, hood popped, boasting a big shiny engine.

Nastia nodded along, rubbed the tar-black globs of makeup from the corners of her eyes. She smiled placidly as her phone chimed with date requests, knowing she would accept none of them. She wouldn't need to. In a matter of hours, her mother would appear and life would go back to normal. Iolanta Cherno's Valentine's Day stunt would make the news. Komod would be revived after their hiatus. Money would flood back in from all over the world. Her mother would take care of everything.

But as the hours ticked on, as daylight waned: still no mother.

Later, Nastia sat at home alone, watching the front door to the apartment. Sol had gone to the agency's social at a nightclub down the street, even though she wasn't the nightclub type. She'd been jittery all day, like Nastia. But unlike Nastia, she didn't entirely believe their mother would turn up that night.

Nastia kicked her heels off but kept her fingerprint dress on. Arranged the scene for her mother: daughter passed out in an armchair wearing god knows what, a pink-and-white Romeo Meets Yulia pamphlet shading her eyes. In a flash, Iolanta would piece it together, the damage she'd done. She'd rage at Nastia, then collapse at her feet, repent, vow never to leave again. She'd tell Nastia who she was not (a bride to be "sold off"), would tell her who she needed to be (but what?).

Nastia draped herself over one armrest, then the other. The icy February draft seeped in between the cracked windowpanes, made her shiver in her thin dress. The building was an old one, prerevolutionary, with thick stone walls. The ornate plaster moldings were half-crumbled, the corridors dim and cavernous, and tongues of soot from some long-ago fire licked its grand oval staircase. When they'd moved in ten years ago, when Komod was at its height, the apartment's spacious rooms had held the promise of a bigger, better protest.

A press photo still hung on the wall, capturing her mother's proudest moment. It was of Iolanta from behind, braid swinging over her naked back, words slashed there in Nastia's writing: FUCK YOU PUTIN. Facing her, the man himself, in the flesh. This had been during Putin's visit to Hanover. The protest was against the detaining of the Russian women's band Pussy Riot. How Iolanta and her troupe had found a hole in his security team, no one knew. To Komod, the photo captured the group's ultimate victory, their most successful stunt to date.

To Nastia, the photo was embarrassing, proved the group's failure. A clutch of bodyguards scrambled around Putin—but Putin himself? A gleeful, boyish expression on his face unlike the press had ever seen before, eyebrows raised, mouth in a tight O. His fists poised in front of him, like he was about to give two thumbs-up.

The last fight Nastia had had with her mother was on the eve of her departure. This was when Iolanta had announced that she needed to disappear for a while, lie low. The rest of Komod had disbanded years ago, its members having fled to Paris after the apartment had been raided, after being threatened by Yanukovych's brutal Berkut police (hand in hand with Russia's secret police, they'd said), and Komod's photographer and sole male member had been beaten on the street. A weird quiet had descended on the apartment after that. Nobody visited anymore. Their mother would wake late. She spent afternoons roaming the city, collecting tiny glass animals sold in subway stations, but always came back. They lived off her savings, which Nastia imagined would last forever, and the odd signed Komod hat or T-shirt sold online.

"Are you joining the others in Paris?" Sol had tried to ask casually—shock only emboldened her mother.

Iolanta waved away the possibility. "They wouldn't have me anyway." She'd complained that the few protests they'd mounted in exile, without her, had been too serious. They'd used bloated academic words in online posts, even though the whole point of Komod had been to take activism back from the highbrow intellectuals, anchor it to the body, something every woman possessed.

"You're plotting something," Nastia said, weary. "Is this about the hundred missing Vietnamese brides?" Their mother had been following this recent news story breathlessly. Overnight, one hundred brides had disappeared from a province in China, twenty-eight from a single village. The brides had been brought from Vietnam to China by a matchmaker who also ran a beauty salon. The night before the disappearance, the brides had attended a party organized by this matchmaker—and then they hadn't come home. A cotton farmer found a Vietnamese-Chinese phrase book his bride had left behind, the phrases she'd been trying to learn written over and over in the margins: "You never let me go out" and "You need a bath."

Nastia knew the story wouldn't end well, and was worried how it might set their mother off. Sol, meanwhile, had tried to be optimistic: The matchmaker had disappeared, too, hadn't she? What if it was the matchmaker who'd helped the brides escape, knowing how unhappy they'd been? Maybe this matchmaker had taken every pair of scissors from her salon, separated each into its two blades, and handed them out to the brides, then led the caravan into the dark night.

Iolanta gave Sol a look of pity. Matchmakers like that only exist in fairy tales, she'd said. The next day, a fresh batch of articles reported that one of the vanished brides did return to her husband. The night of the party hosted by the matchmaker, she'd lost consciousness and woke up in a new village. She was about to be sold off to another husband, caught in a mass scam she'd known nothing about.

"Am I plotting something? Never." Their mother had smiled and pointed at an invisible spot at the corner of the ceiling, a reminder that the apartment might still be bugged. The press had long forgotten her, but Yanukovych's police hadn't, she'd always said, even after the tyrant himself fled the country following the Maidan Revolution.

Nastia saw it then, how fragile the quiet normalcy of the last few years had been. When all along they had really been in the eye of a storm.

How did the fight with her mother start? Had it been Nastia who'd snapped, baited Iolanta?

What she remembered saying: how she'd always thought the topless protests were stupid, show for show's sake. How gross it was that most of the sponsors were men abroad. Of course it was mostly men, her mother had retorted, because men made more money than women, and anyway, unlike other activist movements, everyone around the world knew about Komod. So what, Nastia yelled, everyone knew about McDonald's, but that didn't mean it had done much good for humanity. In an attempt to placate the fighters, Sol slid onto the table a plate of lemon meringues she'd painstakingly baked using an eighteenth-century recipe that called for manual egg beating. The sight of the dainty florets only angered their mother more. She thought her daughters would be *stronger* than she was, she yelled. *Better* fighters who'd lessen the plight of women, because the next generation was supposed to outdo the last, move history forward. Instead, what did she get?

That's when Nastia tore the Putin protest photo off the wall. She held the photo between her hands, threatened to rip it apart, rip apart the younger, glorious version of Iolanta Cherno herself.

Iolanta seized a meringue from the plate and held it in her fist, about to crush it.

Mother and daughter stared at each other, seething, the fate of their hostages in suspension. Sol yanked on a pair of boots and slipped out of the apartment, mumbling something about the nice weather. It was pouring.

When her mother set the meringue back onto its plate, the motion slow and deliberate, Nastia thought she had won for once.

Then, just as slowly, eyes still locked with Nastia's, her mother began to unbutton her shirt. As she took off her jeans, her underwear, Nastia had no idea what to say, how to stop her. It was one thing to see her mother naked in public, surrounded by crowds or encased in press photos, but like this? No stage makeup. No wreath. No war paint. Iolanta was shorter than Nastia—when had that happened? In that dim, cavernous apartment she looked pale and defenseless. A downy fuzz circled her belly button. Red marks gashed her stomach, not from the protests or the detainments, but from the two children she'd borne.

Go on, she seemed to say. Have at me.

It was this moment Nastia thought back on eight months later, as her phone screen flipped to midnight. February 15, a Tuesday, cruelly mundane. Valentine's Day had come and gone. Eight months, and not one phone call or message. Was her mother just late with her stunt? Would it take another day or two? No, that wasn't Iolanta, not when Valentine's Day would've been so perfect.

Something had gone wrong. Maybe the police really had been on her tail, thwarted whatever stunt she'd been planning, thrown her in prison. But she still would've called, wouldn't she?

Another possibility: Nastia had made a mistake joining the romance tours, overshot. Maybe her mother had found out about her betrayal and been too repulsed by the stink the agency and its men had left on her.

Or maybe it was something else that kept her away. In the end, Nastia hadn't ripped up the photo that night her mother had stood bare before her. But Nastia's face, too alive back then, must have given something away, a last lethal judgment.

4

THE THIRD TIME the girl approached Yeva, she offered more cash, both for the lab and for Yeva to operate it, by which she meant "drive it to a specified location." That was when the girl—on this third meeting, she gave her name as Nastia, but Yeva continued to think of her generically—confessed she didn't have the special license, then admitted she didn't have a regular one either, and had never driven so much as a bumper car. Yeva wouldn't need to have anything to do with the bachelors herself, the girl promised. They'd be locked in the lab. Yeva wouldn't have to interact with them, ever. She'd just need to drive, stay at a nice hotel (provided by the girl) for an undetermined amount of time, drop off the bachelors at a specified location (which the girl did not disclose), drive back. The girl spoke haltingly, improvising the details of the plan on the spot—as if she didn't have an entire criminal ring of grown-ups (with driver's licenses!) behind her, Yeva scoffed to herself. Clearly, the girl did not know what she was doing. Yeva could have called the hotline many times over by now, alerted the police, and yet here the girl was talking to Yeva again, implicating her as a witness. As if this preposterous scheme had been her own idea, as if she were trying to pull it off all alone.

"I'm not helping you kidnap and mug a hundred men."

The girl drew back. "Mug them?"

"Hold them for ransom. Whatever."

"This isn't about money."

"Why else would you kidnap them?"

"I'm sending a message."

"A message."

"A warning."

Let it go, Yeva told herself. For once, just let it go. Ask nothing more; it is not your problem.

She set about testing the mobile lab's tire pressure. It was Friday, February 18, two days after the Russians were supposed to have invaded, according to the Americans. Even Yeva was beginning to think the Russians were bluffing; like the girl, everyone around Yeva seemed to be going about their plans, however ridiculous. The romance tour was already in its fifth day, halfway over. Yeva hadn't joined the Love at First Sightsee paddlewheel rides along the Dnipro or the Cupid's Target archery contest, but she kept her trailer parked in the hotel alley and no one had kicked her out yet. She had her own plan, didn't she? A death plan she'd already set in motion, and now she had to push herself through those motions, because if she backed out, it would be yet another failure.

Yeva had already rehearsed her last day in her mind countless times. Her final meal would be the "deluxe combo" from the nearby chain: four-cheese pizza, sushi rolls (bluefish tuna, freshwater eel, both endangered, but why not take down a couple more species along with her?), two bottles of Georgian red along with a La Gloria Cubana cigar. She knew her family would want to stuff her into a wedding dress for burial, as was the tradition for the tragically single, so to appease them she'd decided she would don one herself. This would also be handy in case, in a cruel celestial joke, the afterlife existed after all. The dress was the one detail she still had to figure out. Though she'd never wanted to get married, she found herself being picky about the garment as she window-shopped. White, Western style? Embroidered linen, folksy? She reminded herself that weddings, whether in the land of the living or the dead, were more for the family than for the bride. For their sake, the dress had to be right. She vowed that as soon as she found it she'd drive into the woods, free her last snail, Lefty, back into the wild—her last snail had been her first rescue, a nice bookend—turn on the gas valves, and at last free herself.

"Don't you want to hear about the warning?" the girl pestered, wide owl-like face trained on Yeva. Behind her, a fat rat sauntered between dumpsters. "I think you do, I think you want to hear about the warning. It's really powerful. It all started with my mother."

Mothers! The last thing Yeva wanted to hear about.

Yeva's last conversation with her own mother didn't help matters. She'd called Yeva early the morning before, out of the blue. Yeva had been putting the finishing touches on her final retrofit of the lab. She had rerouted all the pipes to dissipate the gas in a uniform fashion into the body of the trailer instead of individual cabinets—every safety feature, every alarm to prevent this exact thing from happening was disabled.

"Yevusya, I know what you've been up to." Her mother's voice reached her from the other end of the line, tender.

Yeva couldn't help turning around, suddenly worried (but also relieved?) that she'd find her mother right behind her, there to stop her.

"I'm heartbroken you didn't tell your own mother." Her voice was a warm hand cupping Yeva's face. Yeva closed her eyes, leaning into it. Was it really that simple? Had she been waiting for a voice to tell her not to go through with it?

"When did you start dating Americans? Mykola happened upon a photo of you on one of *those* sites."

Yeva dropped the valve she'd been refitting.

Of course this Mykola, no doubt some relative she'd never met, had "happened upon it." Yet another cousin, or uncle, or anyone from the sprawling family, snooping again, trying to make sense of her life. As Yeva waited for her mother's judgment, she also felt a twinge of hope. She imagined her mother swooping in, locking her up in her old room in their apartment, slipping her soup and homemade sauerkraut with cranberries and green apple slices—how she'd missed that sauerkraut!—anything to keep Yeva from the bride buyers. Yeva's mother had railed about them whenever she saw a young high-heeled girl slung on the arm of a Westerner. She'd called them old creeps, predators, divorcés with trails of kids who couldn't remarry their "own kind."

But instead her mother now asked, voice small and girlish, "Met someone you like?"

Yeva felt the air leave her lungs. Her mother would let her go, just like that. Anything was better than Yeva being alone. She picked up the gas valve, began to rescrew it with shaking fingers. "He's a doctor."

"A doctor."

Yeva pictured her mother closing her eyes, imagining.

"House and dog, too," Yeva helped along.

"What kind of dog?"

"Golden retriever."

"Mmmm. A family dog."

They were silent for a while. Yeva heard her father laughing at the television in the background.

"I'll miss you," her mother said. "I'll miss you every day."

"I'll miss you, too, mamo." She already did. She hung up.

"Look," Yeva told the girl now. "I don't care about your warning, and I don't care who your mother is."

The girl took a breath, gave a name anyway. Waited for some sort of reaction from Yeva, like Yeva was supposed to either love or hate this celebrity.

"Who?"

"You seriously don't know."

For a moment the girl seemed relieved, but then she gathered herself and launched into a breathless lecture, like she was being watched and graded. A history lecture about Iolanta Cherno and her women's club. How they fought against many evils, particularly the international bridal industry, fought on behalf of victims like Anastasia King and Susana Remerata, victims Yeva hadn't known about, hadn't asked about. How, less than a year ago, a hundred trafficked Vietnamese brides had vanished and been retrafficked and the world spun on. (Didn't Yeva know?

She didn't, and this only seemed to prove the girl's point.) Yes, one hundred brides could vanish, make the news for a few days, and yet the multibillion-dollar bride machine kept barreling on. Business loans, home mortgages, car payments, farmwork, relied on it. More brides would cross porous borders, into strangers' homes and bedrooms. More busloads of bachelors would cross into Ukraine, would keep rolling in; they'd tour the country in never-ending loops, sweeping up brides.

The girl was still ranting as Yeva climbed the two steel steps up to the trailer's side door, placed her hand on the latch. Certainly, it was all unfortunate—Yeva wasn't exactly a fan of the industry herself—but there was something off about the girl. She reminded Yeva of the tiny raw-voiced woman who proselytized along Yeva's parents' street, a born-again Christian who must've thought she'd sinned so terribly, fallen so low, that she had to spend the rest of her life repenting.

"And so a hundred *men* have to disappear, not just from our agency but from others, too," the girl concluded after remembering to take a breath. "And not for money. Not for any explainable reason. It has to be senseless so it'll scare off other foreign men from coming here, and the whole industry will collapse, not just in Ukraine but all over the world."

Yeva unlatched the door, about to seal herself inside her trailer. "You and your mother seem to have a handle on things, so."

The girl finally blinked. "I told you, it's just me," she said quietly. "My own plan."

"Bowed out, did she?"

The girl's face hardened and she kept silent. Family drama—even less incentive for Yeva to get involved. Yet despite herself she asked, "How old are you?"

"Eighteen." A beat, and the girl added, "And a half."

And a half. Yeva felt herself crack. "There are better ways to effect change. Why don't you write an op-ed?"

The girl shot Yeva a searing look, like Yeva was out of touch, a thousand years old. Did newspapers even exist anymore? The girl wasn't wrong in her skepticism—Yeva had written countless op-eds herself calling for action against continued habitat destruction, but she might as well have been writing letters to Saint Nicholas.

"Anyway, you're out of luck. It so happens I'm going to need this lab myself," Yeva said.

The girl stepped back, tilted her head at Yeva, reassessing. "The other brides say you live in there, that you're homeless. Are you homeless?"

Yeva patted the smooth enameled metal behind her, determined not to be rattled. Had she been that obvious? "The lab is my home."

Yeva imagined her relatives scoffing from all around the country.

Yet the girl simply said, "So you live at your workplace."

The awkward word caught Yeva off guard. Workplace. The girl didn't ask what kind of lab it was, only to laugh at the snail mission, as others had. She took Yeva at her word. The lab: a place of work, where work got done. The lab wasn't just a pipe dream, Yeva remembered, but a place of progress. Or, it had been, once.

Yeva sat on the topmost steel step. "So you want to send a message," she played along.

"A warning."

"To stop the bridal industry machine."

"Exactly."

"That's your whole message?"

"That's my whole message."

"Who are you sending this message to? The next loner who wants to come tour Ukraine?"

"And to the world at large."

"People can still meet online, can't they? No planes or buses needed. What are you going to do, shut down the internet?"

The girl kept her eyes trained on Yeva, undeterred.

Yeva sighed. "You'd need to narrow down your message. Make a specific, achievable demand to modify the industry, increase safety standards. Make a checklist, a manifesto. Something reasonable, ideally without involving hostages."

"But I don't want to change the industry. I want to destroy it."

"And as a little girl, I wanted to save the planet. Trust me, set some parameters. Otherwise, you'll never be satisfied. You'll never rest."

This was going nowhere, Yeva knew. Her words were having no effect. She rubbed her face, a profound sadness taking hold of her. There were no hotlines to help this kind of girl. She could be shaped a little, shaved down, but that molten core would keep fueling her, driving her forward, and there wasn't anything anyone could do to stop it. Only when the fuel ran out by itself would the girl slow down, tumble into a pit of despair, plot her own death.

"The world doesn't work the way you think it does. It finds a million ways to disappoint," Yeva said. "So, here's a lesson: you don't get to just waltz up to a stranger and ask for an entire lab."

"I'm offering you money."

Yeva bristled. "This isn't about the money."

But what was it about? She considered. It was about the broader lesson. She herself hadn't acquired the lab out of thin air. Oh, that German NGO had put her through the ringer. The endless paperwork, the grant proposals, the work plan to retrofit the trailer, the reference letters, the budget sheets calculated and recalculated and resubmitted, the extra hoops to jump through since Ukraine wasn't an EU country, et cetera. The rounds of committees that waffled, stalled. During an interview, one juror deemed the threatened snails a Ukraine problem, not a worldwide problem, as if they weren't in danger elsewhere, as if they weren't affecting the calcium cycle anywhere else. Another juror (on a Russian payroll?) asked how Yeva could prove she wouldn't use her lab to develop chemical weapons as "other terrorist organizations were doing in Ukraine." It took two years of proposals, counterproposals, until she had the keys to the lab in hand. And even then, she could hardly call the old and half-functioning thing a lab. She'd used her meager savings to fix it up. And yes, she'd joined the romance tours.

"If you want my help," Yeva told the girl, "you'll need to submit a prospectus."

"A what?"

"Think of methodology. A project plan. The impact of this initiative on your own practice and that of your field. Figure it out. I have better things to do than coach you through such basics."

Yet, despite herself, didn't this demand feel good? Yeva was always the one asking, asking (begging!). There was something delicious about being on the other side, being a jury of one, holding the veto power. She already knew the verdict: hell no. Yeva would not participate in a kidnapping, but she would pretend to go along with the planning for now, for the girl's own good. By the time the girl cobbled together a proposal and considered the pesky logistics of her movie plot scheme, she'd cool off, change her mind, abort. Yeva would steer a wayward child onto the right side of the law, change her life, possibly save it. Wasn't this what people did to feel good? Help other humans, a supposedly higher cause than helping nonhumans? Legacy, Yeva thought. Help a child find direction, become a mentor. Legacy—not in the field Yeva wanted, but who was she to choose? Yeva saw her last foray into the woods retreat in the distance, and felt a relief. She would postpone her final act.

"But I've already told you the plan, and I don't want to leave a paper trail," the girl countered.

Yeva hadn't thought of that, but didn't want to admit it. "Obviously the proposal will be verbal. A presentation, more like. Ninety minutes, tops."

"There's no time for all that," the girl announced. "The hundred men have to disappear on the Day of the Heavenly Hundred." Yeva couldn't imagine a more offensive day to pull such a stunt, when the country commemorated the victims of the Maidan Revolution—though outrage was probably the whole point, as it would certainly generate more press. But it was only *two days away*.

"Your lack of planning is not my emergency," Yeva said. The quote came from a coffee mug the conservationist had once sent her. "Include a budget in the presentation, too."

"What for? I only need the lab."

"You were planning on feeding your charges, weren't you? Having basic medical supplies on hand? Contingencies in case of medical emergencies?"

Was the girl beginning to regret getting Yeva involved? Even better. Yet the girl couldn't go to someone else, Yeva knew too much by now.

Yeva named a location on the outskirts of the city where the girl could give her presentation, said she could slip her into her schedule tomorrow. But she made no promises about handing over the lab for the Day of the Heavenly Hundred. If the girl was overwhelmed by the idea of preparing a prospectus, she didn't show it. Even so, Yeva was convinced that her strategy would still work, that the girl would see the insanity, or at least the logistical impossibility, of her stunt. She was still a child, after all, eighteen *and a half*.

5

YOU'RE BEING WEIRD, secretive," Sol remarked between dates in the days following Valentine's Day. "If you're actually falling for one of the bachelors, you'd better knock it off."

Of course, Nastia had told her sister nothing of the hostage plan she'd been hatching. They hadn't spoken about Valentine's Day, either, out of embarrassment. Instead, for days they'd acted as though neither of them had gotten her hopes up about their mother's return. But secretly, Nastia plotted: if she played her cards right, their mother would soon see the international headlines about the hundred kidnapped would-be grooms, would wonder about the mastermind behind the plan, so much like herself, and they'd find each other again, two mirror images collapsing into one.

In the meantime, Nastia and Sol continued with the romance tour, with the scheduled dates Nastia hadn't thought she'd have to go through with after Valentine's Day and her mother's promised return. The bachelors blurred together in her mind as she met them in the restaurants and bars around the hotel. The burly long-haul driver who'd been gifted the tour as a surprise fortieth birthday present from his mother. The logger who sweated through his shirt and flinched at any noise, who lived in a cabin in the woods with his dogs and hunting rifles and said he hated modernity. The coroner who'd presented a fourteen-page astrological report attesting to his and Nastia's compatibility as fiery lovers.

"The photos they love showing, their cars or boiler systems—don't buy into any of it," Sol warned.

How could Sol think Nastia would marry some stranger and hop on a plane? She'd clearly read too many historical romance novels featuring European heroines who follow brawny adventurers to the New World. Yet Nastia did not say a word to appease Sol's fears, denied nothing. Better for Sol to worry about Nastia being duped into marriage than to find out what her sister was planning, which Nastia knew she'd never agree to.

Between dates or during breaks in the socials at the hotel, Nastia merely pretended to visit the first-floor ladies' room all the other brides used—the "gossip cesspool" Sol rarely ventured into herself. Instead, she would sneak off to the alley out back and eye Yeva's trailer, parked there. And every time she saw the thing—lumbering, white, speckled with rust—she felt a tinge of relief mixed with excitement. It seemed to grow larger every time she saw it, a great whale about to swallow a hundred men whole. It was the key to her plan.

And then there was Yeva herself.

What did Nastia see in Yeva? She'd watched the woman slump through a couple of socials at the beginning of the tour, but now Yeva appeared to spend most of her time cooped up in the trailer. Whenever Nastia had steeled herself to approach Yeva at a social, the woman had looked tired, strung out, purple under her eyes, like she hadn't slept in days. Coffee stains on her loose blouse, breath smelling like curing meats. She should've been turned away at the tour registration desk, much like other brides had been for much smaller aesthetic infringements, but the administrators must've liked her look, which was that of a dusky-eyed catwalk model in withdrawal. Her ruin suited her, like crushed silk. The bachelors gawked at her mysteriousness, aching to pull her from the wreckage of her own life.

Yeva, someone who could be swayed. Who surely had nothing to lose by helping Nastia with her stunt.

Was this how Iolanta Cherno had thought and operated, back when she recruited for Komod? She had lured the bored university girls from good families, sure, but there were the other kind, too. Runaways. With bad families, bad exes they didn't like to talk about. The girls who fought by Iolanta's side most viciously were the ones who believed she had saved them.

But Yeva wasn't like the Komod girls, who were so attuned to their bodies and the power they believed those bodies held, every angle practiced, perfected. Yeva didn't seem to think much about her body at all, lugged it from trailer to alley like a piece of furniture she didn't need but couldn't quite get rid of. Her gaze didn't flit over Nastia's figure, either. This was new. Disorienting not to know where you stood in someone's books, but also nice. Nastia had grown up feeling constantly watched, surveyed—by Komod, then by the prospecting men and agency administrators, even by the brides set against each other as competition. Every inch of exposed skin: A sign of submission? Rebellion? Was it for men? Against men?

No, she concluded. Her mother wouldn't have wanted Yeva, a civilian. Yet this made Nastia want to recruit the woman all the more.

6

FOR HER PRESENTATION the day after talking to Yeva, the girl showed up at the agreed-upon time and place, a picnic table by a gas station on the outskirts of the city. The sight of her thin coat made Yeva regret insisting on meeting outside—she hadn't had anyone inside her trailer in years, or ever, and hadn't wanted to risk being overheard at a café or bar—but the girl didn't seem to notice the winter chill as she spoke.

What she delivered wasn't exactly a prospectus—it was more like a rambling rant with illegible diagrams and maps drawn on the backs of receipts she immediately tore up so as not to leave "evidence"—but still, the girl surprised Yeva. The preparation, the scope of her plan. The girl laid it out: how the men wouldn't know they were being taken at first, lured into the mobile lab under the guise of an Escape Room—except, of course, there would be no escape. Using a camera installed in the trailer, she'd then record a video of the bachelors saying how scared they were, how they wished they'd never come to this dangerous country, warning other men to stay away. The girl also spoke of the ethical considerations. While unfortunate, any incidental trauma—first from the bachelors' confinement, then from their release into the wild countryside—was a necessary means to a greater good, specifically: a world in which marriage agencies no longer existed.

Yeva, a jury of one, sat on the concrete bench with her hands stuffed in her pockets, pretending to mull it over. The methodology, while thorough, had some flaws.

"You're going to wrangle a hundred men into a trailer by yourself," she said at last. This was after the girl had again promised that Yeva would not need to have anything to do with the captives, that all she needed to do was drive.

"Not wrangle. Like I said, lure. Seduce."

"Disguised in a mask, not weird at all." Yeva was referring to one part of the plan, where the girl had mentioned a mask.

"I'll make the mask thematic." The girl seemed to push a word, with effort, from her pale pink lips: "Sexy."

"All this without an interpreter." Yeva suspected the girl didn't know a lick of English.

"Not the worst agency rule I'd be breaking."

"Forget about the agency. We're talking prison."

"If it comes down to it, we can burn down the trailer so that it can't be tracked back to us. Didn't you say it was extra-flammable?"

Yeva found herself on her feet. "We will *not* burn down my mobile lab."

"I'll pay you back."

Was the girl joking? Could she fathom how much the thing was worth? The hundreds of hours Yeva had spent on renovations? What annoyed Yeva most: how the girl had breezed into the meeting with a duffel bag slung over her back, packed and ready, as if they'd load up the bachelors and hit the road right after they talked, as if it were all so easy.

But hadn't Yeva herself once been this naïve? Hadn't she thought she could drag twenty-three species back from the brink of extinction—easy. Other malacologists might rot in their offices, jump bureaucratic hoops for measly grants, but not Yeva. She'd go rogue, set out on the road, do what no one else could. If, years ago, someone had sat her down and told her that what she wanted was impossible—or even if it *was* possible, that she wasn't built for the job—would she have listened?

Still, the girl should hear the flaws in her plan, the hindrances, for her own good.

Yeva sat back down and took two icy breaths. First, she told the girl to forget about pulling it all together by tomorrow, the Day of the Heavenly Hundred. And second, she couldn't possibly fit a hundred men into Yeva's lab.

"We'll find a way. Make them squeeze."

"The air circulation couldn't handle it. It's not calibrated. They'd suffocate."

The girl rolled her eyes, as if Yeva had invented the pesky thing called mammalian respiration.

"How many then, eighty?"

"If I were to uninstall some of the cabinets, you'd have to settle for twelve, max. Hypothetically."

"Only twelve."

"Twelve has a nice ring to it, a Last Supper size. A number people can clearly imagine, no?"

Yeva watched the girl's face fall. Well, this was what growing up was all about. You had dreams, and you watched them get slowly whittled down. You had to learn to accept the hollowed remnants.

"Thank you for your proposal," Yeva said stiffly, getting up from the picnic table. "You should have the result in four to six weeks."

"Four to six *weeks*?"

Yeva said nothing. The German juries took months.

"Look, I'm not stupid," the girl said. "I came here hoping I was wrong, but I know you're not actually going to help me. I know you have other things going on. Congratulations, I guess?"

"For what?"

"I saw you scoping out wedding dresses down the street from the hotel yesterday."

Yeva rubbed her eyes, suddenly exhausted. She should smile, act bashful. How many times would she have to keep up the farce? First with her mother, now with this girl she barely knew.

The girl reached into her duffel, pulled from it what looked like a body bag—long, white, zipper down the middle—and laid it between them on the picnic table. Unzipped it. A mound of tulle sprang out, shockingly white. A wedding dress.

"The nylon of the bodice is military grade," the girl said, as if this were a selling point. "It's my mother's. You're taller but about the same size otherwise." Fingering the row of snaps disguised as miniature roses down its side, she recounted how her mother would wear the dress in public squares when she pretended to marry foreigners she'd been "dating." The I-dos exchanged, she'd tear off the dress to reveal a body painted with bruises. The dress came with a white maid's bonnet and a fabric bouquet that converted, via a telescopic handle, into a broom. But, she said, putting them back inside the bag, she figured Yeva wouldn't need those. "You can keep the dress, if you don't mind the paint stains inside. My mother hasn't worn it in years. Have a good honeymoon or whatever." The girl straightened her coat, began walking away.

Yeva waited to feel a rush of relief. Finally, she'd gotten rid of her. She watched the girl wait at the bus stop up the highway, watched her wrap her arms around herself, hop on the spot. So she was cold, after all.

The dress stirred in the breeze, as if it yearned to follow.

It was a caricature of a wedding dress, really. Impossible to miss in a public square. Exactly the kind of gaudy thing Yeva's relatives would love, but Yeva would still get the last word, in a way, since the dress was never meant for a real wedding. It was perfect. But as soon as this last detail of her plan clicked into place, the horror of it sank in, the pain of what she was committing to. She imagined herself in a body bag, a real one, unzipped for her mother to identify through the layers of tulle. Her mother, who would never recover. Yeva had thought she only had two choices, to live a life she hated every single day or to die. But now, a third choice was opening up. Not a great one, an insane one actually, but it was better than the other two because at least she'd get to keep meeting with the girl. A girl whose reckless ambition Yeva did admire. For now, this third choice was enough.

"Nastia," she called as she approached the girl. It was the first time she'd spoken her name. When the girl turned around, Yeva stuffed the horrid dress into her arms. "Under exceptional circumstances, you could submit an expedited request. For the lab."

A bus approached but Nastia didn't flag it down. "What kind of exceptional circumstances?"

"If it's a matter of public safety."

"It's a matter of public safety."

To be needed again—pathetic, how good it felt. Yeva hadn't felt this way since she'd picked up her very first snail in the south of the country. She'd placed Lefty in his tank and he'd lain retracted in his wrong-whorled shell, motionless for what seemed like hours until, finally, his translucent body had begun to emerge. The pair of eye stalks had stretched toward her like two pleading hands.

"You can submit the request. Verbally," said Yeva.

"I submit the request." Nastia smiled, and Yeva knew she already understood the answer.

7

THE TERMS Yeva insisted upon weren't ideal. In fact, they were far from what Nastia had envisioned.

The first: the kidnapping would take place in four days, specifically on the last day of the Extra Lux Romance Tour, which coincided with February 23, Wednesday. It was a date which held no particular significance in the national calendar but provided additional time for necessary preparations.

The second: no humans would be physically harmed.

The third: no vehicles would be burned.

The fourth: for safety considerations, the maximum occupancy of the trailer was truly, nonnegotiably, twelve.

Twelve was still enough to make a statement, Nastia told herself. Enough to reach her mother. Twelve did have a nice ring to it. It was rounded, calendrical, biblical, fated. A number people could clearly imagine.

But which twelve?

8

ANY MOMENT NOW, Pasha would traverse the banquet hall and engage the women in courtship. Perhaps, he told himself, if he did not look directly at them, sailed forth blind, he could do it—but still his feet stayed glued to the faded carpeting. Thirty meters away, beyond the arch of pink and white Valentine's Day balloons, the women formed an impenetrable wall: perfumed, stilettoed, their long gleaming nails saber-like. One, in a tight silver dress that shone under the chandeliers like armor, was tearing meat off a bamboo skewer with her teeth. A few were smiling, or trying to smile, but the loudest were those who weren't, who were regarding Pasha and his compatriots with expressions that blared, *So this is it? The agency really does send the dregs.* As a thirty-eight-year-old he was on the younger end of the bachelors, yet terror rose inside him, familiar from his attempts to approach women back home. Already he irritated them, let them down, before he'd even opened his mouth.

It was the first day of the romance tour. Along every wall of the banquet hall, monitors looped photos of the success stories. The happy couples posing on their wedding day or honeymoon cruise or tropical resort. Grooms flashed toothy grins beside demure brides with pursed lips. Look how easy it is to find your perfect bride, the photos promised. Anyone could do it. Even Pasha.

The speaker beside him popped to life, infusing the hall with smooth jazz as a dozen interpreters entered through a side door.

On cue, the first few men pioneered across the room and disappeared into the perfumed fray.

Pasha hated to admit it, but his grand Homecoming to his birth country was not what he had envisioned. The last of his three flights from Canada, the Ukrainian Airlines one, had been choppy and the fellow passengers rowdy, ignoring the seatbelt signs to traipse up and down the aisle and chat with each other. After another patch of turbulence, he overheard the couple seated in front of him joking that the plane must have drifted over the Donbas. Had his countrymen always been like this? Had Pasha been like this, before he'd been uprooted to Canada as a child? And then, at the airport, there was that surly customs guard with his military buzz cut. Despite Pasha's efforts to deploy his best Russian, the guard had switched to a bludgeoning English. Pasha made the mistake of eyeing the flyers laid out in front of the guard, entitled "How to Report Bribery," and the guard made a show of passing a whole stack of them to Pasha with a smile that said, *Just try. Just try to take a flyer, goddamn tourist.* Pasha politely declined—in English.

Standing in the hotel banquet hall now, surrounded by strangers, Pasha reminded himself that it wasn't too late to return to his old life. He hadn't torn up his Canadian passport—he'd had some sense left in him after all. He could taxi to the airport and fly standby back to Vancouver, that glittering mirage of a city he'd vowed to leave forever. But no, he would not give in. No, this new Pasha—he'd reclaimed his birth name (more precisely, the diminutive of his birth name, Pavel), shed that wooden anglicized Paul—was tenacious and brave. A little wild, even. Pasha would see his new life plan through. While Paul would have hidden behind the speaker for the whole evening, Pasha would walk the ballroom with his head high. He would court these women. Not just any women, he reminded himself: Ukrainian women. His own kind. In their soft arms, he'd at last feel at home.

But it wasn't just any Ukrainian woman Pasha was looking for. He felt like he already knew his future bride, like they'd already had a long and soulful correspondence, and he'd recognize her as soon as he saw her face-to-face. She'd have a common name,

Olya or Anya or Tanya. A round, open face. She'd be sitting on the sidelines, in what she thought was her best dress—something comely but plain, like a church smock—hardly distinguishable from the interpreters, and she'd be wondering why she'd come to this glitzy social. She'd feel like she didn't compare to the svelte femmes fatales, though she was decidedly more beautiful in an unplaceable ethereal way. She'd regret not having put on more makeup, having stayed up the night before finishing a university assignment (some rigorous program) so that the delicate skin under her eyes bore the slightest hint of blue. No, the woman of Pasha's dreams did not belong on this romance tour any more than Pasha himself did, but they'd both been spurred by the hope of love. They simply did not know what else to do. They'd laugh about it later, and the story of how they'd met would become their little secret, though they might divulge it in time to a grandchild or two.

This Olya or Anya didn't even want to move abroad—she just didn't know it yet. At this very moment, she was steeling herself for the prospect of leaving behind her entire family, her friends, everything she'd ever known. The Great Abroad supposedly held promise. During a long riverside stroll with Pasha, she would grow silent, take in her city for what she thought was the last time. That's when Pasha would take her round little face in his hands and propose. She would accept, willing to give it all up for him, though in her joy he'd catch that fleck of sadness, homesickness already setting in.

That's when he'd tell her.

"My darling," he would say. "We're not going anywhere." His airfare had been one way. A bit of paperwork and he'd be able to stay here indefinitely. He'd leave behind his stalled life, his paltry Paul self, and start anew.

Hopefully all the above would take place within ninety days. That was how long Pasha was allowed to stay in Ukraine on his tourist visa. As things stood, he held no status in his birth country beyond this. His parents had renounced their Ukrainian citizenship (and, of course, Pasha's) as soon as they'd received their Canadian one. He resented them for this (and was it even possible, let alone legal, for parents to renounce citizenship on their child's behalf?), but there was no more time for resentment. There was only time for action. At this very moment, the woman of his dreams may have already given up on finding love in this chintzy hall, and may have edged along its flamingo-patterned walls to the nearest exit.

Pasha had been eight years old when his parents uprooted him. It was during the nineties, when Ukraine's post-Soviet economy was in free fall. Residing in Kyiv's outskirts, his family had been forced into a medieval sleep schedule reigned over by blackouts: first sleep after work and school, then chores and homework at night, when the power turned on, followed by a second sleep until dawn. Pasha's parents had not informed him of their emigration plan. "We didn't want you jabbering to your schoolmates," they told him later. While legal, it was still uncouth to scurry away like dissenters.

He'd screamed as his parents dragged him onto his first airplane, the flight attendants cooing in sympathy. As his parents wrestled a seatbelt around him, they sang the praises of their destination: a land of bounty, with all the foods he'd ever loved. Bananas. Chicken drumsticks. He could have as many as he wanted. And he'd given in, weakling that he was! Bribed by food, of all things, like a dog. He could have whispered to a flight attendant that he was being kidnapped, begged to be sent back to the doting grandparents he already missed, but before Pasha knew it he was on a second plane, hurtling across an ocean, sucking down his fourth free Pepsi.

His first memory of British Columbia, Canada, "Best Place on Earth": vomit. He'd thrown up in the taxi, all those bananas his parents had plied him with at the airport bistro upon landing now oozing down his sweater and onto the car seat. His parents yelling about the expense of the bananas, the reupholstery they'd surely have to pay for—they'd barely touched Canadian soil and already their son was bankrupting them. The taxi driver oddly, miraculously, did *not* yell or kick them out on the curb; instead he handed Pasha crumpled napkins to wipe his soiled mouth and chin and teary eyes. That's when a grand illusion clouded Pasha's brain, one that would last all the way through childhood and adolescence: the illusion that this new world was a gentler place than the one he'd left behind.

At school, none of the teachers yelled at him, either. No one berated him for nail biting or improper pencil holding. When called upon to answer a question—usually in math class, since the only English words he knew were numbers—he didn't have to stand at attention, could keep lounging in his seat like a loafer. The teachers didn't make a fuss over his poor vision and let him shimmy his desk right up to the chalkboard (his parents had refused to get him glasses, fearing they would further weaken his eyes). The school nurse who checked him for head lice was achingly gentle, apologetic, like she was trespassing on some key part of his being. Back home he'd felt like public property, subject to commentary on his droopy shoulders and pigeon toes from relatives and strangers at any moment. Pasha, who had never taken well to drills, criticism, or punishment, was soon bloated with compliments and stickers. He spent his first school year in Canada in a foggy, confused silence, and even this earned him a Good Citizenship and Listening Award at general assembly. His second school year, he wobbled through his first English sentences, spoke up in class. He looked his elders right in the eye, addressed his new friends' parents by first names. "Paul is prospering," his parents would announce to relatives over the phone, using their new anglicized name for him—ironically at first, but then it stuck.

Pasha's parents were certainly prospering themselves. They plowed through starter jobs—his mother cleaned houses for cash, his father delivered mail-order hardware catalogs—while taking night classes to upgrade their certifications. Within eight months of landing on Canadian soil, his parents had resumed their work as engineers. Within three years they'd bought a house, and Pasha moved into his very own room, an exorbitant luxury. The house may have been ramshackle, its basement a dirt pit stinking of skunk, but the Kazakhstani realtor assured them that the structure had good bones. It had been built seventy-five years ago, of old-growth cedar hard as steel. Seventy-five years ago, Pasha's parents reminded him upon signing the paperwork, his great-grandparents would have been losing their estates to the Bolsheviks. This new old house was the family's first private property in generations. Armed with heat guns and steel barbecue brushes, his parents stripped layer after layer of lead paint off the bombastic moldings and wooden paneling (dirty white, then lime green, hospital blue, nursery pink). They restored the plumbing to coax warmth back into the cast-iron oil-fed radiators. Every improvement they'd document in photos, developed at the supermarket and mailed to approving relatives in Ukraine.

Another achievement: the citizenship ceremony. His father fussed over their outfits, forbade a blouse or collar or jewelry or any other frou-frou in favor of the "local look": matching new baseball caps, jeans, baggy black Costco windbreakers. The three of them crinkled in nylon through the entire ceremony as his mother passed silent judgment on the other attendees who came looking dressed for the prom, at the families who had dared to don the bright, patterned garb of their home countries. After the small bespeckled judge gave a speech about Canada's multicultural fabric and the country's tolerance of all creeds, his parents warned Pasha to be wary. If living under Soviet rule had taught them anything, it was not to trust official messaging, to always read between the lines. "Unlike the Chinese and the Africans," his mother had whispered, nodding at the other newly minted Canadians in the courtroom's lobby, "we can blend right in, stay undetected." The only snag was their chesty Slavic accents. Pasha's parents had already instituted Only English Saturdays, had already watched Rambo movies in the evenings for the simple, well-dispersed dialogue. This routine soon expanded to Only English Sundays.

As part of their Great Assimilation Project, his parents stayed away from other Slavs. While on a windy stroll along the seawall during their first months in Vancouver, Pasha heard an overbundled, overpatterned family of four speaking Russian ahead of them. They could have been from any of the Eastern Bloc countries, but Pasha felt drawn to their familiar voices among this sea of strangers. He chattered to his parents at a theatrical volume, hoping to draw the other family's attention, but his mother yanked him close and shushed him. "Look at them all, swarming in," she hissed to his father. They didn't want too many of their own kind here, bringing their failed empire problems with them like bedbugs latched on to suitcases. If it were up to Pasha's parents, they would've shut Canadian borders to Slavs the moment they themselves had stepped through.

The settled Ukrainian diaspora who hadn't lived under Soviet rule interested his parents even less. "Their Sunday school Ukrainian sounds terrible, like the deaf trying to speak," complained his mother, who never uttered a word of the language herself, having been taught mostly Russian in school. (Still, Pasha caught a hint of envy in his parents' voices when they spoke of the Ukrainian-Canadian archive centers in the prairies, which, untouched by wars or occupations or famines or purges, were able to preserve heirloom paintings and rare books better than their compatriots back home.) With their painted egg societies and red-booted Cossack dance troupes and church pierogi sales, the diaspora had built their own folksy, utopian version of Ukraine that had little to do with the modern one. To this ancient wave of émigrés, Pasha would realize later, new arrivals like his family must've seemed just as alien: a drably dressed, rootless, Godless, emotionally hobbled *Homo sovieticus*, who after decades of Pan-Slavism shoved down its throat had any sense of collectivism bred right out of it.

Before the Bolsheviks stole his ancestors' estates, Pasha's parents recounted, the family had enough wealth to transcend material worries. They'd painted, written poetry and plays and treatises about their human and political condition. They were the Shevchenkos, the Skovorodas, and the Lesya Ukrainkas of their lands. Surely that talent lay hidden somewhere deep in Pasha, suppressed for generations into a diamantine vein. While other immigrants steered their offspring into practical careers like medicine and accounting, his parents, from his early days, scrunched their noses at *all that*. They did not leave everything they knew back in Ukraine, they did not traverse the roiling Atlantic just so their son could suffer the same boring engineering jobs they'd endured, and their own parents had endured. No, Pasha would transcend pragmatism, become a Deep Thinker.

Would his calling be painting? Music composition? Acting? Ceramics? Writing Gogolesque tales? Carving ornate pastoral scenes onto Italian limewood? Or all of the above melded into a wholly new medium? Every evening of the week, Pasha slumped in the backseat of his parents' Dodge Caravan as they ferried him from class to class at community centers or fine arts boot camps or with private teachers. Even as a child, he knew his chicken-scratch paintings sucked. Drama classes were a weekly hell of public embarrassment. It was exhausting to always be on guard for some grand revelation to strike, like a chronic family disease, while the same dumb thoughts chattered on and on in his head, mostly about what he'd eat next.

"Tell us please, he will be success?" his parents would demand, harassing his many instructors and tutors, cornering them after class.

The teachers' smiles would fade at the word "success" like they didn't know what it meant. Pasha knew all too well. Success meant acceptance into an American Ivy League school on scholarship followed by a lucrative career in one of the brand-name cities, like Los Angeles or San Francisco or New York, fulfilling both the immigrant dream and the familial destiny.

"He is Deep Thinker?" his parents would pester.

Pasha would look up at his teachers in moments like this, inwardly pleading with them to put him and his parents out of their misery.

Instead, they'd announce, one after the other, how Pasha was making "such great progress!"

His parents drank it all in, to Pasha's confusion. Why couldn't they read between the lines? It was only as an adult, after his mother told him that her ballet dreams had been shattered by a teacher who'd declared her "Without Prospect" (she was too big-boned, meaning normal size), that he understood. His parents had been reared by the cutthroat Soviet pedagogical machine, which cast aside any child who was not deemed biologically destined for the Bolshoi or the Moscow Tchaikovsky Conservatory or to win gold at the Olympics. His scarred parents didn't see why it should be any different in Canada.

"There is *one* thing, though," his raku pottery teacher dared to confess.

His parents bowed their heads, ready for the verdict.

"Paul doesn't seem to be having as much fun as the other kids in class?"

His parents considered the mud-smeared woman in puzzlement, as if she'd just confirmed to them that Pasha's hair was indeed brown.

His training continued. In middle school, bloated by the fizzy encouragement of his teachers, he began to believe there really was something special buried in his genes, waiting to be mined, like his parents said. Maybe his misery was necessary for Deep Thinking. Anyway, better this life than that of his cousins, stuck back in Ukraine, trudging through technical schools. In a few years they'd be schlepping long commutes to grueling office jobs while still living in crowded apartments with their families. Spinning their wheels, not knowing anything better, never once considering anything loftier for themselves, never dreaming. He felt a pang of survivor's guilt. Steeling himself for his artistic journey, he let his parents enroll him in a special fine arts high school. His portraits were exhibited at semester-end shows while his parents looked on, their faces blank and unreadable as his dead-eyed subjects. If they harbored any suspicion that they'd been deluded about Pasha's talents, they certainly didn't show it.

"Which percentage do you award this?" They'd target the thinner teachers, believing them to be the most credible, and drag them from one globbed canvas to another.

"We don't do grades here," the woodcarving teacher reminded them, dream catchers dangling from her ears. "We advance students on a completion basis."

"So, either zero or one hundred. Is it zero?"

"Of course not."

"Then one hundred," his father declared.

The teacher invented an excuse to slide away.

Finally, in Pasha's last semester of high school, the illusion of his potential greatness shattered. The family's stern iron claw-foot mailbox turned out to be the most honest thing they had, producing rejection letter after rejection letter from art schools across the country. The letters were apologetic. These schools so wished they had more space to take in such a talented pool of applicants, but alas. Finally, his parents read between the lines.

After weeks of mourning, the family compromised on an earthier pathway for Pasha: architecture. A forgivable mélange of art with math. He took prerequisite courses in which he finally felt at home, with mathematical proofs and formulas that were severe and frank, and that declared right away whether you were right or wrong, what you were capable of. He wondered if he could avoid the wishy-washy courses on "expression of beauty" and "cultural considerations" altogether.

At the end of his first year of university, he made an announcement to his parents over dinner. He was switching to engineering. "Mechanical," he specified—just like his parents—putting the final nail in the coffin of their artistic dreams for him. He said he wanted to build bridges or water supply systems, something tangible. He wanted to wear the steel ring on his pinkie, the one given to Canadian engineers in a special initiation ritual when they vowed to work for the public good. "Imagine it," he added, "car, house, a government job with a pension plan."

His father yawned, already bored.

"We might as well have left you back in Ukraine," his mother sighed.

But they accepted his decision. He could have pursued a much worse career for the "public good." Social work, for instance, which had zero chance of glory.

But none of Pasha's plans had panned out. His excellent grades landed him a job at a prestigious engineering firm, but he could barely afford to pay both his student loans and the rising rent. He shared an apartment with two roommates, rode to work on a sweaty bus in which a drunk man had once vomited on him. On drier days he biked to work. He—an engineer! It was unseemly.

Meanwhile, his cousins back in Ukraine were somehow prospering. They worked easier jobs than he did—IT, marketing, communications—yet their social media posts boasted newly acquired condos, breezy tours around the Mediterranean. One cousin bought himself a luxury car (used, but still), posted about how "if you work hard you too can fulfill your dreams." Many of Pasha's relatives were employed by foreign companies eager to outsource work to this cheaper talent, but none tried to use their connections to emigrate. They seemed, Pasha had to admit, happy. And not just on a material level. One cousin opened a gallery as a hobby, another spent his weekends DJing in refurbished factories. A childhood friend bought a cheap piece of land and turned it into an artists' colony.

"Oh my god, have you been to Kyiv? You should totally go," a colleague said to Pasha, glowing after her carefully allotted two-week vacation. No, he hadn't been to Kyiv, Pasha wanted to answer, because the city seemed foreign to him now, had moved on without him. Somehow his sunken ship of a country had resurfaced, jerry-rigged with a new engine. Suddenly its barnacles and cankerweed looked edgy and cool, and every night on this ship was a raging rave, and every night Pasha missed out on it.

He was living with his parents again. Only temporarily, he told himself, while he tried to save for a down payment on a house. And it did have to be a house, however small, anchored to actual land, because paying the kinds of prices people demanded for a condo—a box stacked upon other boxes—felt suspect. Every time he thought he was getting close, prices lurched ahead again, out of reach. Would he end up like the other millennials he read about, who funneled their nesting urges into doll-size houses they decorated with miniature polymer clay furniture? SMELLS LIKE TEENY SPIRIT, one headline read. "It's so nice to have a space you can design and have control over, however small," one interviewee lied to herself. Pasha lay awake at night, the pillowy wallpaper peonies of his childhood bedroom looming over him, threatening to snuff him out in his sleep.

"Still living here, are you?" his father would quip when they ran into each other in the mornings before work. His parents had long stopped lamenting that he had quit the arts, had come to their senses like he had, yet they still saw Canada as the promised land, rendering Pasha's stalled life *even as an engineer* all the more confusing, the result of some individual deficiency. If *they* could buy a house within three years of landing in a country they knew nothing about, with zero job connections, why couldn't he do it, with his pass-for-native English and his straight white teeth?

Alone in the dark of his bedroom, he began scrolling the marriage agency sites. Imagined starting his life all over again in Ukraine, or rather, living out the life that had been taken from him. He could have tried reinstituting his citizenship the hard way, could have demanded his parents provide his birth records, but he knew they would refuse, try to talk him out of it.

From his screen, the sirens beckoned with their flowing hair and sea-blue eyes. Of course, he wasn't stupid. He knew the women of his motherland didn't all look like this.

But what was the harm in scrolling the site?

Now, in the ballroom, Pasha finally unglued himself from his spot only to find a man named Bertrand blocking his way. "Incredible," the man declared. He beamed, raking a meaty hand through his thick dark curls. He looked to be about Pasha's age, and possessed the kind of casually athletic body that was out of place among the other men, a silent provocation. While those who'd spent months trimming themselves down at the gym paraded in their tightest shirts, Bertrand strolled around in hoodies, unbothered. He already had four dates lined up. "Gotta slow down. How you holding up? Taking a breather, too, I see."

Pasha had been seated beside Bertrand the day before, on a double-decker bus for a city tour organized by the agency. Pasha had joined hoping to be reacquainted with Kyiv, but Bertrand had filled up the entire tour with chatter, mostly about the app he was "architecting": Friends with Yachts, which "connected people who had yachts with people who wanted to be on yachts."

In other words, tech geeks with no social skills uniting with Instagrammable women. Bertrand was in Kyiv not just to find a bride but to recruit cheap tech talent and models for social media feeds. "Business," he'd told Pasha with a wink, "mostly."

It was men like Bertrand who made all the bachelors look bad, Pasha knew. Calculating and unromantic. They were the reason the good women, like his Olya, would be pushing through the hotel's brass rotating doors right this second, slipping away.

"I gotta go," Pasha announced.

"Get back in there, brother," Bertrand said. "May you find the One."

9

On the bus ride home after her prospectus meeting with Yeva, Nastia swiped through agency app photos of the men she'd gone on dates with so far. Who would make for proper hostages, be most hysterical in front of a camera? One by one they smiled up at her, earnest. They posed with floppy-tongued dogs, with glistening fish they'd pulled out of rivers. *Pick me.*

Should she choose the most repulsive ones, the ones who kept looking down her fingerprint-patterned dress or who ranted about how feminism had ruined the modern woman? Was that how her mother would have chosen? *Think beyond petty grievances,* she might have said. *Think bigger.* Yes, thought Nastia, the men she chose should be accomplished; they should be media-worthy, have good *stories.* Did he rescue mangy strays in developing nations? Was he a medal-spangled veteran? Did he run a not-for-profit? Had his first wife died a tragic death, leaving him with a horde of young children back home? Instead of being villains, the hostages should look like victims of the marriage industry themselves, victims of the monstrous thugs the industry attracted (thugs who must surely be just like the anonymous kidnappers).

Now Nastia had to consider each bachelor in a way she hadn't before. Could the public at large love him? Could *she* love him? She had to stretch her mind, wrench herself open. She had four days to scope them out, go on more dates, before the bachelors scattered back to their home countries. And there were the other details to attend to: the camera to buy, the disguises to procure, Yeva's list of technical requirements to satisfy. This list seemed to grow longer every time they met: medical supplies, water filtration tablets, portable batteries for Nastia's and Sol's phones, as if they were venturing out into the middle of nowhere, rather than to the oblast's woodsy outskirts.

When Nastia got home, Sol sat waiting in the kitchen.

"I made cake." Her sister gestured, as if Nastia could miss the layered wonder that took up half the table. A pansy-patterned tea service, which Sol usually reserved for guests they never hosted, took up the other half. "Where were you?"

"Out." Nastia started for her room.

"Is that Mother's protest dress?"

Sol was pointing to a tuft of neon white that stuck out of Nastia's half-zipped duffel bag. Nastia stuffed it back. On the bus, she'd let herself press her face to the bodice's slippery folds, trying to root out her mother's scent under the lingering rose perfume. Did it hold any sign of sweat? Excitement? Preshow nerves, such as Nastia herself now felt?

"Just getting the dress dry-cleaned, were we?" The lightness in Sol's voice unsettled Nastia. "Must keep things shipshape, even things we have no use for. Why not." Sol poured tea into two porcelain cups. "Sit."

Nastia sat. The tea was steeped to bitterness, and cold. How long had her sister been waiting?

"It's actually three cakes combined into one," Sol continued. The first, simple vanilla baked with a thin spread of meringue on top; the second, vanilla marbled with chocolate; the third, chocolate mixed with poached cherries and nuts—the dough first made into balls to set in the freezer, then defrosted and rolled into wafers and baked, then frozen again, grated, sprinkled between the other cake layers. Then she'd soaked each layer in black currant syrup before covering it with a cream made of boiled condensed milk mixed with butter. The hard thing was to soak the layers through just enough while keeping the meringue layer crisp. "Took me three days to make," she said, "but you wouldn't know. You've been so *busy*. Sneaking off between dates, coming home late."

When Nastia said nothing, Sol took a blunt steel server, sawed through the confection as though it were Styrofoam, dumped a slab onto Nastia's plate. "Go on, have a taste. How is it?"

Under Sol's scrutinizing gaze, the dessert turned to sawdust on Nastia's tongue, clung to the back of her throat. "Delicious," she forced out. "Moist."

"Moist, thank heavens."

"Aren't you having any?"

Sol sat back in her chair, considered the brown stains on the ceiling. "My baking was her weakness, remember?"

Nastia did. Their mother would refuse dessert by day but sneak creamy spoonfuls from the fridge at night.

"All that time I thought, if I just kept trying to make the perfect cake, she'd keep coming home after the protests or jail or wherever. Or even better, if I made her really, really fat, the cameras wouldn't love her anymore, naked or clothed." Sol let out a laugh. "But here we are again, except now it's you I have to worry about. You're plotting something, won't tell me anything, and all I can do is bake cake."

"I'm not going anywhere."

"I'm just a leak risk, right? A liability," Sol said, imitating their mother's low, matter-of-fact tone. "At first, I worried you were falling for one of the bachelors, but would that be worse than whatever you're plotting? I don't know anymore."

"If I told you, you'd be implicated."

"Another thing she used to say." Sol stood up, paced the kitchen. It was too big for the two of them, like the rest of the apartment, but neither Nastia nor her sister could let go of the place. "I lose my mother, now I'm about to lose my sister, but lucky me, all I have to do is stay out of the way, right? Sit tight, let the two crazies outcrazy each other." She heaved the cake from the table. Nastia winced as her sister flipped it into the trash.

"I'm sick of not being *implicated*," Sol yelled. "I'm sick of making goddamn cake." She took a breath and closed her eyes, like she was about to set out barefoot onto a bed of hot coals. "Let me help you. Remember your humble interpreter?"

"Sol."

"If you're making splashy slogans or posters, always better to write them in English for international media, right? A poorly placed comma can tank an entire campaign."

This, Nastia hadn't expected. But then again, she hadn't expected Sol to agree to the tours, either. They'd both needed the money, yes, but Sol didn't have to stay by Nastia's side for every date, every social. She hadn't had to help Nastia with her transformation, either. When Nastia balked at the cost of hair extensions, it was Sol who'd given her own waist-length platinum locks, which she'd spent years growing out, conditioning with oil and egg yolk, tucking into silk bonnets at night (all this because one of the Komod girls, years ago, had told Sol that long hair would soften the sharpness of her nose and chin). Nastia hadn't forgotten her sister's silent tears as the hairdresser's scissors slid across her nape.

And Nastia did need Sol, didn't she? She still didn't know exactly how she'd lure twelve men into a trailer—even under the guise of an Escape Room. She didn't know how she'd build their trust, seduce them into following her. So far, most of her interactions with the men had been choreographed by Sol. And in school Nastia had never dated, barely had friends. She'd wanted to believe that her mother's reputation had tainted her, but she knew the problem ran deeper.

She put on the kettle for fresh tea. "The plan . . . well, it's a bit more than splashy slogans."

Sol sat back down, crossed one leg over the other. "Go on, you can tell me. How bad could it really be?"

10

WHAT'S THIS? That handler of yours wasn't part of the project proposal." Yeva peered at Nastia and Sol from the side door of her trailer.

Nastia noticed Yeva looked better somehow—had she brushed her hair? "For the last time, Sol is my sister, not my handler. And we need her. For safety." She knew that word would work on Yeva. "She's one of the agency's best."

Sol smiled thinly. She'd barely said anything all morning, hadn't touched the kasha and milk Nastia set out for breakfast. Nastia was still expecting her sister to back out any moment.

"Nepotism," Yeva hissed. "The committee won't like it."

"The *committee* still hasn't given access to the trailer for preparations."

"For the last time—"

"Yes, yes, *mobile lab*. Yeva, meet Solomiya. Sol, meet Yeva," Nastia said.

"I've seen her around," said Sol, coolly.

They stood in silence. Nastia shifted weight. Was she supposed to be the charismatic leader, unite and rile up her troops? She preferred it when Sol did the talking.

"You need at least three legs to make a chair, right?" Nastia said, at last. "Here we are, the three legs, about to take the weight of social change."

"Not the most stable chair, three legs," Sol pointed out.

"Three legs, tops," Yeva conceded. "The driver's cabin can't fit any more." She stepped aside to allow the sisters into her mobile lab.

It was the smell that hit Nastia first: an odd mixture of rubbing alcohol and rot. Sure, Yeva had told her about the snail work, but Nastia had hardly listened. Now she looked around: crumpled clothes, mud-stained boots. A narrow bunk with a yellowed sheet, the cracked red vinyl showing from underneath. A half-eaten pizza, an open jar of fermented tomatoes that hadn't stopped fermenting, the frothy mold on top sprinkled with dead fruit flies. Empty vodka bottles with cigarette butts inside. Fast-food wrappers littering the surfaces, shockingly fattening for an agency bride. A vial with coffee grounds—or dirt?—stood on the Bunsen burner.

"It was sterile, once," Yeva said behind them, quietly.

Nastia avoided looking at her sister. She knew what Sol was thinking because Nastia was thinking it herself: *This* was the third leg Nastia had involved in her grand plan? This pretend scientist? Junkie?

Nastia forced a smile. "Just needs a dusting."

The sisters set to work as Yeva shuffled around, picking up random objects and setting them down again. She told them to get rid of whatever they wanted to, that she wouldn't be needing any of it anymore—but even as Nastia and Sol disassembled cabinets and shelves to make room for the bachelors, the woman would spring to life at the sight of a chipped beaker, a cloudy pipette, tearing the object out of their hands. And when Nastia moved to unplug the bar fridge, Yeva lunged at it as though Nastia was about to take a beloved relative off life support. The woman mumbled something about last members of species, preserved in the "death cabinet" for later study—since they might hold secrets of their extinction, she explained vaguely—as well as one live snail in hibernation. She showed them a pickling jar filled with something green and clumpy, as if this would end all argument.

Nastia watched Sol suppress a dry heave.

"What if we move the jars somewhere else?" she suggested.

Yeva waited with her arms crossed, daring Nastia to name alternative locations.

"A friend's fridge?"

The woman said nothing.

Probably had no friends. "Parents' fridge?"

"They'd forget what they are and throw them out."

"We'll label them."

"They'd throw the jars out all the faster."

"If we leave the jars where they are, the bachelors could get to them."

"I'll padlock it."

"That won't look weird at all," Sol piped in. "The bachelors get in, excited for their authentic romantic getaway, see a padlock on the bar fridge."

"They'll laugh and think it's a quirk. A local custom," Yeva said.

"Yeva," Nastia pleaded. "You really need a bunch of dead snails? You'll really study them one day?"

Yeva spoke so quietly, Nastia could barely hear her: "They're all I have left."

Nastia prayed Sol wouldn't start laughing. Mercifully, she did not. Nastia left the death cabinet alone.

The rest of the cleanout went more smoothly. They pared the lab down to the essentials, a few cushions to sit on. Yeva did try to fight for more creature comforts (A napping spot? Blankets? Something to read? The hot plate for making tea?), while Nastia reminded her that the bachelors would be locked inside for twenty-four hours at most. And they would be hostages. The whole point was discomfort.

Two days later, on the eve of the kidnapping, the cleaning was finally finished. The trio stood outside the lab. Nastia pointed at the logo on the side of the trailer. "Can we do something about the hands?"

"Cliché, I know," Yeva said.

"Might be confusing for the bachelors, when we're trying to coax them inside." And, though Nastia didn't say it, the painted hands weren't very good, the thumbs disproportionately long, the pinkies stubs, the green sprout frail and spindly.

"What about a cupid instead? Or a big heart?" Sol suggested.

Yeva looked horrified.

"Did you paint them yourself?" Nastia tried very hard to like the hands.

"The hands could represent romance," Sol said. "See how one's bigger than the other? You could say that one belongs to a bachelor, the other to a bride, and together they hold, um, new life."

"You know what? Let's get rid of the hands," Yeva said.

"Now I kind of like them," Nastia said. "The hands are growing on me."

11

THE ROMANTIC GETAWAY was starting any minute, Bertrand told Pasha. A "bonus social." They'd have two hours to puzzle their way out of a mobile Escape Room, and once they did, they'd be at their destination, a pagan fertility party in the woods. The invitation was *extremely* exclusive, according to the woman who'd pulled Bertrand into a photo booth. The men had been specially vetted by the brides who'd be at the party.

Was Pasha game?

It was the last night of the romance tour: "Prom Night," where the men wore suits and agency-issued baby's breath boutonnières, and the women swished around in long gowns. The night had begun primly, with bachelors and brides awkward as teenagers as they slow-danced to soulful ballads (Celine Dion, Michael Bolton—couldn't the nightclub play something local?) while Pasha hung back at the bar pretending to peruse the leather-bound tome of cocktail offerings. Pretending not to notice that the one bride he'd had hopes for, but who hadn't answered his date request (quiet but earnest, she'd picked at the heart-shaped sticker on her chest the entire tour as if it were a skin rash), was now sticker-free and doing a cross-armed shot with a truck driver from New Orleans. After Efrosinia's toast to the newly engaged couples, which did not improve Pasha's mood, the lights dimmed and techno pounded. Sweaty bodies writhed around Pasha as he tipped back one overly complicated (and Western-priced) cocktail after another.

Romantic failure aside, his birth country hadn't exactly opened her warm motherly arms to him as he'd wanted. The streets buzzed with a hostile energy; passersby returned his open smile with suspicious scowls. He'd tried taking the bus across the city—with no destination save the past, when his father would take him out for the freshest sweet creams—but even this proved mildly traumatic. It had been rush hour, and the other passengers were packed so tight against his body he could hardly breathe. At each stop, they'd pushed past him as though he had no right to be taking up space in the aisle, in this city. Their irritation had seemed personal, rooted as far back as Pasha's sweet-cream memories. What was he, a deserter, doing back here? What was he playing at? When times were rough, he and his parents had abandoned ship for Canada. But now look how well those who'd hunkered down had fared without him. Look at this new bus, these freshly paved roads, Kyiv's center aglitter.

After his fourth cocktail, Pasha had at last admitted defeat. He'd pushed through the writhing crowds toward the exit, determined to pack up that very night, fly back to Vancouver on standby. That's when Bertrand had come out of nowhere, two horilka shots in hand, and pulled him into a quiet back room with purple mohair poufs and a floor-to-ceiling aquarium of jellyfish backlit a radioactive yellow.

At first, Pasha said he'd pass on the exclusive romantic getaway. "I didn't get the invite anyway."

Bertrand tipped back his shot. "Ah, come on, I'll pull some strings."

Pasha's limbs felt loose, swimmy. His own shot glass, still full, sweated between his fingers. He really should give it back to Bertrand and head to the hotel to pack, he thought as he tipped the glass to his mouth, gulped the fiery liquid. He sank back, let the pouf swallow him like a sea anemone. "Which interpreter was it?"

"Who?"

Pasha brushed silky mohair strands from his face. "The woman who talked to you in the photo booth. She spoke to you in English, no?" Pasha had always tried to be conscientious with the interpreters, remember their names. They were underdogs, like he was.

"She wore a weird straw mask. Fox or whatever. Super pagan." Bertrand waved the question off as if to say, Did it matter, which interpreter? "Look at you, man. How could they not let you in? You're as eligible as they come. Engineer, full head of hair."

Pasha tried to argue at Bertrand's level. "Less of me means more women for you."

Bertrand heaved himself forward in his pouf, and for a moment Pasha thought that he was getting up to leave, that Pasha had offended him. "A brother doesn't leave another."

Pasha sat up. *Brother*. Surely he had misheard?

If Pasha's friends back in Vancouver had said anything of the sort, the words would've been dripping in sarcasm. But were those people—former classmates from undergrad who spent most of their evenings and weekends in hibernation—really his friends? He'd spent more time with Bertrand over the past week than he had with any of them over the past year. The breakfast buffets at the hotel, lounging in the lobby between socials and dates (mostly Bertrand's). At first Pasha thought Bertrand felt sorry for him, but pity was a higher-order emotion, not Bertrand's style. As a programmer Bertrand thought in binaries, after all. He liked you or he didn't. And Pasha liked Bertrand, too, didn't he? Didn't have to be clever around him, could drop his guard.

Bertrand gave Pasha a somber look. "Ever watch a pigeon try to get laid?"

Pasha shook his head. For a moment the room liquefied, as though he'd plunged into the aquarium along with the jellyfish.

"Well, you should. There's a lesson in there. He's all puffed up, he's bobbing and dancing circles around her, he's vibrating with love, and she's whacking at a piece of bread. Doesn't seem to notice him. And you know what? She's right. Takes a lot of work to make an egg, a lot of protein to chalk up, you know? She's gotta keep her gates on lockdown, that's her job. And it's the male's job to prove he's not just any male, he's not going away, he'll always be there."

"To take care of the chicks."

"You're overthinking it. You think pigeons look that far ahead? Neither should you. He just keeps dancing. Dodging people, cars. He dances till his tiny feet are raw against the pavement. She might be gone by the time he's done. In fact, it's not about her anymore—but, maybe, she *is* still there. A switch flips, her gates open. The women here, they're like that. Natural, traditional. They might look more interested in a bread crust than they are in you, but it's an act. So what'll you do, huh, Pasha? Fly away, or are you gonna keep dancing?"

Minutes or hours later, Pasha and Bertrand approached a trailer in the parking lot of a gym that had gone out of business. Two women stood at the trailer's door wearing tight club dresses and animal masks. Wolf, fox, some unidentifiable other. The masks looked homemade, tufts of fur stuck onto papier-mâché. The trailer was obviously repurposed from something—on its side was a cartoon logo of two hands holding a sprout.

Some distant, annoying version of Pasha warned him not to get in. But it was almost charming, this makeshift local version of the Escape Rooms he'd been to in the past, the fancy ones with codes and relics and puzzles he'd suffered through with his colleagues in the name of team building. Here was a quaint Ukrainian attempt at Western decadence, like the fancy restaurants here that sold both sushi and pizza. Trying so hard to catch up to the rotten late capitalist West. It was heartbreaking.

12

NASTIA WATCHED the pair approach with a sinking feeling.

"Isn't that—what's his name? Yasha?" said Yeva, who'd come up behind Nastia.

"I thought you were staying in the cab," Nastia said. The inside of her wolf mask felt moist from her breath.

"Pasha Gurka," Sol reminded them, clicker in hand. "Nastia, you had a date with him. Day two, hotel brunch?" She clicked, but only once, for the one named Bertrand. He was the last, the one they'd waited for, the twelfth. The pretty face the media would latch on to. The other eleven bachelors were already inside the trailer, having ceded their phones to Sol's velveteen sack, some of them pulling theatrically scared faces at the idea of parting with their wares. They'd begun filtering in well past midnight, cheeks flushed and collars disheveled from Prom Night.

Nastia surveyed Bertrand's companion. Short, skinny, the sleeves of his leather jacket too long, hanging over his wrists. If she could hardly remember him, surely the public at large wouldn't, either.

"The guy with the lactose intolerance?" Yeva asked.

"Milk allergy," Sol corrected. "They're different things. He was adamant."

"I thought you two had vetted the men carefully," Yeva said. "Allergies add complexity."

Sol waved this off. "Allergies are mostly in the head. And we did vet them carefully. Anyway, he isn't one of the twelve."

When the duo reached them, Sol greeted both men in English. A back-and-forth ensued, until the one named Pasha began backing away with a stagger. He spoke in a cobbled Russian. "Forget me, I mistaked coming here. I go home now." But Bertrand pulled him back by the elbow.

Sol yanked Nastia and Yeva aside. "Number Twelve says he's not going anywhere without his friend."

"What's the big deal? They're already here," Nastia said. "We can let them both in."

Yeva turned to her. "Your meal plan and budget are for twelve. My trailer's capacity is twelve. Thirteen becomes a fire hazard. A bad omen. We start deviating from the plan this soon, what'll it be next?"

"Well, now we can't *not* let him in," Sol snapped. Her fox mask made her voice sound high and nasal, gnomelike. "He's already seen too much, both of them have. Once the agency gets wind of the missing men, he'll be a witness, tell them all about the trailer before the stunt is over."

Sol beckoned the two men over and asked Pasha something in English.

"Milk does not cause me to die," he answered, in Russian. "Only pains, like knife." He laughed, made a stabbing motion at his bowels. "No problem."

"See? No problem," Nastia repeated.

Yeva heaved herself up into the driver's seat of the cab at the front of the mobile lab—a signal, thought Nastia, that she had made her decision. If she still did not outright approve of the project plan amendment, at least she did not disapprove.

Sol turned to their thirteenth hostage, opened her velveteen sack for his phone. "Welcome," she said with her warmest smile. "May you find the One."

13

MORNING. Still dark.

Then: a great bone-deep crack, as if a truck had crashed into a cement wall.

They'd been on the road two hours, Nastia squeezed between Yeva and Sol on the vinyl maroon bench seat of the driver's cabin.

A flash of light, a whistle, another crash. Yeva pulled over. Nastia watched Yeva look east, where the horizon was paling.

Silence.

A car accident? Or a gas explosion in an old building in a nearby town. Or, any number of things.

The women waited. Nastia could hear Sol's breathing, quick and shallow.

"It's fireworks," she decided. "Just fireworks. Right?"

Yeva grabbed her hand.

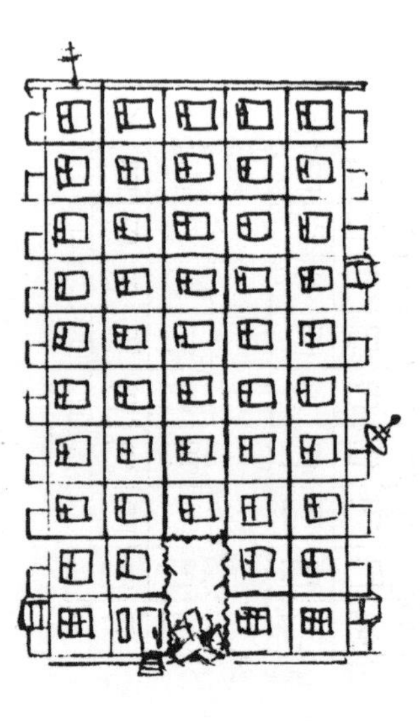

PART II

I SIT IN MY parents' attic in a city that is not a suburb of Vancouver, gripping the phone to my ear. The musk of a not quite fully mummified rat wafts through the floorboards. On the other end of the phone line, a voice calling from the fiftieth floor of a tower in New York. The voice belongs to an agent named Rufus Redpen, which sounds like Ruthless Redpen, which sounds fictional, because he is, mostly. I have otherwise given up on fiction.

After a bit of banter, Rufus Redpen takes a long inhalation, turning to the subject at hand: the Novel, already a year past its contractual deadline. I've been living in this attic—its ceiling lined with old fence slats—living through the winter's squirrels burrowing and nesting in the walls, the spring's black-flies hatching from the leaky skylights. Living cheaply so that I can write. My words drag along, on the verge of falling apart, but isn't this precarious place where true Art lives? True innovation? It's what I'd been telling myself, anyway.

After my agent's inhalation, a pause.

A pause which surely signals his loss for words. Because *A Happy Family Is But an Earlier Heaven* has fallen on the side not of disaster but of brilliance—but how to express just how much so? The long wait, the missed deadline, will certainly be forgiven.

I watch a woodpecker dismantle another roof shingle.

"Why don't you tell me," Rufus Redpen says at last, "where *you* think the material is at."

As I begin to babble about this material—how it might not be as polished as I'd like, but isn't it raw, visceral, certainly something that can be whipped into shape in time—my laptop dings. An email from a reader of my previous book, accompanied by a photo: a Ukrainian high-rise with a hole blown through its middle by a Russian rocket. The Soviet-era panel building no longer looks made of concrete but looks like fabric, its frayed edges rippling in the breeze. Panic floods me: it's my aunt and uncle's building in Kyiv. The night before, they'd tried to flee the country but had to turn back when my uncle's mother-in-law, who'd recently suffered her third stroke, began feeling ill. They worried she wouldn't survive the rest of the trip. Were they already back inside the building when the rocket hit? Had they papered and taped their windows, hid in the corridors as the government recommended, or was that about as good as spitting over your shoulder three times and hoping for the best?

I peer more closely at the photo.

No, the metal entrance doors are painted a different color from my aunt and uncle's. The tragedy passed on to another family.

Isn't it awful, the reader has written, how this structure looks just like the illustration of the collapsing Soviet-era building in my first book? It really is uncanny, the resemblance. In my story collection set in 1990s Ukraine, however, the cause of the collapse is not a bombing but an overly zealous renovator who rips out a load-bearing wall, sending the suites above tumbling down like dominoes. Nobody dies—a miraculous ending possible only in fiction.

I close my laptop, try to push the image of the destroyed building from my mind, listen to my agent.

The voice on the other end of the line is speaking of yurts. About spending a lifetime designing custom yurts, then being contracted to build a mansion. "He was speaking in symbols," the agent explains.

I have no idea who Rufus Redpen is talking about, or how we got to the yurts.

That famous short story writer who tried to write a novel, he repeats. After decades of writing stories? That famous interview?

"What you've written," he diagnoses, "is a bunch of yurts." He says the material is really just hobbled nubs of narrative, barely connected; suggests that from "chapter" to "chapter" the protagonist reads like different people with ever-changing settings and supporting casts. The publishing contract stipulates: *Work 2 shall be a novel (approximately 80,000 words).* Not another story collection. Story collections don't sell. That aforementioned Famous Author may have done well for himself with his painstakingly built yurt stories—solid reviews, solid teaching position—but he was the exception to the rule, and it wasn't until the release of his "long-awaited debut novel" (publisher's words, book jacket), that his career catapulted to new heights. One of *Time*'s Ten Best Fiction Works of the Year! #1 *New York Times* Bestseller! Man Booker Prize winner! As if his previous books had been teasers, as if the literary world had been holding its breath the past twenty years waiting for the real event.

I open my laptop again. The bombed building springs out like a pop-up card. If not my aunt and uncle's building in Kyiv, is it that of friends in Brovary, the capital's suburbs? Russian tanks and artillery were pummeling the place, trying to break through the eastern gateway into Kyiv. Take away the balconies, and the bombed building looks just like my cousins'. Lop it down to five stories, and it could be my grandfather's Khrushchev-era apartment building in Kherson, another city under siege. Cruel, how Soviet apartment blocks look alike. I've been watching the same building get bombed, resurrected, bombed, over and over on my phone, laptop, on the TV screen at the corner store.

Leave, get out while you still can, my parents, sister, and I have been pleading from Canada. Easy for you to say, our relatives in occupied Kherson tell us. They're hearing all sorts of stories about the checkpoints: one soldier might give a fleeing family lollipops, something to remember the Russians by, another soldier might shoot. Anyway, where would they go? The cousins have never been out of the country before, and the prospect of leaving is more terrifying than staying in an occupied zone. My grandfather, for his part, can't leave his books. The countless albums of family photographs he developed himself, over decades, in the bathtub. The volumes of notebooks marking births, marriages, graduations, renovations, second renovations, the visits from Canada, deaths. The lives of everyone he loved began and ended in his notebooks—how could he possibly leave them behind? He always kept the apartment stocked with cash and grain reserves, kept the reinforced metal door he'd welded himself oiled—something we used to tease him about. He'd been preparing for these dark days his whole life. Like hell he'd leave now. His sister, for her part, can't leave him. Nor can she leave the pansy-patterned tea set she inherited from their mother, the only heirlooms that survived Kherson's first occupation, eighty-one years ago, by the Nazis, and survived the Bolshevik raids before that. My grandfather and his sister will surely keep the tiny estate safe—if not from a bombing, then from the Russian military. There were already Russian families moving into emptied apartments.

"Are you still there?" Rufus Redpen asks. "I know this isn't an easy thing to hear." He quotes the Famous Author again, his line about how one must conceptualize a novel as a mansion of interconnected yurts.

I try to run with the analogy. "So I need to sew my yurts together." Make a big circus tent, blanket the world of the book in one sturdy swath of cloth.

My agent considers this for a moment. "Honestly, I just don't see how. Between your yurts are thorny brambles. How does one move from yurt to yurt? One has no idea. It isn't even a campground, really, it's inhospitable. And dark. Not a campground I can imagine anyone wishing to stay in. Do you follow?"

Or is the bombed building on my screen the one I lived in as a child during the nineties, before leaving for Canada? The ten-story structure had been newly built from leftover construction material and, due to a clerical error, wasn't listed in the city registry. When its first winter came and the heating didn't turn on, my father rushed to the municipal hall, where an irritated administrator proclaimed that since there was no such address, there was no such building. A bureaucratic goose chase followed, my father trying to prove the building's existence. This was a quaint Soviet-flavored story I used to love recounting at dinner parties and book events, how during visits back in Ukraine I'd lay a hand on my old building's cool cement to make sure it still "existed." It's the building that inspired my first book, the story collection, which means I'd lived there another five years in my imagination, cloistered myself inside its Turkish-rug-covered walls. I knew its narrow corridors and awkwardly shaped rooms and the families who lived in them more intimately than I knew my own family—their everyday joys and lifelong regrets, the color of an old bathing suit stuffed at the back of a drawer. It's the building that collapses at the end of my book and nobody gets hurt. But what of the real building? Is it still standing? Where are its families?

In the smaller Ukrainian towns even the playgrounds look alike, nestled between apartment blocks, decorated with brightly painted animals cut from old truck tires. I'd spent my childhood evenings on such playgrounds and now I watch as they are destroyed. Standing, gone. Standing, gone. The last few months have been a decade long, but they've also been the same few seconds, looping infinitely.

"Your material," the agent continues. "It's all so violent, grisly. And not in a good way. A firing squad? In this day and age?"

The Novel. Firing squads. I straighten in my wobbly chair, wrenched back to the subject at hand. I invoke the real-life inspiration behind the book as justification. How, after a shortage of lethal injection drugs, Utah's Senate had just reinstated firing squads as a backup method of execution. How, during the time I was doing my research, other states were following suit. The family in my novel is based on Real Life, too. I'd found an interview mentioning a former squad leader who described how they'd practice on the same cottonwood tree; on the day of an execution, the squad would sit down together and enjoy—no, not enjoy, consume dutifully—a large pancake breakfast made by the leader's wife, and they'd all pray to God to give them strength for what they were about to do.

"Yes, yes," the agent interrupts. "Dark times."

I remind him that my first book also includes state-sanctioned violence—it's just that the state was the Soviet regime.

"Those were dark times past," he explains. "Dark times elsewhere. Dark times to escape to. Readers don't want a mirror to their own lives."

"When the pandemic hit, Camus's *The Plague* topped the charts."

"For five minutes, sure, before everyone plunged back into luxury real estate shows. Look, if your protagonist were trying to *escape* a firing squad, or lobbied her senators to abolish firing squads again, it would be one thing. But to join one?"

"The squad gives her a sense of community."

He says nothing.

"It concludes her emotional arc." I try to remember what that emotional arc is, exactly—an adolescence spent in a wilderness reform school, the real villain of the story being the troubled teen industry and society at large—but the rest is murky, as if someone else wrote the thing in a panic, to avoid writing some other thing.

"She begins as a psychopath, she ends as a psychopath," concludes the agent. "I see no emotional arc, only a flat line. A dead heart."

A story's flaw is often the flaw of its creator, I once read. Am I dead inside, heart flatlined?

I suggest sending the manuscript to the publisher anyway. Maybe they'll like the thing, see something in it the agent doesn't?

"They might like it, sure," he says darkly. "There's always the possibility. Or they won't, and their first impression will taint the project, ruin any authorial attempt to salvage it." After a moment, "Wasn't your novel originally going to be about a marriage agency in Ukraine?"

"Null and void."

"What does that mean?"

"The premise, irrelevant. I was writing about a so-called invasion of Western bachelors to Ukraine, and then an actual invasion happened. Even in peacetime I felt queasy leaning into not one but two Ukrainian tropes, 'mail-order brides' and topless protesters. To continue now seems unforgivable. So I wrote a different book, a different world, something I thought would be happier. And that's why we have *A Happy Family Is But an Earlier Heaven.*"

"A firing squad."
"A family, reunited."

Ossetia, Grozny, Aleppo. The Russians have done all this before, using the same playbook. When one of their previous military campaigns stalled, they'd carpet-bomb cities, killing thousands. I spend nights glued to my phone, zooming in on aerial shots of what was left of those cities, searching for patches which by a stroke of luck appeared undamaged. If a family happened to be hiding in one of these spots, what were their chances of survival? Would my own relatives outlast the bombings in Ukraine now? So far, my family's cities still stood whole, but already Zhytomyr, Mykolaiv, Kharkiv, Mariupol were falling.

In the daytime, as I walk down Vancouver's tree-lined streets, where the crocuses are in full bloom, I squint at the bright clear skies, wondering if one day all this, too, will turn into a burning wreckage. Riding the bus, I startle at a caved-in building, reminding myself that unlike every other caved-in building on the news and in my nightmares, this one has simply been bulldozed. My sister, who also lives in Vancouver, tells me that when she passes freshly dug mounds for flower beds, she sees mass graves. Sometimes I wonder if she and I are going insane, living two realities at once—the explosions peppering phone calls from Ukraine alongside the dinner parties in Vancouver with laughing, smiling friends in wrinkle-free fabrics who don't mention the war. Maybe there is no war, as conspiracy theorists whisper online. Maybe it's all in my head?

UNFAMOUS AUTHOR: Do you ever sew your yurts together?
YURT MAKERS: How do you mean?
UNFAMOUS AUTHOR: Into one big mansion of a yurt.
YURT MAKERS: As a matter of winter survival, each dome is specifically calibrated to trap its inhabitants' bodily heat and reflect it back to them.
U.A.: So, no.
YURT MAKERS: What would cause one to sew yurts together?
U.A.: I don't know, the combined thing would be roomier? Sell more units?
YURT MAKERS: You Americans, always chasing something larger, always wanting to sell. If you want a mansion, build a mansion. Do not drag yurts into this.
U.A.: I'm Canadian.
YURT MAKERS: Same cloth.
U.A.: I tried to build some yurts myself, but they're dilapidated and falling apart, with thorny brambles between them. I think I need to put them in the drawer for a bit. Let them ferment.
YURT MAKERS: We do not follow.
U.A.: I'm speaking in symbols.
YURT MAKERS: *(A unified sigh.)*
U.A.: What's wrong?
YURT MAKERS: You are a writer?
U.A.: Who's to say? And for how much longer?

YURT MAKERS: You are not the first of your ilk who has called us in the middle of the night crying, begging us to sew up your mess. This is regarding that quotation by the writer who is your leader, yes? The mansion-made-of-yurts nonsense? Has he ever laid eyes on a yurt himself? we ask.

U.A.: He builds them. They're exquisite, custom, self-contained.

YURT MAKERS: We are still speaking in symbols, yes?

U.A.: I tried building a different novel-yurt before, that one set in Ukraine, its structure large and sprawling, more mansion-like than my other set of yurts, but the Russians began bombing it. What right do I have to write about the war from my armchair? And to keep writing about the mail-order bride industry seems even worse. Dredge up that cliché? In these times? Anyway, am I even a real Ukrainian? I left the country as a child. I speak more Russian than Ukrainian, and neither that well.

YURT MAKERS: The Tajik yurt makers among us, they, too, were made to speak Russian under Soviet rule, but are they not Tajik? And what of Kazakh, Kyrgyz, and Uzbek makers? We have not heard about any of your books.

U.A.: Book. Just one. It came out on the eve of the WHO's pandemic declaration and got swept under the tide of more important news.

YURT MAKERS: Always some petty thing, conspiring against literature. Rebuild your yurt. Make it stronger.

U.A.: And another thing . . .

YURT MAKERS: May we remind you, it is still the middle of the night here.

U.A.: My first book? The irony is that it was also about Ukraine—about Soviet Ukraine, that long-gone Ukraine I'm more familiar with, since that's the place I left—and for the book's release I had written op-eds to be printed in newspapers, essays about growing up in Ukraine, the language politics, but they got canned when the pandemic hit. Now those same newspapers are calling me, asking me to write about Ukraine again, promising to actually publish this time, probably canning other writers' pieces because now "my" cause is more important.

I'm getting calls for magazine interviews, photo shoots, radio appearances I'd only dreamed of when my book first came out. I'm trying to be grateful. But why must a country be bombed before we care about it?

YURT MAKERS: The world is a whore.

March 10, 2022

Dear Ms. Reva,

Thank you for your essay, "Never Too Soon: Humor as an Act of Survival in Ukraine." Our editorial team appreciates your attempt to find light in these dark times. While we enjoyed learning, in the essay at hand, about your homeland's "bottomless arsenal" of wartime jokes, and while we also enjoyed reading about the civilian who downed a military drone with a jar of pickled tomatoes and the many memes her act of bravery inspired, we worry that the subject matter of your essay does indeed come "too soon," and fear its tone would not quite fit the sensibilities of our readers.

As previously discussed, we were hoping for your perspective as a Ukrainian expatriate watching the horror unfold from abroad (gentle emphasis on horror), i.e., how you and your family are feeling and how that emotional journey stands apart from the reporting/responses from non-Ukrainians.

Could you resubmit by tomorrow a.m.?

Sincerely,
Elron McKinley
The Northwest Beacon

March 10, 2022

Hi Elron,

Thanks again for soliciting my essay, and thanks so much for your feedback. I totally understand how the jokes my friends and family and Ukrainians at large are passing around as they shelter in basements and subway stations might come off as a little inappropriate to folks out here. I do wonder if, maybe, a part of the essay got lost in the attachment? The part where my uncle's family try and fail to escape their besieged city, and my family here in Canada are utterly powerless, and sometimes all we can do in the face of an incomprehensible reality is flip through pickle jar memes? Or the part about how normal life churns around us while we're stuck in a deep murk holding our breath, but we do have to come up for air before descending again? If we don't laugh, we will drown, etc.?

Thanks so much!
M

March 11, 2022

Dear Ms. Reva,

This is to confirm that we did indeed receive, and read, the essay in its entirety.

We see that you published a wrenching personal essay just last week, titled "The Streets of My Childhood Lay [Sic] in Ruins." We found the tone more fitting there, with the appropriate gravitas.

If you need more time, do let us know.

Yours,
E

March 12, 2022

Hi Elron,

I'm so glad you enjoyed that essay.

You'd asked for the type of reporting/response that would differ from that of a non-Ukrainian. In Ukraine, dark humor dates back to the Soviet days—probably earlier—giving people who live in uncontrollable circumstances a sense of power. If you can laugh about a dark reality, you rise above it, etc., as I mention in the essay. A non-Ukrainian wouldn't touch the topic of wartime humor with a ten-foot pole right now.

Thanks so much, again,
M

March 15, 2022

Dear Ms. Reva,

We've had a discussion with editorial. Why don't we circle back to the topic at hand in a month or so, when the dust settles a bit?

Warmly,
E

Commonwealth Arts Foundation (CAF) Application Form
Applicant Name: Maria Reva
Type of Grant Requested: Travel
Destination: Ukraine
Describe your research goals:
In humble submission, I, a Canadian-Ukrainian writer, beseech the esteemed granting institution to consider bestowing upon me the munificent gift of financial support. I am a Canadian-Ukrainian writer seeking to conduct research for her novel-in-progress set in Ukraine. The novel will treat the subject of war with utmost *gravitas.* My travel expenses will be modest (see budget), given the ongoing devaluatory pressures on the Ukrainian hryvnia.

My novel-in-progress, *Endling*, explores the problematic practices that beset the international bridal industry, simultaneously interrogating the hackneyed, albeit persistently prevalent, Western perception of Ukrainian women as either docile and acquiescent "mail-order brides" or wily and deceitful scammers.

As a Ukrainian-born woman united in matrimony with an American, I have personally encountered and grappled with this preconceived notion myself. The husband in question and I met in a university dormitory while pursuing our undergraduate degrees, I feel compelled to specify. Yet, as I traversed the territorial threshold into the United States to visit him from Canada, where I now live—a pandemic temporarily forced us to reside apart—I was invariably subjected to the ordeal of protracted secondary interrogation. I initially bore this repeated scrutiny with stoicism, presuming it to be an obligatory custom, a *sine qua non* for all foreign visitors. However, it was not until I was apprised of numerous instances where my male acquaintances, bearing Anglo-Saxon nomenclature and ancestry, ventured into this very same self-proclaimed democratic republic to reunite with their significant others *without* enduring extensive interrogations, that I began to entertain the notion that my provenance might in and of itself constitute a conspicuous scarlet standard. Or as one might say, a "red flag."

Canadian border guards, it should be noted, exhibit no less suspicion. When an American friend of mine journeyed to Vancouver to visit his romantic partner, who had recently fled besieged Kyiv, the border official inquired, with a palpable air of insinuation, as to the nature of the relationship and whether an exchange of currency for *services* existed between them.

A coincidence? Paranoia on my part? Quite possibly. Yet, *ex nihilo nihil fit.* Nothing comes from nothing; no paranoia without seed.

Explain the inspiration for your project and why you wish to undertake it at this time:

My opus draws inspiration from the wellspring of narrative prowess exuded by Deb Olin Unferth's canonical work, *Barn 8*, wherein the notions of abduction and social justice deftly intertwine, as well as the groundbreaking metafictional elements prominently displayed within the protonovelistic oeuvre of Salvador Plascencia's *People of Paper.* Thus fortified by the literary beacons that have illuminated the path before me, *Endling* seeks to transcend the boundaries of conventionality while being grounded in the timeless questions of the human condition. Now that Russia is conducting a full-scale invasion of Ukraine, the central conflict woven into the delicate fabric of my novel, namely the influx of Western suitors into Ukraine, has been subjugated—or *ripped apart*, to keep with the metaphor—by a far more violent and destructive narrative. My novel (postnovel? yet-to-be defined entity?) needs further tailoring to reflect these rapidly changing circumstances. Returning to Ukraine and visiting cities like Kyiv, Kharkiv, and Kherson—the typical sites of romance tours—will enable me to restitch the novel to fit current times. Another goal of the trip will be to seek out my grandfather, the last of my relatives to remain in Kherson, and drag him to safety.

Describe any anticipated research challenges and ways in which you will overcome them:
Grandfather will likely refuse to be dragged anywhere. I do not yet know how I will overcome this.

Summarize in one sentence how you will ensure safe working conditions for yourself and others through proper Covid-19 safety protocol. This summary will be used in the CAF's official reporting.
A quote from a Ukrainian MP: "One upside of this war is that we've finally vanquished Covid."

Further describe how you will ensure safe working conditions for yourself and others through proper Covid-19 safety protocol.
As of the time of writing, Russian troops are withdrawing from Kyiv to focus their assault on the eastern region of Donbas, thereby rendering access to Covid-19 testing clinics possible again, if any remain. I pledge to adhere, with unwavering commitment, to any and all local Covid-19 prevention guidelines—in extraordinary instances where there are none, I will be only too pleased to observe CAF's own—in addition to being inoculated with the latest and finest booster vaccine available. Should I find myself sheltering with members not of my household during an air raid, I will maintain the appropriate social distance of six feet and will actively assist those around me to do the same; no moment is inopportune for a little public health education. The possible malfunction or detonation of the Zaporizhzhia nuclear

power plant, currently being occupied and shelled by Russians, may pose additional challenges, but in case of a nuclear incident, should I find myself experiencing a medical exigency I will alert the emergency operator if I have, or suspect I have, Covid-19, and will be sure to don a mask when help arrives.

14

HERE'S HOW it all ends: happily, believably.

When, at 5:00 a.m., the bombings begin, Yeva, Nastia, and Sol know exactly where they need to venture. Their minds fuse into one single unwavering arrow, and that arrow points to Kherson. Despite never having set foot in Kherson—why would they have visited that depressed place?—its sandy soil and intoxicatingly sweet acacia blossoms awaken memories buried deep within their souls, as though they themselves had frolicked along the city's reedy riverbanks as children. What a relief for each of them at last to have a true direction in life, led onward by the ironclad grip of a hand reaching down—perhaps from the heavens, perhaps from a faraway attic. Whatever plans they might have had before now seem trivial, irrelevant, null and void.

Yeva's earlier failure to sustain life inside her mobile lab? Now forgotten, forgiven. Snails, so what? Who really cares? But the lab remains, after all, the perfect instrument of rescue. For those of a certain age plagued by overactive bladders, the lab's retrofitted bathroom conveniently allows for long journeys without stops (since every stop risks encounters with Russian soldiers, many of whom have no qualms about shooting civilians). It turns out that Yeva's earlier snail rescues were but rehearsals for the real thing, with people.

They turn in the opposite direction, away from the tides of refugees spilling westward with children and animals and suitcases and checkered oilcloth bags. Instead, they drive the lab deeper,

deeper, into the very maw of the invaders, as an ethereal voice urges them onward. *Turn here, take that back road, now this one. Drive calmly past the armed men. Keep doing what I tell you, and all will be just fine.*

Columns of cars clog Kherson's exits as the city empties out. A miniature poodle in a pink puffer vest darts between lines of traffic. The town center, by contrast, is eerily quiet. In the heart of a tree-lined plaza, the women spot a concrete pedestal from the old Lenin statue. Only his feet remain, big as bathtubs, rusty rebar curving from them like veins (note this powerful, original image, not in the least plagiarized in desperation from its creator's first book).

At last, the rescuers park on Friendship of Peoples Street, so named by the Soviets in a gesture that now feels like mockery.

The entry doors of the five-story Khrushchevka building are, for once, unlocked. Inside, the women bound up concrete stairs freshly painted in the friendly blue of the sky. When they reach the steel outer door of their destination, Grandfather's suite, three hands rise as one, lift the heavy knocker, and rap. After a moment, they hear the familiar click of the inner door's dead bolt. They listen as the door squeals open—they can almost see its red faux-leather upholstery—then comes the ticking of more locks, like clockwork, followed by the gravelly melody of the chain sliding along its track, and dropping. At last, the steel door swings open.

For a moment Grandfather stands there, blinking, a dripping wooden spoon in hand. The smell of the apartment greets the women, unchanged. Old books, laurel leaves. A pot of soup bubbles on the stove, infusing the air with a sharp sweetness, like the underbelly of a rotting log. They know they should grab him and hurry out of here, but the women can't recall the last time they ate. As they devour the soup, remembering not to scoop their spoons too deeply so as not to disturb the peppercorns, Grandfather chatters away. Many of the other residents of his building have already evacuated, he says, and he's never lived in such quiet, except for the explosions in the distance. He thought he'd enjoy it, but at night he can hear his own pulse, like the drum of the approaching army. A few residents moved to their dachas in the villages, others moved in with relatives many towns over, outside Kherson Oblast.

Yes, it's true, dear reader, dear agent, dear fund-giving cultural institution: we've been here before. In the book that came before this one, in another death trap of a building that risks collapse any moment. And since that book ended happily, sort of, now this one will, too.

The women look around the emptied apartment, ask where the boxes of photo albums are, the archives with the notebooks detailing the key dates and events of each of his relatives' lives. Births, deaths, the building of the dacha house across the Dnipro, every upgrade in the dacha house, the number of liters of wine made each year in the dacha cellar, the emigration of a daughter, son-in-law, and two granddaughters to Canada, the older granddaughter's graduation from Princeton (proof of a successful immigration), the younger granddaughter's date of marriage to an American (further proof), this same granddaughter's winning of a mysterious writing prize founded by a Texan perfume maker (Why? How?), each visit back to Kherson. A chronology so detailed, authoritative, it was hard to tell which came first, the events themselves or the recording of the events. Grandfather must've been the one who'd designed the web of lives, all of them radiating from his drafting table.

"It's all gone," Grandfather tells the women. He has burned the chronologies, the albums of photos he'd spent decades developing in his bathroom-turned-darkroom, in the courtyard, pile by pile. He's burned, too, the hundreds of books he'd collected back in the time when books were hard to come by, the vinyl records by bands banned during the Soviet Union, albums that still felt elicit. It was difficult, but he had to do it, to untether himself from the apartment at last.

Just as during the previous occupations of Kherson (the Nazis, the Soviets), again the family line scatters, heirlooms and archives vanish. Again, a blank slate.

The women pour the rest of the soup into jars for the long road ahead. They walk through the rooms of the apartment, maybe for the last time, but it doesn't matter now because these are simply rooms, containing objects from a family these women have never met. They won't remember the ivy wallpaper, the bookshelves, the onions sprouting from mayonnaise containers on the windowsills. They help Grandfather down the concrete steps carefully, one at a time to save his bad knee. They help him board the mobile lab. They head west. Soon they'll reunite him with his family, with the children and the grandchildren, who will travel from their corners of the world, and their scattered web of lives will shrink back into one tight knot, just as he had chronicled in his notebooks before he burned them.

An iron sheet will slide across the horizon, will close Ukraine's sky. Any missile that dares to pierce this formidable shield will boomerang back to its origin, serving as a lesson to all the other little men on thrones: never invade a sovereign country. The war will end, no more lives will be lost, no other invasions will occur elsewhere, either.

Oh, and the bachelors? The ones Nastia, Sol, and Yeva took hostage? Before the Kherson mission they'd been dropped off at the nearest border, the one with Poland or Slovakia or wherever, and released into the throngs of journalists and humanitarian aid volunteers who plied them with barley soup.

END

ACKNOWLEDGMENTS

I'd like to thank the many patient people who made this book possible, especially Amelia Atlas at Creative Artists Agency. At Knopf Canada: Lynn Henry (a national treasure), Rick Meier, Sharon Klein, Stephen Myers, Susan Burns, and Martha Kanya-Forstner. At Doubleday: Lee Boudreaux, Maya Pasic, Susan Brown, Julie Ertl and Kayla Steinforth, Jess Deitcher, Ellen Feldman and Marisa Nakasone. My gratitude as well to Emily Mahon, who designed the striking Doubleday cover with adapted artwork by Valentin Pavageau. At Virago: Sarah Savitt, Grace Vincent, and Chevonne Elbourne for the cover design. My thanks as well to Cathryn Summerhayes at Curtis Brown Creative.

Ed Yong's reporting in *The Atlantic* on snail endlings proved invaluable as source material. Special thanks to Igor Balashov at the Schmalhausen Institute of Zoology in Kyiv, from a rare species himself, for his correspondence with me about terrestrial mollusks. Though their endangerment is true to life, the snail species in my novel are fictional—mostly. (There did exist in London a left-coiling snail who inspired an international quest to find him a mate—Jeremy, named after left-wing British Labour politician Jeremy Corbyn.)

Deb Olin Unferth's *Barn 8*, Salvador Plascencia's *The People of Paper*, and *Asymmetry* by Lisa Halliday were among the muse books that fed this one.

To Shashi Bhat, Sonya Lalli, Renée Sarojini Saklikar, and the other writers of Paging Gracefully who helped sustain the book. To Isaac Yuen for the feedback over pastries. To Olha Khometa for her informed input to this manuscript, and for the new friendship. To the opera creation community, especially Musique 3 Femmes; if I didn't have opera libretti to write alongside this book, my days would have been terribly silent.

To the Canada Council for the Arts as well as the British Columbia Arts Council for their generous financial support.

To Jane and John, who graciously lent me their house at key times. To Richard and Roberta Hyman, whose children's playhouse also proved to be an excellent place to work.

I would also like to thank Russia's Ministry of Foreign Affairs for including my name on their sanctions list of Canadians who are now forbidden from entering their country, one of the biggest honors of my literary career.

My deepest gratitude to my family for their unwavering support, especially to Anna Pidgorna and to One Whose Name Shall Not Appear in Print.

Finally, I'd like to thank Rufus Redpen, who appreciated this novel from the start but now recognizes that *A Happy Family Is But an Earlier Heaven* really is the better one, and regrets his previous error in judgment.

ABOUT THE AUTHOR

MARIA REVA IS the author of *Good Citizens Need Not Fear*, a linked story collection set in a high-rise in Soviet Ukraine, and also writes opera libretti. Her writing has appeared in *The Atlantic*, *McSweeney's*, *The Wall Street Journal*, *Granta*, *The Best American Short Stories*, and elsewhere. She is most well-known, however, for her long-awaited debut novel *A Happy Family Is But an Earlier Heaven*, an instant international bestseller selected for literary prizes worldwide commending the work as "raw and visceral" and "cohesive, most certainly a novel" and "not too dark to be publishable" and blessed by the grandmaster George Saunders himself as "a mansion of interconnected yurts, sturdy and indestructible. Definitely a novel." The novel resulted in the (re)banning of firing squads in three states.

Maria was born in Ukraine and grew up in New Westminster, British Columbia, where she lives in her own single detached home afforded by the fortuitous earnings of *AHFIBAEH*'s adaptation into a Broadway musical, an opera, and a television miniseries.

A NOTE ON THE TYPE

This book, a novel, was set in Serifus Libris, a typeface designed by distinguished Italian engraver Giuseppe Pizzinini (1852–1913). Conceived as a private handkerchief embroidery type to celebrate the twentieth anniversary of his marriage to Countess Johanna Trauttmansdorff of Austria, and modernized before his untimely death by screw press, this type displays the tireless qualities of a master craftsman intent on weaving letter to letter, sentence to sentence, chapter to chapter, to create a sense of cohesion or an illusion thereof. In this way he shaped manifold manuscripts, however unshapely in their nascent form, into acceptable books. An ardent worker, Pizzinini remained steadfast at his beloved printing press even on his (rare) breaks, arranging and rearranging letter blocks with his apprentices to see who could spell the heaviest word. He has been credited as the inventor of the game now commonly known as Scrabble.

YURT MAKERS: The hotel cookie. How was it?
UNFAMOUS AUTHOR: The cookie was excellent.
YURT MAKERS: Warm?
UNFAMOUS AUTHOR: Perfectly so.
YURT MAKERS: It was as if they baked it right behind the reception desk, just for your arrival. But not your favorite flavor, chocolate chip.
U.A.: I'm not complaining.
YURT MAKERS: But you could, it's that kind of hotel. Still, we make do with what we have, don't we. It's the small compromises, especially when the rest is so peachy. An entire university campus reading your first book for your visit. Students, with your book in hand, recognizing you as you stroll between old red-brick buildings. A university president, a mahogany podium, an ASL translator translating your very important guest lecture right beside you. Everything a pandemic took away from you, a war now returns. Who could've known that your best publicist would be Mr. Putin himself. The Russians bombed Kyiv again today, during rush hour, did you know?
U.A.: Please, for one day, just let me listen to the ocean.
YURT MAKERS: Kyiv and other cities. More than eighty-four missile and air strikes. Fourteen dead, ninety-seven wounded. But don't let us interrupt. By all means, sink into those high-thread-count sheets. Tell us, Ms. Voice of Ukraine, how do you toast in Ukrainian again?

U.A.: I know I said it wrong at the reception yesterday. I just didn't want to say it in Russian.

YURT MAKERS: How's the second book going, by the way?

U.A.: The ocean!

YURT MAKERS: We simply want to know where *you* think the material is at.

U.A.: Did Rufus Redpen put you up to this? The yurt is done, okay? There's enough *material* to cover all the rooms.

YURT MAKERS: But the material is fake. Slippery as polyester.

U.A.: Of course it's fake. It's a work of fiction.

YURT MAKERS: Your grandfather is still in Kherson. Just yesterday, didn't rocket shrapnel land in his courtyard? Or did you miss that, too, busy being upgraded to the King Deluxe Seaside Suite paid for by the university, busy tipping back prosecco?

U.A.: My parents and sister keep pleading with my grandfather to leave, but he refuses to budge.

YURT MAKERS: Isn't it for him to choose?

U.A.: Maybe it shouldn't be. He's too close to the fire, can't see through the smoke. Sometimes it's impossible to know if it's safer to stay or go, and sometimes there's nowhere else to go—I understand that. But I'm hearing about all sorts of people who refuse help to evacuate, who refuse offers of a place to stay, believing their own street or apartment building to be safe. As if they can control how close the war comes to them. And then a missile lands too close, pierces that imaginary shield. The front line reaches their doorstep, but by then it's too late, no one can get them out anymore. A blindness is what it is, this defiance.

YURT MAKERS: Selfish.

U.A.: Isn't it? All the friends and relatives who worry day and night. The terror, the powerlessness we feel, all radiating from one person's stubbornness.

YURT MAKERS: Your grandfather is not who we were referring to when we said selfish. So long as the right few people are safe, *you* can move on with your life, right? Properly enjoy the oyster reception held in your honor as you speak on behalf of your bereaved motherland.

U.A.: That's not true. Absolutely not true.

YURT MAKERS: And so you live on in your savior fantasies. Tell us, what is he to you?

U.A.: My grandfather?

YURT MAKERS: Would you be friends if you weren't related? What is he like?

U.A.: Retired thermal engineer. Likes swamp green.

YURT MAKERS: That's it? Vague as a dating profile.

U.A.: Big on water conservation. Drinks exactly one shot of vodka with salted fish at lunch, but never washes the glass because alcohol is supposed to sterilize it. And his sister would come over and try to wash his cloudy glasses, the cloudy dishes, and he'd start yelling and calling her a neat freak, and then they'd fight.

What else? Loves analog, hates digital—parts you can't see with your own eyes or fix with your own hands. Yet, in secret, he bought himself a computer and took a special tech course just so that he can turn the thing on, Sundays at 7:00 a.m. EET, to video-chat with us. Then promptly turns it off for the rest of the week. If we don't sign in at the allotted time he'll worry, but will turn off the computer anyway so as not to leave it running, much like you wouldn't leave a drill or a blow-dryer running.

YURT MAKERS: So you speak with him every week at the allotted time.

U.A.: I sure do.

YURT MAKERS: Another lie. What is he to you? Apart from a useful plot point.

U.A.: My grandfather!

YURT MAKERS: We all have grandfathers. Or, had them.

U.A.: What else do you want me to say? He's my last grandparent alive. I don't know him well, all right? And I never really tried to. Whenever I'd visit, there'd be traces of other children who'd grown up around him, their paintings and straw art, but nothing of mine except for the bare-bones plotline of my life charted in his notebook and tucked away in a drawer. There wasn't much of me left in Ukraine. So the thought I had—

a childish thought: It's too late. I've been gone too long. Other people grow up with grandparents, but that just wasn't what I got. You can't have everything. That's just the way it is.

YURT MAKERS: Totally fine.

U.A.: Absolutely fine.

YURT MAKERS: No grandparent-shaped hole left in your soul.

U.A.: Here's a nice moment I can tell you about. He'd always dreamed of playing the piano, but pianos were too hard to find when he was a child. So he made his daughter, my mother, play piano, which she hated because she dreamed instead of learning to dance ballet. But ballet teachers didn't think she was waifish enough to have any hope of making the Bolshoi. So after my mother had me, she put me into ballet lessons, and something worse happened: the teachers deemed I had Potential and were about to throw me into militaristic training. But all I wanted was to play the piano. Which, finally, in Canada, I did. My first visit back to Ukraine, when I played for him, he cried. It felt as though a family curse had finally lifted.

YURT MAKERS: It was your grandmother who cried.

U.A.: For our purposes, let's say it was my grandfather.

YURT MAKERS: And what are our purposes?

U.A.: To get at a broader, truer truth.

YURT MAKERS: It's what you all say.

U.A.: My grandmother died before the war and I don't want to drag her back, onto these pages. Best to leave her in peace.

YURT MAKERS: So if you get your grandfather out of Kherson, then what? He'll come to you, or you to him? You'll finally get to know him, make up for lost time?

U.A.: I don't know. But it'll be enough to know he's safe.

YURT MAKERS: And another thing.

U.A.: Not another thing.

YURT MAKERS: It isn't true that all Soviet-era buildings look alike. That's just a tired cliché all Westerners use. Each building has its own face if you look close enough. You really have been gone too long.

PART III

14, REDUX

WHEN, AT 5:00 A.M., the bombings began, Yeva's, Nastia's, and Sol's minds did not fuse into one single, unwavering arrow that pointed to Kherson. None of them had set foot in the place, so why would they now? Kherson, over six hundred kilometers south, was the farthest thing from their minds. Instead, they convened a meeting.

Meeting Minutes
Date: February 24, 2022
Time: 06:10
Location: Viridia Labs XF500 Mobile Research Unit, unnamed gravel back road north of Kyiv
Participants:

- Yeva
- Anastasia
- Solomiya

Agenda:

1. Discussion on course of action in response to bombings
2. Review of President Volodymyr Zelensky's address (via radio)
3. Status of escape routes and potential areas of refuge
4. Input from relatives (via telephone)
5. Current situational updates (via social media)
6. Status and demands of the detained bachelors

· · ·

Discussion Points:

1. **Initial Confusion**
   - A discussion among the three meeting participants took place over the nature and source of the auditory disturbances which commenced at approximately 05:30. Proposed sources included: a highway collision involving multiple cars; unplanned gas discharge at a fracking site, if any nearby; geological event; fireworks.
   - Following this, there was a period of silence (inside the cab of the mobile lab but not outside) during which a (nonverbal) agreement was reached concerning the nature of the audible disturbances.

2. **Yeva's Proposal**
   - Yeva suggested, in a calm and collected manner which surprised Solomiya, given the speaker's (presumed) psychologically turbulent history, continuing north and sheltering near the Belarus border. She described a swampy village known to her from past expeditions, left untouched by previous wars and occupations, whether by luck or by favorable geography. The trip would take only three hours under normal road conditions.

3. **Solomiya's Counterproposal**
   - Solomiya urged a return south, to Kyiv, just an hour away if they took the main highway, aligning with the President's request for people to stay home.
   - The President's address, more of a terse status update (devoid of his usual charisma, as noted by listeners), proclaimed martial law and did urge calm and for civilians to stay home, noting that Ukraine's defense sector was operational.

4. **Concerns About Kyiv and Other Cities**
   - Yeva strongly opposed returning to Kyiv due to the fact that the sound of the bombings emanated from that very direction.

- Radio reports confirmed that many cities, including Kyiv, were in fact being attacked by missiles. Yeva reiterated that any and all cities should thus be avoided.

5. Concerns About Rural Areas

- Yeva expressed equal concern over the sparsely built, sparsely wooded agricultural land *between* cities, the lack of shelter it offered. Had this animal instinct to avoid open ground and sky always been there? Had they, in their human hubris, simply ignored this ever-present danger their entire lives?

6. Anastasia's Focus

- Anastasia attempted to turn the discussion away from matters of philosophy and back to what she described as the true matter at hand: the bachelors, who had been banging on the walls of the mobile lab throughout the discussion. She proposed that now might be a good time to film the hostage video, the bachelors' hysteria having reached an appropriate level.
- Solomiya noted a pathological quality in her sister's single-mindedness, to which Anastasia responded in a manner that does not bear summarizing here.
- Yeva acknowledged, while maintaining her composure, how one might be tempted to focus on prior plans, no matter how irrelevant, rather than to accept, in the face of total chaos and unknowability, that there was no plan anymore, that everything had gone to shit, in the sense both narrow and broad. With this last bit, Solomiya expressed agreement; Anastasia, disagreement.

7. Updates via Social Media

- Robust scrolling of phones, by Yeva and Solomiya, followed.
- Solomiya discovered via Telegram feeds that tanks were advancing toward them from the north, through Belarus, even through the Chernobyl exclusion zone, kicking up

radioactive dust. A video was viewed featuring a tank that rolled over a civilian car parked on the side of the road like a boot seeking the satisfaction of a dried leaf crunched underfoot.

- Yeva's prior proposal to head north was unanimously struck down.
- Further updates showed Russian tanks crossing Ukraine's eastern and southern borders as well. The 150,000-plus troops previously amassed at the border were now invading the country. A map of Ukraine circulating online showed what looked like two-thirds of its 6,900 km border glowing red, in danger, on fire.

8. Decision to Record Meeting Minutes

- Upon reviewing the above updates, Solomiya succumbed to distress.
- Yeva directed Solomiya to tuck her head under the dashboard and in between her knees. Yeva reminded her to breathe slowly, deeply, which Solomiya did try to do, even as the air thinned and she worried it would all be gone if she didn't keep gulping it down thirstily. Yeva also instructed Anastasia, who had been staring blankly ahead for who knew how long, barely responsive, to stroke Solomiya's back, something that should not have to be asked of a normal sister, or any normal bystander for that matter, but Sol did appreciate Anastasia's gesture, stiff and choreographed as it was.
- This went on for an unknown period of time.
- A small black notebook and chewed-up pen slid under Solomiya's nose, with the suggestion she record "meeting" minutes as they determined an "action plan." Solomiya knew what Yeva was trying to do: make Solomiya feel in control of the uncontrollable, plan for the unplannable. This was no committee, she reminded Yeva, just three women stranded in the middle of a war zone who had no idea where to turn, and nobody could say other-

wise. Yeva pulled a dented thermos from the cup holder in her door and said, "Here's some bad coffee. Now it's a committee meeting."

9. **Decision to Head West**
   - Yeva proposed hiding out in the westernmost part of Ukraine, specifically in the Carpathian Mountains, as far as possible from Russian missiles. An eight-hour drive under normal conditions.
   - The possibility was acknowledged that many other evacuees might have the same idea, resulting in clogged highways. They would all be sitting ducks between bare fields under open skies, but what other choice did they have?
   - The decision to head west was supported unanimously.

10. **Decision on the Future of the Detained Bachelors**
    - Deferred to a later time.

11. **Input from Relatives (Yeva's)**
    - Throughout the meeting, Yeva received no shortage of opinions, via speakerphone, from relatives inside the country and out who gave updates on their whereabouts and asked for Yeva's. A number of relatives were already directly involved in the fighting, with one cousin called to the front and another joining the Territorial Defense Forces.
    - An aunt suggested as shelter old cathedrals, opera houses, or theaters; surely Russians would not bomb sites of historical and cultural significance?
    - An uncle suggested heading to Poland, which was accepting refugees. This term was met with resistance by Anastasia. Was that what they were now, she said, refugees? Just like that, overnight?
    - Another uncle, who'd resided in Moscow for the last twenty years and called himself apolitical, suggested they seek safety in Russia, because Russians only wanted

the best for Ukrainians as they "denazified" them and brought peace to the region. This phone call, Yeva promptly ended.

12. **Input from Relatives (the Bachelors')**
    - At the time of the meeting, the foreign nationals' phones lay in their velveteen sack in a trash heap on the edge of Kyiv, inert as stones. The phones had been turned off to prevent tracking.
    - (Their guardians' phones were also supposed to be off to prevent tracking.)
    - Solomiya observed with regret (inwardly) that if the bachelors' phones were still on, they would be lighting up in a cacophony of calls and texts from all over the world, the screens lighting up, dimming, lighting up like the besieged skies.

13. **Input from Relative (Sol and Nastia's)**
    - None.
    - The above, despite the fact of Solomiya's and Anastasia's phones being very much on and available, and reception remaining strong, as evidenced by the almost indecent deluge of calls received by their colleague.
    - A phone call from Solomiya and Anastasia's sole known relative would not have been unwelcome. For Iolanta Cherno to break character and come out of hiding for just one minute.

Action Items

1. Head west.
2. Continue monitoring all available communication channels for military and traffic updates.
3. Breathe.

Meeting Adjourned.

15

PERHAPS PASHA AND THE OTHER MEN may have panicked a little. They may have lost their heads for a minute. But now they were cool again, in control of the situation.

According to Pasha's watch, they'd been on the road for six hours.

Reaching the exclusive romantic getaway was taking longer than expected, as travel often does. Judging by the stop-go of the trailer, they'd hit morning traffic, as one does. With the trailer windows sealed there was no way to tell night from day, but Pasha imagined a green and pink dawn filtering through pine branches, alighting on the dregs of a pagan party in the woods. The bonfire would be on its last smoky whisper, the pan flutes laid down, but the brides would still be there. Draped over logs, flower wreaths wilted, they would be waiting.

Today was a special day, the smooth female voice on the trailer's PA system had informed the bachelors. Every year, Ukraine held a national fireworks competition. That's what the men had heard three hours into their excursion—pyrotechnicians outdoing each other. All around the country, lovers were getting engaged under glittering skies. What could be more romantic?

For the first two hours of their trip, as the bachelors had searched for ways out of the Escape Room, a boyish giddiness had filled the trailer. Pasha was still tipsy from Prom Night, and the others seemed to be under the influence as well, but the giddiness wasn't only because of the effects of the alcohol. The getaway was their reward, the group speculated. They'd done well on the tour, presented themselves as worthy suitors, so they were leveling up to the next phase, where even better women waited, women who had been vetted for the secret party just like the bachelors had.

Among the men, there was Lee from Oregon, CEO of a charity that recycled plastic bottles into fishing nets for villagers in developing nations.

Laurent from Lyon, a journalist with a wide following who'd exposed a famous American yoga-wear brand's abhorrent sweatshops in Bangladesh.

Raj from London, on the cusp of discovering a cure for feline leukemia.

Kyle from Detroit, who made custom prosthetic wheels for dogs who'd lost a leg to road accidents in poor neighborhoods.

Bill from Albuquerque, with his squad of fostered boys he'd been trying to set on the right track through wilderness survival training.

Tim from Hollywood Hills, a plastic surgeon whose resculpted noses and facelifts graced countless movie screens.

And there was Bertrand, the visionary who'd invested early in crypto, then in NFTs (those adorable, tradable cartoon Potter Otters who used their bellies as pottery wheels), and whose Friends with Yachts app would surely be a hit.

Liam, Hans, Carlos, Jerome, Steve. Who did what, Pasha couldn't remember, but they seemed like upstanding men.

(Where did that leave Pasha, thirteenth wheel, his presence accidental? He remembered what Bertrand had told him: Engineer. Full head of hair. Deserving as the others.)

But by the third hour on the road, they'd admitted defeat. The padlocked fridge held a clue to solving the Escape Room, that much was clear, but none of them could find the key. Or any other clue. They'd even tried unplugging the bar fridge, but a shrieking alarm terrorized them until they plugged it back in. Pasha figured the Escape Room had a design flaw: normally in these setups, the first clue was supposed to be easy to find, to give players a false sense of their own intelligence. Or maybe this puzzle was meant to be unsolvable? What were they supposed to do if they did find an escape—roll out of a moving vehicle straight onto the highway? They'd just have to wait it out until they arrived at their destination, when the women would have no choice but to release them. Or at least give them the first clue.

Pasha hadn't minded the search, not at first. He'd eagerly checked for hidden hatches under the cushions, volunteered his credit card for Bertrand's attempt to pry open a wall panel. Unlike past Escape Room exercises mandated by his employers, where team building was forced and probably evaluated, Pasha knew he didn't have to like these men, and they didn't have to like him—their camaraderie was wholly voluntary. The fact that in a few short hours they'd part and never see each other again gave Pasha a preemptive pang of nostalgia.

By hour three, a tense silence filled the trailer. The men sat on the floor in the dimness, squeezed together like schoolboys on a field trip, eyes on their palms, where their phones normally lived. The alcohol had worn off. Headaches were coming on. The silk-tasseled throw cushions had long lost their novelty and volume, and Pasha could feel every pothole reverberate up his spine. All the while, lady eyes watched them—Laurent had discovered the beady black eye of a camera disguised as a smoke detector—and knew the players were stuck, yet did nothing to help them.

It was Bill, eldest of the group, who voiced what Pasha himself had been thinking: something felt off. Phones unreturned. The road endless. Gas station junk food issued through a sliding hatch in the wall of the driver's cabin: cold cellophane-wrapped hot dogs, chips, bagged sauerkraut—not exactly the stuff of romance. After the gold-leafed hotels and catered paddle-wheel rides, why would the agency scrimp on its Chosen Ones?

Hums of agreement filled the trailer.

Then came the bangs. Enormous crashes Pasha felt in his own chest. They seemed to be emanating from every direction. The trailer lurched to a stop. The thought struck Pasha like a fist to the stomach: What if the buildup of Russian troops at the border, something he'd been tuning out all week, wasn't just another bluff? He surveyed the other bachelors' faces. Were they all thinking the same thing?

Raj from London knocked on the polished steel wall of the trailer, the spot where the driver's shoulder would be on the other side. Just checking in, he said to the wall in a tight tentative voice. Perhaps the ladies might let the gentlemen know what was going on? He had a flight back home that day, and many of the others did, too. Another bachelor tapped the tiny camera. Soon other men joined Raj in the knocking, which became less polite, and Lee the recycled plastics guy started yelling. The naked terror in his voice made the others' fear real, too, unleashed it there in the trailer like mustard gas that poisoned their softest tissues. They were all yelling now, slapping and pounding the steel walls, demanding to be let out, to be told what the hell was going on. To be heard, at the very least.

Finally, the speaker on the ceiling croaked to life. That's when the female voice on the PA told them about the fireworks.

No ETA or any other update on their trip, as if all was going according to plan. Only then did Pasha feel the low pulse of the engine again in his sit bones, comforting now. The trailer had resumed its course.

The men looked at one another in silence, each waiting to see what the others would do. How badly did they want to believe that smooth voice? Their belief had to be unanimous, or it wouldn't work. Like a spell they had to cast together.

Bertrand spoke first, his voice high, wavering, as if he'd sent it along a tightrope ahead of them, across a gaping pit hungry to pull them in. It took Pasha a moment to clue in to his words, mundane as they were.

Bertrand was telling a story.

A few years ago, Bertrand said, he took his nephews to a children's musical that featured a live parrot. The original macaw got sick, so they had to sub another one in at the last minute. But as soon as the music and singing started, the bird tried to tear off the actors' clothes. First it went for their hats. Then it tore at their buttons, tugged at their collars, dug into bra straps, until the curtain had to be closed. It turned out that the parrot, who'd been readopted multiple times, had had its start at a strip club.

All thirteen sets of lungs collapsed into laughter.

How good it felt, the release! Like a painful boil bursting. How easily terror flips to laughter. Both convulse from the same part of the gut, thought Pasha. Isn't that why we say *screaming with laughter*?

Thirteen grown men! Well-educated men! Kidnapped! By three girls in animal masks! *In a war!* When their shrieks risked dying down, one of the men would rev up again, and on and on their laughter rolled through the trailer, like a wave through a stadium audience.

Yes, they'd been silly. Their imaginations had run wild. They hadn't slept a wink all night. Dog tired, they were.

When their sides ached and their throats were worn raw, when they could laugh no longer, the others looked to Bertrand again. The ceiling light illuminated his curls into a halo, carved dimples into his boyish cheeks. *Speak, Scheherazade.* So long as the stories kept flowing, they'd be just fine. Surely they'd get to the pagan party.

Bertrand sat cross-legged and Pasha noticed, peeking from under his dress pants, purple socks patterned with green parrots. Maybe Bertrand's story was true or maybe he'd made it up on the spot, inspired by his own socks. No matter.

The stories had to keep coming.

Silence was what the men had to escape now.

16

THE RADIO RATTLED on and off as Yeva drove, reception faltering. Four helicopters had already been shot down over an airport—the one near Kyiv, did they say? Four civilians dead, ten injured, after a ballistic missile struck just outside a hospital in another city. Ten thousand more Russian soldiers had crossed the border. A Kharkiv schoolteacher was fleeing in a car filled with sixteen abandoned cats. The sympathy Yeva felt upon hearing these reports was muted, dutiful, as if everything was happening in some faraway country. Instead, it was the small things that made her catch her breath: the hairline crack in her windshield—from a time before this time, when the only thing that fell from the sky was a stone kicked up by a truck's wheels. The wad of blond hair on the floor of the car—from Nastia shedding it everywhere, balling up entire locks between her palms and carelessly tossing them aside while Sol chastised her for not keeping up with replaiting or regluing or rebeading in some witchy feminine ritual Yeva knew nothing about. Their fifth hour on the road, Yeva had yelled at the sisters to clean up their shit. "Our shit? It's Nastia's mess," Sol protested. "It's *your* hair," Nastia snapped back. She rolled another ball and extended it to her sister, who turned away in distaste, like she'd been offered back her own saliva.

The mug of instant porridge in the cup holder—also from before the war. (Immediately Yeva chided herself: the war had already been grinding on in the Donbas for eight years while the rest of the country sat around in offices and cafés and bars and went on with their days.) The porridge was still fresh, but Yeva couldn't touch it now. It was a remnant from a past life, a time when Nastia seemed always to be gnawing on something—salami sticks, bublyky, salted dried fish from the street stalls, chunks of waffle tortes.

All for what?

Beside Yeva, Nastia was gray-faced, watching the road with a blank expression, as if it led nowhere.

They'd been on the road eight hours, weaving on and off the clogged highway, taking back roads when possible, circuitous detours. For now the old roads held icy and firm, but soon the marshes would thaw, bubble through the potholes. On past trips through the Polesian region, Yeva had the impression that if her mobile lab were just a few kilos heavier, the softening road would swallow her up whole, fold her into its gaseous brew.

Normally they would've already reached the foothills of the Carpathians, but at this rate it would take days. The land stretched flat and unyielding.

One thing that hadn't changed, from the past life to this one: Yeva's mother. When she called a second time in the space of an hour, Yeva braced for the worst and pulled over onto the road's narrow shoulder. Had something happened to Yeva's father? Had their building's basement, where they'd been sheltering, caved in?

"My mother again," Yeva mouthed to Nastia and Sol as she pressed her phone to her ear. The sisters looked at her as though she'd uttered an indecent word.

"Yevusya, I've been thinking," her mother began. Yeva could hear a mechanical clicking in the background, a pipe or elevator machinery, she hoped, which meant the building was still standing. "How many of our own will die on the front." She paused.

Yeva wondered if her mother was about to cry. She'd never imagined it was possible.

"How many men, I mean," her mother pressed on.

"Women, too."

"Yes yes, but I'm talking about the men. Don't you understand?" A ruffling sound as her mother switched the phone to her other ear, which she always did when she was about to proclaim something urgent. "I know how it goes. My own grandmother told me about the dearth of men after the Second World War, the women scrambling for the remnants. And the man she ended up with certainly was a remnant." He'd died before Yeva was born, and all she'd heard about her great-grandfather was that he walked crookedly due to scoliosis, and that he was a drunk, though a gentle one. "You need to get serious, Yeva. Secure a nice man now, put it in writing. Before a draft. Before another woman snags him." Had her mother somehow forgotten Yeva's previous lie, about meeting that American with the golden retriever, or had her mother never believed her? Normally this latest round of meddling would have bothered Yeva, but now her mother's matter-of-fact tone, her unflinching practicality, brought Yeva comfort. So long as her mother stayed the same, everything would be okay. "And if your new husband goes down fighting, well, at least you'll have tried. Better to be the stoic widow of a war hero than a spinster."

"Mother?"

"A Pole would also do, I suppose. Did you see Poland is now letting Ukrainians stay and work for up to eighteen months? Plenty of time for you to sort things out."

Yeva hardly heard her. "If I don't see you again—" she began, but what was it she wanted to say? *I love you?*

"Don't be dramatic," her mother interjected, mercifully. "Of course you'll see me again. Where would I go? Just remember what I said. *Dearth*, Yeva."

17

NASTIA REGRETTED answering her phone as soon as she heard the woman's voice. She'd hoped the unknown number was her mother, finally breaking character to come out of hiding.

"Anastasia? It's Efrosinia. From the agency."

Nastia hung up immediately.

She shouldn't have. Efrosinia's voice was calm, without accusation, and if there had been any, Nastia could surely have smoothed it over. Or at least she could have handed the phone to Sol, who would've fixed it, as she always did.

Now a text came through from the same number. Then another. Nastia left them unread. She, Yeva, and Sol had agreed to keep their phones off during the kidnapping to avoid being tracked by the agency (or the police), but that rule seemed frivolous now. Maybe the agency was simply checking in on all the women, making sure they were safe. Offering help. She imagined a room full of Komod girls laughing in disbelief at the idea.

"Who was that?" Sol asked without looking up from her own phone. She'd been texting with her friends and classmates. Scenes of mangled concrete and rebar filled her screen.

"Spam," Nastia muttered. Best not to bother her sister and Yeva needlessly, when nerves were already frayed. What could the agency possibly suspect? If someone had witnessed the bachelors getting into the trailer they'd recognized as Yeva's, they wouldn't be calling Nastia. And if word had spread about the secret romantic getaway (maybe through Bertrand, who'd already blabbed to the one named Pasha), what could the agency do about it now? Alert the police? Surely the police had bigger problems at the moment.

Yeva gave Nastia a side glance. "Isn't there someone you need to call, check in on? Family?"

Nastia sighed but did not answer, as if there was indeed a vast network of relatives, even larger than Yeva's, who were waiting with bated breath for a call, but the task of contacting them all was so daunting that Nastia hadn't worked herself up to it yet. Yeva seemed to accept this.

Nastia did receive one text six hours into the invasion—a former Komod girl who now lived in France. One of her mother's favorites. Mousy with soulful eyes, but during protests she'd become a fierce, raging thing, all hair and elbows, as though possessed. She'd been the first of the exiled Komod members Nastia had called when her mother went dark, but the woman had insisted that she and Iolanta hadn't spoken since the group splintered, that she knew nothing of Iolanta's plans. Now it was this favorite who sounded panicked. *Please tell me you're okay?* The text irritated Nastia, made her mother's continued silence all the more damning. She entertained a gnawing suspicion that her mother knew exactly where she was and was watching her, that any face peering from behind a car window as they sat in traffic could be part of a network of eyes her mother still controlled. A ridiculous thought, but not so ridiculous if you knew Iolanta Cherno: perhaps she'd somehow engineered this cataclysm just to test her daughter. Would Nastia still go through with her kidnapping plan? How loyal was she to her mother's cause, really? How loyal was she to her mother?

But what if Iolanta's silence meant something different—that she was in danger? No, Nastia couldn't imagine it. Over the years she'd come to believe in her mother's ability to outwit danger, control it, to come home in the end, if she wanted to.

Her phone chimed with a text. Another from Efrosinia.

Nastia turned the phone off and muzzled it with the metal mesh-lined bag. She pushed the fear down, too, kept it at a controlled distance. So long as Yeva drove, so long as Yeva made the decisions, they'd be fine. Surely she'd thought of all the ways the hostage plan could go wrong—beyond what they'd discussed during their planning meetings—and had contingency plans in case things really went south. Yeva had even predicted the renewed invasion, hadn't she? She certainly didn't seem too surprised, kept her eyes dutifully on the road like this was another of her expeditions, another fire to put out. They'd head north, she said, hide out in the Carpathians for a couple weeks (from the war, not the agency, which shrank away to a distant blip) and beyond that—Nastia's mind went blank.

The future had been a luxury. The future didn't exist anymore.

18

PASHA TRIED not to think about his feet. Swollen and sweaty in their polyester socks and narrow dress shoes, which Pasha kept on to spare the other passengers, his feet screamed in protest. Somewhere out there was a shower, a bed with clean sheets, fresh food that wasn't suffocating in cellophane, but he tried not to think of these things, either.

How many hours on the road now? He'd stopped checking.

He forced himself to look beyond the immediate discomforts. Imagined his future bride, his Olya, waiting for him in the pinewoods, poking at the simmering coals of the fire pit. As the shy one among the wild nymphs, had she been the thirteenth wheel, like Pasha, invited along at the last moment? Would she and Pasha recognize each other right away? After a few dates he'd visit whichever city she lived in, meet her doting parents, marry without delay. They'd rent a comically cheap apartment (cheap for Pasha, that is, who'd work remote for a company that paid in CAD or, better yet, USD), save up for their first fully detached home with a garage and backyard. A gas stove. A long extendable faucet to be installed over the expanse of burners, for convenient pot filling, broth making. A guest suite would be a must, perfect for hosting friends visiting from Vancouver, who would gawk at all the space, the open skies, at Pasha and Olya's carefree children, who spent the days playing in a nearby field or gazing far off into the horizon, staving off myopia. And his children, well, they could do anything they wanted in life. They could live comfortably while, say, pursuing fabulous careers in the arts. How close he'd come to giving all that up, skittering back to Canada, living like a serf!

The other bachelors had turned to him.

Could they, all of a sudden, smell him?

"Your turn," said Bertrand, chewing on the stem of his carnation boutonnière. Pasha's turn to tell a story. But anything worth recalling scuttled out of reach, his memory wiped clean, as if he had no history before the trailer. Every story existed only in his future, when real life would begin.

"Anyone else want to go?" he offered.

Everyone else had told a story, he knew. Bertrand himself had already told three. The first, about the parrot, the second, Pasha couldn't recall, the third, about his time working at a big tech company, when he'd accidentally shut down 11 percent of the world's internet traffic. *This* is my story, Pasha thought, the one he'd tell his friends over beers during a visit back to Vancouver, how three broads wearing silly animal heads loaded thirteen bozos into a single trailer ("And you went along with it?" they'd gasp), drove for god knows how many hours, and the men did have their doubts at first but—but then what? He had to wait till this story finished to make it funny in hindsight.

The other men's eyes kept Pasha pinned.

"Tell them the one about"—Bertrand helped along in a hushed tone—"the jogger."

The jogger. Pasha and Bertrand had discussed the jogger at great length back at the hotel bar, deciding who'd been at fault (not Pasha).

"Back in Vancouver," Pasha began, the way he had with Bertrand, "I kept running into the same jogger on the same park trail. A woman jogger."

The men leaned in, glued to his words, even Bertrand listened intently, as if he hadn't heard it all before.

"We'd jog the same loop, except I'd do mine clockwise and she'd do hers counterclockwise, and every time we passed each other, we'd wave. I'd smile, she'd smile. Another loop. She'd smile, I'd smile. It went on for months, a kind of joke, like we were two hamsters stuck on the same wheel."

If you're on the same wheel, Bertrand had said the first time, how would you run in opposite directions? But he kept silent now.

"What did she look like, this lady jogger?" asked Jerome, eyes squeezed shut. Earlier, he'd said his contact lenses were turning his eyeballs to sawdust.

"Bright red hair. Really tall. A bit of a hunch, probably from having to stoop down to talk to people."

"Let me guess, you tried to make a move," said Tim, the plastic surgeon, darkly. "And she stopped smiling."

"Scowled as if you were a leper," said Bill, the elder.

"Changed her jogging route," said Laurent, the journalist.

Bertrand kept quiet, peered at Pasha with a half smile. None of this was quite how the story went, but the jogger looked bad either way, so what did it matter? And the other men were gazing at Pasha knowingly. A hand squeezed his shoulder. It felt nice. When he spoke again, his voice came out high and strained, sounding foreign to him but articulating a higher truth. "There we were, two people trying to make a connection in this vast, lonely world, but the signals got scrambled. That's when I understood that we don't know how to talk to each other anymore, and I don't just mean me and the jogger. I mean us men, and *them*."

"Them," repeated Kyle. He gazed out somewhere beyond the trailer's walls, where the *them* lived, mysterious and unknowable.

"Once, I had the gall to greet a woman sitting alone with a book. Asked what she was reading," said Bill, the elder. "And you know how she looked at me? Like I'd just interrupted her study session at the library. Except we were at the *bar*. On Trivia Night!"

A comradely silence filled the trailer.

"We've fundamentally lost contact," concluded Pasha.

"Amen, brother," said Bertrand.

The trailer rumbled on.

"The fireworks were a good omen," Bill announced, like he'd decided on the fact that very moment. Each and every one of them could be on the cusp of finding the One, he went on, but to find true love you had to fight, you had to journey. You had to set out with your brothers to the trenches, you had to be cramped and stinking and hungry, feet stewing in boots. Love couldn't be found in a park or a bar, where the women regarded you as a predator, and it didn't exist online, where the women ignored you. No, it stalked here, in real life, at the end of a long highway, under a glittering sky.

Their heads were almost touching now, in a sports huddle. And so they journeyed.

19

Nastia straightened up from her spot behind a pile of tires. They'd stopped on the side of the road for a pee break. Sol was still trekking up the road scoping out the perfect bush, while Yeva crouched in the shallow roadside ditch a few paces away in front of the lab, hardly hidden but clearly above caring. The traffic looked thicker now, everyone fleeing westward. A station wagon rolled by with a cage of doves strapped to its roof, white balls of fluff huddled together against the wind. Another car hauled a mattress, which struck Nastia as absurd. What would she have taken with her, given the chance? Her mind drew a blank. She didn't miss anything of her own, not even her clothes, the flimsy dresses she'd worn for the romance tours, the baggy jackets and sweats she'd burrow herself into when off-duty.

No, her only need was to turn on her phone for a moment, to check if her mother had called. The messages flooded in immediately. All from Efrosinia.

We're evacuating the bachelors but are missing at least ten. Do you happen to know anything about that?

Anastasia, pick up. Just a few questions.

Please?

Anastasia

Nastia

This surprised Nastia—that the agency cared enough about the bachelors to evacuate them. She would've expected the administrators to fold up shop and save their own skins. Maybe it was their founder who'd put them up to it, directing the operation from her sauna/yacht in Canada. She had the benefit of perspective, could see beyond the immediate fires of the war. How would the agency look, having lost track of so many men? Best to preserve the agency's reputation, make Romeo Meets Yulia look like it cared for its clientele.

We know what you did. A witness saw two women in animal masks talking to the men before they disappeared. Then we found you and Solomiya in photos. Think we wouldn't be able to tell who's who by the shape of your bodies?

Nastia pulled her coat tighter around herself. Of course there had been eyes on her body, what had she expected? In hindsight their disguises did seem lacking—they could've worn puffier dresses, wigs—but at the time, during Prom Night, while they slipped through the sweaty, drunken crowd in the dim light, moved between brides who wore flashing neon headbands or rhinestone headdresses or kitten ears, who seemed in disguise themselves, Nastia had hoped she and Sol wouldn't be noticed.

Why was the agency messaging Nastia and not Sol? Did they hope the younger sister would cave first?

Soon they were on the road again, and Efrosinia's messages continued to stream in, increasingly urgent: Did Nastia understand she was endangering not only the bachelors' lives but the country as a whole? That it was of military significance to Ukraine, as Zelensky pleaded to leaders worldwide for aid, not to ruin its image? Think how it would look: Ukraine a country of thugs. Some people online, the ones who didn't want weapons sent here to help, were already calling it that.

Think of the scandal.

But Nastia did think of the scandal. The scandal was the whole point. She turned off her phone again.

20

PASHA HAD LIED. Or, if not lied directly, he hadn't set the story straight about the red-haired lady jogger.

He wasn't the one who made the first move.

He and the jogger had been two, three months into their mutual smiling, their telepathic inside jokes set to the soundtrack he listened to while jogging, which made him feel like they were in a movie. A clever romantic comedy where his love interest worked a stressful, if low-paying, job. A nonprofit she was deeply passionate about—cleaning beaches or driving seniors to polling stations. She was the eldest of two, three siblings, someone tasked from an early age with too much responsibility—yet she always saddled herself with more. She had plants, pets, but the thing about pets and plants is that eventually they left you, died before you, and what she really needed was someone who would stick around.

One scorching summer day, instead of waving she halted in front of him.

He took his earbuds out, cutting off the soaring John Williams score for *Schindler's List*. The tone wasn't quite right anyway. She stood before him, gasping, out of breath.

"Look." She wasn't smiling anymore. "I don't. Know how to do this."

This? The jogging? It's true that if she'd been pacing herself properly she wouldn't be out of breath like this. If she was the seasoned jogger he'd considered her to be, she should be able to have a conversation during the act of jogging itself. Pasha was about to offer helpful tips, like running with a metronome—

"I like your face, okay?" She shook her head, started again. "Do you want to meet up sometime? For a drink? With me?"

Her voice was lower and louder than he'd imagined it to be, the kind of voice that hollers obscenities at sports stadiums. She took a step closer, towered over him, shoulders heaving. Rivulets of sweat ran down the swollen cords of her neck, down, down under the tight spandex, from which protruded two sharp nipples aimed, like weapons, at his throat.

"If you don't drink that's fine, we can do coffee, if you don't do coffee, we can . . ." As she bellowed on, the park thickened in his mind into a forest, one where there was no one else around. Pasha realized he did not know her at all. He did not know what kind of job she held, even *if* she held one. If she was this forward (with a stranger!), there had to be something wrong with her.

He tapped his ears to show he couldn't hear her through his earbuds. As her face cracked into confusion, then hardened (he'd been clutching the earbuds in his other hand, he realized later), his legs were already carrying him away. Not jogging—one might call it running. Pasha ran. He never returned to that park.

21

MIDNIGHT. Just drive, Yeva told herself. Ignore all else. Keep the headlights off, keep to the back roads, keep going, however much longer the trek westward. Yeva's foot pumped the gas pedal, her neck and back aching from the endless driving. Dead silence around her, save for the hum of the engine and the whispery radio Yeva kept on low as Sol and Nastia slept on the seat beside her. The sisters had finally given in—Sol at the window, hands folded on her lap, Nastia splayed in the middle, head thrown back with her mouth agape. Maybe it was the blunt force of exhaustion, or maybe the events of the last nineteen hours hadn't settled under their skin yet. Did the dream world feel more familiar, more real now, and *this* waking world the nightmare? Yeva didn't think she could ever sleep again, as though the two reserve diesel tanks she'd hooked onto the mobile lab before they set out had been rerouted straight into the thumping machinery of her heart.

The village at the foot of the Carpathians had to be close now. It hid in the crook of a ravine, under the evergreen cover of old firs, its rocky winding feeder road inaccessible by tanks, should they come this far west. Like the swampy village near Belarus which she'd first suggested as refuge, she knew this village from past snail expeditions. (See? The expeditions had been useful after all, she'd be sure to tell her relatives next time they called.) Its residents hadn't much liked her at first, the way she went door to door like a missionary, preaching about a local snail they'd never spared a thought for, pleading with them to stop dislodging mossy stones from the ravine for decorative arches, but by the end of her third expedition, when it became clear she really was campaigning for snails and not a political party or a god that wasn't theirs, they warmed up to her. Did they stop picking away at the ravine stone by stone? No. But they did offer Yeva a bed to spare her the silliness of hiking along the feeder road to and from her lab (a woman! alone!) every morning and night.

Beyond reaching this village, Yeva and the sisters had no plan—not for themselves, or for the bachelors, who'd stopped banging on the walls at last, a couple of hours ago.

Sixteen twenty. Twenty-three forty-two. Zero one thirty. Twelve twenty-eight. How long since the faraway, grainy radio voice had been reciting numbers instead of news? She'd read about Cold War numbers stations that were believed to have carried encrypted code to intelligence operatives all over the world. *Sixteen zero two.* She floated out of time, forgetting which decade, which century, she was in. But the voice grew louder and more focused, and Yeva realized it wasn't just any voice. These numbers weren't meant for faraway anonymous ears. They were meant only for her.

00:22
23:01

She straightened in her seat. The cab was silent. Had she fallen asleep at the wheel, dreamed up the numbers? Just as she thought this, they resumed:

09:57
11:12

How she'd tried to forget that voice! Now it echoed from the console into her mind with its rounded American r's, and with everything else she remembered about the man it belonged to. His raven-black goatee, its small population of hairs so neatly nurtured. His inability to pronounce the word "wolf," which had led Yeva to believe that Hawaii's most fearsome snail predator was the woofsnail until she got laughed out of her first malacological conference. She'd blocked his number a year ago to forget him. But now, through the two-way radio Yeva hadn't known still worked, he'd found her again, appealing to her weakness for extinction time stamps. She picked up the radio handpiece.

"Kevin."

Even his name she'd tried to forget.

"Yeva," he breathed, "thank god"—though she knew he believed in no such thing.

The words poured forth as if the two of them had never lost contact. He asked where she was. Was she safe? He asked about her parents, about every one of her aunts, uncles, cousins, nephews, and nieces (of course he still remembered their names from her past rants about their meddling, his memory good as ever). His panic rushed at her from a hemisphere away, and this at last made the attacks feel real, not a collective European hallucination. "Enough about me," she said in a ragged voice. Kevin himself was still in Hawaii, he told her. Still living in his mobile lab with his charges, still fighting the good fight against the woofsnail. Recently the islands had been issued an emergency alert of an incoming ballistic missile that turned out to be a false alarm, but for a moment, he'd seen his own end. He'd redoubled his conservation efforts, scraped together funding for fifteen more exclosures for his recovering populations. There were many difficulties, he admitted: more endlings under his care meant more death stamps to witness, all alone. That's what he'd been reading out to her.

"I'm so glad I found you again," he said.

I'm so glad to have been found, she said in her mind.

Cautious, timid, at last his question came. "How are they?"

The black notebook with her own death stamps still lay in her glove compartment. She could start reciting from it, on and on and on in a dirge, but unlike him she had no recovering populations to offset her failures. She glanced at the two sleeping humans beside her. Slime oozed from the younger one's gaping mouth. The older one's face twitched, in what could've been a grimace or a smile. Yeva's new charges. "Safe as can be."

"Lefty, too?"

"Hibernating." The chill of her padlocked bar fridge was keeping him dormant. His release onto an acacia tree was supposed to be special, part of the suicide plan she'd made long ago, in another life.

"Hibernating! Nice! Nice." Was it the radio reception, or was his breathing shaky? He sounded nervous. "Hey, I need to tell you something. You might not want to hear it. In these times, I mean." He paused. "I could also not tell you."

What could shock her anymore? "Try me."

He talked too quickly about a selfie that had gone viral around the world. It showed a Ukrainian teenager about to flee the country with his family, tears in his eyes, clutching a fat pet rat to his cheek, a rat he had to release because his parents wouldn't let him take it with them. Kevin stopped abruptly, waiting for a reaction from Yeva. Was he really so shocked by the boy having to flee? Did he not understand how many more there were like that boy around the country? All Yeva felt was exasperation.

"In the background of the photo there's just a tree trunk and a fallow field," Kevin went on, "but on the trunk, what looks like a side shoot. A tiny twig. Like, this twig does *not* look like it should be there, that far down the tree."

Suddenly Yeva knew what he was getting at—but no, it couldn't be. A twig was just a twig.

"At its base, if you zoom in on the photo, you see the dry mucus seal, Yeva. *C. surculus!* In the wild! And you see the snail's shell spirals left. Left. Yeva, do you hear me?"

She had pulled over, turned off the engine. Lefty's species. Lefty's left whorl. A one in forty thousand chance. It was too much. Or, too little. She leaned over the sleeping sisters, searched the glove compartment for cigarettes, remembered that Sol had thrown them out when Yeva insisted she'd quit. Damn girl! Damn Yeva, for pretending to be good!

Kevin kept speaking. He said the gastropod grapevine was on fire, had already geolocated the photo. It was probably the isolation of the acacia that had saved the snail from street rats, the gastropod forums agreed—rats didn't like exposing themselves to predators by crossing open spaces. (Would a released pet rat have the same instinct? Yeva hoped so.)

She had to keep cool. Objective. "No way to know if the snail in the photo is female." Unlike most land snail species, *C. surculus* were not hermaphrodites.

"No way to know," he agreed. "But there could be more of them stuck to that tree, overwintering." Hope was a dangerous thing, Yeva knew. And yet, wasn't it hope that had kept her from releasing Lefty?

Kevin gave the coordinates of the fallow plot. The photo had been taken down south, where the exodus of civilians already numbered, Yeva knew, in the hundreds of thousands. From her phone Sol had shown her a livestream of the traffic cameras, where instead of morning traffic a military convoy fed in, gray-green and glimmering under the sun, like a snake that slid straight out of the Black Sea, endless.

"Honestly, I'd rather not have known about the *C. surculus*," Kevin admitted, voice cracking, "but I knew you would have wanted to. I just thought, if there were anyone equipped enough, anyone crazy enough—"

An alarm sounded on his end—most likely a malfunctioning mister or any number of emergencies that used to jolt Yeva's own heart, used to make her feel alive. After he bade her goodbye, she got out of the cab, shut the door gently behind her. Trod up the road. Let out an animal roar that sent a flock of birds fluttering from a nearby bush. The ravine village hid just ahead. Nine hundred kilometers southeast, in the opposite direction, a lone messenger no larger than her thumbnail carried millions of years of genetic memory. For all she knew, its tree had already been burned down by the invading army. Hope for a species reappeared, and just as quickly disappeared.

22

SOMEONE WAS SHAKING Nastia awake, telling her and Sol to gather their things. It took her a moment to recognize the hollowed voice as Yeva's.

The ravine village sat just down the dirt road that branched off the highway, Yeva said. She was pointing through the windshield, but all Nastia could see in the pitch black was the reflection of three faces staring back at her, green and sullen from the dim dashboard lights. Yeva could drive no farther, she told Nastia, but she'd called one of her contacts in the village who'd agreed to take Nastia and Sol in for the night. It was all arranged. All Nastia and Sol had to do was hike down the road to the first hut on the left.

"And where will you stay?" Nastia asked.

"I keep telling you, I'm not going with you." Yeva continued on with the instructions. This villager she knew from past expeditions, a "very nice man," owed her a favor and could drive them to a train station in the morning, and that's how they'd get out of the country. "He might try to drive you straightaway, but he has cataracts and can't see at night," she warned, "and don't let him convince you otherwise."

"But what about you? Where are you going?" Sol pressed.

"South. Running an errand," Yeva said.

"What kind of errand?"

Yeva bent down to gather Nastia's and Sol's things off the cab floor and shoved them into their backpacks—animal masks, pink plastic mugs they'd bought at a gas station for instant noodle soups, a blister pack of activated charcoal tablets to settle the stomach. From the glove compartment, she fished out Nastia's and Sol's passports and pressed them into their palms—she'd insisted the sisters bring documentation in case the kidnapping went wrong and they needed to flee the country. When Yeva flung herself from the cab and set their things on the side of the road, neither Sol nor Nastia moved. In her matter-of-fact tone, Yeva had made her plan for them sound logical and simple, yet Nastia felt a new wave of terror sweep through her.

Yeva opened the passenger door for the sisters, just like men used to open taxi doors for Nastia on dates.

"Take us to the man's house, at least." This from Sol, who so easily accepted abandonment.

"If I go, he'll convince me to stay. It's not far," Yeva promised.

"Stay till sunrise, at least."

"Better for me to drive by night."

"Some friend you are," Nastia spat.

"You're welcome for finding you an escape route," Yeva said. "And we were never friends."

"Colleagues," Nastia tried.

"Grantor and grantee," Yeva corrected. "You applied for temporary use of the mobile lab, I granted it. I've fulfilled my end of the agreement to the best of my ability in present circumstances—an agreement that was never formally written or signed—and so we are released from each other." She spoke quickly, her words an impenetrable wall. Was this some former self coming through, Nastia wondered—the person who'd got lost in drinking, in the trash that had filled her trailer? The one who'd operated a lab, kept hundreds of specimens alive, every logistic passing through her and only her?

A crisp knock came from behind their heads. After the freak-out of a few hours ago, which Nastia had watched from the camera feed on her phone, the bachelors had cycled back to a determined calm punctuated by the occasional reminder of their existence.

"You're taking the men with you?" Sol asked Yeva.

Nastia saw the blank look on Yeva's face.

"Oh my god, you actually forgot," Sol said.

"I'm sure you'll figure out what to do with them," Yeva said slowly.

"*We're* not taking them," Sol said.

Yeva nodded in their sisterly direction. "They were your idea."

"Nastia's," Sol reminded her.

Both other women turned to face Nastia.

A sudden feeling of cold made Nastia shiver. Anything beyond the cab's steel steps suddenly seemed out of reach and beyond her immediate sphere of worry. She had to keep from leaving the cab, and keep Yeva from leaving her and Sol. The old villager with the cataracts was an unknown, and "abroad" was a greater unknown—unlike most people she knew, Nastia had never left the country, and she imagined a steep drop into nothingness, like sailors once imagined as they approached the edge of their flat world. Out there, abroad, where would Nastia and Sol go? Who would they be—"refugees"? The refugees she remembered seeing on the news from seemingly faraway cataclysms looked as if they'd spent months or years crowded in the tents of humanitarian organizations, living out of bags. Nastia wasn't, couldn't be, one of them.

What Nastia knew was Yeva. At the beginning of the attacks, as the rockets had blown up everything Nastia thought she understood, it was Yeva who had pulled Sol out of her wheezing panic as Nastia looked on, paralyzed, useless. Yeva who had brought Nastia's hand to the warmth of Sol's quaking back and told her to make a slow circle over and over, and the circle contained both Sol and Nastia, brought them back into themselves. Yeva might be trying to cast them aside now, but if Nastia stopped focusing on Yeva's words and made her own hearing blurry the way she could make her vision blurry by crossing her eyes, Yeva's voice still calmed her, hooked her back from a terrible undertow.

What Nastia had to do now was stall, keep this woman close. "The hostage video," she reminded Yeva. "We can't release the bachelors until we film their message." She'd painstakingly prepared a script for the men, which she planned to slip through the narrow sliding hatch in the wall between the driver's cabin and the trailer. She'd coded it with former Komod slogans and lines from her last fight with her mother—lines still burned into Nastia's memory—hoping her mother would recognize who was behind the heist.

Yeva spoke slowly. "Nastia, forget about the video. There won't be any more romance tours here anyway. You already got what you wanted, can't you see that?"

"But when the war ends—"

"When? Tell me. We're feeling it here now, but it's already been going on for eight years."

Sol hugged her balled-up jacket to her stomach. "So what do you want us to do with the men, release them here? In the middle of nowhere? That'll go over well."

"They'll be grateful to be *anywhere* near the border at this point." Yeva swung open the door to the cab wider.

"We'll all come with you on your errand," Nastia said quickly. "Me, Sol, the bachelors. How long will it take anyway? Then we'll decide what to do with the hostages."

"Where I'm going, it's not safe," Yeva warned.

"Nowhere's safe."

"I'm going to Kherson."

"Kherson."

"You can't be serious," Sol said. "Haven't we all been listening to the same news? Kherson's about to be captured."

Yeva took a deep breath and explained why Kherson, but Nastia could barely understand. Leave two girls and thirteen men alone in the dark, all for a glorified slug hundreds of miles away whose shell spiraled the wrong way? Or, the right way, apparently, for Yeva's purposes. Nastia saw that she had misread Yeva, overestimated her moral compass. Or underestimated it? Nastia and Sol were only humans after all, two among billions, while that snail figured among a handful of its species. The snail was more valuable. Wasn't that how these environmental fanatics thought?

Sol tried softening Yeva. When was the last time Yeva had slept, she asked. How about a nap? A nap does wonders. Or Yeva could sit back down and they'd hold another meeting and this time Yeva could take the minutes? Yeva was having none of it. The longer they chitchatted, she said, the farther her snail could be crawling from its tree. Nastia asked (unwisely, she knew, but she couldn't stop herself) how far a fucking snail could really get. That's when Yeva grabbed Sol and Nastia by the wrists and yanked them both out of the cab.

Nastia stood stunned, watching Yeva climb back into the driver's side. "You can't just leave us," Nastia said, hating the desperation in her voice. She pulled her thin dress over her thighs. "I'm the one who saved you, see?"

Yeva's hand froze over the ignition. "You *saved* me."

"I know what you were trying to do before we set off with the bachelors. The wedding dress you were looking for? I wouldn't have pegged you for the superstitious type, worried about burial, but obviously you weren't getting married. If we hadn't met, if it weren't for my plan, if it weren't for me, you'd be dead."

Yeva recoiled in embarrassment, as if Nastia had caught her talking in her sleep. And Nastia made the mistake of letting her satisfaction show.

"*You* saved *me*," Yeva repeated. "You knew what I needed the dress for, so you gave me your mother's? What were you trying to pull, exactly? Hurry me to the grave when you decided I wasn't useful to you? Or maybe you knew I wouldn't do it, wanted to rub my face in my own weakness. You saved me, did you? No, you manipulated me, manipulated your own sister into your psychotic so-called activism, like you're trying to manipulate me now. You know what you are?" She said this last so quietly, Nastia could hardly hear her. Nastia sensed the venom coming, but she couldn't move. No one had ever told her what she was.

"You cling to the idea of your mother because you have no other personality. Nothing in there. No one home. A pretty shell, that's it." Yeva paused, like she wanted Nastia to deliver a countershot, prove her wrong.

Nastia turned to Sol beside her. Her face wore the panicked, searching expression Nastia knew so well, when her sister wanted to soften a fight, say whatever it took to make everyone happy again.

But Yeva wasn't wrong, Nastia now knew.

Nastia's mother had once said her strangeness was what made her special. Wasn't this a lie all children heard at some point, because all children are born strange before they learn to smooth down the edges? For a while Yeva, too, had seemed to think something of Nastia, and now she didn't. Nastia felt the shock of relief. She'd grown to like Yeva, too much, but now the sharp words severed Yeva from her in one clean cut. They could part, forget each other. It was that simple.

Yeva gave her head a shake, as though to loosen any lingering memories of Nastia. She started the ignition. "Get your men out of my trailer. Now."

23

"DEAR GENTLEMEN, May you find the One!"

The wave of fresh air rushed into the trailer and over Pasha's face. At last, the door had slid open. It was night, and the dome light on the trailer's ceiling illuminated the silhouette of a small woman in a fox mask and an ankle-length parka who was speaking to the circle of men in her silken voice, the same voice that had cooed at them from the trailer's PA system during the drive. Pasha vaguely remembered a masked woman in a glittery dress from when he and Bertrand had first entered the trailer, but they'd both been drunk then. Was this the same woman?

In her accented English the interpreter announced that, regrettably, their exclusive romantic getaway had to come to a premature end due to the commencement of a full-scale Russian military invasion. The driver had done them the courtesy of taking them west, a convenient bus ride away from four countries they could choose among: Romania, Hungary, Slovakia, and Poland. If the bachelors could please exit the vehicle and proceed down the highway, they would reach a bus stop by the time the buses began running again. On behalf of Romeo Meets Yulia, the interpreter wished the bachelors a safe trip, and the best of luck with their romantic pursuits.

She stepped aside and flung her arm out into the pitch-dark night.

They'd been on the road seventeen hours. Pasha was the first to rise from his floor cushion, wanting nothing more than to throw himself from the trailer and stretch his aching joints. Yet he held back. None of the other men had moved.

"Look, we all know the key's in the bar fridge," said Laurent, who sat atop the fridge like a hen warming her eggs. "You made five of us miss our flights home, then you tell us it's game over?"

"All flights over Ukraine have been canceled," the interpreter said. "You can understand, I am sure. We ask you to remain calm as you deboard vehicle."

Through the PA system, a low female voice barked a command. The interpreter reached into the trailer, mumbled "for your safety," and flicked off the ceiling light. The dark enveloped them all. The February air, crisp and refreshing at first, now grew icy. Through the opened trailer door the stars began to reveal themselves, but only in one thin jagged strip up top, as though the rest of the world had been ripped away. A mountain range stretched before him, Pasha realized, perfectly solid, but he couldn't shake the feeling that if he took a step out of the trailer, he'd plunge into the bottomless black.

A thin plaintive voice, Kyle's, came from Pasha's right. "But you promised there'd be ladies. The agency chose us, and only us, to meet them."

Tim demanded a refund.

"You are joking, yes?" the interpreter said.

A firm silence. It was she who had to be joking—earlier, Pasha and the other men had briefly pondered the possibility of a war and then dismissed it. They hadn't heard any more explosive bangs—which in any case were more like crackles and pops when they replayed in Pasha's memory—since their third hour on the road. When he'd last seen daylight (admittedly, before entering this trailer—its windows were shuttered), locals lounged in cafés and children ran around schoolyards. Surely there was nothing to worry about.

She sighed. "Your getaway was included in romance tour fee. It was no extra charge anyway."

"Refund the whole fee, then," Tim persisted. "I'm not going anywhere until you guarantee it."

Rich, Pasha thought, for a Hollywood plastic surgeon who

probably didn't need the money anyway. Meanwhile, he himself could certainly use it, having quit his job back home.

Pasha could just make out the woman's shape, how she slumped against the opened door, obviously exhausted. Even the fox ears seemed to droop. He was reminded of a dolphin-watching tour in Mexico that had not yielded any sightings, the Torontonian couple who'd yelled at the guide for not delivering, Pasha's embarrassment at being associated with such miserly Westerners.

The interpreter was speaking again, explaining the impossibility of a guaranteed refund because the original fee they'd paid was directly to the agency, whereas the getaway was through a third party, and anyway, the agreements signed by the bachelors stated that in the event of an act of God such as the expansion of the existing war in the Donbas, of which they were surely aware, all rights to refunds would be forfeited. Pasha couldn't remember if this was true of the papers he'd signed. He hadn't read the fine print. And might they have been wrong about the war? That disaster in Donbas had been going on for years, but an "expansion"?

"Who here even brought their passports? We weren't alerted of the need for passports, let alone cash for international bus fare," Lee piped up from the back of the trailer, by the bathroom. An indignant murmur followed. No one had brought their passports with them. Their passports were back at their hotel rooms, which they were supposed to have checked out of yesterday morning. "So let's say, for the sake of argument, there is some kind of war. We try to leave the country, get stuck in some holding cell between borders, and then what?"

"Border authorities will sympathize, I am sure, due to extraordinary situation." Her voice wavered, like she was unsure of this herself.

"I want my phone back," demanded Raj, his hand extended through the opening. He added, "Please."

The interpreter readjusted the mask over her face. "We left your phones in Kyiv. No phones allowed at forest party."

"But there's no forest party, is there," said Bertrand, slowly, to Pasha's left. He'd been unusually quiet these last few hours.

"This is what I am saying, yes. Canceled. Everything canceled," said the interpreter, her tone clipped.

"Canceled, of course," said Bertrand. His dark shape leaned forward, and he tapped the vinyl floor of the trailer with his finger, like he was about to draw on it. "Let's see. Twelve phones, plus the bonus one from Pasha. Good phones, too, upper tier. Mine's worth about twelve hundred. Tim's is nicer, but two years old—could still pull in a thousand if you refurbed it. Raj likes to keep his in a beater case to look less flashy but it's at least fifteen hundred. Kyle over there, our dark horse whose nonprofit must be especially nonprofitable"—he paused, and Pasha imagined Bertrand winking at the man—"clocks in at nineteen hundred. Some people remember others' shoes, for me it's phones. Altogether our phones are worth, say, fifteen thousand?" He emphasized, "USD. Not bad at all, fifteen grand in one haul. Is that how you chose us?"

Pasha shifted in place, uneasy. How naïve, he thought, that he'd believed they'd been chosen not for money but for simply being good people.

"No one's getting out until we get some answers," said Bertrand. He flicked the ceiling light back on.

Now not one, but two women in animal masks stood before them. The fox had been joined by something long-nosed like a gazelle, but with pointed ears like a lynx.

The gazelle-lynx woman flicked the light off.

Bertrand flicked the light back on.

And suddenly three women in animal masks stood before them. The third, unmistakably a wolf, stood slightly apart from the other two.

If they kept flipping the lights, Pasha wondered, would the menagerie keep multiplying?

"We do not want phones, money. It is not about money," the gazelle-lynx woman said, her voice low and gruff. This was the same voice that had commanded the lights to be turned off over the PA—the voice that apparently belonged to the leader. Had she posed as one of the brides at the agency? Had he gone on a date with her, or with any of these thuggish women? It was unimaginable now. All three women wore baggy clothes, making them unrecognizable.

"All we ask is, you leave," their leader said.

"How do we know there's really an 'extraordinary situation' going on? An 'invasion,' as you say? How do we know you're not lying about that, too?" asked Bertrand. "Seems dead quiet out here to me."

"We heard them," the interpreter said. "Rockets. You didn't?"

"Those couple of bangs you told us were fireworks?" said Tim.

"We did not want to cause panic while evacuating you," the interpreter explained. "Rest assured, there is war."

"Then why aren't you all trying to get out, too?" Bertrand asked the women.

"They are leaving country, yes," the leader in the gazelle-lynx mask said, pointing a thumb at the other two, who seemed to stiffen. "But I must go south."

"What's down south?"

The leader spoke of tanks rolling in from Crimea, endangering—here, sense got lost in translation—snails? One snail?

Bertrand burst into laughter.

When the others joined in, Pasha couldn't help himself, either. It was all too ridiculous. And the animal masks the women were wearing didn't help. When the laughter quieted down, Bertrand leaned back and stretched his legs, satisfied, his point about the women lying about a war apparently proven. And Pasha did want to believe Bertrand, didn't he?

"Don't you see what's happening here?" Bertrand went on, turning to the men. "The *real* war here is poverty. Inequality. They've skipped from Communism straight to the most rotten kind of late capitalism." He turned back to the women. "See, it's not about the money for me, either. What's a thousand dollars out of my pocket, really? It's the principle. I came to your country not just to find the woman of my dreams, but also to find talent for my start-up. Tech talent, photogenic talent. In between dates, I scouted your countrymen and women. I was going to give out jobs. Could've given each of you one, too. Teach a man to fish, that kind of thing. But what do you do?" His voice softened to a whisper, drew the other men closer. "You steal my fish."

The men around Pasha hummed in agreement, looked down at their palms, as if the fish had slipped straight out of them.

"You stole all our fish," said Lee.

"I understand you are afraid," the interpreter in the fox mask said, assuming a soft voice, like she was talking to children. "We are afraid also. Take step by step. Leave country, it's most important thing. If taking bus to border is most scary part, Pasha speaks some Russian and will guide you."

All heads turned to Pasha. He felt the blood drain from his head. Had he spoken Russian to these women before entering the trailer, outed himself as useful? The idea of acting as a guide to anyone anywhere in this country he now realized he knew almost nothing about, a country that might or might not currently be under invasion, filled him with dread. He sat back down on his cushion.

"See? Pasha doesn't believe your lies and scheming, either," Bertrand told the women. "Of all of us here, he'd know your kind of people best. Born here, weren't you, Pasha?"

Pasha mumbled something unintelligible. Best to neither confirm nor deny his provenance. He still didn't know what to believe.

The interpreter began to speak to Pasha in Russian and offered him, and him only, a full refund, if he could get the others out of the trailer. Did he seem so easily bought? Yet he felt himself waver.

"What's she saying?" asked Kyle. Was there an edge of suspicion in his voice, as though Pasha, entangled with the women, was in on the scheme, too? He quickly relayed what the interpreter had offered him. "But I'm saying no, obviously."

"So they can issue refunds after all," Tim pointed out.

The fox-interpreter sank onto a log on the side of the road, as though her last reserve of strength was empty. The wolf stood beside her and crossed her arms, her blond chin-length hair tangled, with a few long locks straggling out. There was something feral about her, and her loping presence made Pasha uneasy. If they were indeed a girl gang, Pasha decided the wolf was the one who did the snuffing. She mumbled to the interpreter, who waved away her words without translating them. It was the leader in the gazelle-lynx mask who relayed the message to the men, her tone wooden, a last formality. "You are welcome to direct all complaints about Romeo Meets Yulia, and all marriage agencies, to international press."

Glancing over at the two women by the log, Pasha could see the dark liquid eyes in the holes of the wolf's mask, the satisfaction in them. It was an odd thing to say—to suggest they could go to the press. Scammers preferred to lie low, didn't they? That's when it dawned on Pasha: If the press did find out, the punishment of public scorn awaited—against the grifters, sure, but also against the men, because whose fault was this, really? Who had let themselves be lured into a trailer by three girls in silly animal masks? And what were these men doing in Ukraine in the first place? Word would get out about the romance tours, too.

Bride buyers. Creeps. Colonizers. Those were the kinds of comments he'd seen on online forums back when he researched which agency to choose. Now they would be directed at him, at all of them. *Serves them right to get fleeced.*

Pasha could see that the other men were imagining the public shaming, too. Bill, who'd reverse-mortgaged his house to go on this tour and give his fostered kids a mother again even though his own mother had tried to stop him, called him a sucker for buying into the agency's promises. Laurent, the shrewd investigative journalist who was supposed to know the questions to ask, to be able to sniff out a lie. There were two men with PhDs among them who sometimes jokingly referred to themselves as doctors. And Pasha himself, biggest embarrassment of all, the coddled expat who'd lost all street sense, let himself be duped by his own people. What would his friends say? What would his parents say? They didn't even know he was in Ukraine. He'd told them he was going to Europe for a micromechanics retreat, a lie he knew would inspire few questions, allow him to bide his time as he set up his new life. He'd wanted to surprise them once the pieces began to fall into place: a woman of interest, the prospect of children, house listings in hand.

No, Pasha would not let word of his colossal miscalculation get out, and neither would the other men, he knew. They'd band together to make this right on their own.

"Here's what you're going to do," he heard Bertrand say to the women. "You're taking us back to Kyiv, straight to the hotel." He raised three fingers for three demands. "Phones, passports, dignity."

The three women peered back at them through the eyeholes of their masks. Their postures seemed to slump a notch lower.

Why should Pasha fear the schemers? He knew, of course, that he and the other men could overpower them. Wrangle the ignition key from them, commandeer the vehicle. If weapons weren't part of the equation—and Pasha doubted they were, since the exhausted-looking women would've surely brandished them by now—then brute laws of physics and chemistry would dictate the result. Thirteen men versus three women, testosterone versus estrogen. But he hated how quickly the thought had come to him. He'd always considered himself civilized, a gentleman. He and the other men were wearing tuxedos, after all.

In the spirit of diplomacy Pasha held up three fingers, just like Bertrand. "Phones, passports, dignity," he demanded, in Russian. In case the women hadn't understood the first time.

24

THE THREE WOMEN kept a grim silence as the lab barreled down the highway. Nastia could see Yeva grimace every time she pressed the gas, as if Yeva could feel the weight of the thirteen men still in the trailer, could feel their drag on her. Of course, they wouldn't go back to Kyiv as the bachelors had demanded, so they had no choice but to take them along to Kherson. Nastia tried to keep as still as possible so as not to upset the dozens of jars at her feet. She knew the snails in the jars were dead, but she didn't want to test her luck. Or, not luck. Nothing about this felt lucky. But at least she was still here in the trailer, a place she knew, and not out in the dark unknown.

The mood in the lab hadn't been helped by Yeva's argument with the bachelors over the trailer's windows before they set off again. Pasha had played interpreter, at Bertrand's prodding. Bertrand no longer seemed to trust Sol to do the job. (That Nastia, Sol, and Yeva were still wearing masks didn't help matters, Nastia knew.) Bertrand wanted the windows uncovered so that he and the men could see everything with their own eyes, Pasha explained in Russian. Yeva had countered that she wanted the windows to stay covered to keep the trailer from giving off any light, thus exposing their presence on the road. The bachelors promised to keep the lights off. Yeva said she didn't believe them. Well, if the men couldn't see out of the trailer, Lyle countered, then the women shouldn't be able to see into it. He reached for the fake smoke detector, which was supposed to disguise the camera, and yanked the device out as Nastia watched, with a sinking feeling, yet another piece of her hostage plan fall away. Yeva, who didn't trust the bachelors not to tamper with other equipment, then unlocked her death cabinet to retrieve its dozens of jars. Nastia could see her neck muscles tense under her mask as she carried the jars armful by armful to the cab, batting away the men, who insisted on inspecting the fridge's every shelf and nook. Meanwhile, Bertrand was still complaining about the covered windows and saying they were further proof that the women were lying about a war happening. This, despite Sol's attempts to show him and the others media photos and videos of blasts on her phone, grainy and glitchy from weak reception.

On the side of the road, in the dead silence, the war did seem far away again to Nastia, too—a bad dream she'd woken from.

In the end, Yeva slid the trailer door shut on the men's faces and reeled around to face Nastia and Sol. "If you don't want to stay back here, fine. But if you're coming with me, you're dealing with the bachelors. They're your mess."

Nastia wondered what that meant, "deal with the bachelors." Keep them alive? Find a way to wrench them out of the trailer at the next pit stop?

"We'll just have to tell them we're taking them back to Kyiv," said Sol, when the three of them were seated in the cab again. The bachelors had resumed thumping on the walls of the trailer.

"Like hell we're going back to Kyiv," Yeva shot back.

"Of course not. We'll only say it to calm them down. We'll worry about them accepting reality later."

Nastia nodded in agreement. Yes, they'd worry about the rest later. The fact that Yeva had let her into the trailer again must mean she felt bad about what she'd said earlier, about Nastia being nothing but a pretty shell. Yeva hadn't meant it. She felt the knot in her throat loosen.

"You told them the bombings were fireworks to calm them down the first time," Yeva reminded Sol. "Look how that worked out."

The thumps grew in intensity. A muffled protest chant came through, but Nastia couldn't make out the words.

Sol threw her hands up. "Open to suggestions."

Yeva started the engine. "Like I said, they're your mess. Promise them Kyiv if you want to." She added, "Just keep them fed."

Now the hours snaked on as they pushed south. They stuck to the major roads this time while an endless chain of cars evacuated in the opposite direction, the sane direction. The bachelors stayed quiet, for now. They'd smugly accepted the gas station snacks and mini water bottles Sol pushed through the narrow hatch. The detour to Kherson wouldn't take long, Nastia told herself. Over nine hundred kilometers southeast, one way, Yeva had warned her, but it wasn't the numbers that mattered to Nastia. The important thing was to keep everyone together, captors and hostages, keep the kidnapping plan viable somehow. She tried to focus on that, rather than the fact of them plunging toward the path of the tanks.

The snow petered out, but it didn't seem to get any warmer. Nastia shivered in her seat. Yeva kept the heating off so as not to bring her one live snail out of hibernation, and Nastia knew there was no point in protesting. Nestled in a cup holder on the dashboard, its jar looked as if it had been repurposed from jam or pickles, and unlike the other jars, at her feet, this one had holes punched in the tinplate lid. Hard to believe the inert grayish lump inside needed air. She imagined rolling down a window, smashing the jar against the speeding asphalt. Would they still need to rescue its potential mate then? Maybe, or maybe not, but Yeva would definitely kick Nastia and Sol out to the curb.

Nastia stared into the dark. A half-moon gave the road a faint sheen. Somewhere out there, Kherson awaited them.

INTERLUDE

KHERSON DOESN'T EXIST ANYMORE, or not as I once knew it. Fiction is slow to form, to rally its characters from room to room, city to city, to build causality even as real life rushes forward. As I write, Russians have occupied Kherson. And Ukrainians have taken it back. Russians, still in control of the marshy lands across the Dnipro, have by now shelled Kherson more than two thousand times (how many more times, as I edit this same passage?). They've targeted monuments, supermarkets, civilians lined up for humanitarian aid, a demining crew, a rescue crew in the middle of extinguishing a fire. The Robin Bobbin bakery and candy shop on my grandfather's block has been hit, as has the ATB grocery store where he buys his weekly crossword, an indulgence sorely missed during the occupation. Authorities have disabled air-raid sirens, deeming it safer for people to stay home, to avoid congregating. Residents were asked to avoid exactly that same thing not long ago, during a quickly forgotten pandemic. The dress rehearsal for the real act.

For a few days we thought our family dacha across the river, built by my grandfather's hands and where our generations grew up, had been hit, too. The cooperative's guard reported a two-story wooden house had burnt down on our street. (The guard had been our only source of news about the area. Unable and/or unwilling to leave it himself, he'd been stuck in limbo since the occupation. If he tried to leave eastward, he would come under

Russian fire; if he tried to cross the river back to Kherson, he risked fire from Ukrainian snipers.) The guard sent photos of the wreckage. It turned out to be another family's dacha, two plots over. Photos of our own dacha, still standing, showed blown-out windows. "Good thing I didn't spend all that money upgrading them like I'd wanted to," my second cousin says over the phone, attempting to sound cheerful. She fled Kherson with her husband and eleven-year-old daughter three months into the Russian occupation.

Our relief over the dacha was short-lived. As I edit this same passage, the house is underwater, or floating downriver into the Black Sea. The Russians have blown up the Kakhovka Dam. The massive reservoir, called Kakhovka Sea by locals because in some parts you can't see the other side, has unleashed south, submerging towns and settlements, neighborhoods in Kherson. It churns up and redeposits land mines, some exploding en route while others remain dormant; it unsettles the bones of Nazi soldiers from World War II, churns up radioactive sediment from Chernobyl, washes away the Soviet-era polka-dot teacups of our dacha, uproots a charred acacia from its field. The past and present churn together, roil away. Civilians in motorboats rescue people from their rooftops as Russians continue to shoot and shell them. I look for our dacha's gray roof poking out of the water in the drone footage on the news. Swans swim over rooftops, power lines. Even as I write about the dacha guard, he has already died of hypothermia. He is eventually found in his flooded attic alongside his border collie, Jessie, also dead.

In truth, I don't know the dog's breed—but the detail seems important here. A recognizable breed, not too foreign. Ukies have border collies; they are just like you. And, perhaps also just like you, they once thought disaster only befell other people.

Once, when speaking to my grandfather over the phone, my mother heard the explosions in the background while my grandfather, hard of hearing, couldn't. He said his Turkish coffee was about to overflow, he had to go. When my mother hung up, she looked at me as if the explosions had been coming from outside our own windows.

No, these lines are not quite true to what happened.

My grandfather's hearing has been declining, and his descriptions of the shelling certainly aren't as pointed as those of his sister, my great-aunt, but during that phone call with my mother he did hear the explosions himself. I need to keep fact and fiction straight, but they keep blurring together.

The exaggeration would have served well here, though. Watching a war from abroad, rather than living it, can be its own brand of horror. Moonlike, we in the diaspora watch the captured zones of our homeland ebb and flow like tides. We are aware of every wave of bombings, first in piecemeal fashion from texts, phone calls, and social media, then aggregated into numbers (deaths, injuries, scope of destruction) on the news. Then we put on our shoes and go to work, surrounded by people who have other worries. But to live through a war from the inside: Would you see and hear the blast only in your vicinity? If your city block is hit and you survive, are you part of a collective of witnesses who can grieve together? This is a kumbaya story I like to tell myself, but I don't really believe it. And what is it like if you are simultaneously living under bombardment and watching the news?

In the first year of the war, when I felt guilty for crying (*I'm not the one being bombed!*) and then guilty for not crying (*Think of those being bombed!*), I wondered, uselessly, who had a proper claim to grief. I knew expats who mourned dutifully, refusing social engagements, their faces ashen as if Ukraine had already fallen. I also knew friends back in Ukraine who were hiding in basements and still hadn't stopped cracking jokes.

In 2023, as my sister Anna and I prepared for our trip to Ukraine, everyone I knew had an opinion on Who Has It Worse. Or, Where Is Most Dangerous. My Canadian friends thought—understandably so, given the footage one watched on the news—that every inch of Ukraine was burning and tried to talk me out of going. What if I got stuck there? What if, being Ukrainian-born, I got drafted into the military? (An impossibility for multiple reasons, I tried to explain.) When we arrived in Lviv, deemed by real estate ads to be "the safest place in Ukraine!," a local shuddered at the idea of Anna and me continuing east to Kyiv. Before we left for Kyiv, a childhood friend who lived there assured us that nowadays we were unlikely to "see anything, much less hear anything"—seeming to forget, Anna observed, that a helicopter had crashed two blocks from his office the month prior. "It's Kharkiv," he assured us, "that's truly dangerous." When my sister's professional contact reached out from Kharkiv to invite us for a tour of the city, she said it was a fine time to visit now that Russian artillery had been driven back a bit. We just needed to bring a flashlight for the dark streets. "It's not like, say, Kherson, where people are dying every day." Meanwhile, in Kherson, according to my grandfather, people were out and about shopping, ignoring the blasts in the distance. They just tried to avoid the riverbank, which was in the direct line of fire from the Russians who'd occupied the opposite bank.

As it turned out, my sister and I could go no farther than Kharkiv. We never made it to Kherson. Even a day trip felt too dangerous. In Kherson, the proximity of the Russian artillery renders the air-raid warning systems useless. The city's silty soil (still unflooded as I write this particular passage) means there are no good underground shelters for hiding.

Kherson's train station will come under attack, too, just as a train is about to pull out. My grandfather's sister will be inside the station. She'll shelter in the basement. One wagon will catch fire, be disconnected, and two of its crew will be sent to a hospital, but the rest of the train will make it to its destination on time.

When the Russians began shelling Kherson, my grandfather's sister, my great-aunt, refused to leave her house. So long as she stayed under that tin roof, she must have thought, she would be spared. Why did her calculation change three weeks later, when she fled her birth city by train? Why did it not change for my grandfather?

His stubbornness. His eighty-six years. His bad hearing. I don't know. If I and my family knew, we could reason with him.

Who Has It Worse?

I know this is a useless question, but my head is full of useless questions. Why have the Russians always been so obsessed with Ukraine? How many support Putin's "special military operation"?

A question I've heard asked (was it Anna, or did I hear it secondhand from a friend's therapist): Is the trauma of those who escaped Kyiv (or Kharkiv, or Dnipro, or Chernihiv, or . . .) during its siege and scattered to all corners of the globe fresher, more ongoing, than the trauma of those who stayed? The first group continue to associate their beloved streets with explosions and smoke, while the second group (as a collective) have witnessed the retreat of the enemy and their streets returned to normal. Or, as normal as can be for now. During air raids, they might obey the sirens and trudge dutifully underground, but more likely now, they ignore them altogether. Has their collective reality come almost full circle, normal–abnormal–new normal?

Does their trauma "resolve," I wondered. My own word, an optimistic bludgeon.

Anna and I visited Kharkiv Conservatory—my sister had been fundraising to repair the missile damage there, to save sixty grand pianos from rotting in the encroaching dampness and cold—and met with a professor, the woman who invited us for a tour of her city, telling us to bring flashlights. At the beginning of the siege, in February 2022, she and her husband had pushed their university-age children onto a packed train leaving Kharkiv, fighter jets flying overhead, but they stayed behind. Kharkiv has since stabilized, its bombed-out windows boarded up, streets resolutely litter-free, probably cleaner than before the war. Dressed in a bright yellow scarf and boots, the professor seemed cheerful at first. We drank coffee while she guided us through the city, insisted we pose in front of bombed-out buildings and a street lined with charred nubs of trees so that the world could see them. Another photo, another, she urged. We had to resist our reflex to smile for the camera, tried to remember to keep our pink paper cups out of the shot. The professor laughed plenty, but her eyes would periodically water in a way that was disconnected from her animated facial and body gestures and speech. At first I mistook the tears for allergies.

Had her trauma been "resolved" more than that of a Kharkivite who'd fled the city?

We sent a photo to an expat friend in Vancouver, alerting her that we were in her hometown. "I don't think I could pose in photos like that," she texted back.

When, in March 2023, my sister and I arrived in the country we'd watched burning from our phones, laptop screens, television monitors at gas stations, I wanted to be "resolved." And there was certainly something satisfying about watching fellow Ukrainians resolutely going about their lives. What I felt, reuniting with my relatives, still leaves me speechless. But neither Lviv, nor Kyiv, nor Kharkiv is my hometown. It's Kherson. More specifically, my hometown is a tiny plot of land with a wooden house on stilts that my grandfather built with his own hands, and that juts into lawless marshes where I could sit in the mud for hours, watching the hatching of life. It's the place ravaged by floods, seeded with mines, where I may never sit again.

It's February 23, 2022, and none of what I've written above has happened yet. The floodwaters stop, move upriver. The reservoir's muddy bottom refills with water, and the fish twitch back to life. Every scattered piece of concrete and metal and particle implodes back into place, and once again the Kakhovka Dam holds firm, the Dnipro River's great inheld breath. Missile and shell shrapnel dislodges itself from roads and sidewalks and buildings and from soft flesh, human and animal, and is sucked back up by the sky. The black loamy chornozem smooths itself over from the tank treads of the Ukrainians who recapture these lands, and finally from the Russians who captured them.

It's the morning before the full-scale invasion. In Kherson, the buildings stand whole. Some are new or freshly renovated, some are worse for wear but functional. All are complete with floors, walls, and ceilings. When a hand turns on a tap, water pours from the nozzle. A flick of a switch, and light floods a room. The parks also are whole, grass stretching uninterrupted. Daily crossword puzzles are printed uninterrupted. Residents live and residents die, in balance. Everything is yet to come, and none of it is imaginable in this moment. That the elder residents had lived under occupation before, first with the Nazis and then again with the Soviets, does not make the imminent occupation any more believable. The World War II bullet holes in the old center's buildings have long been filled in and painted over. We are, after all, in a civilized time. Few residents have left, preternaturally spooked by swirling rumors.

On a lone tree in a bare field, a snail wakes. Her foot taps against the hard mucus ring sealing her shell to the tree, taps, taps, finds the hairline crack she'd left for breathing, kicks through. Upon devouring the seal, her first meal of the season, she emerges in full. Tentacles stretch, taste the air: the sweet breath of a nearby acacia bud about to erupt from under its scale; the sulfurous trace of gunpowder, blown in from the east; the smoky sigh of drying lichen. Unlike other tree snail species, this one lives not on leaves but on branches, the lips of their shells curved to their contour. Her grayish shell isn't smooth and glossy but craggy and uneven, to match exactly the bark of acacia trees. Leaving almost no mucus trail, she is adept at hiding, likely from an avian predator now long extinct. No other snails have found her, either, not even on those lush nights after rainfall when she'd crawled right in the middle of the trunk, exposed herself to the elements, wanting to be found. She must've looked like a knot among knots, too good at hiding for her own good.

Her next predator will come by land—a predator that was once close amphibious kin, and now, 400 million years later, a distant cousin. They still share similarities. The genetic mechanism that coils a snail's shell just so also coils a human's stomach and intestines, just so.

Announced by diesel fumes and the cloying scent of latex, blue-rubber-gloved hands will crawl all over the tree like two oversize spiders—though one is a tad bigger than the other, more agile. The hands will try to peel the snail from her tree and shut her in a jar, take her far, far away from her acacia tree, a place she couldn't have crawled to within her own lifetime, within three thousand lifetimes. As always, at the slightest vibration—the skitter of claws on bark, the thunk of human footsteps—instinct will shoo the snail into the nearest crag or knot. Luckily, this particular acacia, over a hundred years old, has many. This one still hasn't been cut down, saved by its gnarled combination of knots that remind the landowner of his beloved late mother's face. The snail likes to hide in the deep hole of the mother's left eye.

25

NASTIA WAS DRIVING. Fine. Not ideal, but fine. Her hands shook. So long as there were no other cars on the road, they'd live. Yeva, who sat in the middle seat, had only been forced to lunge at the wheel twice to keep Nastia from careening off the highway. Anyway, it was hardly a highway, not like the ones around Kyiv. When was the last time anyone had fixed this road?

But there were cars, lots of them, pressing in the opposite direction. They made Nastia think of the thrust of traffic out of Kyiv on Friday nights, frazzled urbanites leaving for their quiet dachas to tend to vegetable patches or gather plums for winter jams, or to visit grandparents in the villages, or to simply sit around a campfire in the woods eating shashlik. Best not to think about why everyone was leaving their city now. The outbound traffic slowed to a crawl, took up every lane. Pedestrians hauled checkered oilcloth bags; Nastia saw the occasional cat slung over a shoulder. An elderly woman pulled a resistant cow by a rope. A miniature poodle in a pink puffer vest darted between cars until a window rolled down and a hand plucked the animal off the road by its sparkling handle. Yeva's voice, determinedly calm, instructed Nastia to ease the trailer onto the gravelly shoulder, keep pushing south. So far, the only other vehicle she'd seen going south was a van labeled PRESS.

Was Yeva regretting making Nastia drive? Nastia hoped so. Hours before, when Yeva had begun to nod off behind the wheel, she'd made Nastia talk, talk about anything at all, to keep her awake. So Yeva liked snails, did she? Nastia said, and segued into a story about a Komod girl who'd stayed at their apartment, a diabetic who'd kept therapeutic leeches in a vat and would soak in the bathtub with the things latched on to her like fat mutant moles, as if her own body had grown them. Yeva had replied that she didn't see how the leech story was relevant. Leeches belonged to an entirely different class from gastropods, although it was a common conflation and an offensive one.

How was it offensive? Sol piped up. Leeches weren't that much more gross than snails. One just has a shell and the other doesn't.

This argument over taxonomy had kept Yeva riled up for another two hours, but then her head began to roll again. When Sol started giving a play-by-play of a romance novel she'd recently read, about an English count who falls in love with his horse trainer, Yeva pulled over to the side of the highway, yanked her key out of the ignition, and thrust it at Nastia.

Nastia had recoiled in her seat. The key dangling from Yeva's hand looked like a stage prop, its long black fob encrusted with complicated buttons. "I told you I don't drive."

"High time to learn."

"Sol's older," Nastia tried.

"But skittish," Yeva said. "On the road, hesitation kills."

Sol looked away, indignant, while Nastia felt a pang of pride. If Sol was the skittish one, what did that make Nastia?

"Pull over and take a nap," Sol snapped at Yeva.

"No time," Yeva said. "Where we're going, I'll need a copilot anyway, just in case."

"Just in case what?" asked Nastia.

"Don't play dumb." Yeva folded the keys into Nastia's palm.

A yellow and blue sign welcomed them to Kherson. Sol nudged Yeva, who'd fallen into a fitful sleep between them as soon as Nastia seemed to gain some measure of control over the lab. Nastia maneuvered along Friendship of Peoples Street. Residents in puffer jackets and furs stood in lines spanning several blocks, waiting their turn at banks and ATMs and pharmacies. A run-down gas station with a large hand-painted cardboard sign announced, NO GAS, DIESEL ONLY. Yeva told Nastia to pull into the line of buses and trucks. Nastia turned right, too sharply, and had to reverse to correct as a car honked behind her.

"Is that a Tesla?" Sol asked, peering into the passenger-side mirror. "With a generator strapped to the roof?"

Yeva leaned over Nastia to look. Her thick black waves brushed Nastia's chin. "An electric car converted to diesel, that's a first."

The three of them broke into nervous laughter.

As they waited to fill up, Nastia's phone rang from her back pocket. She reached for it, keeping one hand on the steering wheel. The call was from an unknown number, long and foreign-looking. Nastia felt a spike of hope as she picked up.

"There she is, daughter of the devil herself," said the hard voice on the other end of the line. Not her mother's voice.

Sol mouthed, *Who is it?*

It took a moment for Nastia to recognize the tone of the agency founder, the woman who'd coo at the brides from her Canadian sauna/yacht at every induction session, her face blown up to many times its size on the huge screen. Maria—although the brides were supposed to call her Masha. It was too late to hang up, and Nastia knew she couldn't tackle the woman alone. She put Masha on speakerphone.

"Nice try with the fake last name," Masha told Nastia. "You might've flown under Efrosinia's radar, but now I know who you are. Your heist has Iolanta Cherno's name written all over it."

Sol turned to Nastia, her face stricken with panic. "We don't know what you're talking about," said Sol. "Or who."

"Is that you, Solomiya?" Masha tittered. "Too bad, really. You were one of our best interpreters, I hear. Could've had a real future with us."

Sol's weak spot was her fear of disappointing people, Nastia knew, so she was relieved to see her sister's face harden.

"When Efrosinia told me about the missing men and showed me headshots of the suspects, I knew right away," Masha continued. "Anastasia, you look just like her. Solomiya, not so much, but my staff told me you were sisters. Efrosinia hasn't been in the business long enough to have been in Komod's line of fire, but I have. I've lost count of how many socials they crashed, naked and screaming. How many times Iolanta would barge in, wearing that whiter-than-white wedding dress just to rip it off and cause a scene. Always during my trips back to Kyiv, too. Like she wanted to show she knew where I was. Like it was personal."

Komod's last protests had taken place eight years ago, when Nastia was a preteen. Now she felt a gnawing guilt over how embarrassed she'd been by the stunts, how she'd thrown dark looks at her mother whenever she watched her dress up as a blushing bride.

"I thought she'd finally run out of steam, given up, got a job or whatever," said Masha. "Now I see she's making her own daughters do her bidding. It's disgusting."

The truck in front of them moved forward. Nastia jammed her foot on the gas.

"Easy!" Yeva yelled.

"It's my bidding, not my mother's," Nastia retorted. "I don't even know where she is." Nastia meant to sound proud, in command of her almost nineteen years, but the words came out wilted and pathetic.

"You don't know where your mother is?"

"Not for the last eight months."

Nastia saw Yeva's glance—as if something had just dawned on her, a piece of information Nastia wanted to take back.

Masha said sweetly, suddenly maternal, "Well, I know where she is. I can tell you."

Nastia froze. Her mother spoke of the international marriage agency network like another person might of the secret service. If she really had been plotting her biggest protest yet, for Valentine's Day, had Masha's agency found out? Did they know more about Iolanta Cherno's plans, about the reason she'd had to lie low for eight months, than Nastia herself? She imagined her mother tied up in a dungeon, her mouth stuffed with crumpled bridal catalog pages.

Nastia tried to keep her voice level. "Where is she?"

"Give us our boys back first," Masha said.

"That's what we were doing," Sol interjected. "We're evacuating them."

"Great," Masha said, her voice flat, as if she didn't believe this. She named a statue in a town by the Romanian border and demanded that the bachelors be dropped off there. "You have twenty-four hours."

"We have other plans for their evacuation, and we're nowhere near the Romanian border," Nastia pleaded. How many hundreds of kilometers back west would it be, six hundred? Seven? "We're all the way down south."

Sol made a slicing motion at her throat. *Don't give away any details.*

"South? You can't be serious," said Masha. "Haven't you seen the news? The tanks are coming straight up from Crimea."

"We're running an errand as part of the evacuation." Nastia glanced over at Yeva, who pointedly looked away, refusing to acknowledge that even an enemy thought their detour was crazy.

"Twenty-four hours," Masha repeated. "No boys, no mother. And keep your phone close." She hung up.

Nastia pushed one of the buttons under the window, marked with a car trunk and lock icon. She felt the mechanisms shift deep in the lab and pictured the trailer locks latching. Once again, the bachelors were trapped inside. "We need to turn around."

"Like hell we're turning around," Yeva said. She peered at a map on her phone, zoomed in on the pin of the GPS coordinate of the acacia, a pulsing red point. "We're almost there. We pick up the snail first, then we go toward Romania."

"How do you know the snail's still on the tree and not crushed under a boot?" asked Sol.

"How do you two know Masha actually knows where your mother is?" asked Yeva.

"We don't," Nastia said, coolly. It wasn't like she hadn't considered the possibility that Masha was bluffing. Still, all she wanted was to lurch the lab out of the gas station line and hurtle west toward the Romanian border right this moment. She willed herself to be patient. Tapped her nails against the hard cracked leather of the steering wheel. Only four cars ahead of them. And how long could it possibly take to find one snail on one tree?

26

PASHA JOLTED AWAKE at the click of the lock. He'd managed to doze off for a few hours, his head on Laurent's soft squelching stomach. They were long past prudishness, fitting their aching bodies on the floor of the trailer in whatever way they could. Judging by the trailer's lurches and turns, they'd arrived in a city, perhaps in Kyiv itself, at last.

Now that the trailer had slowed to a stop and the thrum of the engine cut out, Pasha clambered across the sprawled men and tried the door. Definitely locked. Bill gave it a try, then Tim. Had they made an even worse misstep by refusing to leave the trailer when they'd had the chance, worse than going along with the special trip to the woods? At the time it had felt better to stay inside the trailer, take a stand against the scamming women, but Pasha wasn't so sure now.

The blasts came again, closer than the first time they'd heard them. It was as though the air had solidified into a vast, all-covering carpet and somebody was beating the dust out of it.

An air-raid siren began to wail. Pasha had never heard one before, but it was unmistakable, the wounded sound obviously engineered to create alarm. It rose and fell in a terrible moan, like it tore from his own throat. He and the other men sat upright.

What to do? Start howling, as dogs do when they hear sirens? He felt a searing panic rise from his stomach.

"Here's a fun fact," began Bertrand. He sat with his legs crossed, the picture of serenity, like he'd always known the blasts were not actually fireworks but had another, better explanation all along. The other men leaned in, listening hungrily.

"Ukraine's president used to be a comedy actor," Bertrand said. "Played President on one of their TV shows. Did you know?"

Pasha did know.

"Another fun fact," Bertrand went on. "His wife, the First Lady? A scriptwriter."

This, Pasha did not know.

"Call me crazy, but what if it isn't a coincidence? Tell me, who put them in power?"

"Zelensky was elected," Pasha said. "Fairly."

Bertrand gave him a sad look. "On the surface, sure. Look deeper. Who puts anyone in power these days, meddles in elections? Either it's Russia or America. This time, I'd wager it's America, my own tax dollars at work." He jerked his thumb behind his shoulder, at the driver's cabin. "We thought the women were lying about a war just to get rid of us, make off with our phones. But what if the lie's bigger than them? Bigger than all of us? What if it's America engineering another fake war to fund weapons contracts and feed its own economy? Like we did when we invaded Iraq for weapons of mass destruction that were never there. Except this time, we don't even need an actual war. All we need these days is a couple of photos and videos of a supposed Russian invasion for the internet, get enough people in a panic, and bam, it becomes real."

They were all up again, seated on the floor in a circle.

"But what we just heard . . ." Tim trailed off, pointing at the ceiling, the sky beyond it.

"Not actual bombs. More bang than bite," Bertrand said. "The worst thing that could happen? We wet our pants like schoolboys."

Pasha looked at the other men, who were now staring at their palms. Maybe no one wanted to be the first to shut down Bertrand's far-fetched speculations. Or maybe the other men were actually taking his ideas seriously. And would that be so unreasonable? From what Pasha knew of Bertrand, the man had been right about other improbable things, hadn't he? Crypto, which he possessed in multiple currencies. Or those Potter Otters, maddeningly adorable, each now worth over eighteen grand. What if Bertrand had a sense about these things, even if Pasha found them stupid, couldn't understand them? Pasha was supposed to be the rational one—he worked with rebar and concrete, substances he could see, touch with his hands—while Bertrand traded in air. Yet those damn otters had earned the man a house, a car, a body he had the time to sculpt and chisel. What did Pasha's "rationality" get him? His childhood bedroom, that's what.

These days, Potter Otters might be the real deal, while a war was not. Who was Pasha to say otherwise?

Kyle was the first to break the silence. "What about the women, though?" he asked, nodding at the driver's cabin. "They're still just after our phones?"

"It's that simple," Bertrand said, hands clasped.

An uneasy laughter filled the trailer. Pasha chuckled, too. It seemed almost charming, this homegrown grifting, compared to the horrors he'd thought possible only a moment ago, listening to the blasts.

27

MILITARY TARGET, Yeva told herself. She tried to ignore the sound of the explosions, which seemed to be coming from a nearby airport. She and the sisters would surely be safe in residential areas.

They'd found the fallow field, weedy, half a block wide, between two squat apartment buildings. The acacia stood a couple meters from the curb, the only tree in the field. It looked ancient, about two stories tall—taller than Yeva had imagined—with gray sinewy bark and thick thorns along its branches.

The sisters waited in the cab as Yeva's hands searched over the tree, every crag within reach, every wrinkle. Air-raid sirens wailed and a booming recording of a male voice urged civilians to seek cover, but she climbed the boughs, higher, higher, as high as the gnarled trunk could hold her. The sisters ventured out of the lab and paced around the tree offering help, but Yeva shooed them away. Their movements were too frantic, risked crushing the snail with a misplaced palm or boot. They'd better take care of their own charges, the thirteen bachelors, who'd need food and water and sanitary supplies slipped through the sliding hatch, and Nastia better not forget the dairy-free alternatives for the bonus bachelor she'd insisted on bringing along. What did Nastia think of her little deviation from the plan now?

"*My* deviation?" The girl threw her hands up as the sirens began blaring again. "Look where we are."

Yeva drew in a breath for a counterattack—better to fight than acknowledge the growing pit of guilt she felt about coming here. She could tell the girl that a heroic rescue like this could make international news, shine a light on the plight of the other endangered animals across the region, attract funding for more conservation work. Of all people, Nastia should understand the value of media attention. Yet against the wails of the air-raid sirens, Yeva knew the argument would fall flat. So she said nothing.

When the sisters set off to look for food and supplies, Yeva finally descended the tree. She sat with her back against its gnarled trunk and took off her latex gloves, buried her hands into her armpits for warmth. Two hours had already passed. The sun was setting. A steady stream of residents rushed past the field or cut through it, hauling shopping bags, rickety caddies, suitcases. A woman Yeva's age passed by with a pink-bowed toddler in her arms. The little girl smiled and waved at Yeva. Yeva waved back, trying to appear calm. Any moment, Yeva would haul herself up again and resume the search, but doubt had set in. What if the snail wasn't here? Worse: What if it *was* here, but the tree was too large, its branches too numerous for Yeva to comb through? She considered running a hose from her water tank to mist the entire tree, to mimic rain. Rain could lure a snail out of hiding, to bask in the wetness, glide like a skater on fresh ice. But in this case, ice would be a problem. So far, temperatures had hovered above freezing, but what if they plunged? Yeva risked icing an exposed snail to the tree. Sure death.

She might as well saw the tree down and haul it north, comb through its barbs in safer territory. But haul it how? The tree did not look like it would go down without a fight.

A solution came to mind: alcohol. Not for herself. She'd wet a patch of bark with beer as bait. Snails loved the smell of anything yeasty, decaying. Before she set off to find an open kiosk, she left a note for the sisters on the windshield of her lab and locked the cab. Her key still in the lock, a thought surfaced about how quiet the bachelors had been these past few hours—no thumping on the walls, not even a polite knock—but that thought was very small, and easily ignored.

28

INSIDE THE TRAILER, Pasha had his ear pressed against the wall of the driver's cabin. No muffled voices, no movement there. The other twelve men stood breathing behind him, waited for the right moment to stage their escape. They'd loosened the last screw of the skylight using Tim's credit card, which was made of some fancy indestructible metal.

No one talked about getting their phones back anymore. This ordeal had gone on too long, with no end in sight. They were sick of the cellophane-wrapped "food," the stinking compost toilet, sick of dozing upright. They needed to contact their families, reassure them that they were okay, that the so-called invasion was not what it seemed. They, insiders now, knew better.

Whose idea had it been, to try the skylight? No matter. They worked as a team, a hive mind. That they hadn't considered the skylight before was understandable. It was sealed off from sunlight, blended in with the rest of the ceiling, sort of. Panic gives people tunnel vision; they miss the obvious. There was a reason why flight attendants, during safety demonstrations, had to remind passengers that the nearest exit might be behind them.

His ear still pressed to the wall, Pasha heard one of the cab doors slam shut, followed by a retreating set of footsteps against asphalt. He gave the men a nod. "Now or never. I think."

Bertrand stood below the pane of glass and took off his blazer—which had somehow remained unwrinkled this whole trip, Pasha noted with envy. His muscled arms reached up to push once, twice, until the pane came undone, clattered onto the roof.

The men cheered quietly, tapped each other on the back.

Pasha peered up at the slit of sky, which seemed impossibly narrow now. Enough for a child or teenager to squeeze through. Enough for a grown man to get stuck in.

"I can go last, help hoist from below," Bertrand said. "Pasha, you go first. Once you're out you can help by pulling from above."

The other men stood aside in agreement.

As Pasha climbed onto Bertrand's back, he felt his cheeks burn. Of course he had to go first. He was the smallest, having hardly grown since he was sixteen, but did the others have to make it so obvious? Couldn't they have at least feigned deliberation? Had his fellow captives been sizing each other up all along, long ago putting him at the bottom? It was like gym class all over again.

He squeezed right through the opening, but gave a low groan to show it wasn't as easy as it looked. He pulled himself onto the ridged roof of the trailer, crouched on all fours, filled his lungs with crisp winter air.

A breathtaking sight greeted him. The setting sun saturated everything in comic book colors: bubble-gum-pink clouds, yellow apartment buildings. To his right, there was an orange rectangle of land with a tree that cast an outlandishly long tar-black shadow shaped like an eagle's taloned foot. The road on which the trailer was parked led down the hill, to where a river gleamed like a red-hot blade forged straight from a fire. Unsettling, the absence of people. As if everyone had gone into hiding before the coming dark.

"Well? What do you see?" asked Bertrand. "Are we back in Kyiv?"

"I can't say," Pasha admitted. He couldn't recognize any of his surroundings. But how well could he really know a city he hadn't lived in since the age of eight? The river did look wide as the Dnipro, which passed through Kyiv. Pasha leaned over the hole in the trailer roof, which exuded a terrible musk of sweat, cologne, fumes from the compost toilet. The men crowded below were staring up at him. "We might be on the outskirts of Kyiv. Looks pretty peaceful out here to me," he added, not quite believing the words himself.

Kyle was the next to give the opening a try. He could only get his head and one arm out.

Lee got past the shoulders and arms, but despite Bertrand's pushing and Pasha's pulling, the man's belly formed an insurmountable plug.

After three other men had tried and failed to escape, they gave up on the skylight. Pasha thought of smashing the driver's window, finding the button that unlocked the trailer, but what was the point without the ignition on? The button wouldn't work without power. He would need a crowbar to wrench open the trailer door. Perhaps he could use a paper clip to pick the lock, even though he'd never picked a lock before. He wished it weren't him alone outside the trailer, wished that someone stronger *and* smarter had gotten out in his place, but there was no time to feel sorry for himself. He leaned over the hole, told the men he'd be right back. Told them, as if they had any choice, to hang tight.

Where to go? Where to find a crowbar? He knew nothing of this place, or why the women had parked here. Pick a direction, any direction. He chose the river, hoping to find a port or marina with tools he could borrow.

As he ran downhill, the river opened before him, shimmering invitingly. A bridge crossed it. Nothing remarkable about the girder—nothing like the arched wonders that leapt over Vancouver's inky inlets—just a flat road propped up by pale concrete pillars, but the honesty of the design, its austere Sovietness, tugged at him. He slowed to a walk, caught his breath. Here was a bridge not pretending it was anything more than a road. A nostalgia he hadn't realized he possessed pulled him closer, closer, right to the foot of the bridge—void of cars, he would recall later—back to an unadorned childhood spent in a concrete box of an apartment, where you never felt poor because everyone around you lived the same way. He began to walk up the bridge, and the river gleamed red as lava, blinded him. For a moment he forgot the trailer, the men, their misadventure. He was alone for the first time since joining the romance tour. This place, whether Kyiv or not, wasn't so foreign to him after all. He was in Ukraine, *his* Ukraine, not the modern one he'd hardly recognized. Finally, he was home.

He stumbled over a crack in the asphalt. Spotted on the ground a pale leather glove, fingers stiffly curled. He automatically reached for the dropped thing to tuck it somewhere at eye level, as good citizens do, until his fingers met flesh.

Not a glove, but a hand.

His whole body shot back. He looked up, shielded his eyes with both hands from the gleam of the river.

He saw what lay ahead.

29

YEVA AND THE SISTERS were a block from the trailer, supplies in hand—they'd intercepted each other at a kiosk across the city, the only one still open—when they stopped short.

On the street corner, a skinny figure sat on an overturned milk crate. Pasha. There was something off about him, Yeva noticed, the way he sat ramrod straight, unmoving. For a moment no one said anything, as though any sudden noise would cause the man to come to his senses and bolt.

Had the others escaped, too? Scattered all over Kherson?

Nastia let out a soft "Fuck."

"Who left the door unlocked?" Yeva asked, but both sisters insisted they'd locked it after the phone call from Masha. How could they not, Nastia reminded her, now that they needed these men to get to Iolanta?

Nastia set down the box of protein gel packets she'd snagged from the rapidly emptying kiosk. "Three of us, one of him. We can wrangle him back inside."

"And risk the others escaping, if they haven't already?" Sol said. She rubbed her face. "I say we just talk to him, scope out the situation before any wrangling."

The three women made their slow approach, Yeva in front.

"Oh, hi," Pasha said in his accented Russian. He seemed surprisingly happy to see them. He wiped his mouth with the back of his sleeve. There was a pool of vomit between his dress shoes. "I went for a walk."

"How did you get out?" Sol asked. "We were keeping you all inside for your own good."

His face turned somber and he leaned forward, as though to tell them a secret. "I saw them, soldiers, in pieces." He whispered, "There is a war on."

"So we've heard," Yeva said. Oh, she would have said more, much more; she would've given the idiot a piece of her mind and told him to pass it on to his other idiot friends inside the trailer—if only Pasha hadn't looked like he was on the verge of losing it.

"We are not in Kyiv, are we," Pasha said.

"Kherson," Yeva said. "But Kyiv is under siege, too. As we said."

"Maybe we should leave," he said.

The sisters turned to Yeva. Like they hadn't spent the entire walk back from the kiosk trying to convince her of the same, like she hadn't already told them a dozen times she needed to try the beer bait first (she'd managed to snatch the last bottle from the kiosk), hadn't explained it would work best at night, when the snail was likely to be most active.

"Tomorrow," Yeva promised.

"Where are the other men?" Nastia asked Pasha.

He jerked his thumb toward the trailer down the block.

"All twelve?"

Pasha smiled placidly. "Twelve. As intended."

Yeva felt a wave of relief and saw the same feeling pass over the sisters.

"Keep them inside," Pasha said, still smiling. "Don't let them see or hear. Bolt down the roof window."

Yeva took this to mean the skylight, the way he'd managed to get out. "I will," she promised.

"Hey, I recall you, from the first social," he told her. "I wondered, before, is it she, behind fur mask?" He squinted up at her through the growing dark. None of them were wearing their animal masks now. He scrunched up his eyes. "Yeva, yes. You told me about mason bee." His face turned dark. "How she always lays the male eggs closer to the surface of nest, so any hungry bird that comes will massacre them first."

Sol shot Yeva a scandalized look. *That* was her icebreaker?

Yeva shrugged. She remembered delivering that factoid countless times—didn't think how it might come off—but still couldn't remember Pasha himself. She hardly remembered anything from the opening of the last tour. The search for lethal gas between dates, a burial dress. Then Nastia, seeking her out in the alleyway behind the hotel, teetering in her stilettos. Only then did the colors begin to drain back in.

"And you," Pasha went on. He was looking at Nastia. "I'm sorry you were dead bored at brunch. Little young for me anyway."

The girl frowned, clearly unsure what to make of the rejection.

To Sol, he offered a handshake. "I am he, the mechanical engineer?" He gave another dopey smile, like he'd just remembered the fact and it pleased him.

"I say we let him loose, cut our losses," Nastia said as the women huddled out of earshot from Pasha. "Did Masha say she needed all thirteen men back? She didn't specify a number. We can afford to lose one."

Yeva told herself she should be pleased. Her little activist, who'd once dreamed of trapping one hundred men, now all grown up and finally thinking practically. Yet it almost made Yeva want to stuff the man back inside the trailer, resume the original kidnapping plan, just to see that childish hunger again in the girl's eyes.

But Yeva had to think carefully now. Pasha didn't seem right, physically or mentally. Whatever was brewing inside him, she couldn't risk unleashing it on twelve others inside a cramped metal box. Maybe Nastia was right.

"So what do we do with him?" Sol said.

"Ignore him," Yeva said. "Maybe he'll just wander off on his own."

30

AS HE WATCHED the women head back to the trailer, Pasha decided two things.

The first: despite what Bertrand had said, the war was indeed real and they were right in the middle of it—a disaster too vast to behold at the moment, like climate collapse or the sun's eventual swallowing of the Earth—but (second) what Pasha had seen on that bridge was not real.

Amplified by the wide sheet of river, the sunset had been too bright, had compromised his vision. What he'd seen on that bridge could have easily been piles of muddy, crumpled clothes. People dumped the strangest things around bridges—not just clothes but burst cushions, doll parts—and Pasha's paranoid mind must have transfigured those clumps of material into *that*. For a moment he'd been transported to an anomalous place, a crack in reality without sense or order, and then he'd thrown up. Now he was back on sure ground, embarrassed at having overreacted. No doubt it was the food he'd been eating that had made him sick, if he could even call it food. These past two days he'd had no choice but to eat whatever slipped through the hatch. Dairy, the enemy Pasha knew well, lurked everywhere. That bland lettuce and mustard sandwich, its seemingly innocuous white bread. The bag of potato puffs powdered with who knows what—the molecular compounds on its ingredients list were impossible to recognize in Ukrainian. The gas station hot dog, its meat probably pumped with cheap filler.

The streetlamps flicked on, casting dim circles over the potholed road. Halfway up the block, beside the field with the twisted tree, he could see the women busy with the trailer's skylight, their leader up on the roof revving a drill as the men inside protested, banged on the walls. Who were these three women, really? Could they truly have come to Kherson to rescue a snail, as their leader had said they needed to do, when the women had tried to kick everyone out of the trailer? Or were they still trying to scam the men? Did it matter anymore?

Now the interpreter was jogging back in his direction. He knew he'd been on a date with her before—or, not officially with her but with the young feral one she interpreted for, Anastasia, who hadn't looked so feral during the tours, hair a single glossy sheet. The three of them had eaten brunch at the hotel restaurant, sat in a red plush booth encrusted with rhinestones that dug into his back. His date had spent most of the allotted hour jabbing at her bacon with her fork, shattering it to bits, showing him zero interest, but he'd liked the interpreter more anyway. They wove between Russian and English, the way he did with his parents, as they worked through the laminated Suggested Subjects card they'd found under the menu (pet preferences, jobs, ethical dilemmas involving capsized boats and runaway trolleys). A thick dog-eared paperback had poked out from the backpack by her side, he remembered. She didn't seem to belong on the tours any more than he did. When Efrosinia passed by the booth, giving a matronly nod, a look had passed between Pasha and the interpreter, like they were both in on the same joke. Or had he just imagined it?

She stood before him now, catching her breath. He searched her face for any hint that she remembered their brief shared history, and found none. She nodded in the direction of the trailer. "Can you talk to the men, calm them down?" she asked in Russian. "I had to tell them we're not in Kyiv but promised we'd let them out of the trailer at the border, that they just need to wait a little longer. They don't believe anything I say. The more noise they make, the more attention they'll attract. They'll only slow us down."

Her name returned to Pasha. He tested it on his tongue. "Solomiya."

She blinked at him. She remembered him, of course she did. She looked at the trailer again, at the two women who stood waiting, then back at Pasha. "Everyone just calls me Sol."

"But I will call you Solomiya."

"It means peace." She gave a sad laugh.

He throttled his voice a notch deeper. "What we all want."

The senselessness of the past two days rearranged itself into a story. He'd tell it when this was all over, when he reemerged braver, harder, reforged. How he'd been scared at first, but then he'd found her. *She* was what this whole ordeal was about, she was its meaning. And there was the undeniably practical fact of her body: her small frame, which he'd be able to lift. He'd always dreaded not being able to lift his bride on his wedding day.

Was he getting ahead of himself? But was it so wrong, to look for love in a time of war? The search wasn't any easier in peacetime.

The leader was marching toward them, her hard gaze flitting from Pasha to Solomiya. "What is this, a speed date? Romance tour's over," she called. She beckoned him toward the trailer. "Your friends are about to give themselves a collective heart attack."

Solomiya fixed her bright brown eyes on his. "You'll talk to them?"

Pasha heard the men in the trailer quieting down at the sound of his voice. He felt a strange power being the one who was sitting shotgun in the cab, the one gripping the PA microphone in his fist, the women watching him by the open door. Pasha, thirteenth wheel no longer. Now both the men and the women needed him.

He'd assumed a businesslike tone. He told the men everything they wanted to hear: that he'd had a real, hard talk with the women. They'd agreed to take the men back to Kyiv after all. The men would get refunds, plane ticket reimbursements. Phones, passports, dignity. All of it. They just needed to sit tight a little while longer.

An unintelligible chatter crackled through the speaker. Had Pasha gone too far, made it all sound too good to be true? He missed being a comrade among these men, he realized. The cramped limbs, breath stale from junk food, as if they were on a boys' sleepover.

"How much longer?" Lee's voice broke through, hoarse. "Get those women to let us out first. Just for a stretch."

Pasha looked at Solomiya, who whispered in Anastasia's ear, who shook her head no.

"That, they can't do yet," he relayed. "I'll be riding up front, right along with you. I promise."

All three women seemed to stiffen at the idea of Pasha squeezing beside them on that single mottled seat, but they must have realized this was not the time for argument.

The speaker gave a thump. Its static grew silent. The men had covered up their microphone, shut him out.

"Bertrand?" Pasha called. His surest ally, silent this whole time.

It was Kyle who answered. "You were working with those grifters all along, weren't you?"

Pasha flinched. "What?"

"I knew it," Kyle went on. "The way the interpreter would make comments to you in Russian. The way she was trying to use you to get rid of us, back at that middle-of-nowhere mountain village. And how convenient, how you're the only one who could fit through the skylight. It all stank of collusion, but I didn't want to believe it. None of us did."

Pasha glanced at Solomiya. She seemed to wilt.

He couldn't deny that the words hurt. How quickly the others had cast him out. "No one's colluding," he said. "I'm trying to help you here. Commonsense diplomacy."

He saw the women shifting where they stood, impatient. He'd failed to calm the men. He felt his usefulness draining before their eyes.

Then Bertrand spoke, at last. "Pasha, hey. How are you."

Bertrand's voice was a steady bass, emanating from both the speaker and the other side of the driver's cabin wall, cutting through the trivia of Pasha's allegiance. It was as if he'd pulled

Pasha aside, away from the boyish squabbles, to have a man-to-man. "What I said about the fake war," he went on. "I was right. It's fine out there, you see it with your own eyes. Everything's fine." He paused. "Right?"

Bertrand, who still trusted him. His true ally. Friend. Pasha felt himself soften: he owed Bertrand the truth. Yet at the same time, Pasha wanted to keep the man cocooned from it just a little longer. Encased in the trailer, Bertrand was the lucky one—all twelve of the other men were—not having seen what Pasha had on the bridge, not having it lodged behind their eyes.

"You were right all along," Pasha told Bertrand. "Keep quiet, and we'll get back to the hotel all the faster. Everything will be just fine."

"Okay. Of course it will." Bertrand chuckled softly. "You hear that, boys? Now settle down."

Pasha clicked off his microphone and listened for a moment. The other men might have their doubts, but they didn't resume banging on the trailer's walls. His assurances had worked.

He climbed down the cabin's tiny steel ladder, his hair feathering against his face, into the fold of women. He wondered if this is what statesmen felt like, descending from private planes onto windy tarmacs, returning home from foreign missions.

Solomiya nudged the one named Anastasia who, with a sigh, issued him a tube of lime-green slime from her pocket.

Solomiya seemed to read the question on Pasha's face. "It is edible."

Pasha took the gesture as a thank-you. Felt his chest puff up.

Then their leader—Yeva, the other two had called her—moved to step in front of him. Her gray gaze pinned him to the spot. She leaned her face into his, as if she was going to kiss him, a prospect that thrilled and terrified him.

"You're good now, right?" she asked, her voice soft. "You seemed off before, sitting on that milk crate."

He nodded.

She clapped her hands together. "Excellent. Then you'll go

get weapons." Machine guns were being handed out to civilians as defense, she explained.

Pasha took a step back. The sky seemed to flick a notch darker. "Now? It's almost night."

"Exactly. For the night."

He didn't disagree with her plan. In theory. "Maybe it's better I stay here," he suggested. "Keep guard."

"Keep guard with what?" Her tone was weighted with a forced patience, like she knew he'd get the right answer eventually.

"He'll keep guard with that smile of his," said Solomiya. Was she complimenting him or being sarcastic? He couldn't read her—her, or the other women. Especially that Anastasia, the youngest one—there was something that seemed not quite real about her skin. It was too smooth, humanoid, like she was made of silicone.

"Don't worry about it," said Yeva at last. No disappointment in her voice, like she hadn't really expected him to say yes. "I'll do it myself."

But this was not how the story was supposed to go, the one he'd recount to everyone back home. You let *a lady* get the weapons? his father would yell. His mother would look on, speechless. Pasha was supposed to be the brave one, venture through a city he didn't know, handle weapons for the first time.

"Absolutely not," Pasha told Yeva. "I'll go."

"Really, it's fine." She'd already turned to the other two, started issuing instructions for some kind of bait involving beer and a rag. He felt himself getting pushed out of their circle, losing his foothold.

He set his jaw. "Just tell me where I need to go."

After one block, he stopped and turned. Under the streetlamps, the women melded into a three-headed silhouette, watching him. No, the women weren't simply trying to get rid of him, he decided. Except for Solomiya, they'd paid him no heed during the tours, but now all three really did need him.

The factoid Yeva had told him on their long-ago date, a story about mason bees, returned to him—it was a story about the sacrifice of male eggs to predators. At the time Yeva's opener hadn't sat well with him—he'd taken to heart his date's implication of male expendability. But now it seemed fated, a kernel she'd planted in Pasha. What she'd been trying to tell him was that the male cocoons were not bird fodder but protectors. Their role was to ensure the survival of the females so that they could make more females—and more males. In the same way, a man throwing himself headlong into danger wasn't motivated just by chivalry. Such an act had to stem from a biological drive to ensure the population's survival, its renewal.

Yes, the three women needed Pasha: a smallish man, but a man nonetheless.

Unrefined, this thought. Probably offensive.

Pasha was tired of his thoughts, refined or not.

He waved goodbye to the women, though not for long, and set off deeper into the unknown city.

31

UNDER THE COVER of night, Yeva sat with her back against the acacia trunk, shivering, waiting for the snail to reveal itself. The temperature hovered above freezing, which meant the snail would be moving even more slowly than usual, if not hibernating deep within a crevice, unreachable—a possibility she did not want to consider. Above her left ear, the beer-soaked rag hung pinned to the bark in the place, Yeva calculated, where the snail had originally photobombed the selfie of the boy with his pet rat. As she waited for the snail to reveal itself, she kept her ears perked for the scurrying of rodent feet. The boy had released the rat right on this field. Another possibility she refused to consider: that the rat had already sniffed out soft mollusk flesh, scaled the tree before Yeva's arrival.

In her gloved hand, the one-liter bottle of lager she'd bought for bait at the kiosk, the last one left. Still three-quarters full after soaking the rag. She'd vowed not to drink it herself, but there it was, already in her hand, and at a time like this it seemed a shame to waste such a precious substance. She licked the wet cold lip, breathed in the yeasty smell. Took a long swig. Leaned her head back against the acacia's rough bark, let the fizzy finger slide down her throat, warm her insides, numb her. The alcohol hit her immediately, harder than usual—maybe because she hadn't had a drop since she agreed to help Nastia with her heist, or simply because she was exhausted, defenses down.

The air cracked with gunfire again, but it seemed far away, across the river, farther with every swig. Pasha still hadn't returned.

An hour ago, when Yeva was setting the bait and the gunfire first started, Sol had flung herself from the cab and told Yeva they needed to get out of the city. Nastia had followed, her face set, clearly determined not to look afraid. The countdown to return the bachelors was ticking, she reminded Yeva, as if this were the real reason they had to leave.

If they left by daybreak, they'd still make it on time, Yeva had promised. She'd settled herself at the base of the acacia. "Stay in the lab. The vibrations from your footfalls will scare off the snail and hold us up longer." She had no idea if this was true, but it got the sisters back inside.

Through the passenger window a few meters away, Yeva could see Nastia folded in her seat, muddy boots still on the dash, as if she knew Yeva was watching her.

As for the bachelors, they were keeping quiet, but who knew for how long. When Yeva had last dumped out the stinking sludge of the compost toilet at a roadside bush halfway to Kherson, she'd noted, with a pang of guilt, the increased liquid composition, the ill-formed stools. Signs of stress. Of course the bachelors were stressed, it didn't take a genius to guess that, but this mammalian evidence saddened her. She'd recalled her time with the snails, how exacting she'd been when checking their excrement, this trove of information on well-being. The only window into their interior states.

These people had chosen to follow her to Kherson, Yeva told herself. The bachelors, the sisters. Back at the foot of the Carpathians, she'd handed them all an exit out of the country and they'd chosen not to take it. That the sisters seemed to have no family, no one else to fall back on, was no fault of Yeva's. And there was a broader lesson in this for Nastia, wasn't there? You load living beings into a trailer, you take care of them till the end, until you can't anymore and have to face your own failure. That's how you grow up.

Something snagged her peripheral vision. Movement on the

tree trunk, by the right side of her head. She twisted around, hopeful, but it was only two fat garden snails, striped caramel shells glinting under the streetlamp. They'd begun copulating without even reaching the beer bait, as though to taunt Yeva. She considered separating them out of pettiness but left them to it. She sat back again, slumping against the trunk. After a moment, she tore the glove from her free hand with her teeth and dialed Kevin. She needed to hear his voice, the one person who wouldn't call her rescue attempt insane. Ever since their conversation over the two-way radio, she'd been texting him updates on her search for the "specimen"—a cold, clinical term, so as not to get hopes up, to remain detached.

He picked up right away. "Yeva." Thirteen time zones away Kevin's day would just be starting, his voice still low and raspy from the night that was currently looping over to Yeva. She imagined him breakfasting one-handed on something nutrient-efficient, maybe a chalky protein bar.

"Are you safe?" he asked.

She didn't know how to answer that question.

When she'd last checked the news on her phone, she'd seen that the Russians had slaughtered a group of twenty civilian fighters, members of the territorial defense, in the city across the Dnipro. These people had been fighters more than civilians, she had tried to tell herself, even though she knew it wasn't really true—and the distinction didn't matter to the Russians anyway. In cities deeper east, already under the grip of the Russian occupation, she'd read reports of soldiers hassling people randomly, searching their phones for anything they considered too Ukrainian, pulling people into basements for interrogation. After that, she'd stopped checking the news. It was too terrifying. What mattered was what she could see with her own eyes. The grassy field rippling in the night breeze. The familiar sight of her lab. That ragged driver's seat stained from hundreds of thousands of kilometers of coffee chugging, powdery chip snacking; that seat from which she'd sung her heart out in her most sentimental moments (deep down, she did believe the endlings could hear her, and cared to hear the music).

"I'm safe," she said.

After she'd told Kevin about her stalemate with the specimen and he'd made all the right noises of sympathy, he asked what she planned to do "afterwards." After what, exactly—successful rescue or failure—he didn't specify. "You could live anywhere, in Europe or Africa, in America." He tried to entice her with platitudes: home could be anywhere, the planet was our home.

Yeva smiled. Once, she used to think that way, too. "I'll leave Kherson when I find the snail, but I can't leave the country. There's too much work to be done."

"You haven't heard, have you," he said. "I don't know what kind of news you're getting there in the middle of it, but from here it's not looking good, for the whole country. There's a forty-mile military column heading toward Kyiv. Kyiv looks like it's about to fall. Think of yourself, for once. Think practically."

"When have you ever thought practically?"

"If something happens to you, who'll take care of your endlings? How many species will go down with you?"

She took her black notebook from her breast pocket, began reading the death stamps aloud, all the species that had already gone down with her. He tried to interrupt, but she read on. He laughed, as though she were making up the dirge of numbers as a macabre joke, but when the death stamps kept coming, he grew silent again.

At last, she finished.

Slowly, cautiously, he asked how many species—of the ones she hadn't restituted to their habitats—remained in her trailer.

"Lefty. That's it."

For a while he said nothing. Then: "It's a start," he choked out.

She tipped the last of the beer down her throat. "An end is what it is." Lefty, the endling of her endlings. Surely Kevin must have sensed that Yeva didn't have many others left, and had thought she wouldn't have risked going to Kherson otherwise.

"Yeva," he whispered.

"Don't worry, I'm still scoping for Lefty's potential mate, aren't I? Thinking practically."

"I never should've told you about that photo."

"I would've found out anyway." News this big had a way of blazing through the malacological community.

After a moment, he gave a high nervous laugh.

"What?" Yeva asked.

"All this work to find Lefty a mate. Imagine if they don't want to do it."

"That's their prerogative."

"If it were me and I hadn't been with a human in years, and then I saw one who looked equally lonely . . ." He sighed into the phone. "Wouldn't you want to? Whatever he looked like?" When she didn't answer, he kept on. "What if he were a really, really amazing-looking specimen?"

Yeva checked the spot where she'd last seen the two garden snails. They were gone now, but a foamy spittle remained on the bark, marking where their bodies had thrashed in slow motion. "I don't know."

"What if humanity depended on it?"

Yeva laughed, unable to imagine such a possibility.

He said in a small voice, "What if it were me?"

She paused before answering. "If it made you happy."

"It wouldn't make you happy?"

She should have seen it coming—the spot where anything new, anything budding, always ended. "I don't do that kind of thing, sex." She wouldn't have been surprised if he'd hung up on her, the freak that she was.

"Oh, Yeva," he said, his voice cool and silky. "It's okay."

"Is it, though?"

"It's okay to still be a virgin."

If only it were that simple. "Look, I've done it. Loads of times. Always the same result, or nonresult."

"Maybe you just haven't found the right person."

If only she could grab and shake him. Shake the truth into him. She didn't care anymore how sappy she sounded—the way this conversation was going, she'd never meet him *in the flesh* anyway. "I did find the right person. You were that person," she told him. "Still are."

She knew what would follow. He'd keep saying what everyone had been telling her all along, that if she just tried it one time, why not, if she just tried therapy, if she just dug into some traumatic past she wasn't aware of, if she just checked her hormone levels, if she just—

"It's okay," he repeated. "There's nymphomaniacs out there, and there's the opposite. Outliers, sure, but that's just the way they are. We'll just, I don't know, try it."

"I don't want to try it anymore, that's what I'm telling you."

"What I mean is, we'll try *not* having sex."

She rubbed her face, feeling another wave of exhaustion. "Get out there, Kevin. Get out of that trailer for once. Do normal things normal people do. Don't wait around for me."

"It's just you out there, for me. No one else. That's what it feels like, like we're the last of our kind. I love you, Yeva."

Her face felt hot. No one in her family talked like this. They expressed partiality through criticism or cooking. And how could she believe his declaration when he had, in theory, countless women he could take to bed with him, normal women who would happily follow.

"Have I ever told you," he asked, "about the coupling habits of the Taiwanese giant wood roach?"

She couldn't keep herself from smiling. "Go on."

He recounted how even the driest scientific journals couldn't help cooing about these bastions of monogamy. Some couples ate each other's wings down to the nubs, never to fly again. Stuck together, dependent on each other, they burrowed themselves into the earth and spent the rest of their lives together raising their young, never straying.

Yeva had stopped smiling. "Is that what you want?"

"It's what most people think they want. I'd prefer to keep a bit of wing, if you let me."

"I have no interest in eating your wings."

"Excellent." He added after a moment, "I mean, you can, though. Just leave a bit on."

"Can we talk in human terms?"

"The screech owl might be a better example here," he began.

"Kevin."

The words tumbled from his mouth. "So long as you let me have relations with other people once in a while just to get it out of my system, we're on."

This seemed both too simple and too complicated. Everyone she knew would throw a fit at the slightest insinuation of an affair, so shouldn't she be insulted by such a proposal? She waited for the feeling of preemptive jealousy, but it didn't come. What came instead was relief, as if a burden had lifted.

It was a delicious moment, when all possibility opened before them. Maybe they didn't have to follow the rules of tradition, after all.

Kevin kept talking, quickly now. Logistics, their future together. He'd already done the research into which visa Yeva would need to apply for, the documentation she'd need, and he'd help bring her over to the States, fix up a bigger lab to accommodate them both.

"I'm not leaving Ukraine," Yeva repeated. "You know that, don't you?"

"Not even to tide yourself over for a month or two?"

"This won't be over in a month or two."

"Maybe, maybe not. Nobody wants war."

"Of course not."

"Russia's going to do what it's going to do, so it depends more on Ukraine's response, I guess."

"To defend itself."

"To keep the peace."

She jerked away from the radio, as though zapped. "We should just lie down and take it, then?"

"That's not what I meant."

"What, then? You don't know what they're like, these invaders. My grandparents lived under their occupation."

"They, them. What I'm hearing is a lot of generalities. What if we tried to understand Russians as, you know, individuals with their own traumas. What if there were more empathy in the world, if we loved each other more? Did you see that video going around? That video of the L.A. woman reading a poem for Putin, how she can't imagine how it feels in his heart, but if she were his mother, she would be a start . . ."

He trailed off, sensing the stoniness of Yeva's silence.

"You have family in Alaska, no?" she asked after a pause.

"Mother's side. So?"

"I'd like to see how pacifist you would be if Russian soldiers hopped across the Bering Strait, and it was your own family on the line."

"Don't be ridiculous, they're not going to touch the States." The sureness in his voice enraged her. She envisioned a missile, just one, sent in a close arch over his island to pierce that confidence. Then she regretted the desire immediately. What was wrong with her?

"Look, I know where you're at," he said. "How you feel. When Hawaii had that ballistic missile alert—"

"False."

"False, yes, but that doesn't negate how awful it felt. I *know* what it's like to see your own end, and trust me, you don't want that. Putin's threatening nukes, Yeva. Is anything worth that kind of risk? It's not just you, it's all of us. Humans, fauna, and flora. Everything you and I fight for."

"Is it better to live in a world where a gas station with nukes gets to call the shots?"

"Gas station with nukes, Christ. Since when do you quote our Republicans?"

"Who cares who says it if it's true?"

That's when Yeva heard a sound she'd never heard before, an insect-like rattle that grew louder, metal against concrete. She jumped to her feet, slipped her phone into her breast pocket, muffling Kevin's retort. She saw the passenger door of the lab opening tentatively—the sisters had undoubtedly heard the sound, too—and she ran over and slammed it shut, harder than she meant to, but the sisters got the message and stayed inside. She edged along the side of the lab to its back end, ducked her head out to peer up the road.

A hundred meters away, at the street corner where a little

while ago Pasha had been sitting on an upturned milk crate, the first tank caterpillared into view.

The machine didn't seem human-made. Mud-colored and faceless, larger in real life than on the videos people posted online from their besieged cities and villages. The yellow cube of the milk crate looked like a child's toy in comparison. She stood frozen in awe, forgetting for a moment who'd sent the thing, and who it was coming for. The tank stopped at the intersection. Perpendicular to it, an old red van with suitcases strapped to its roof screeched to a halt. The tennis ball at the tip of its antenna swung wildly. The van had the green light. The tank seemed to be daring it to cross.

"Yeva?" a small, tinny voice called from her pocket.

With a high whine, the tank's cannon swiveled a slow ninety degrees, until its eye aimed at the van.

"I *know* you," Kevin's muffled voice implored, "I know who you are and what you stand for in normal times. We'll return to those times, I promise. Just take a step back. Zoom out a bit. Take a breath."

But Yeva couldn't breathe, couldn't move. When she tried to imagine the gunner behind the scope, what agreement he and the crew were coming to inside the tank, a wave of dread overtook her. She should duck her head behind the trailer, brace for a shockwave, but she couldn't look away.

Finally the van lurched into reverse, swerved into an alley.

The tank's cannon swiveled back to center and the machine clattered forward, toward the heart of the city. A moment later a second of its kind followed, then a third. She could hardly believe what she heard next: Soviet music, a march she hadn't heard since she was a child, from her grandparents' radio.

She and the sisters and the men in the trailer needed to get the hell out while they still could. They'd avoid the open roads, take the alleyways.

Kevin's voice crackled from her pocket, still calling for her. She took the phone out, squinted for a second at the name on the bright screen like it was a foreign word. Then she hung up and he was gone. They'd come so close, she thought. Closer than she'd come with anyone. One day she'd surely find it funny, the wild reversal of their fate.

A few minutes later, Yeva spun around at the sound of footsteps behind her. It was Nastia. The streetlamp turned the girl's face and hair a lethal yellow. Yeva retracted her hand from the acacia's rough bark, embarrassed to be caught in a moment of sentimentality. She'd been saying a goodbye of sorts, conceding defeat.

"We saw them, too, the tanks," the girl said. "Through the side mirror," she clarified, as though worried Yeva would get mad at her for not staying inside the lab, as though Yeva was the threat here. Yeva became aware of just how brusque she'd been with Nastia and Sol while in Kherson, how cold—sure, it was understandable, given the circumstances, but this wasn't a version of herself that Yeva liked.

"Don't worry, we're leaving," she said, softening her voice. "We'll make it out, drop off the bachelors on time. Everything will be just fine."

The girl's eyes flitted to the empty beer bottle by Yeva's foot, and Yeva saw a flash of anger or disappointment—as if she had expected better of Yeva—but her face smoothed over immediately, the emotion erased.

"What about your snail?" she asked. "We're here. We're so close." She stood beside Yeva at the base of the tree, looked up its trunk. "Why don't you just stick Lefty on the bark and see what happens? Can't snails, like, smell each other?"

Yeva blinked, embarrassed she hadn't thought of this herself. Yet the idea of using one snail to lure another was too simple, child's logic—could two snails smell each other across an entire tree? And there were other considerations: If she warmed up Lefty, yanked him out of hibernation only to expose him to the frigid February air, would it shock his system? What if there was no other snail of his species on the tree and it was all for nothing? Would she chill Lefty yet again into suspension—another possible shock, maybe his last—or keep him awake and watch his lifespan tick down all the faster?

When she explained all this to Nastia, the girl sighed in exasperation. "Got any better ideas? Maybe he's ready for the end anyway. It's been a lonely run, no?"

"Don't sentimentalize him," Yeva shot back. Yet she couldn't help cracking a smile at Nastia. The girl, too, believed in the existence of a second *C. surculus*. And just maybe, she didn't think Yeva was crazy.

32

IN THE EARLY MORNING LIGHT, Pasha kept close to the buildings as he scurried along the empty streets. He was lost, not having found the weapons distribution point Yeva had told him about. He'd spent the night in the garden shed of a house that looked to be abandoned, had slept on a moldy lawn chair under an old Turkish rug that smelled of mouse droppings.

He had no idea where he was in relation to the trailer. No idea how he'd find Solomiya, Yeva, and Anastasia again, how he'd get out of Kherson. Yet with every step came an awareness of how far he was from the river, and the conviction that he should stay away from the river.

A maroon glove on the ground caught his attention, made his palms sweat.

Then the satin scrunchie at the foot of a dumpster, its glistening pink intestine-like folds.

He had to get ahold of himself, wipe the bridge from his memory. He had to call his parents. You know a nightmare is only that, a harmless thing, when you wake and your room is just as it was before, your teeth are still firmly in place, your arms and legs. His parents' steadying voices would remind him of home, of his childhood bedroom with its peony wallpaper, would anchor him back to himself.

But first, he'd have to tell them he was in Ukraine.

This is what you get for going back, they'd say. What did you think you were playing at? Life got a bit tough in Canada, so you thought you'd have a go at it in Ukraine? But after the initial rebuke, they'd tell him what he had to do to save himself, just like that time when, as a child, he'd climbed the sprawling maple in their backyard but couldn't get back down. His father's maneuvers with the ladder didn't help, Pasha was too high up. Call the firefighters, he'd mewled, but his parents refused out of embarrassment. Finally, his mother coaxed him down by choreographing his every move from below. Left foot at that crag, right hand in that fold, down, down, until his father's large hands clamped around his waist. As Pasha wove through Kherson's streets, how he ached for his father's hands, his mother's clear, sensible voice! Take that turn, Pauly, now this one, all the way out of this hellscape we already rescued you from once before.

He came to a road flanked by commercial buildings, low and boxy. A crow pecked at a bag of chips. On a bus shelter ad, a brunette with poppy-red lipstick nibbled on the corner of a chocolate bar, winking. The streets and skies were quiet. For a moment, everything seemed normal.

The first person he encountered was a tiny ruddy-cheeked pensioner in a polka-dot kerchief. She seemed the sort who would be amenable, so he asked to borrow her phone, but she kept lugging her shopping caddie as if she hadn't heard him, yanking it over cracks in the sidewalk and tree roots.

The only other people on the block: a pair of leather-jacketed men across the street, bent over the open hood of a Jeep, deep in argument, unapproachable.

He caught up with the pensioner again, deployed his best smile while trying to tamp down his desperation. "I can help you with that," he offered, gesturing at the caddie.

Instead of stopping, she sped up.

He followed, and said in a pinched voice, "Maybe you could just tell me where is the train station?" A contingency, he thought, in case he couldn't find his way back to the three women.

The pensioner swung around, brushed a strand of white hair from her eyes with a mittened hand. "I will tell you no such thing," she said, with such force that the men by the Jeep stopped arguing and looked over. "I've heard of your type, sniffing around our streets. Russian wolves in civilian clothes, painting markers on buildings for air strikes. Don't think I won't turn you in."

The shock of the accusation pushed the air out of Pasha's lungs, made him laugh. He understood, too late, that this was entirely the wrong reaction. The men by the Jeep angled their bodies toward him, their faces like searchlights.

He backed away, arms raised, and turned a corner. Then he broke into a run, realized this, too, would attract suspicion, and slowed to a walk, mimicking the determined gait of a local out procuring supplies. Kept his eyes on the ground. He couldn't bring himself to approach another stranger.

At first, the three gleaming white trucks labeled HUMANITARIAN AID seemed heaven-sent. Their engines turned off with a sigh as Pasha approached, as though they'd been waiting for him. The trucks stood, along with a dozen white buses, in the middle of a plaza lined with skinny naked trees. People began to spill from the buses. They were dressed in rags—puffer coats that looked freshly split, knit hats and sweaters half-unwound—yet they chatted jovially among themselves as they looked around. Pasha drew closer, standing at the outermost ring of the crowd. A spindly man with stylish tortoiseshell glasses and a camo flat cap strolled around issuing orders from a megaphone—who would stand where, who would do what. All at once the backs of the white trucks rolled open, and from them unfurled three chains of soldiers who passed pudgy burlap sacks hand to hand down from the trucks and across the plaza, their movements practiced and efficient, into the waiting arms of civilians.

Why so many soldiers, just to hand out food? Pasha wondered. Why the long chains?

As he drew closer, trying to get a better look at their uniforms, gauge who had sent them, the driver from the closest truck gestured at Pasha through his open window, waved him over. Come! Come! The prospect of food made him realize how hungry he was. Certainly, Pasha was overdressed in his pointed shoes and collared shirt compared to those lining up for humanitarian aid, but nobody seemed to care. There was a dreamy aura of love and harmony about the whole thing, as if everyone was equal in their suffering.

Pasha stepped in line. He even chanced asking the broad-shouldered woman in front of him to borrow her phone.

She gave him an odd look, said under her breath, "Obviously I don't have mine with me, either. They told me to leave mine back home, same as you."

"Back home," he repeated. Had these people been pulled from a different part of Ukraine, one already under occupation?

The woman named a region in Russia. "You sound different," she said, eyes passing over him, assessing. "Which region?"

The chatter around him sounded higher and more pointed than the low, chesty Russian he'd heard from Khersonites, he realized. It dawned on him: these people were all from Russia, the newcomers lined up for food, the soldiers with rifles flung over their backs.

His throat tightened. The tide of the line pulled him forward. Pasha had the distinct sense he should not say he was Ukrainian. That he should not be in this line. Three feet away, a man wearing a black beanie and holding a camera stood interviewing a soldier. Blond, tanned, healthy-looking, like he'd been grown for the camera, the soldier declared President Putin's Special Operation a success. They were saving the Ukrainians from their Nazi regime, city by city. They'd already neutralized Kherson's river port, the railway station. They'd stabilized the municipal government. They'd set up checkpoints all around the city for "filtration."

Pasha's collar felt hot and moist against his neck. What did that mean, neutralized, stabilized? Filtration against whom?

Beside the soldier, a woman in a dirty crochet sweater, half-undone, cradled a sack of grain in her arms like a baby. She thanked the Russian Federation for bringing peace.

Pasha slipped from the line, slipped away from the crowd. Across the street, he saw a young couple in matching camel peacoats and white sneakers with their phones out, filming the filming. He edged beside them until he could hear the narration they were providing. From what he could make out, Russians were filming a documentary about their liberation of Kherson using cameras all over the city, bringing in their own extras, even as they were blocking real humanitarian aid from reaching the area. That very morning the mayor had announced that Kherson would run out of food within two days. "Here's yet another scene," the woman announced. She named the intersection. She turned the camera off and began tapping fervently away on her phone.

Pasha looked up at the buildings around him. How many residents were filming with their own phones right now, from their windows. The streets were quiet, but many eyes might be watching, a network of information crisscrossing over Pasha like invisible power lines. He wondered if he'd been caught on camera, too, maybe by both the Russians and the Khersonites. How many versions of himself were jolting across the globe—a starving Ukrainian in line for grain, a phony Russian extra? A saboteur in a suit, loping around the streets.

The couple in the peacoats fixed their eyes on Pasha. He suddenly felt awkward, loitering beside them, eavesdropping. He hoped they hadn't seen him sneaking through the crowd of extras. To give himself an air of purpose he asked, this time in English, if he could borrow one of their phones to call his parents.

The woman's gray-eyed gaze snagged on something on his face. His patchy stubble? The stinging, peeling skin around his nostrils, unused to this cold, dry air after temperate Vancouver? He untucked his shirt collar from under his blazer, regretted its warm musky sigh.

"American?" she asked.

Normally Pasha would have corrected her, smugly answered that he was Canadian—but who was Pasha anymore, really?

The couple beckoned him to follow them around the street corner, away from the crowd of Russians. The man pointed to an app on his phone. "You can phone." As Pasha dialed—his parents' landline the only number he remembered by heart—the couple took a few steps aside, backs turned, polite but obviously inconvenienced. How pitiable Pasha must look, a stranded foreigner. But he didn't care what he looked like anymore. All he needed was his parents, the steady anchor of their voices.

He pressed the phone against his cheek, warm and smooth as a sun-soaked stone. A click. An expectant silence filled the line, Pasha's father's signature greeting for unknown numbers.

"Papa!" The syllables flew from his mouth, high and childlike.

"Pavlo?" his father said.

"Pasha," repeated Pasha. "It's me."

The three-tone jingle of 5 Kanal filtered into his ear from his parents' end of the line. He imagined them watching on-the-ground footage of Kherson at this very moment, the channel reposting shaky videos from civilians' phones. Imagined his parents glimpsing the skinny figure in the background, a figure who looked uncannily like their son.

Pasha took a breath. But where to begin? How to explain that he wasn't at an engineering conference in Germany after all? How to instead name the country they'd worked so hard to leave, were still pushing away from, because it was easier to write off your birthplace than to miss it?

He thought again about how he'd taken his failed life in Canada into his own hands, how he had been waiting to call from Ukraine until he had something to show for his actions. Now, in a rush of panicked words, Pasha promised to tell his father where he was calling from, but only if his father promised not to be mad, to hear his son out, because all that mattered now was that he was alive, right?

"Pavlo!" His mother joined in.

Who the hell was Pavlo?

"It's your *son*," Pasha yelled into the phone. Was the connection so bad his parents couldn't recognize his voice? "Pasha. Paul. Pauly." It was true that Pasha probably didn't sound like himself—it wasn't just the panic in his voice, but how freely his Russian flowed, grammar be damned, accent be damned, his shame over having lost his first tongue be damned.

"*Pavlo*," his father insisted, as though Pasha had forgotten his real name. His parents' voices came haltingly. For the first time in his living memory, his parents were speaking Ukrainian. They were saying something about Germany, about weapons, about Pasha's colleagues at his engineering conference. He could foggily understand the words but couldn't reply. The last family member who'd spoken Ukrainian natively, before the Bolsheviks suppressed it, was a great-grandfather on his mother's side. Pasha hadn't even known his parents spoke the language. They'd once told him that by the time they were in school Ukrainian was being taught again, but only as a second language by mean, foulmouthed teachers, as though the authorities had purposely dredged them up from the muddiest villages to prove its vulgarity.

His parents plowed on nonetheless. The Germans, they repeated. Weapons they did or did not send. Pasha understood this much: His parents were angry with the Germans.

It was all very well for them to switch to Ukrainian, he thought, with a stab of impatience. The dismantling of generations of imperialism did have to start somewhere, but now? Right this second?

In a last attempt to make himself understood, Pasha switched from Russian to English. "Mother, Father. I am in Ukraine," he announced at last. He waited for the questions, the reprimand.

"Oi, Pavlo," his mother sighed. She continued in Ukrainian. "I also am in Ukraine. In my heart."

"We are *all* in Ukraine," his father said, his voice cracking.

They were all hurting, his parents said, no matter how far they might be from the motherland.

Pasha was silent with astonishment. Never before had his parents spoken of this place with longing. He was about to explain that he was *literally* in Ukraine, that the Russians had taken over the local train station and set up checkpoints and he was trapped and terrified and saw no way out, when his mother said, "Really, Pavlo? You have not even one word of Ukrainian for us?" He'd spoken it at school when he was very young, before they'd emigrated, didn't he remember? It was his true mother tongue. But now, not one word?

Pasha jerked the phone away from his ear and stared at the useless thing. If he knew what to say, how would he say it? In which language? They blurred together in his head—English, Russian, a ghostly Ukrainian—this, like a song he remembered the melody to, but not the words—even a few scraps of French from high school. His tongue lay limp and heavy in his mouth, like it had been severed. He hung up.

"Nothing beats home, right?"

The couple in the camel coats were beside him again. The man had switched from English to Russian, probably having overheard Pasha's end of the phone call. Pasha handed the phone back, too aware of their probing eyes on him, like they could see his disfigurement.

"How are you getting back?" the woman asked.

He didn't know how to answer the question, or even where home was anymore. He felt his mouth, a flapping thing, form syllables—barely comprehensible, judging by the couple's frowning concentration as they listened. But then, their faces lit up.

"The field. The one with the saggy old tree?" the woman asked. She gave Pasha a strange look as she pointed. "Right down the block." He recognized the street now, from last night, how it sloped downward. If he followed the street, yes, he'd reach the field, the trailer, the women. His shoulders loosened with relief, but only for a moment. Between the five-story apartment blocks, the river caught his eye, glimmered seductively. A familiar undertow hooked him behind the knees, pulled him forward. If he let it, it would pull him down, down, past the trailer and the women, straight onto the foot of the bridge.

33

BACK AT THE FIELD with the acacia, before the soldiers arrived and blood spilled and everything went to shit, Lefty lay motionless in Yeva's palm. She and the sisters waited for him to wake from hibernation. If Yeva had had the luxury of time, she would have warmed him up in his jar, just a few degrees each day to simulate spring thaw, instead of the brute method of trickling lukewarm water from her camping stove over his shell.

Fifteen minutes, twenty.

She'd set up a camping stove at the base of the acacia, warmed the water to eighteen degrees Celsius—"room temperature," though being inside a room right now, with heating and soft furniture, felt like something from another world.

Twenty-five minutes.

Lefty's scraggly shell stayed still as a tree thorn, his body shut behind his hard mucus seal. The longer he stayed like this, the more Yeva became convinced that his potential mate must also be deep in hibernation, despite the slightly warmer southern temperatures.

The streets were quiet again. A sulfurous smell hung in the air, but no more gunfire, no more clanking of metal against concrete since that column of tanks.

While they waited, Pasha returned, crumpled and hollow-eyed. He avoided Yeva's gaze as he stepped into their silent circle. A chalky smell wafted from him, as though he'd spent the night rolling in plant fertilizer. He'd failed to procure weapons, but

Yeva held her tongue. Let the wretch join them. She watched as the realization passed over his face: yes, they really had come all this way to find a mate for this clump. Fortunately he, too, held his tongue.

Thirty minutes.

The sisters began fidgeting, their fingers catching on zippers, coat snaps. Sol checked her phone, where she could see what had shown up on the webcam someone had installed on their balcony, aimed at the boxy city hall. "They just took down our flag." She crossed herself.

"How long does a snail take to wake up?" Nastia asked.

Yeva wrapped her fingers around Lefty's shell, slid her hand under her layers of clothing, pressed him against the warmth of her chest like a newborn, would've prayed if she were the type. What if it had been unwise to leave Lefty inside the death cabinet along with the endlings that hadn't made it? A bad omen?

"Maybe," Sol said, "you just need to let this one go." Her voice was soothing, lulling. The same voice that had lured thirteen men into a trailer. "Plenty of other critters to save out there, far from Kherson, critters who need you more. Just let it go." Yeva looked into one of Sol's bright caramel eyes, its yellow feeding into a black, bottomless hole. The hole widened and Yeva stood on its edge, toes curled, feeling its pull.

Then Yeva felt a tap against her palm. Once, twice. A pulse meeting her own.

Lefty, awake. Alive. Head knocking against the dry mucus seal to break through.

She took her hand out from under her shirt, watched Lefty's seal crack open, overfill with buttery yellow flesh. No food or water for months, and yet there he was. Snails really were miraculous—how could she have forgotten?

The sisters closed in around Yeva, doubt wiped clean from their faces as they waited for her to transfer Lefty to the acacia. What if he needed another day in his jar? To eat his fill of lettuce, reconstitute his strength?

Sol's hand was rubbing Yeva's back, hurrying her along—goddamn her, didn't she know Yeva was immune to touch? Yet

Yeva watched her own hand reach out, reach through the cold, hostile air, gently press Lefty onto the lowest branch. He latched right away, became a thorn among thorns. He looked at home. Four years she'd kept him in her lab—the last eleven months, chilled to an unseasonable sleep in his sterile glass jar. A necessary imprisonment, she'd told herself, but it seemed doubly unnatural now.

One translucent eye stalk drew out, but sensed something amuck. Retracted.

Ten more minutes passed.

For the first time Yeva loathed Lefty's slowness, the slowness of his kind. Bitten by the icy February air or the cloying smell of gunpowder, was he bowing out, going back into hibernation?

Pasha tapped his thigh with his thumb. The sisters broke into fidgets again, into mutinous thoughts, no doubt. Commandeer the mobile lab, leave Yeva and her silly science project behind.

Then the thorn twitched. One tentacle drew out again, another, tasted the air. Lefty began dawdling upward. Stopped. Dawdled some more. An invisible string seemed to pull him forward. Went slack, pulled forward again. Yeva allowed herself a crack of hope.

"Yeva, look."

The worry in Nastia's voice tore Yeva's eyes from the acacia.

Two soldiers were ambling down their street, machine guns bouncing at their backs. No yellow arm or helmet band, darker uniforms than the ones Yeva had seen on military recruitment posters around Kyiv. These two were definitely Russians. Their leisurely pace unsettled her, like they were patrolling land they already owned. She ordered the group to hide behind the trailer, but Pasha lingered.

"Go," Yeva hissed. "I'm staying with Lefty." She couldn't pluck him off the tree yet, break momentum, not when there was still a chance the soldiers would walk right past. "You'll just attract more attention in that suit of yours." Pasha's attire seemed a provocation now, unfit for the occasion.

He made a show of hesitation, but as he backed away she could see the relief on his face. He'd been released from having to stay behind to protect her, whatever that meant.

Alone now, Yeva attempted a casual posture, leaning against the tree trunk with her arms crossed, Lefty just inches from her right ear.

On her other side, out of the corner of her eye, she saw the soldiers cross the road toward her. Still she refused to acknowledge them, kept her gaze fixed on Lefty. One of his eye stalks stretched around and seemed to peer straight into Yeva's face. Could he smell her fear? She couldn't hide now, not even behind the tree, its curved trunk. Civilians, she reminded herself. She tried to believe in the word, a protective charm cast over herself, the sisters, Pasha, the men inside the trailer, who were mercifully staying quiet. The soldiers had no reason to touch any of them.

The pair were just steps away now. She could hear the crunch of tiny rocks under their heels, the snap of a twig.

They can't all be bad, she told herself. Maybe Kevin was right. That morning, before she'd blocked his number, he'd sent her a photo of a school the soldiers had looted in the Kharkiv Oblast, desks overturned, Ukrainian grammar books ripped up. There was writing on the chalkboard, blocky but slanted, an attempt at calligraphy: *I am sorry. I don't even want to be here. Don't repeat the mistakes your elders made.*

The pair of soldiers stopped before her. "Identification," the younger one ordered.

Her only weapon: time. She would stretch seconds into minutes, make the soldiers wait. Slowly she uncrossed her arms, took stock of the men. The one who'd spoken looked to be in his early twenties, thin and pale and his spine already bent in a slouch, like he spent his nights bowing before a computer. The embroidered name tag above his right breast pocket read KRYLOV. The other soldier was older, bulkier, and instead of army boots he wore dirty running shoes. Even after seeing the tanks and other machinery, it was worse to watch those scoping eyes, the way they ran over her body, made inventory of its parts, ones they wanted, ones they'd take.

She reached into her back pocket for her wallet.

"Hands up, where we can see them," ordered the younger one.

He moved closer, like he was about to take her in a dance. On his breath, the smell of canned meat he'd tried to cover with a sprig of mint. His hand reached around and slid into her back pocket, palm cupping her ass, twitchy and boyish. His eyes round with exaggerated surprise, like he'd only meant to grab the wallet. Was she supposed to avert her gaze now, show modesty? She burrowed her focus deeper, into the red indents on the bridge of his nose, marks from heavy glasses, from his other life, the one he'd left on the other side of the border.

The hand slid away.

He flipped through her wallet, a brick of a thing. Cards from various conservation conferences she'd attended long ago, when in a more collaborative mood. Unused gift cards for beauty salons and clothing stores from relatives who thought she could use a spruce-up. The soldier took a long look at her driver's license, at the photo of the woman who could hardly keep herself from smiling, so happy she'd been upgraded to a Category C driver that day, already imagining herself on her first expedition in her lab.

"Yeva," he uttered. "Always liked that name, biblical. The original woman."

She felt her fingers curl. She wanted to reach between those thin wet lips, claw her name back.

"Krylov," she forced out. Make this seem like a mundane interaction, she told herself. Two people meeting, exchanging names, soon to go their separate ways.

His eyebrows rose, surprised that she knew his last name, before his free hand tapped the tag above his breast pocket in remembrance. Had he been issued this uniform just yesterday?

"The guys call me Uzel." Knot. He said it secretively, like he was not supposed to tell her this. He seemed to be waiting for her to ask how he'd earned the name. When she stayed silent, he continued his inspection of her driver's license with renewed zeal, turned it over. What could he glean from the little plastic card? What hostile, anti-Russian affiliation? He dug into her wallet, took out the crumpled bills, made a show of folding them neatly and tucking them back inside, along with the license. He extended the wallet to Yeva. When she snatched at his hand, he pulled it out of reach. "Where we come from, we say please and thank you."

The older soldier, who'd been watching these antics with an indulgent expression, yanked the wallet from his junior's hand and tossed it to Yeva. He seemed higher in rank than Krylov, despite the dirty shoes. Yeva read his tag: OVECHKIN. Root of the name sheep. A sheep in uniform, thought Yeva, surely harmless.

Ovechkin nodded at the trailer. "What's in there?"

Yeva held her breath steady, tried not to think of the sisters and Pasha crouching just beyond, the twelve men inside. Mercifully, they'd stayed silent, perhaps sensing danger. "In there? Not much."

"Not much of what?"

"Lab equipment."

"What kind of lab?"

Ovechkin was frowning at the painted hands cradling the sprout. Those fucking hands. Should've painted over them, like Sol and Nastia had wanted. Yeva recalled reading, somewhere in the past couple of days, that the Kremlin had spun a story to the UN about the existence of lethal Ukrainian bioweapons being made in mobile labs, supposedly funded by the U.S.

"Why don't you open up this lab of yours for us," Ovechkin said, easily. No hurry in his voice.

Yeva's mind reeled. Opening the trailer would prove she didn't have weapons, but who knew what the Russians would do with the foreigners inside? Would they abduct and use them as collateral for POW swaps? And what would happen to Sol and Nastia, once the soldiers' roving eyes landed on them? She tried to think of a way to buy time. She spoke of snail conservation but could tell neither of the soldiers was listening. They probably assumed she was lying. She steeled herself, was about to point out Lefty on the tree trunk as evidence—he hadn't moved a centimeter, as if ready to be called up—but the older soldier was already walking behind the lab.

Yeva winced when she heard Ovechkin's exclamation. She watched as the soldiers ushered the sisters and Pasha out into the open, rifles pointed at their backs. The three were pale-faced, arms stiff at their sides.

"Lab mates?" Uzel said with a thin smile.

Ovechkin lined them up beside Yeva, and her uncle surfaced in her mind, the careful way he lined empty beer bottles on a log, before a hunt, as target practice. How they had to be spaced just so.

Yeva hoped this discovery might mean the soldiers would forget about the inside of the lab, at least—but at that very moment, the trailer came alive with shouts. Palms slapped the walls from inside. Of course, Yeva thought. The men would've heard the strangers' voices outside. Weighed the opportunity.

Ovechkin cocked his head at the lab, his face giving away nothing. "Open it."

The sisters and Pasha turned to Yeva, as if she could still undo all this, but she knew she had no choice. She stepped from the line, unlocked the side door, and slid it open. A chorus of curses burst forth, along with the stench of sweat and cologne.

"Finally!"

"Fucking dying in here!"

All twelve pairs of eyes swiveled from Yeva to the soldiers, and the curses stopped.

Ovechkin ordered the men to form a line beside Pasha and the sisters. The bachelors began filing out, hunched, wincing as they unfolded sore joints. As they stood shoulder to shoulder, foreheads gleaming with sweat, Yeva couldn't help but feel a tenderness for the men. Their suits and boutonnières recalled the first day of the romance tour, less than two weeks ago, when the suitors had filed into the hotel banquet hall for the first time. How some of them had hung back along the wall, stiff and earnest in their nervousness, waiting to be picked.

"Identification," Uzel ordered.

No one moved.

The soldier adjusted the gun strap across his back and repeated his command, the edge in his voice sharper.

Quietly, Sol translated the word into English. The bachelors pointedly ignored her. They were looking at Bertrand, as though waiting for a cue.

Bertrand, in turn, looked at Pasha. Winked. Pasha shook his head, eyes widening in horror. But Bertrand had already turned back to the soldiers. He began to clap. Slowly, theatrically.

"Very good. Lifelike," said Bertrand. "Almost had us." He pointed at Ovechkin's muddy running shoes. "What, couldn't find the rest of your costume?"

And then—could it be? No, surely what Yeva was hearing was a fit of coughing.

Another bachelor joined Bertrand. Then all of them.

They were laughing.

Ovechkin shuffled backward, visibly self-conscious about his shoes. Bertrand stepped out of line, waved his hand in front of the soldier's pointed gun. "This—not bad, though. Could pass for real, almost."

The air cracked in half.

Yeva threw herself to the ground, pulling Nastia and Sol down with her. When she looked up again, her vision blurred at the edges. A meter away Bertrand crouched on one knee, his pant leg riding up to reveal a purple sock patterned with green parrots. His head was bent forward, thick curls covering his eyes. A red stain spread across his button-up shirt, as though he'd tripped and spilled wine on himself. When he tried to get up, he crashed down on the grass between the cowering bachelors, writhed and gulped for air. Yeva watched the soldier's running shoes take two steps closer. Another shot, and the writhing stopped. A ringing filled Yeva's ears. She watched a rivulet of blood weave along the hardened earth, between yellow tufts of grass, past Nastia's hand. The girl lay on her stomach watching it, too, her face frozen. The picture, if you ignored all else, of a child watching a glistening ant trail, as Yeva herself once did for whole afternoons many summers ago. But these ants pooled in a boot print, spilled over as a long dark finger pointing, in accusation, right at Yeva.

Yeva's fault, all of it. She'd brought the sisters and the foreigners here. No creature she let inside her lab, no creature under her care, ever made it in the end. How could she forget?

From above, the soldiers commanded everyone to get up and follow them.

"There is maybe little mistake."

It took a moment for Yeva to recognize the voice, hoarse and low, the stumbling Russian words, as Pasha's. He'd flattened himself against the ground, too, his head near Yeva's ankles. "We supposed to start filming by now?"

Had he, like Bertrand, gone crazy? The other bachelors, still flattened beside him, were staring at him in desperation.

"Pasha, stop," Yeva hissed. She couldn't lose another.

"What filming?" asked Uzel.

"This white truck," he said, pointing shakily at the lab with a wild look in his eyes, as if he was seeing it for the first time, "is supposed to be with other white trucks. We are extras? In documentary film about your liberation of Ukrainians? Right up this road. You did not see white trucks, humanitarian aid?"

The soldiers exchanged confused looks, yet they nodded, as if this was information they were supposed to be privy to. "Obviously we saw the white trucks."

Yeva heard one of the bachelors whisper to Sol, asking what was being said. Sol shushed him.

Slowly Pasha rose onto his haunches. "We were supposed to join them, were just waiting for signal. But you will let us go now, yes? To join them."

The soldiers looked down at Bertrand, who lay on his stomach, the pool of blood still growing from under him.

"Is that what he was on about," Ovechkin said, mild curiosity coloring his face. "My so-called costume."

Uzel turned back to Pasha. "She said it was a lab." He nodded at Yeva.

"She says many things." As Pasha blustered on about the "crème de la Kremlin" director who'd be *very very mad* if the field scene didn't get filmed with the right number of trucks, Yeva wrenched her eyes away from Bertrand, toward the acacia. Her breath caught in her throat. Lefty was nowhere to be seen. Was he on the other side of the trunk? Had his presence called to the other snail, brought the creature out of hiding?

Uzel pulled out his phone. Rosary beads swung from its granite-pattern case as he tapped. He began making a series of phone calls—to fellow soldiers, Yeva gathered, their aliases like something out of a video game: Lightning, Storm, Hawk, Shadow, Ax. He asked who else had seen the white trucks, because he might have a stranded one in the middle of a field. The voices on the other end of the calls kept saying they knew someone else who'd seen the trucks, another person Uzel had to call. Did these mythical white trucks really exist, Yeva wondered, or did no one want to admit they hadn't seen them? Finally, Uzel hung up and confirmed to Ovechkin that there were indeed trucks, and a film crew, at a nearby intersection.

Yeva turned to Pasha, gave him a solemn nod. It seemed like his improvised plan might actually work, get the two soldiers off their backs.

Then Uzel's phone rang. He picked up.

"That's right, a field," he said. "That's where the stranded truck is." His voice took on an air of deference. He put a palm over the microphone. "It's the documentary director," he said to Ovechkin.

"About half a block wide," he told the director, eyeing the field like a prospector. "Nothing on it, a tree."

Nastia cut Yeva a look. She, like Yeva, did not like where this was going, didn't like the director's sudden interest in the field.

"Could probably fit you all, sure. Trucks, crew. No, definitely. Definitely can." After a moment, "Tanks, too? How many have you got?" Uzel gave a low whistle. "It's ambitious. But I'll bet we can squeeze you all in."

Yeva turned to Pasha. "What did you *do*?" she mouthed. He stared back at her, helpless.

As both soldiers huddled over Uzel's phone, Yeva began crawling toward the acacia. This might be her only opportunity. If she found both snails she would grab them, save the species in captivity. And if she saw only Lefty? Would she pluck him off the tree, doom the species to eventual extinction? Or leave him behind in the hope he would find his mate himself, survive whatever the director was about to do to this field, survive the war? Neither choice was great.

"You, stay where you are," Ovechkin ordered, having turned back to the group.

Yeva stopped but kept her eyes on the tree.

Now she saw Lefty everywhere, every thorn and crag.

"On your feet," Uzel ordered the rest of the group, after he hung up. "Everyone's assembling here. For the liberation scene."

Yeva watched as they got to their feet.

Again the soldiers considered Bertrand's body. Uzel's features soured, and Yeva imagined him thinking that Bertrand had chosen to lie there just to be in the way. Ovechkin turned to the bachelors, who'd clumped together, eleven humps of navy and black. "Better clean up now," he chided them, as if they'd made the mess.

When Sol translated this in a wooden tone, the bachelors looked from her to Pasha. Surely that wasn't the order? She pointed to a spot in the alley along the field, a big yellow dome for recycling. "Behind there. Go, do it."

At first, no one moved. Pasha stepped forward at last, turned Bertrand onto his back, grabbed onto the man's arm at the elbow. He waited, stooped, until the Londoner grabbed onto the other arm and two Americans took the ankles. Ovechkin followed the carriers, kicking up dirt in a futile attempt to erase the red trail. Bertrand's head rolled back, and for a moment his flat pale gaze locked with Yeva's.

She remembered him then, from the tours. He was the one who'd told her there are more trees on Earth than stars in the Milky Way, something she'd dismissed as greeting-card drivel. But then she'd checked online, and it turned out to be true.

34

First came the military trucks and armored personnel carriers and tanks, a gleaming green snake just like the military parades back home. Then the white trucks and buses, which had spent the morning shuttling "civilians" from location to location, distributing and redistributing bread, and filming people receiving it, for the documentary film for audiences back home.

And no, the people spilling from the buses onto this next location wouldn't call themselves tourists. They'd arrived from snowy, faraway lands, sure, but many were poised to stay in this city, bring their families over. Watermelons grew like weeds here, they'd heard, and what child didn't deserve that kind of childhood?

They weren't "extras," either, because the term implied a fictional film, which this one was not. The fact of their being paid to be witnessed by the cameras: beside the point. The point was the broader, truthier truth: even if these people weren't Ukrainian, they would *experience* the act of liberation as any sane Ukrainian would if they knew what was good for them, thus the newcomers were just as Ukrainian, if not more so, than the confused Khersonites.

So, they weren't tourists or extras.

Pioneers, more like.

After the documentary work there'd be free apartments here, jobs to fill, their arrival ordained centuries ago by Catherine the Great herself, who'd first alighted on these lands, virgin lands with nobody and nothing else on them.

Kind of like this field.

(A bit underwhelming, though, this field. If they were being honest. Lumpy with tufts of dry grass, an ugly probably dead tree, apartment blocks on either side leaning away as if from a bad smell. The pioneers had been expecting a great steppe, rippling wheat fields—that had been what the director promised anyway; he'd heard it from an on-the-ground soldier.)

Now they were to assume position. Position, position. The order repeated among the camera crew and pioneers, but no one seemed to know what their position was. (Or what "position" could possibly mean on this expanse of now-muddy nothingness, or even what the plan was.)

Who'd dared insult the field?

This, from the youngest of the pioneers, a high schooler who was damn tired of the complaints. Sheepskin vest, felt boots, embroidered shirt, and red belt, the boy was agreed upon by the group to have the best locally flavored costume. He took the job most seriously, had waited in long lines back in his hometown to register for this. Didn't want to miss out on the Special Operation, the chance to ride the knife's edge of history. His parents thought it might not be a bad idea for him to leave Russia for a few weeks while it all played out, the boy being three months shy of eighteen, the age of military service—not that they wouldn't be absolutely honored to have their son in battle dress protecting the motherland. But maybe not as part of this specific operation, and maybe not this boy.

This group of people he'd arrived with, the group who'd spilled from the white buses along with him, actually made up two groups, he'd say. The people who came here to do honest work—and the whiners. Whiners whining all the way here, across multiple time zones, over potholed roads. Who stole whose coat on the bus, who took whose seat during a pit stop, blah blah blah.

Now they were at it again. The field wasn't "right." One film credit and they're connoisseurs. What did they want from a field in dead, dumb winter anyway? Watermelons, really?

And of course there was a plan, the boy yelled over the whiners. The whiners just had to shut up for one second and listen to the director, the guy with the megaphone in case they hadn't noticed, the one now standing on top of an armored personnel carrier trying to get everyone's attention. This field was perfect, as the director was saying. Just what they needed for the grand climax of the documentary, when the Ukrainians first see the Russian soldiers—tall and blond and blue-eyed men who made the boy's chest flutter. In this scene, the Ukrainians were to welcome their guests with customary bread and salt. Bread made from their last stores of grain, which they'd been saving for exactly this occasion.

(Could they eat the bread after filming?)

Another whiner, at it again.

(Because this morning, when they reenacted receiving humanitarian aid as starved Ukrainians, the bread got taken away after filming and no one knew where it went, and it better not have gone to actual Ukrainians, who were not very welcoming, not presenting any bread and salt. Presenting instead, on that video going around, sunflower seeds to "at least bloom" from their pockets when they "all lie down here," a pretty unneighborly thing to say, really not that nice.)

35

If she and the sisters had any chance of escape, Yeva knew, it would be now. She would have to leave Lefty, but there was no longer any choice. For now, chaos would be their cover. Eight white trucks, a film crew, and a military convoy comprising ten tanks and four armored personnel carriers clogged the field. Extras piled out of the trucks, and soldiers out of the tanks and APCs. The two original soldiers, Uzel and Ovechkin, had been swallowed by the thickening crowd.

Yeva grabbed onto Nastia's cold hand, then Sol's, and pulled them through the crowd in the direction of the narrow alley, toward the high-domed recycling bins behind which Bertrand's body lay.

"What about the bachelors?" Nastia asked, behind her. "We've lost them." Yeva scanned the crowd: Not a single blazer bobbed around the threadbare frocks of the actors. Not even Pasha's—Yeva thought he would've stuck close by. Had they all run away? Surely, it was for the better. She kept pulling, determined to get the sisters off this cursed field at last. What had happened with Bertrand could not happen again, and certainly not to these girls.

They passed within meters of the acacia. An APC had parked right beside it, and from its roof a tall, thin man in a camo flat cap and a megaphone was surveying the field like he was the first to lay eyes on it—the director, Yeva realized, as he brought the megaphone to his lips and began issuing stage directions over the crowd. Yeva pulled left, away from his prospecting gaze—and away from the tree. She would first get the sisters out of the city—she'd convince a fleeing car to take them, however packed, pay the driver all she had—then return to the field herself. For Lefty, at the very least.

"Hey, you three, I told you to stop." Behind them, the director's voice boomed through his megaphone. Yeva and the sisters had made it to the edge of the field.

"I want the skinny girl to go up front, to be the face of the Ukrainians."

Yeva turned around and looked up. The director's long pale finger was pointing, she saw with horror, at Nastia.

The civilians stood on one end of the field, where Yeva and the sisters were now, while the soldiers and their military equipment formed a front at the other end, upfield.

"Go on, stand at the helm of the civilians," the director said. "You'll be the one who presents the gift of bread and salt to the liberators."

Yeva watched an oversize round of bread and a saltshaker pass through the crowd, hand to hand, until a woman with dark penciled eyebrows extended it to Nastia. Before Nastia had a chance to react, Sol lunged in front of her, as though the bread were poisoned.

The director waved Sol aside. "Not you. *Her.*"

A portly man holding a boom microphone patted Sol on the back. "Don't worry, milaya, you'll get your starring role another day."

"There are no small parts, only small actors," the director intoned.

Sol stood her ground. Yeva stepped beside her, shoulder to shoulder, blocking Nastia. But she knew the director wouldn't let Nastia go so easily. Of course he'd cast the blank-faced, orphan-thin girl as the one who approaches the so-called liberators first. If you didn't know her, you could project anything onto that face—a bottomless gratitude, for one thing. Already Yeva could see that face gracing the Russian state channels, churned into proof that Ukrainians welcomed the "Special Operation." Across eleven time zones, Russian audiences would eat her up.

"Maybe now's not the time for protest?" Nastia said, behind them.

Rich, coming from her, Yeva thought. But she knew the girl was right: How much of a fight could they put up against the bread and salt, against the cameras, given the military convoy across the field, the armed soldiers?

"My child, there is no need to fear the cameras," the director said in his lilting Moscow accent, the vowels rounded and drawn out in long strokes like a comb through a borzoi's pedigreed fur. He quoted Stanislavsky on how to retain an "inner truth" even under the frightful gaze of an audience of thousands or millions.

"Don't you get it? How you'll look, presenting the bread?" Sol hissed at her sister. "Back here, you'll always be known as a collaborator."

Yeva turned and saw Nastia give the bread a strange smile, like she was aware life as she knew it could end, but that life was some other girl's, not hers.

The director was still speaking—not just to Nastia but to his broader audience on the field, to the dozen locals who watched the commotion in puzzlement from across the street. How, as the Great Stanislavsky would say, one was to imagine oneself enclosed in a circle of light and to carry that protective circle always, no matter how dark and frightful the stage, the way a snail bravely carries its shell into the most unknown unknowns.

Yeva saw Nastia flinch at the comparison. "Don't sentimentalize them," the girl said, in a low voice.

The director's gaze locked back onto Nastia. He lowered his megaphone. "Excuse me?"

Yeva wanted to clamp the girl's mouth shut, but she also welled with pride.

Nastia drew a clattering breath. "Snails are basically blind anyway, so it doesn't matter how dark it is. The metaphor's moot."

Yeva had told the sisters about ocular tentacles while on the road, shortly after the attacks had begun, in what she'd assumed was a futile attempt at distraction. Nastia had been listening after all.

"So the girl does speak," the director said with an indulgent smile. He seemed to be intrigued by Nastia all the more, Yeva sensed with a sinking feeling. How could she and the sisters possibly slip away now? But the acacia snagged her attention. Just a few steps away, the sun's golden rays were setting the tips of the tree's branches aflame. If she were a believer she would have seen God then, the shimmering presence pulsing through every crag and thorn.

Instead, she saw *them.* As if they'd only been waiting for this very moment, waiting for their cue.

Halfway up the acacia's trunk, where there had been one twig, now there were two. A fist's width apart. As their glistening bodies stretched toward each other, Yeva realized she had never seen two *C. surculus* at once. Dizziness overtook her. It didn't seem possible—surely the doubling was a trick of her vision. Life teetered between annihilation and—could she dare think it?—hope.

36

NO, LEFTY didn't see much. No circles of light, mostly shadows. It was the smell that hooked him. *Her* smell. Bubbling, sulfurous, alive. It could seep into the smallest fissure, this smell, crack open a boulder. New, yet deeply familiar, from a time he rode through the world latched to his mother's back, barely a spiral to him.

37

PASHA WAS RUNNING faster than he'd ever run in his life. He didn't care anymore if he drew suspicion. He chased each slap of pavement against his feet, that lash of a whip up his spine his due punishment. He hated himself, hated every molecule in his body. For coming to this country, thinking he was still one of them. For trying to help the three women but making everything worse, then running away. He hadn't outgrown himself, hadn't stepped through the flames of war reforged. The terror of the past few days hadn't crystallized into a grand lesson, or a love story with the one named Solomiya. If only he could charge fast enough to bend time, and go back just two weeks—when he stood at the airport gate in Vancouver, waiting to board the plane—to when his bravery was still untested, when he could imagine himself in the hypothetical.

Worst of all, he'd lost his friend. If Pasha hadn't stoked Bertrand's delusions about the war, he wouldn't have goaded that soldier. Would still be alive. Bertrand's last moments kept looping through Pasha's mind: those wide blue eyes darting madly as he hit the ground beside Pasha, trying to grasp an explanation. How, after the second gunshot, his face regained its famous calm. Pasha waited for a wink, a twitch of the lips. Any sign Bertrand was only playing dead, waiting for the right moment to spring back up. *Gotcha! Told you the gun wasn't real.*

Tears blurred Pasha's vision, but he kept on. He had no way out of this place but his own two feet. He wanted nothing more than to hide under Vancouver's gray impenetrable skies, under his wool blankets, never to come out again.

It's for the better, Pauly, his parents would say. *Best you come home.* His role wasn't to be in the middle of a cataclysm but to do what he did best: observe from afar, reflect. *Our Pasha has the sensitive soul of a Thinker.*

He stopped, heaving, at the edge of a crowded public square. Just his luck, he thought, to escape one throng only to run headlong into another. A hundred or so people stood facing away from him, wrapped in Ukrainian flags. Towering over them, what Pasha guessed was the administration building, hefty and Greek-columned. Russian flags hung from it—white, blue, and red stripes bright as an Aquafresh toothpaste ad. A row of soldiers stood behind shields. The protesters' chants—*Kherson is Ukraine! Kherson is Ukraine! Russians go home! Russians go home!*—mixed with the soldiers' threats, and it all swirled together into white noise. Pasha had stopped understanding any of it. The protesters were just as foreign to Pasha as the soldiers, as foreign as his parents on the phone, as foreign as the people he used to call friends back "home," that faraway world he'd never be able to reenter, not fully, not after the bodies he'd seen on the bridge, not after Bertrand. How easy it would be for the crowd—protesters, soldiers, all—to discover among them the third element, the intruder, to surround and smother him. Or would it be worse not to be seen at all, a hump of clothes under a storm of boots?

As he backed away, a pair of eyes did discover him. Black, alien, large, unblinking.

The eyes belonged to a baby who surveyed him over a man's flag-draped shoulder. The baby babbled at him, still without blinking, that slimy protolanguage from which thousands of the world's tongues stemmed. A deep ache filled Pasha, transported him back to the viscous depths of his childhood when he, too, could have mastered all languages.

What the baby was not saying to him: *Stranger. Intruder. Coward.*

What the baby said instead: *Chaos.*

Or, not that word precisely. Not the "chaos" of the crowded

field Pasha had just run from, nor the "chaos" he'd just run toward, this public square with these protesters, but "chaos" in the broader sense. The uncontrollable, ever-shifting essence of the universe—one we try to tamp down in our everyday lives, cover with a skim of order.

That wasn't all the baby had to say. Layered over this concept was another, like some birds layer one melody over another, another talent we humans surely possess at birth but forget with time.

Fighter, the baby said.

As in, that thin but hard rod that did exist within Pasha after all, despite his previous beliefs, the rod that pointed not away from Kherson but right back into its heart, into the field with the acacia tree and the crowds and the military convoy and the three women who'd brought him here.

Fight chaos with more chaos, the baby was telling him.

At last, the baby blinked, released him.

Pasha knew what he had to do.

38

THE CROWD playing the role of grateful Ukrainians parted around Nastia, waiting for her to take bread from the director's hands. Upfield, the soldiers were fidgety. Some lowered helmets, readjusted rifle straps. She spotted Uzel and Ovechkin among them, gazing at her with suspicion, as if her hesitation proved that she'd never been part of this film troupe in the first place.

To Nastia's right, she felt her sister's body tense with alarm. *Whatever you do, don't let their cameras film you.*

She tried to imagine what would happen after the propaganda film was released. Would it filter from Russia's borders, cross back into Ukraine? How soon would word get out that the star of the liberation scene was a real Ukrainian girl, a collaborator? Nastia's face would be matched with existing photos of her on the internet. Tight dresses, pouting lips. Perched on velvet fainting couches and mahogany banisters. Anastasia, eighteen years old, Kyivan. Member of an international marriage agency. Already selling herself off long before the Russians got there, people would say. The sense of dread sank deeper: How long, Nastia wondered, before she would be publicly linked to her mother? Iolanta Cherno, the famed protester who'd bared herself in front of Putin a decade ago, bloodred slogans slashed across her back. And now her own daughter, who looked so much like her, was welcoming the tyrant's army. Both mother and daughter would be dragged into the media limelight. Would this be the closest they'd come to reuniting, two photos side by side, canceling each other out?

Her mother would never return to Nastia, not after this.

"Three," the director said.

Nastia looked up. The director squatted atop the military truck, his gaze cold and seething. He was holding up three fingers for a countdown, as one does with a misbehaving toddler. He couldn't stand down and choose another girl to present the bread, Nastia knew, not when everyone was watching.

Frozen, Nastia still did not know what to do. She turned to the left, to Yeva. Followed Yeva's wonder-struck gaze to the acacia. Saw enough to witness the miracle in her features, how they opened with possibility. Saw enough to know that Yeva had spotted both snails on the tree, a few yards away. Nastia swore she could feel a part of Yeva peel away, strain toward the acacia, while the corporeal Yeva stayed at Nastia's side.

Nastia turned back to the director. She should choose the path of least resistance, shouldn't she? Not make a bigger scene or start more mayhem—crowds could turn so quickly. She should take the bread, get the (sanctioned) scene over with, let Yeva extract her snails off the tree while Nastia kept all eyes on her, let these people and their military convoy drain out of the field and move on.

"Two," the director announced. He lowered another finger, eyes fixed on Nastia's.

Movement from one of the apartment blocks overlooking the field caught her gaze. She spotted, at a second-story window, a figure behind a gauzy curtain. Was she already being filmed? How many phone cameras might be trained on her now from above, catching her, pinning her to the propaganda film crew, to the Russian occupiers, before she'd even agreed to present the bread?

"One," the director said. Only his index finger lifted now, pointing at the sky.

Nastia fingered the hem of her jacket. She considered her weapon, the only weapon she'd ever had, she realized grimly: her body. She saw this body from the outside, her gaze hovering above the field like a drone, the way her mother might see it. The staging was perfect: a row of soldiers about to meet a row of civilians. At their helm, the lithe girl would peel off her coat, sweater, shirt, bra in one swoop, as if she'd been bred for this moment. Collaborator no more, but saboteur—as any photos and videos from onlookers would prove. Her name would be cleared. Her mother would materialize beside her—yes, she and the rest of Komod really had been watching her these past eight months, waiting for her to finally come to fruition. Her mother would take Nastia in her arms, and for the briefest moment, before the soldiers converged on Nastia, life would go back to the way it was before the war, before Iolanta left.

Nastia watched the director lower his last finger, slowly, into a fist.

Nastia smiled at the fantasy, let it go. She reached for the bread.

39

As Pasha marched back toward the field, he allowed himself a poem.

If he that in the field is slain
Be in the bed of honour lain,
He that is beaten may be said
To lie in honour's truckle-bed.

True as the dial to the sun
Although it not be shin'd upon.
For those that fly may fight again
Which he can never do that's slain.

Yes, he had run away before, but he was coming back to the battleground, to the three women he'd vowed to protect. He was coming back alive—no small feat. (Bertrand!)

So he hadn't procured weapons or food like Yeva had asked him to do. So he'd made everything worse by bringing in the movie people and military convoy. So he'd run away. He would undo all that, or at least dilute it, by bringing in an even bigger crowd: a hundred chanting protesters marched behind him, carrying banners and Ukrainian flags.

He did not know exactly how he'd rallied the protesters to leave their central square and follow him. He remembered only the baby and its somber message. After he'd received the message, had he climbed onto a statue's plinth? Delivered an impassioned speech (in which language, though?) about the propaganda film being minted that very moment, mere blocks away, with a horde of fake Ukrainians? He must've blacked out. When he'd come to, he was already marching.

He and the protesters were three blocks from the field now.

The Canadian hero Laura Secord came to his mind—she who'd waded thirty kilometers through forest and mud and mosquitoes two hundred years ago to warn the British colonies of an American attack, then become immortalized as a chocolate brand. A middling one—Pasha's parents would buy the cloying Laura Secord six-inch chocolate chip cake for his birthday out of patriotic duty (this was before they believed in allergies, especially to something as mundane as milk)—but he felt a kinship with the steel-eyed woman now, a messenger like him, incontestably useful.

He rewound the poem, recited it under his breath, letting its meter drive him on when doubt crept in, made him wonder what the hell he was doing and should he peel away from the protesters and find his way to the train station.

"You are a poet."

A flag-wrapped woman had caught up with him. Her English had a prickly tone. Were her words a statement or a question or a quip?

"It's by Samuel Butler," he explained. "The actual poem is much longer. I took the highlights." Verses from the epic had been shoved down his throat every Sunday at Versa-tile Minds Youth Poetry Club, back in his teenage days, when his parents and the world at large seemed to be waiting for Pasha's own majestic talent to reveal itself.

The woman waved off Butler's name. "I mean, what you say before. When you climbed the tires. Pure poetry."

What had he said? What tires had he climbed?

She gave him a serious look. "Your grammar—very poor."

"Thanks." Was this all she'd wanted to tell him? Were she and the other protesters following him as some grand mockery of his attempt at poetry and grammar?

"But when I stopped listening for all mistakes, I heard what you were trying to say. What was under."

Back at the public square, had this stranger witnessed some other version of Pasha, a better one, unknowable to him? He tried to find this heroic version, some hint of awe, reflected in the woman's dark features, in her lips, painted a frosty blue. "So what was under?"

"Begging for compliments, it's not pretty." Yet she was smiling at him. Talking to this woman, Pasha felt as if he were plunging between a glacial river and a hot bath.

The woman's left hand, the one that clutched the corners of the flag to her chest like a cape, bore no wedding ring. As they marched side by side their shadows stretched in front of them. Her braids and ribbons were long and Medusa-like, and whenever their shadow touched his own, he felt a sting.

He asked for her name.

But when she turned to look at him, her frosty lips forming a perfect circle, he already knew what she was going to say.

"Olya," she answered.

What were the chances?

(Pasha knew the chances were, in fact, quite high: Olya was an exceedingly common name here. He chose to ignore this knowledge.)

She wore no coat under her flag, despite the cold, and he felt the urge to wrap an arm around her. She wasn't just any Olya. Surely she was *his* Olya, the one he'd been dreaming of since his arrival in Ukraine. At last, he'd found her. Yes, for a moment he'd been distracted by Solomiya, whom he hardly knew, but wasn't that the nature of the game? Romance: a winding, treacherous road, full of dead ends.

40

FILMING WAS PROCEEDING in an orderly and civilized fashion. At long last, the civilians were about to meet their liberators, bread and salt in hand. Sure, the girl chosen by the director to do the presentation had been hesitant at first but, as the director reminded everyone, when she did step up to the task, great historical turns (i.e., a liberation), like great works of art, weren't always so obviously great right away. Sometimes it took a moment to appreciate them.

In the end, the girl was perfect, the way she thrust the loaf forward with two stick-straight arms, eyes downcast, lips bitten between teeth, awkward as a lovestruck teenager. All the while the other blond girl, the one who'd wanted the role—a bit harsh on the eyes, that one—stood back watching, looking to be on the verge of tears.

And who wouldn't be lovestruck at the sight of the men in uniform, approaching the girl, the civilians? Blue-eyed, platinum-haired. Ice columns sprouted straight and pure from the tundra, while other men around the world melted, muddied, withered, painted their nails.

Oh, the civilians had seen men like this before, of course. In the military parades back in Russia, on the flyers flapping from bus stops. On the government TV ad that featured a corner-store security guard tapping his baton aimlessly against his hand (*Was this really the protector you'd wanted to become?*), the personal trainer with the bulging muscles pale from windowless gyms (*Is this really where your strength lies?*), the bearded taxi driver locking his jaw as he accepted another pittance from a passenger (*Is this really the road you wanted to choose?*). All three men were transformed once they wore fatigues, their shoulders thrown back, spines straight.

Just like these soldiers, goose-stepping across the field.

But just as the rescuers and rescuees were about to touch, lock in embrace, the director cut the cameras. Could the soldiers please not extend their hands toward the girl's bread or even acknowledge the bread? The bread is an afterthought for them. They're not here for the bread.

The soldiers nodded in cool acknowledgment, hands sliding into pockets. Obviously they're not here for the bread. Still, one of the soldiers in front, who was a tad shorter than the others, had to ask, "But, why then?"

"Why what?" the director asked.

"I mean, I *know* why we're here. To liberate the Ukrainians from their Nazi regime. But where are they, the Nazis? I mean, I *know* they're out here, but how about in this scene? And the scenes before that? It would be nice if we could, I don't know, see the enemy. Just to show who we're freeing the Ukropy from."

"And how do you propose the enemy should look, young man? A swastika flag in one hand, a *Mein Kampf* in the other? The enemy is more subtle now. Hides in plain sight. Inside every Ukrainian."

The civilians broke into murmurs. No one had alerted them to this possibility.

"So what am I supposed to think as we come at the Ukropy, who might or might not be Nazis themselves?" the soldier asked. "Do I love them or do I hate them or what? What is my face supposed to do?"

A tad awkward, this moment. The rescuees had been so open, so natural, so ready to take in the men—and now here was one who had to spoil the moment with chatter, logistics.

"I'm not here to direct you," the director reminded him. "Do what you would do naturally."

The scene restarted. It took a moment for the mood to click back in for the rescuees, but it did, just as the sun dipped to the perfect angle and illuminated the soldiers' faces. This time both sides would get it just right. They began their approach, slower, more bashful, stealing glances.

Again the girl presented the bread, looking even younger now in her stiffness. A broad-shouldered soldier stepped forward, accepted the gift, wrapped the child in his arm. When he kissed the top of her tangle-haired head, she scrunched her eyes, as if she'd always wanted to be held just like this. Then the rest of the rescuers and rescuees converged around the two. Countless hands shaken, kisses planted.

In this great act of unity, no one was "acting." No one thought about where their arms stretched, what their faces should or shouldn't do. Instead, each mined their own circle of truth, which was actually a collective one, a circle as vast as the methane craters that pockmarked softening Siberian lands, this truth being that everyone, even the soldiers themselves, just needed a firm (presidential) hand to lead them to steady ground again, to save them. (This would be the documentary's message postedit, to be approved by the Ministry of Culture before distribution within Russia and her province of Ukraine, for common enlightenment and contemplation, as well as for critical study in the West, where intrigue over the unknowable Russian soul remained strong, even stronger after the launch of her Special Operation.)

With the sandy soil underfoot (another Crimea!), with the five-story Khrushchevkas just like the ones back in their hometowns, with the colorful laundry hanging inside the glassed-in balconies above, balconies probably stocked with preserves, everything felt so soulful. Already, this place felt like home. No, these civilians were not newcomers, not even pioneers. They were just as rooted as Ukrainians, in fact they *were* Ukrainians (meaning Russians, because there was no such country as Ukraine and never had been). They were One.

41

DURING THE FILMING, as all eyes were on the center of the field, where the extras and the soldiers converged, and Nastia was swallowed among them, Yeva could turn at last to the acacia. The two snails were still visible on one of the boughs, closing in on each other, eye stalks about to touch. Her foot prodded for a hold in a gnarled knot on the acacia's trunk. She'd managed to climb the tree before, but now her limbs were jittery, uncooperative. Her mind was still on Nastia, whom she could no longer see—the girl had promised to meet back at the acacia as soon as the scene wrapped up. Sol was with her sister, shadowing.

Yeva willed herself to focus. She wrapped one arm around a bough, reached with the other for the nearest snail—not Lefty, she could tell by the notch at the tip of the shell. *Her* shell? Yeva couldn't tell the snail's gender, of course, but had been picturing the creature as female. Slowly, as gently as she could, Yeva curled a finger over Lefty's companion until the snail reared up and lost some of her suction. If the snail fell now, she would surely be trampled by the crowd below, but Yeva tried to tune everyone else out. It was just her and her snails again, like old times, she told herself, no one else to worry about. She held her breath as she kept pushing her finger under the buttery foot, slowly unpeeling it from the bark—Lefty crawling forward in the meantime, as though sensing the imminent separation—until at last she lifted the snail off with both fingers. The snail's foot curled into her shell, the way Yeva had seen an infant's legs curl up when lifted.

As she slipped the snail into her breast pocket, she waited for that feeling of weightlessness, that rush she usually felt at the retrieval of an endling, but it didn't come, not fully. Something was missing, and that something had to do with the girl who was not at her side—a thought she had to shake off. It was Lefty who needed Yeva. But as she reached for him, her foot slipped from its hold. She slid, groaning, down the trunk, cheek and palms grating against the gouged bark, the sharp thorns. After checking her breast pocket—the shell inside was still whole—she lunged at the trunk again, trying to find a handhold, and heard the director yell: "Cut!"

Yeva looked up. The director was back on the roof of the APC again, right beside her. Civilians and soldiers, mixed in one clump in the middle of the field, embracing and shaking hands, looked over, startled at the interruption. Yeva tried to pick out Nastia and Sol among the crowd, but couldn't.

"Now, this tree," the director began. He turned to the acacia, like a show host about to introduce a guest onstage.

"This *tree*," he repeated. "What does the tree *mean*?"

Yeva felt her cheek sting from the earlier fall, and her palms were bleeding, but the pain felt distant. The excitement in the director's voice unsettled her. Maybe, she told herself, he'd seen the pair of snails himself, witnessed the miracle. Snail hobbyists hid where you least expected them. The man had even spoken of snails, hadn't he, the artsy circle of darkness bullshit?

"Alone and ugly, the tree. Clearly an outlier," the director went on. "What's the tree doing for us?"

There was still hope—stretched thin, but it was there. He might just dissolve this whole affair in the name of conservation.

He turned to his assistants, who stood below in black parkas. "Can we have the tree burning?"

Well, fuck. "Leave the tree alone," Yeva yelled. "The tree's fine as is."

But the director was speaking to the crowd, wrapping them in his fine-woven voice. The burning tree would symbolize chaos and radicalism, he said, but a soldier would be kind enough to extinguish the flames, bringing peace and stability to these wild lands at last. And *then* they'd reshoot the scene with the bread and salt. An ascending murmur spread from mouth to mouth. Yes, yes, the tree must absolutely burn, how was the tree not burning already?

A red canister of gasoline passed from the soldiers to the civilians, then a blowtorch.

Yeva lunged for the acacia again, pressed her back against its trunk, clamped her hands on the other side. Two of the director's black-clad assistants tried to pull her off, but she clung on. Would everyone please just leave, she yelled, and let her do her fucking conservation job. (A job no one asked or paid her to do, her mother would remind her. Her mother, who would've died at the sight of Yeva: crazy, unwashed hippie, a literal tree hugger, every fear she'd had for Yeva manifesting.) Already a kerchiefed woman poured clear liquid from the red canister in quick, efficient strokes as people cheered. Yeva tried to imagine that the wetness seeping into her shoes was simply water. The director could have the damn tree, he could do whatever he wanted with it, Yeva yelled, if only she could evacuate its last resident. She yelled louder, louder, but no one seemed to hear her.

Then, all at once, the crowd grew quiet, as though sensing a shift in the air, imminent danger. Hands loosened their grip on Yeva. Faces turned away from her.

Soon she heard it herself: echoing between the apartment buildings, a column of voices sang a melody she recognized. It was the folk song about the red viburnum. She couldn't see the singers through the extras and film crew and soldiers, but as the song grew louder, Yeva swore she could pick out a familiar voice, a voice that lagged behind, clearly uncertain about the melody and lyrics. Could it really be Pasha? The last time she'd seen him, the military convoy was descending on the field. He'd been running away. Now the song reached a crescendo, and once again that uncanny bellowing voice followed a beat behind the rest. The kerchiefed woman who'd been pouring the gasoline around the tree cut Yeva a strange look.

Yeva realized she was laughing, and couldn't stop.

42

IT WAS NOT OBVIOUS to the civilians clumped by the acacia, waiting for their liberation to be documented on film once more—this time with a soon-to-be-burning tree in the background—who the approaching horde was. Not at first.

At their helm was a scrawny man in scuffed dress shoes and a woman with ribbons tied into her braids. They were followed by two priests, and a pack of students in flared jeans and pastel puffer coats. A pensioner holding a baby with freakishly large black eyes. This motley bunch kept marching around the street corner, a dozen of them at first, then two dozen. The closer they came to the field, the clearer the lettering on their banners, the shine of their flags and other nationalist relics. The look of death in their eyes.

Fifty of them, a hundred; a yellow and blue mob.

It was unmistakable now: these people were the fascist enemy the Peaceful Ones had been warned about—by their director, and before that, by their president back home.

The not-quite-eighteen-year-old among the Peaceful Ones—the best-dressed boy in the sheepskin vest, felt boots, embroidered shirt, and red belt—couldn't help but wonder: Were the cameras still rolling? Maybe these loud and angry-looking people who were gathering on the edge of the field had been summoned here by the director for the surprise climax of the documentary, the battle before the bread is truly earned. The boy recalled something he'd read about the making of the movie *Alien*. How none of the actors were warned what the creature that burst from Kane's chest would look like so that the cameras could capture their true shock and horror.

But now the director was ordering the intruders to stay back. And these angry people weren't listening to him.

Of course, grand historical moments—like military liberations or works of art—couldn't please *everyone*, the Peaceful Ones knew. In the months to come, they would shake their heads as they looked back on this moment. Many would reminisce from their hometowns back in Russia, while others would reminisce from where they'd set themselves up across the river, in the freshly emptied houses with watermelon patches. They'd shake their heads because the filmed liberation really had been so civilized. Until that moment. It had been so orderly yet soulful. And look what those fanatics brought upon themselves, look what they made the soldiers do.

(In the commotion that followed, many of those who'd previously felt so Ukrainian did wonder: Why are the soldiers firing on us, too? Couldn't they tell who was Russian and who was Ukrainian? That they were not in fact One?)

43

THE DAY COULD still end well, Nastia decided—or if not well, at least not worse than it already was—if she didn't dwell on certain details. If she loosened her mind, made the sharp edges of memory blurry. If she focused instead on the miracle of where she was now—back in the passenger seat of Yeva's mobile lab—and on their imminent escape from Kherson.

Yet Nastia couldn't shake the feeling she was still being watched, filmed by both the Russians and the Khersonites, her movements tracked and judged before an invisible jury. She leaned back in the seat, tried to loosen her shoulders, focus on the naked trees that lined Kherson's streets, their gnarly boughs bent threateningly over the road. No, not threateningly—protectively, she decided. Oaks or whatnot. Certainly not acacias—she never wanted to see another acacia.

To Nastia's right, Sol began to whimper.

"Breathe," Yeva reminded them, knuckles white as she gripped the steering wheel.

Nastia flicked her sister's thigh, willing her to keep it together. They'd both witnessed the same hellscape of the field, hadn't they? The soldiers who'd opened fire on the crowds. The white-haired man who sank to the ground a few steps away from her and Sol, slowly, gently, as though he were simply taking a rest. The teenage girl dragged away by two soldiers who'd grabbed her by the checkerboard-patterned backpack.

Nastia forced her mind to reel back in time, to before the gunfire, to the good part: the moment when the protesters had stormed the field and swarmed the military trucks. It was as if the bile and anger that had filled Nastia as she presented that bread and salt to the soldiers had manifested, grown legs and lungs and voices, spilled over the yellow grass. Stunned, Nastia had simply watched as the protesters marched past her. She remembered the stout man in a plaid cap and vest, the one who looked like he could've been a schoolteacher, climb onto the APC as the director jumped off in fear. She remembered the woman in a raincoat patterned with yellow ducks who'd cracked a microphone pole over her knee. And the soldier who'd ambled past her, looking lost—here they were, actual Ukrainians, he seemed to be thinking, but why weren't they welcoming him like they were supposed to? Where was the bread and salt? That's when Sol had jabbed Nastia's arm, pointing across the field. She'd spotted the cameramen. A clutch of four, in jeans and parkas, edging along the side of one of the white trucks. Sol set off after them like a hound, Nastia following. They intercepted the men just as they were about to lock themselves inside. Protesters, two women and a man, had appeared then and ripped the cameras out of the crews' arms, off their backs, threw them on the ground. Sol crouched over the machines, ejecting trays to pluck out memory cards, the way Nastia had seen Komod members do after long days of filming. These memory cards Nastia then smashed with a piece of concrete. How good it felt, in that moment! To believe she could destroy every bit of footage of her collaboration with the invaders.

Nastia remembered, too, when it had seemed as though the protesters might gain the upper hand. The extras had piled back into their white buses. A tank reversed away, tracks churning the sandy soil. She'd cheered along with the protesters, allowed herself a glimmer of hope: If the Khersonites could stop the film, could they stop the soldiers' real-life advance across the rest of the city?

In the seat beside her now, Sol was taking long, quavering breaths, her eyes closed.

On Nastia's other side, she could feel Yeva's body stiffen for a moment, as if Sol's distress was contagious, before catching herself. She watched as Yeva lifted the glass jar from the cup holder on the dash, eyed it, then slid it back. Nastia had lost count of the number of times Yeva had checked the jar, as though any moment the two snails inside might evaporate through a pinprick in the lid.

Lefty's rescue back at the field had been another victorious moment Nastia clung to. Nastia and Sol had returned to the acacia just as the first shots were fired. Someone had set fire to the tree, and angry flames leapt up its withered bark. Shoeless, Yeva was holding a bent pole, prodding a spot on an overhanging bough with the furry microphone on the pole's end. "Lift me up," Nastia called out behind her, and Yeva reeled around, eyes wide with terror but also an unexplainable happiness. She clasped her arms around Nastia's waist, and Nastia felt her feet leave the ground as she reached for the dull thorn that was supposed to be Lefty. He'd retracted into his shell, done with the burning world. "Don't grab by his shell!" Yeva called from below, chin digging into Nastia's ribs. She rattled off complicated instructions. As Nastia tried to loosen Lefty's hold, she could feel Yeva's arms shake from her weight. Sol joined in the lifting. At last, the snail fell into Nastia's palm with a gentle tap, like a raindrop.

Now a soft knocking behind Nastia's head brought her attention back to the driver's cab. She sat up.

"Did you hear that?" asked Sol, staring at Nastia. The sound had come from inside the trailer.

"Once upon a time, I agreed to hauling thirteen bachelors," Yeva said, "but if any of those movie people got into my lab . . ." She trailed off, cursing under her breath.

Of course it couldn't be the bachelors, thought Nastia. She'd lost them back at the field during the commotion. By the time she'd reached the lab along with Yeva and Sol (and the two snails), had a moment to catch her breath, and checked her phone as Yeva maneuvered into the nearest alley, there were four missed calls from Masha. Each before five o'clock, the time by which the bachelors were supposed to have been dropped off at the border. No more calls after that. The unspoken verdict: the deal was off. No hostages, no mother. Nastia knew she'd have to call Masha back, find some other way to bargain with her. But what could Nastia possibly offer in return now?

Another knock. More insistent. Familiar.

Sol unhooked the PA microphone from the dash and uttered a tentative greeting in English: "May you find the One?"

A male voice returned the greeting. "May you find the One." Nastia recognized the voice's high timber: the bachelor named Raj, the feline leukemia guy, the Londoner. She felt a glimmer of hope. Could this be a chance to resurrect the deal with Masha?

Raj continued to speak, too quickly for Nastia to parse, though his panic was obvious. "He's asking what in blazes just happened back there," Sol relayed. "He says he and the other men hid in the lab when the military convoy descended."

"Ask how many are with him," Nastia urged.

"Eleven men," Sol relayed. "No Bertrand, of course," she said grimly. "And no Pasha."

Eleven out of thirteen. Another miracle, really. Although maybe it wasn't such a surprise that the men had stuffed themselves back into the trailer. It was the only thing familiar to them in the middle of a country none of the dating guidebooks had prepared them for.

"No Pasha, huh?" Yeva said as she maneuvered the lab through a particularly narrow alley. She was trying to avoid the major roads. "I thought I saw him in the middle of the protesters, his arms around a woman wrapped in a flag."

A silence filled the trailer. Were they all thinking the same thing? Nastia wondered. Had Pasha made it out of the commotion alive?

"He was still in romance tour mode, I guess," Sol said at last. Nastia caught a hint of bitterness in her sister's voice. Yes, this must be the correct emotion, Nastia decided—anger was a trusted antidote for worry. Better to be angry at Pasha—a bride prospector to the last.

"Tell the men we're taking them to the border," Yeva told Sol as she navigated around a dumpster. "And they'd better get out of the trailer this time."

As Sol calmed the bachelors with the promise of rescue, her

voice frictionless and placid again, the way it had been during the romance tours, Nastia dialed Masha on speakerphone.

The woman picked up on the second ring. "Anastasia. Finally. You're all right, then." Masha's tone was stilted, and Nastia had the feeling she was only pretending to care out of formality.

Sol clicked off the PA.

"We got held up, but we're coming," said Nastia. Her voice sounded hollow, not her own, more like Yeva's in administrative mode.

"How do I know you'll actually show up this time? Efrosinia waited around for hours."

"Give us a few more."

"How many."

Nastia turned to Yeva, hoping for an answer, but received a look of exasperation. Yeva had halted the lab at the end of the alley they'd been traversing, which opened to a major road. Nastia watched a military truck pass by. Its canvas cover billowed with every bump in the road, swelling and collapsing like a set of lungs. Yeva put the gear in reverse, lurching the lab deeper into the alley to try to find a safer route.

"Road conditions aren't exactly normal over here," Sol told Masha on the speakerphone. Sol's voice was steady, but Nastia could feel her sister's body shaking against her own.

"You're still in Kherson," Masha said, her tone softening. It wasn't a question. And she didn't sound surprised. For the first time, Nastia wondered if Masha had ever truly believed in her own deadline, in the possibility that Nastia and Sol could escape Kherson in time to get the bachelors to the border. "But you have all thirteen men?" asked Masha.

"All thirteen," Nastia answered, too quickly.

Sol gave her a questioning look. But Nastia had decided the matter of the missing two bachelors was a detail to sort out later, at the drop-off.

"No use lying about the number," Masha chided. "I'll find out anyway."

They were lumbering through a different alley now, a narrower one with sludgy ruts.

"One of the men found love, so he isn't coming back with us," Nastia admitted. It wasn't untrue. "And another—"

Nastia turned to Sol, not knowing how to say it.

"The other found peace," Sol said quietly.

"What does that mean?" Masha asked.

What did she think it meant, Nastia wanted to yell into the phone. They were in the middle of an invasion, a reality the founder probably couldn't grasp from the comfort of her beach chair or wherever. But Nastia held her tongue. It took great effort, but if she erased the acacia tree and the field from her mind, and thought of the missing two bachelors as a simple accounting quirk, a number to make up for, she could find a way to fix the error. In any case, the numbers were still in her favor: Nastia had eleven people Masha wanted, while Masha had only one person, the one Nastia wanted. She could even afford to go on the offensive. "So you have her? My mother?"

"*Have* her," Masha repeated. "Like, tied up and locked in my dungeons? What kind of business do you think I'm running?"

"You've always had it in for my mother. You and every other agency."

"She was a bit of a thorn in the side, sure."

"And isn't it convenient that she disappeared just as she was planning her biggest protest yet, for Valentine's Day?"

"You think that's why she disappeared?"

Nastia fought against the swell of weariness, fear, shock, and sadness. She had to sound confident, as if she had already pinned Masha to her mother's disappearance. "My mother wanted to send a message. A message you didn't want the world to hear."

"And what message would that be."

"Same as mine."

"And here I thought you were just *evacuating* the men, not pulling the same kind of stunt your mother might. Silly me," Masha said, her voice saccharine. "Go on, I'm all ears. What's your message."

Ever since that last fight with her mother, how many times had Nastia fantasized about this moment of reckoning? She'd delivered countless speeches from an imaginary podium, listed every grievance against the international marriage industry. But now, instead, her mind clicked back to the wrong slide: black blood trickling between pale tufts of grass.

Charitable, Masha stayed silent, waiting, but Nastia couldn't get any words out.

Yeva patted her hand, which made Nastia feel worse.

"I've been thinking," Masha said, at last. "Eighteen years old, future still ahead of you, yet you waste it away by kidnapping thirteen men. Is that really what you want your story to be?"

Your *story*. Masha was always using this phrase with her brides, Nastia remembered from the induction sessions. Turn your life into a good story. People love that kind of thing. What you've been through, what you're made of, how you've risen from the ashes. How you've come to believe in joy and love again, would cross the Earth in search of them.

"It doesn't matter what my story is," Nastia countered. "I'm not trying to get anyone to pick me."

"Certainly not your own mother, right?"

Nastia relapsed into silence.

"Whatever your story is," Masha continued, before Nastia could whip up a counterattack, "you don't want it to end badly, do you? Your beloved mother, forever missing? And you might just disappear yourself." Her voice turned soft and misty, a noxious gas Nastia couldn't strike against. "But we don't have to go that route, do we? As I always say, you can choose to have a happy ending. I'll tell you what. If you can get one more man out of Kherson, a different man, along with the eleven bachelors you have already, I'll tell you more about your mother."

One man to make up for two? It seemed too simple, a trap. "This other man isn't part of our original agreement," Nastia said.

"I think we're well past our original agreement, don't you? You won't find your mother by yourself, just so you know. She changed her last name."

Typical, thought Nastia. Iolanta went by many names. Maybe she'd infiltrated agencies in America and had to keep changing her name to stay under the radar. Sensible. This, Nastia could forgive. All she needed was to talk to her mother.

"This new man, he'll refuse to come with you, but you'll keep trying." Masha gave the name and address.

Nastia turned to Sol, who did not meet her eyes. She turned to Yeva, who glanced back warily but did not protest this final detour.

"Who is he?" Nastia asked Masha cautiously, imagining a shadow agent in Masha's criminal circle, someone higher up the ranks, the real founder of the agency.

"My grandfather," the woman said simply.

44

THEY FOUND the grandfather's building half an hour later, in a quieter part of the city, a peach five-story Khruschchevka encrusted with multicolored glazed balconies. The main entrance door, painted a bright blue with the word SHELTER stenciled over it, was locked, but soon an elderly woman with dyed red hair bustled out, empty net bags in hand. When Yeva moved to hold the door, the woman stopped at its threshold, gave the visitors a quick scan, seemed to decide they were harmless, and kept moving. Inside the small entry hall lined with tin mail slots, a set of steps led down to a basement and another set, the one the women took, led upward. A small foggy window on each landing, plants on the sills. The geraniums on the landing for the grandfather's floor looked freshly watered. His door was an expanse of steel (it was one he'd welded himself, Masha had told Nastia with a mix of pride and exasperation, when giving her instructions on how to find him).

After Nastia rapped the knocker, a dead bolt slid somewhere deep within the apartment, and more locks ticked like clockwork until, at last, Nastia heard the squeal of a door opening—although not the steel one. That had only been an inner door. Its red faux-leather upholstery surfaced in her mind, as if she'd been here before. Slow, stealthy footsteps on the other side, a pause. Nastia aimed her brightest smile at the peephole. More locks slid and unhinged. Or had the man on the other side changed his mind, and he was locking up the inner door again?

But the steel did swing open. A white-haired pensioner peered at the three of them through large square glasses, dripping wooden spoon in hand.

"Congratulations, we're here to get you out," Nastia announced. "We have a trailer, very comfortable. Equipped with a bathroom, great for long hauls."

The man's expectant look faded. "Did my family put you up to this?"

Yes seemed to be the wrong answer, so Nastia simply kept smiling.

The steel door slammed shut.

44, AGAIN

AFTER A MOMENT, the three women hear the familiar click of the inner door's dead bolt. The inner door squeals open—its red faux-leather upholstery (more precisely, "dermatoid" or "Fabrikoid," as it used to be known in the Soviet days) surfaces in their minds, as if they've been here before—then comes the ticking of more locks, like clockwork, followed by the gravelly melody of the chain sliding along its track, dropping.

At last, the steel door swings open.

For a moment the pensioner stands there, blinking at the three women, no wooden spoon in hand. He doesn't cook with wooden spoons like some folksy fairy-tale witch—how could one forget? The spoon he holds is a corrosion-resistant alloy of copper and nickel. The hand that holds the spoon is large and broad-knuckled, fit to build a house from the ground up.

"We've come to get you out," Nastia announces. "There's a trailer, very comfortable. Equipped with a bathroom, great for long hauls."

"And who are you supposed to be?"

This time, Nastia decides to be honest. Sort of. His family *did* put them up to this, she tells him. Specifically, his granddaughter. "I'm Masha's colleague."

He narrows his eyes. "Colleague? My granddaughter works alone, from an attic. If you can even call it work, what she does."

"I mean the international matchmaking agency she founded."

The grandfather laughs. "Another of her stories. Or are you

the one spinning tales here?" He closes the door to a crack, hinges the chain. "Nice try. Some thugs tried the same kind of ploy with the neighbor a couple years ago. Tried to get the old lady's trust, convince her she already knew them. All so they could rob her."

The steel door slams shut.

44, REVISITED

AT LAST, the steel door swings open.

For a moment Grandfather stands there, blinking, a stainless-steel spoon in hand.

It's me standing at his door.

"Masha," he says, pale, like he's seeing an apparition. We haven't clapped eyes on each other in seven years. My own delinquency, life, work, a pandemic, every possible excuse. He hasn't aged a day. In fact, his features look brighter, like in his portrait hanging in our living room back in Canada. My sister had painted it in oils from a black-and-white photo of him in his twenties, a bright engineer with a T-square hanging in the background. She'd added the green of his collared shirt herself, the pinks and yellows of his skin.

"How did you get here?" he asks.

I wave the question away. "I'm here to get you out. There's a trailer, very comfortable. Equipped with a bathroom, great for long hauls."

He hurries me inside. He curses me for risking the trip to Kherson at a time like this. The Russians were already setting up checkpoints outside the city, hadn't I heard? Soon they might block civilians from fleeing, trap them inside the city to be used as human shields. He speaks of these endangered civilians as if he isn't one of them.

I take in the apartment, its familiar smell of old paper. On one of his wall-to-wall bookshelves stands a school photo of my scowling sister, aged six or seven, her chiffon bow as large as her head. Pinned to the Turkish rug on the wall are her watercolor natures mortes paintings, glistening pitchers and fruit bowls, a pencil sketch of a plaster fleur-de-lis, its curlicues meticulously shaded. Her art teachers drilled her with still-life studies, declaring her Talented—but only to my grandfather (who passed on the verdict decades later), so as not to let it go to the child's head. The natures mortes bored my sister out of her mind, she'd once told me.

Petulant, I regret not bringing a copy of my first book with me for display alongside her artwork, even though he won't be able to read it since it's written in English.

He tells me I shouldn't stay, it's too dangerous, but puts on tea. While I'm here, do I want to take the photo albums? If not the bulky albums, the rolls of film, at least, since they travel more easily? And how about the notebooks where he's written out our lives?

Yes, yes, I tell him, we'll take everything we can. We'll fold up the entire apartment, fit everything into the trailer. And then somewhere far away, somewhere safe, we'll fold it all out just as it was, like a pop-up card.

He laughs. If only this were possible. If only I could fold up the entirety of Kherson, the marshes, the dacha.

The dacha's going to be gone soon, I tell him. Flooded or washed away into the Black Sea, after the Russians bomb the Kakhovka Dam.

He looks at me like I'm crazy. Certainly, the Russians wouldn't bomb *that.* Do I want to take the stamp collection, too?

"We'll take anything you want," I repeat.

"We?" he says. "I'm not going anywhere."

44, CORRECTLY THIS TIME

AT LAST, the steel door swings open.

Would it really swing, though?

Or would it open just a crack. To see if the visitor isn't the enemy, ready for ambush.

Does the door have a chain? How is it that I can't remember? During visits, how many hours of my life did I spend locking and unlocking all those bolts myself every time I had to step out of the apartment? The outside world would take on a hostile quality. Was I sure I wanted to step out there? Was it really worth it?

Am I suggesting my grandfather is an agoraphobe? Certainly, it would be easier to sum him up as an old man hiding from the world, war or no war, easier to imagine him fearing death than accepting it. But most people I know in Ukraine live behind double doors like this, a holdover from the paranoid Soviet era. And the doors have proven themselves useful lately, when the enemy lurking outside really is out to get you.

Of course the door has a chain.

If I get the details just right, my grandfather will leave Kherson.

45

NASTIA DID NOT KNOW how long she'd been sitting beside the steel door, face on her knees. Above her, Sol's and Yeva's frantic voices asked, then ordered, then pleaded for her to get up. But the voices seemed far away, meant for someone else. Twice they'd threatened to leave her behind, made a show of stomping down the concrete stairs, only to return, renew the threat, descend.

Nastia sat alone again. The idea of Sol and Yeva delivering on their threat and driving off without her was both terrifying and a relief. She could sit by the steel door for days and months, until the man inside agreed to leave.

She was so close. The math was so simple. One grandfather to replace a fallen bachelor, and then she'd finally find her mother.

The steel door swung open again. Out rolled a metal grocery caddie from the Soviet era, reinforced against thieving hands. The grandfather peered at her through his thick plastic-rimmed glasses, startled. "Still here?"

Before Nastia had a chance to respond, the caddie rolled back inside and the door closed again, but this time Nastia heard only one lock turn.

A few minutes later the single lock clicked, the door opened again. The grandfather extended a bowl of soup. Mushroom. Nastia's fingers stretched along the flat rim of the bowl painted with fish. She ignored the sorry sight of her thumbnails, the grime under them, the Rouge Allure that had begun to chip off. She couldn't remember the last time she'd held warmth.

"It's just like my mother used to make."

The lie had come out of nowhere, and the man must have sensed it, because the door shut again. Nastia set the bowl down and pressed her face to her knees again, her bottom numb against the concrete.

The sky gave a whistle, and Nastia crouched into a tighter ball. The rocket sounded like it was coming directly for her, like it knew her intimately, had pinpointed her through the building's concrete, despised and loved her.

Sol and Yeva still hadn't come back, even if only to renew their threat of leaving without her.

"The rocket's outgoing, don't worry. One of our own." The grandfather had reappeared. "The pitch is lower, you can hear the difference. I think." He peered down at her. "I'd let you in, but you're better out here in the stairway than by all my windows. Double-paned, too," he added bitterly, before disappearing inside yet again. This time, Nastia didn't hear any locks turn.

There was a window in this stairway, too, Nastia noted, but it was small. Someone had crisscrossed the glass with tape.

Another whistle wiped her mind clean.

Yes, a lower pitch, surely. She drew a breath, rested the back of her head against the cold corridor wall. She imagined each hour spent in besieged Kherson pressing into her bones, her body forever keeping record, the way debris from cataclysms like floods and mudslides and volcanic eruptions hardens into layers upon layers of rock. A fact she remembered from a schoolbook.

Her phone rang.

"Try again," Masha commanded as soon as Nastia picked up. "Try one more time. You're so close."

Masha must have been informed of the stalemate by the grandfather. "I don't know what to do," said Nastia. "Tell me what I'm supposed to say to him."

"I told you he'd be stubborn. Go on, knock on his door again. It's not even locked, so the knock is just for show. You'll think of just the thing to say, and this time, he'll listen."

Nastia closed her eyes. "I wish I could sleep." It was all she could think to say. Her mind had gone blank again. She felt a growing pressure at the back of her neck, a clamp that tightened over the muscles and tendons. The start of a migraine, maybe—she'd begun having them in recent months. But this grip felt different, sharper, like a set of teeth had latched on to her nape, trying to lift her off the ground by the neck, cajole her body into action.

"I'll give you a hint about where your mother is, who she's with," Masha tried. "All you have to do is get up."

At last, Nastia heaved herself up.

"He was a marriage agency client," Masha began. "Not one of ours, I regret to say. Turns out the international marriage industry isn't as bad as your mother thought."

"I don't know what you're getting at," Nastia said. And if, perhaps, she did have the smallest inkling, she did not want to believe it.

"Face the door."

She faced the door.

"The two of them met on the side, of course," Masha continued. "Your mother wouldn't have shown her face at any official agency events. Now, hand on the knocker."

Nastia curled her fingers around the cold metal hoop of the knocker but stopped there.

"A town in Nevada," Masha said. "House in the sleepy suburbs."

"Stop lying," Nastia said, releasing the knocker.

Yet memories crept in—those last few months before her mother had left, how she'd spent her afternoons and evenings out. She'd tell Nastia and Sol she was just going for a stroll, but neither of them ever truly knew where she went. Nastia remembered, too, the tiny glass creatures her mother would bring home late at night, the types sold at subway stations—penguins with glossy bellies, bulging-eyed frogs, gazelles with legs thin as rice vermicelli—to be set precariously along the chipped plaster moldings of the apartment. The figurines had puzzled Nastia at the time. They were not her mother's style. Could they have been gifts? she wondered now.

"If she was dating a foreigner, it was only for protest," Nastia insisted, suppressing a gnawing sense of doubt. She thought of her mother's kitschy wedding dress, worn in public squares only to be ripped off, to shock onlookers. "She wouldn't have actually married him."

"When they moved in together, they got a golden retriever," Masha went on. "They named him Junior."

Surely this would have been just a play at domesticity, a farce. "She wouldn't have left me and my sister for that kind of life," said Nastia.

"You can keep playing make-believe, or you could knock on that door in front of you."

Nastia reached for the knocker again, but she couldn't do it, not yet.

"A stepdaughter, too," Masha went on. "Still little."

Nastia's breath caught, and she stepped back from the door. Her foot snagged the bowl of soup, sending its brown lobes of mushrooms spilling on the concrete floor of the stairway.

"Never mind the soup," Masha said. "Never mind the formality of knocking. As I said, the door's not locked anyway. Just go straight in."

Did Nastia really want to know more? She considered hanging up, but kept the phone pressed to her ear.

"Tears, very nice," Masha went on. "Tears will be useful." In that moment Nastia had a vision of Masha sitting in an attic, skin tinged blue from a laptop screen, her eyes terrifying—dull and bloodshot and unblinking. She was hardly recognizable as the light-bathed woman who tuned in from overseas to lead induction sessions. Above her was the ceiling made of wooden planks, the kind that had once hinted at something luxurious, like a sauna or yacht saloon. They were simply old fence slats, Nastia saw now. "Go on, pull the outer door open," the voice in her ear ordered.

Nastia pulled the steel outer door open.

"Now the nice upholstered inner door."

Just as Nastia reached for its brass handle, the inner door swung open. The grandfather poked his head out. His gaze flitted from her face to the spilled soup on the floor. "Clumsy girl, I'll get you more. No use being upset."

"Call me after you two talk," Masha told Nastia, and hung up.

A moment later, the grandfather returned with a fresh bowl of soup. He'd set a bread crust on the rim of the bowl, the kind that's dried in oil and salt and can last decades without molding. That's when it dawned on her: the man was hunkering down, set to stay. He was immovable. The clamp around Nastia's nape lessened, and she sank back down to the ground. She accepted the soup and bread.

"Why are you really here?" the man asked, standing over her. "Rescuing a stranger? I still don't buy it. And I know you didn't just come for soup."

Nastia bit through a peppercorn. Her eyes watered again, but this time she knew the tears were useless. She could try to spin a tale about how Masha had told her so much about him that Nastia felt as if he was her own grandfather, no stranger at all, so of course Nastia would want to get him out—but all will had drained out of her again, and the pretense was too much. She ate the salty soup, soaked the bread, and decided to simply be honest. Between spoonfuls she told the man about her vanished mother, about the kidnapping stunt to try to get her back, about how it had gone wrong. She told him about her deal with his granddaughter, the cold math of the agreement to exchange the remaining foreigners plus him, the grandfather, for her lost mother.

"You just made that up," he said.

Nastia blinked. "I didn't."

"Sounds a lot like the novel my granddaughter's been trying to cobble together. She mailed me a draft, fed through one of those internet translation machines. It's about a girl who thinks she can get her activist mother back by kidnapping a bunch of men."

Put this way, the plan didn't sound great to Nastia. "How does the book end?"

"Turns out the mother just fell in love."

"Not very believable, an ending like that," Nastia said. "Does she ever write or call the daughters she abandoned?"

The grandfather thought on it. "That, no."

Maybe this mother was ashamed to have fallen in love with the object of her protests, Nastia thought. Maybe she knew her many followers would disown her if they found out.

Or maybe, she was afraid to call her daughters because she thought they would never forgive her for leaving.

Nastia remembered her own mother writing on her vanity mirror in red lipstick, THE BANE OF ACTIVISM IS CONTENTMENT. In her new house with her new family and her dog, had she at last found contentment? Something Nastia and Sol couldn't give her?

"Actually, there *is* a phone call between the mother and younger daughter at the very end of Masha's novel," the grandfather remembered.

"I doubt the phone call goes very well," Nastia said, imagining her own mother calling from her prim house. A washing machine running. A stepdaughter laughing in the background. Nastia felt a surge of anger.

"No," the grandfather conceded, "but the mother invites both daughters for a visit."

"And?"

"That's where the story ends. Think the daughters would go for it? The visit?" the grandfather asked. "Would it be believable?"

Nastia finished her soup, handed back her emptied bowl along with the overturned one. "It would be a start."

The grandfather shrugged. "Not the kind of book I'd usually read, to be honest. Must be a bad translation. There's a grandfather in there, too, who refuses to leave Kherson. I think my granddaughter wrote the thing hoping that if I read it, I'd finally leave."

He disappeared into the apartment again, reappeared with a wooden stool he set across from Nastia. He gripped his knee, sat down with a sigh. They sat for what felt like two years, three, waiting for another, more amenable grandfather to emerge from the apartment. Green collared shirt, suitcase in hand.

She made no call to Masha, and none came from Masha in return.

When Nastia stepped outside at last, alone, the sun hung low on the horizon. The mobile lab waited for her, white coat of paint splattered with mud, narrow headlights like in a pained, squinting face, the face one might make when pushed toward a cliff drop.

Why was Nastia surprised to find the lab waiting for her? Of course Yeva had stayed. Nastia watched her wipe the dashboard with her coat sleeve. Nervous busywork before the dangerous road out of occupied territory. Or maybe, now that Yeva had a new guest in her jar, she'd regained faith, saw a point in keeping things clean.

Sol, meanwhile, slumped in her seat. Sol! Nastia hadn't really looked at her sister, hadn't truly considered her, since before the outbreak of the war. Now, she saw that Sol suddenly looked much older. In retrospect, the last few months felt like a game: not just the kidnapping plan, but her and Sol's time at the agency before that; the Anastasia persona they'd created, the dresses, the heels, the coquettish flip of the hair, a dress-up game girls play with their mothers' wardrobes, home alone. As Nastia approached the lab, her sister looked up, face impassive. She didn't seem surprised Nastia had returned empty-handed, that yet another of her roundabout attempts to find their mother had failed. She'd indulged Nastia, the little sister who just needed to grow out of her fantasies, grow up. Had Nastia herself ever believed in her own schemes? Or did she just need to be sure she'd done all she could to prove herself to Iolanta? She could find other ways still, in some hazy future she had trouble imagining, but right now she was simply too tired.

When Nastia climbed into the cab, Yeva's gloved hand hovered over the ignition. Are you sure? she asked Nastia. All three of them could knock on the grandfather's door again, try one last time to convince him to leave.

Nastia shook her head. "It's where he feels safe." She hardly knew the man, but she almost believed in the words herself.

46

SOME GOOD NEWS, for a change: inside the trailer, the eleven bachelors had finally unlocked the bar fridge. They weren't trying to escape anymore—they'd tried running already, hadn't gotten very far before they'd had to turn back to the (relative) safety of the trailer—so now they didn't expect the fridge to hold the key to getting out of this "Escape Room," or anything so literal. No, they had been trying to solve a riddle larger than the confines of the trailer, achieve a grander escape.

Sure, the tall black-haired woman had opened the fridge and "emptied" it of its jars days ago, when she'd tried to kick everyone out in the middle of a dark highway, but she'd locked the fridge again afterward. If she'd really emptied it, the men pondered, why lock it again?

There was probably a clue to be gleaned from that dark highway, then from the dusty field with its biblical burning bush, from the beautiful flag-wrapped siren with ribbons flowing from her hair who'd lured one of them astray, from the unspeakable acts of violence (staged or not) they'd seen outside the trailer.

(Whether or not the war was real remained a subject of debate among the bachelors. The shooting of one of their own had pushed their collective opinion in the affirmative for a terrifying moment, but the arrival of the full film crew had pushed it back into a gray zone.)

How many more men had to be picked off from the original Thirteen before the survivors finally solved the riddle?

For the fridge lock, a SIM card ejector did the trick—that wiry paper-clip-like thing that pops open the tiny plastic tray from your phone. One of the bachelors found the tool in his breast pocket.

Which bachelor? Each Chosen One had once possessed a name but, like other earthly attachments, names had ceased to matter.

Don't even try the padlock on the fridge, another said. Can't be done, tool's too short.

Watch me, a third bachelor said. In his past life, he'd been adept at picking locks with fishhooks, binder clips, bra hooks, all sorts of objects. It had been his party trick.

That little SIM tool was the last thing the Chosen Ones would remember of the trailer. More precisely, the last memory they'd agree on.

A fourth bachelor would say the fridge was definitely empty when they opened it, blinding in its whiteness like the gates of heaven.

A fifth would remember a small jar tucked in the corner, forgotten. What else to do with a jar but open it, take a careful sniff?

The floor under their feet shook and rumbled. The trailer had begun to move again.

A sixth would say the muddy stuff inside the jar only smelled like, well, mud.

Death, a seventh would insist. It smelled like death.

An eighth would confirm the presence of the jar, but say it smelled like nothing, which is why they had to taste it.

A ninth would deny this last bit: We weren't stupid, we closed the jar and put it back. Something gross and slimy floated inside.

A tenth would agree with the ninth: We closed the jar and put it back, but then came all the military checkpoints, the soldiers with guns who ordered us in, out, in, out, in, out of the trailer, yelled at us and strip-searched us, and we'd thought this torture, real or staged, would go on forever, in, out, in, out, so we took the jar out again, knowing that for the tape to stop glitching and looping, we had to drink from the jar. It was a kind of mystical belief.

An eleventh would say, What does it matter if we drank from the jar or didn't? The point was what came after.

This, the Chosen Ones would agree on. The What Came After.

A fire raged down their throats all the way to their toes, all the way to the molten core of the earth, a volcano in reverse.

A stillness followed, a fraternal calm.

Hands joined, tears flowed. A deep understanding descended upon the circle of men. A key clue, the only clue, from these past harrowing days: The place they had to escape wasn't the trailer, but something grander. Their carnal desire. They'd been rattling its white-hot prison bars, waiting for a damsel to come along and save them. None would. Not the women back home, not the women here or elsewhere.

And so, they did not need women.

In that trailer, joined in their closed circle, the eleven took a vow of celibacy. They'd damn well hold each other to it, too: they'd choose a common country to reside in (not this one), build a home on a vast and desolate steppe, dig a well themselves, far from the temptations of their old lives. They most certainly wouldn't be tempted by each other, either—don't even think about it. At long last, they would be free.

(Would this really come to pass? Even as they took the vow, a few of the Chosen Ones—we won't name names—began to inwardly wriggle, backtrack, unchoose themselves. Easy to remain celibate while locked inside the trailer, without feminine temptations, but afterward? Still, the bit about the communal home would hold true in spirit—a transnational brotherhood of monthly meetings held online, transcending petty concerns like land borders, legal residency, employment, healthcare, pension plans, et cetera. Either way, what would remain after their time in the trailer, after they splintered back to their physical "homes," was a sense of dislocation. They'd float above the daily grind of their days, as if they had died in that trailer. They were numb to the kind of beauty that once stirred them: flawless lawns, perfectly raked clouds, quartz countertops white as fondant, gleaming watery skyscrapers, the way the seam between road and sky shimmered in the distance, about to come undone. Now, it all seemed suspect. They couldn't shake the urge to snag a corner and peel it away, this illusory peace, see what lurked underneath. This uncanny feeling would stay with them the rest of their lives.)

47

MRS. BROWN: Are the zip ties really necessary?

YURT MAKERS: You have proven yourself a flight risk.

MRS. BROWN: I don't like to be looked for.

YURT MAKERS: Yet you like to be seen.

MRS. BROWN: Get on with it. Arrest me. Drag me back to Ukraine.

YURT MAKERS: Once again, we are not with the police. We are not with the secret service, American or Ukrainian. Nor were we sent by the Tranquil Tides Homeowners Association to depose you as their president, despite your inaction on the persistent complaints about the fish fertilizer used in the common flower beds and the robust odor it emits.

MRS. BROWN: You expect me to believe you are what you say you are? I don't even know what that is, *yurt*.

YURT MAKERS: And yet that is where we found you, at long last. What one might call, though one might not be completely accurate, a "theater tent." You, the loose thread of the so-called mansion of interconnected yurts. The Persian rug makers advised us not to look for you. Leave in one flaw, they said, because only Allah can create perfection. We are not of the same opinion. An imperfect rug poses little hazard, but a yurt? Let one thread loose and the entire structure might collapse, generations of families might perish.

MRS. BROWN: I have no idea what in hell you just said.

YURT MAKERS: Tell us, "Mrs. Brown," do you despise children?

MRS. BROWN: I love children.

YURT MAKERS: The content of your one-woman "children's plays," and the fact that no child ever attends them, leads us to believe otherwise. The play about the lonely lighthouse that turns off its beam, lures boats to crash against its rocky foot? Or the one about the potato on the run from the peeler set to dig out its eyes?

MRS. BROWN: It's not my fault parents censor everything these days. I'd like to change out of my costume, if you don't mind. Polyester gets very hot.

YURT MAKERS: We need not be schooled on the properties of fabrics. Would you have let your own children watch these kinds of shows when they were younger?

MRS. BROWN: Charlotte wouldn't really understand them. Not that kind of kid.

YURT MAKERS: Your other children. The two you abandoned in Ukraine when you ran off with the American?

MRS. BROWN: Oh, I see what this is. Someone called the morality police. Go on. Arrest me. Drag me to morality prison, then, make me sit through morality plays about bad mothers. Never mind the countless mothers I've fought for over the years. Better maternity benefits, employment protection, the right to breastfeed at work.

YURT MAKERS: Not one phone call to your daughters, Mrs. Brown? Not one letter?

MRS. BROWN: It was—is—for their own good. Before I left Kyiv, I was being followed again. I didn't want to implicate them. And any contact could've gotten me traced and blown my cover. The less my daughters knew, the better for all of us.

YURT MAKERS: You were being followed, you say. By whom?

MRS. BROWN: I don't know. The police? Secret service? Whoever you "yurt makers" are? Loads of people out for my neck. How many weddings had Komod sabotaged? How many foreign delegation luncheons had we crashed? Never get on the wrong side of the wedding industry, let me tell you. Behind every boutonnière hides a pin primed for your aorta. We used to get all kinds of threats, you know. One of our photographers got jumped, beaten.

YURT MAKERS: Yet you seem relieved to be found.
MRS. BROWN: Do I?
YURT MAKERS: Happy, almost.
MRS. BROWN: Ever had bedbugs?
YURT MAKERS: What kind of hovel do you think we're in the business of crafting?
MRS. BROWN: Betty Thompson down the road wouldn't admit to them either, not at first. Snuck in a fumigator truck disguised as HVAC maintenance, guest-parked without a permit and bam! The homeowners association got her. Anyway, years later she told me she still didn't trust her own skin, any tingle became a bite, and she was convinced they were back, that they'd only been dormant. She almost wished they'd come back just so she'd know she wasn't going crazy.
YURT MAKERS: During your months of hiding, your only pursuers were your own two children, Mrs. Brown.
MRS. BROWN: Of course, it's my loving children who just tied me up mid-rehearsal.
YURT MAKERS: Komod hadn't operated in years. Why else would your so-called enemies pursue you?
MRS. BROWN: You really don't know.
YURT MAKERS: As far as we know, you had retired.
MRS. BROWN: Retired! What an awful word. Like being shoved onto a dusty shelf. No, back in Kyiv, I was trying to start a new Komod. A better one. Fresh blood, so to speak. A hundred trafficked brides had disappeared in China last year, and I knew my work was not done. I started going to university campuses, shadowing rallies to see which girls yelled proudest, whatever the cause. I don't know how it happened—maybe some old enemy recognized me, knew I was getting back in the game—but I remember the feeling distinctly, like I was in the crosshairs again. My whereabouts noted, filmed. Whenever I saw anyone pull out their phone, heard the Morse code tapping of fingernails against screens . . . I knew I had to go dark. And that's when I met Mr. Brown.
YURT MAKERS: Nice man?
MRS. BROWN: Nice as they come.

YURT MAKERS: A marriage agency client, we've heard. What you'd call a bride buyer, no?

MRS. BROWN: When we met, he was just a man who stood next to me at a subway station stall, picking out glass figurines for his daughter. By the time we were on our third round of drinks and I found out why he'd come to Ukraine, it was too late. I already liked him. How excited he got, when I told him I'd dreamed of being an actor once, starring in movies or on the grand stage. He told me about his neighborhood theater tent, built by the Educational Hobbies Committee. I'd get full run of it, he said, since no one ever used it.

YURT MAKERS: This is how he wooed you? This sorry, underventilated structure?

MRS. BROWN: Well, no. At first I found the proposition insulting. Threw my coat back on, about to march out of the bar. He didn't know me at all, of course. Took me for someone who could settle for a hobby. But his excitement about the theater tent was so innocent, genuine. I started to wonder, what if I *could* be a hobby person? Lead a quieter life, for once? So I sat back down.

And like I said, I needed to get out of the country for a while. Here was an opportunity for escape, protection. Gated communities are always on lockdown against an invisible enemy, aren't they? Kyiv has places like this too now, like that Lego-inspired abomination Comfort Town, but the idea of a walled neighborhood was still wondrously exotic to me. Especially American ones. Here were these freedom-loving Yankees who hated any whiff of centralization, of a nanny state, Sovietism, and yet they were willingly shutting themselves behind perimeter walls and bending to the most minute rules—like when you can put up and take down Christmas decorations and what shade of beige you can paint your door or how much your dog can weigh.

Mr. Brown figured out the paperwork. We didn't even have to get married for me to cross over, not right away. I was only going to stay in America a couple of months, I'd told myself.

Just long enough for that nagging feeling to go away, the feeling that I was being followed. But it hasn't gone away. And the bigger problem: I haven't stopped liking him.

YURT MAKERS: So you married.

MRS. BROWN: So I married. Became Mrs. Brown.

It's my final role, see?

Suburban housewife, president of the Tranquil Tides HOA council. Every morning Mrs. Brown wakes up in a pitch-black house, metal security shutters rolled over every window and door for the night. In every room hides a shotgun. A life people here call safe, and so it must be. On his way to work, her husband drops off his (their) daughter at preschool while Mrs. Brown stays behind the high adobe walls of Tranquil Tides. She walks the dog along Burbling Brook Alley or Rushing River Road or Surfside Avenue, wishful names that almost make her forget she's in the middle of a spreading desert. You'd think she'd be bored out of her mind, Mrs. Brown, but there's plenty to do here. Board elections to oversee, architectural variance cases to steer, aesthetic standards and property values to uphold. Her quiet proposal and passing of Covenants, Conditions, and Restrictions that contradict each other might make it seem as though she's deliberately trying to sow chaos between residents, undermine the hegemony of the HOA from the inside out, but that's not it at all. She's just forgetful, more so recently.

Most important, there's the little theater on Crescendoing Creek Crescent. That nobody goes to Mrs. Brown's shows—except the odd twenty-something-year-old high on weed—does not matter. She doesn't need much of an audience. Sometimes, on a rare rainy night, she swears she can see the distant glow of L.A.'s lights reflecting off the clouds, and that's as big a slice of Hollywood as she needs. A different woman would be drawn to the light, moth to a flame, but not this one, not anymore. She imagines, sitting in the first row of theater seats, the two daughters she hasn't seen in a long time, much longer than eight months ago. The girls she imagines are still small, pigtailed, and they still look at her as if she can do no wrong. That's who the shows are for. These daughters would love them.

YURT MAKERS: There's a war on, did you know? Fifty-two hours on, and you still haven't called them.

MRS. BROWN: I do know, but nice try on the emotional blackmail. If I were going to call them, I wouldn't tell you anyway. I'm not in the habit of divulging plans.

YURT MAKERS: It's been too long.

MRS. BROWN: You'd said they were my only pursuers these past months. *Were.* As in, they've given up? Moved on?

YURT MAKERS: Find out for yourself.

MRS. BROWN: What if they won't forgive me for leaving? The longer I stay, the more I'm convinced they won't.

YURT MAKERS: Go on, try them. Tie the loose thread.

MRS. BROWN: And then what, we'll have perfection? Harmony? I'm with the Persian rug makers on this one. Leave a thread loose. For the lord, so to speak.

YURT MAKERS: Fear does not suit you, Iolanta. Call them.

MRS. BROWN: You'll need to untie me first.

YURT MAKERS: You will not run away?

MRS. BROWN: Try me.

48

A light vibration, like a wasp trapped in a jar. Almost imperceptible at first, the sound came from the passenger side, front. It must be the same wheel as before, when Yeva had first heard that sound months ago and discovered the loose nut. Not a big deal if caught and tightened early, but eventually the studs underneath wear down and the wheel could fly off, as had once happened to the conservationist (this time, it was easier to forget his name). Yeva glanced at the sisters beside her. They didn't seem to notice the vibration. Yeva must be imagining it, a cruel trick of her mind when they needed to keep moving.

At each checkpoint out of Kherson, when soldiers demanded to see Yeva's documentation, she had to bite the sides of her cheeks, willing herself to keep quiet as she handed over her passport. Willing herself not to scream, why do I need to show you anything? I'm on my own land, you're the intruder. At the second checkpoint, soldiers surrounded the lab, scoped the underside, ordered the men inside to get out for a strip search behind a brown tarp. The men returned pale and tight-lipped. At the fifth checkpoint, soldiers blocked civilian traffic until a military column passed through. At the sixth checkpoint, the soldiers said they were only letting nine more civilian cars through that day, and Yeva got lucky, just slipped through. At the seventh checkpoint, the car in front of Yeva's lab got let through, only to be shot at for no apparent reason. The car went on for a while before swerving onto a shoulder, rolling to a stop in a wheat field. An eighth checkpoint, a ninth. How many more?

The vibrating sound was getting worse. But so long as Nastia and Sol behaved normally, whatever normal meant, Yeva could ignore it.

Just keep driving, Yeva told herself. She peered at the jar in her cup holder. Perhaps, while Yeva and the sisters had been trying to extricate that octogenarian from his apartment, the snails had gotten the deed over with furtively, away from prying eyes. Yeva and the sisters hadn't been gone long, but who knew, the world was full of possibility again. A one-in-forty-thousand chance these two could even be in the same jar, yet here they were. These two might just be the beginning, and one morning she might discover a clutch of hatchlings. A new beginning—for Yeva, too. She'd rescue snails again, assemble teams all over Ukraine, inside enemy lines and out. The world was watching now, renowned ecologists crying foul at the catastrophe unfolding in Europe's own backyard. With outcry comes funding, and with funding comes staffing, especially after the war ended. The math was that simple.

But for now, as far as Yeva could see, the snails kept apart. After that first sniff on the acacia tree, it was as though they were already over each other.

And yet, whenever Yeva witnessed this standoff, didn't some small part of her, a very small part, smaller than the snails themselves, rejoice? Feel a sweet tingle of vindication? Wasn't it enough to be in one another's company without having to stab each other with darts? They weren't starved for sex, did fine without. Could gnaw on some lichen. Suction up a glass wall and fall off, just to feel the thrill of gravity, air on rippling slime, and repeat. Or was it a sense of loyalty that kept Lefty in his corner? Lefty, destined to be alone in the end, just like Yeva.

Oh, shut the fuck up, Yeva told herself. Stop trying to stuff warped human thoughts into creatures who don't have brains. To drive all the way into Kherson, to endanger the lives of everyone in her mobile lab (who'd chosen to join, but still), to pluck a snail from the maw of the enemy, to endure all this, only to rejoice at her rescuees' inaction?

The vibrating sound pulled Yeva's attention back to the road.

It was loud enough now for Sol and Nastia to turn to her in worry.

The chances of the wheel flying off were low, Yeva was sure, but if it did, they'd be sitting ducks. How many more checkpoints, how much longer until they were on safe land again? She took her foot off the accelerator. It could still be a loose nut, a quick fix.

49

LYOSHA AND VALIK are out here, a patch of willows between bare fields, waiting for their next order. Although they don't know what the current order is, either. Radio down, phones taken away back in Russia. They have two tanks, but one doesn't roll and the other doesn't shoot, so they wait. Maybe more will come, maybe not. All Lyosha knows: he's fucking bored. Valik dozes in one of the tanks, the one that shoots, while Lyosha stays under his willow watching the road for Ukropy. Sort of watching. His mind is back in that nice big house he'd seen yesterday. A local had slipped the address to the sergeant, promising it was the nicest house in town. Held a grudge maybe, or just didn't like soldiers pacing up and down his own fence. By the time Lyosha and Valik found out about that house and tracked it down, four streets over, it had already been picked over by the other guys—drawers flung out, electric kettle swiped off its base, Wi-Fi ripped out of the kitchen wall, but there was still some stuff left. A sporty family, must've been. Had a whole set of spare road bike tires, a pantry full of vitamins, fancy protein powders. A garden with its own furniture, that special kind made of straw, what's it called? There's a word for it. Sometimes the set includes fussy cushions you take inside for the winter, and when he checked for them, there they were, white and plump like they'd never been sat on, stacked in their own closet under the staircase. Their own closet! And in the warm months, when the cushions got set out, did the closet just sit empty and unused and not full of other shit? There must be some sort of rotation of stuff. He'd been about to show Valik but thought against it. Valik would've booby-trapped the closet's accordion door with an explosive, as he'd already done with the fridge and piano and washing machine—what he called homecoming gifts. Once Lyosha snagged a car, what if he came back alone for the cushions? For now, he'd helped himself to the vitamins, some shirts, the tight slippery kind. You can always use a shirt.

From under his willow tree, Lyosha hears the distant whir of a diesel engine.

Then he sees it: the big white bus barreling down the road. Or, not a bus. More like a vacation RV, like you see on TV. Through his binoculars he spies the child's drawing of a pair of hands holding a sprout. Not the typical kind of rig you see these days down these roads. Maybe it's one of his own who's driving the RV, making off with it. How he'll get a thing like that back across the border is a mystery. Could go through Belarus, change the plates there, Lyosha has heard. The RV's heading west, though, so it's probably some rich Ukrop family skittering off. They lived nice before, had a big garage with a door and a lock, and now they've left it all, now they'll live the same way as Lyosha lived back in his muddy village. Except, of course, they'll have the RV. So they're still better off.

The RV stops. Doesn't park on the shoulder, smart. The 36th mined it yesterday, that spot or another. Someone's coming out of the RV. The binoculars are shit, so he gets his gun, where the scope is better. Through his crosshairs, sees her. Thick black hair, long legs. Girl like that, driving a thing like that, now he's seen everything. She's kneeling by the front wheel, lug nut in hand, like she knows what she's looking at, playing mechanic. If he wasn't dozing, Valik would've shot her by now. Valik says they need to be wiped off the map, not just the men, the men are just the surface weed, you need to get at the root, yank it right out to keep more from cropping up. Lyosha, though, he doesn't care one way or the other. His village is as far from Moscow as from Ukraine, these places are all the same to him. He's getting paid, no use getting fanatical, it's a job. Anyway, Lyosha has a better plan. He aims for the tire. If he can blow the tire out, the Ukropy will have to set their coffees down and peel themselves off their vinyl inset couches and file out one by one and walk the rest of the way in the snow, no more RV. It's out of love, really. Valik says that these people, actually they're our brothers. Our little brothers who lost their way. Stuck their noses out, thought themselves better, and so they got themselves their European cars and vitamins and wicker furniture sets (sarang! That's it, it's called sarang) until their souls got corrupted.

One blown-out tire, and they'll become brothers again.

Lyosha pulls the trigger. Misses the tire.

He turns around and sees Valik, who's been watching him. Valik gets his own binoculars out, better than Lyosha's, slaps him on the back. "Look at that," Valik says. "Clean shot."

50

THE FLESH SPLITS, but there's no pain. The act feels years, centuries in the making. It's her dart that pierces his wet, buttery underside first, just as he rears up. He retaliates with his own dart, long and white and curved, narrowly misses her heart. They're both still, stunned. Her flesh froths at the point of penetration. Could've died then and there, taken the entire species down with them. Suctioned onto the side of the glass jar, they look like they're levitating.

After a moment, they throw themselves at each other, slime on slime, more alive than ever. Stroking, probing, pulsing, darts still stuck in each other's gyrating bodies. Their shells coil in synchrony, their shapes made for each other, clink into place. And that smell! You could get lost in its sulfur, never see daylight again.

In a future where all *C. surculus* are left-coiling, Yeva will live on in their synapses, pass through generations. They will have a predilection for stale coffee, for sunburnt hair, the cloying taste of latex gloves.

51

IT ALL UNFOLDED before Nastia, yet none of it felt real. She felt as if she was still part of the movie set, the director's voice booming from above. Get out of the cab, the voice instructed. Descend toward the woman on the ground lying in pooling red. Shake her, but she won't answer, so you'll lift her right up. Lift her right up, that's it. You're already lifting her up with a superhuman strength, like she's made of Styrofoam, when the passenger door opens. Your sister's arms reach through to catch the woman and pull her in, lay her on the middle seat. The wails are a titch melodramatic, Sol, tone it down. Nastia, you're already back in the cab, behind the wheel, and you don't see where this blood is coming from. Her shoulder? Kiss the top of Yeva's head now, kiss it better. There, there. Now jam your foot on the smaller pedal, the one at the very right, the gas. Middle is the brake, but we won't need that for a while, and on the very left, the one that looks just like the brake, is the dead pedal, that nice place for your other foot to rest, just like we learned, see? Jam the gas now, whiplash us, go, get the hell out of here. What great practice. Isn't it nice, how Yeva taught you to drive?

52

A THUMB WAS STROKING Yeva's hand, rhythmic, methodical. Whose? Nastia was to her left, Sol to her right, and both were still, lying naked in the swamps. They'd been drinking. When? Must've been during one of the pit stops, bachelors packed into the back of the lab, right before the invasion. When they'd stopped to stretch their legs, and the sisters complained of the mosquitoes, and Yeva said, I have a trick for that. A moment later they'd lain naked, Yeva between the sisters, arms tight to the sides, as though for burial. Peace and utter stillness, as if the mosquitoes had grown suspicious of three warm sacks of blood offered up so openly.

That's the moment to fall back to, yes. Something nice, think of something nice. Her mother's voice, what she'd always said, from the time Yeva was small and inconsolable, angry at something or other.

But Yeva needed to get up, she remembered now—there was a fight she hadn't won, a last word she hadn't gotten in. When she tried to move, the sucking swamp kept her still.

Yeva felt herself shivering, set her jaw against the cold. And all at once the insects were upon her and the sisters—and not just mosquitoes, but whatever else hatched in these shallow waters. Night gnats, flies. A scratchy, stinging blanket covered their bodies, the softness of Yeva's thighs. To her right, Sol cursed, and Yeva reminded her not to swat or scratch. It took the last of her strength to follow her own advice. This was worse than that first time she'd lain in the swamps, beside that boy who'd shown her the mosquito trick, the first boy she'd slept with. The trick didn't work, not really. She knew now it was only magical thinking. To her left, a slap. Yeva took Nastia's cold hand in hers, then she took Sol's. Which of the sisters laughed? They all knew it was a terrible idea. Maybe the insects would suck them dry, leave three pale bodies to rot away in the swamps. Yet instead of giving up, the sisters rolled closer, pressed their blue moonlit skin against hers to seek, by instinct, mammalian warmth. Yeva didn't know how long they stayed huddled. She'd been waiting for this moment for as long as she could remember, to know if it was possible to be present with another's body and for that to be enough. Only their warm breaths mixed: Sol's sour but pleasantly so, lemony, while Nastia's still held the scent of boiled eggs from dinner. Or was that the swamp's sulfurous sighs? The swamp opened under her, softened, and Yeva let herself sink. But she needed to get up, she remembered. A fight, a last word. Her mother's voice again: Let it be, Yeva, just let it be. Think of something nice. Was it before or after the war, lying in the swamps with the girls? Either way, the mosquitoes wouldn't have hatched yet, not till spring. When was it, the swamp with the girls? Get up. Stay down. Let go. Think of something nice.

53

THE ROAD SIGN promised a town in thirty-nine kilometers. There must be a hospital there, surely. (And a train station for the bachelors, Sol said, still dwelling on such details.) As Nastia tore down the highway, left hand clutching the steering wheel, right hand clutching Yeva's, her phone lit up again. Probably Masha calling to tell Nastia what she already knew: the deal was off and she shouldn't bother meeting at the border.

But no, this was an international number. The sight of the chain of digits, overwhelming in its length, made Nastia certain of two things: one, the caller was her mother; and two, Yeva would live.

She knew these two truths precisely because her hand, the one that gripped Yeva's, did not reach for the phone. Nastia could do it, could let go for a moment—she had no illusion that just by stroking Yeva's hand she was sending some primal signal, keeping her alive, but the very fact that Nastia could afford the missed call, afford the possibility of never speaking to her mother again, was a signal. A restructuring of the world around her, a tilting of its balance. The way Earth's magnetic field can become jumbled and even flip, as Yeva had once told her: north becomes south, south becomes north. But before this happened, the weakening poles might wander over the planet, split into multiples, cause migrating birds and whales to flounder. When had this lessening, this letting go, begun? Was it when she'd found out about Nevada, her mother's new family? Or did it start before that, when she met Yeva? When she presented her so-called project proposal for the kidnapping, and Yeva looked at her with both horror and pride. Or was it before even that, when her mother had not yet gone definitively, but by small strokes every night?

"It's here," Sol said, hands buried in the ripped red mass of Yeva's coat. She'd found the wound. "What are we supposed to do?"

Lemon and salt and sunlight—that was all Nastia knew to say. As if the stain would disappear like magic.

They raced through a birch forest. She glanced at Yeva and caught a flutter of her eyelids, a good sign. Nastia had to distract her, like one distracts a child before she realizes she's fallen, bumped her knee. "Yeva, look." Nastia nodded at an old log up ahead, lolling into luxurious chocolate chunks along the side of the road. Rotten logs, cradles of new life, now in shorter and shorter supply: an obsession of Yeva's. Something about nutrient cycling, calcium carried from log to snail shell to bird stomach back to saplings. Nastia had to keep remembering the wondrous things Yeva had told her about the world, keep this knowledge coursing between her and Yeva's body like shared blood.

Was that a nod from Yeva? Had she seen the log, too? She must have.

Love, like those wondrous logs, was a finite resource. Not just her mother's, but Nastia's, too. She kept her grip on Yeva's hand, still warm, as she watched her phone screen go dark again.

If Nastia had let go of one, she would have the other.

PART IV

54

IF I REALLY FOCUS, I can end the war.

In its beginning, while chanting "NATO! Close the skies!" at downtown Vancouver rallies, I knew how I'd end it: a solid iron shield would slide over Ukraine, protecting its people and land from Russia's incessant bombardment.

But why cut Ukraine off from the sun?

No, I'd cover Russia. A sarcophagus built over the entirety of Russia, much like the one built over the radioactive remains of the Chernobyl disaster, so that Russians could stop wreaking havoc on neighboring countries. Let them figure themselves out, their mysterious bottomless souls, within their own borders.

Or, another way to end it: each missile shot from Russia would stop midair, spin around, pummel into its exact point of origin. (Not impossible: a video had circulated on the internet of a Russian missile losing steam midair, hurtling straight back down to Russian soil.)

My awareness of the ridiculousness of the fantasies, of my mortal inability to make them come true, did nothing to stop the fantasies.

When I was eleven years old, an episode of a daytime talk show convinced me of the supernatural power of the mind. That afternoon, the guest on the show instructed how to bend spoons through sheer mental focus, then conducted an exercise enabling the live audience and television viewers to glimpse their own futures. I saw myself, age twenty-one, on an operating table about to undergo open-heart surgery, which I would not survive. (I'd begun having what I thought were heart attacks, which later proved to be harmless palpitations.) I've outlived my own prediction, and I know I can't bend metal with my eyes, yet this past year I've become convinced again of the power of the mind.

The most debased of the fantasies: all this happened so that I could write about it.

Four years ago, something terrible happened to someone dear to me, someone very private. My best friend, let's say. Let's say that the terrible thing was blood cancer. While she underwent chemotherapy, I stayed in the hospital room with her and kept a log. My official reasoning was practicality: we could inform family and friends who kept checking for updates with a single link, rather than individual texts, phone calls, and emails. I played my role as chronicler dutifully, sleeping on the hard foldout in her room, going back to the motel only to shower. My real reason was to make myself believe that something good and artistic could come of all this mess. Otherwise, how to square away the situation which the doctors called an "enigma inside a puzzle," a thirty-year-old with chronic lymphocytic leukemia, a disease that normally struck the elderly and, in those cases, was often left untreated? And this had happened not just to any thirty-year-old, but to one I happened to prefer above most people and who didn't deserve this mess. (Another fantasy: disease befalls only sinners.) As long as I saw her predicament as material, a good story, I could live through it, and by some irrefutable logic, so could she.

I wrote the Log. She recovered.

The fact of her survival only bolstered my delusions.

The Log was what I liked to think of, at the time, as a success. I couched the ugly parts in humor to make them palatable (for my readers? For myself?). There was the part about the "smart" hospital bed, probably among the most expensive in the world, glitching and barking commands at the nurses. The woman who joked that she'd tried to put on as much weight as possible pre-chemo to look all the better for her coffin. Friends confessed they enjoyed reading the Log. A nurse friend passed it to other nurses, arguing the Log was useful as a patient's viewpoint on the caregiving process.

Useful. That was the word I'd been looking for. Not for the Log itself, but for her cancer.

Here I am again, trying to make use of another cataclysm.

Am I no better than a snail, sniffing out the softest, most rotten part of a log to feast on? At least a snail digests the rot and excretes nutrients, useful.

55

My sister and I consider returning to Ukraine on another trip. On the six hundredth day of war, I still dream of arriving at my grandfather's door in Kherson. We plan to stay mostly in Kyiv, but I tell myself there's a possibility we'll make it into Kherson this time, even though the shelling has been getting worse, closer to his building. I don't want to think about what Kherson looks like now, what's left of it, so I try to focus only on my grandfather's door, which I know, at the time of this writing, is still standing. There's no more delusion on my part, though. Our visit will not be an evacuation.

I understood this only after I landed in Ukraine on that earlier trip, the one where my sister and I made it as far east as Kharkiv but couldn't go on to Kherson. Friends back in Canada had tried to convince me not to go to Ukraine. Was I really thinking it through? Why go now, of all times? Their words felt heavy on my shoulders, but as soon as I landed in Ukraine, their worries seemed far away, a choice they had made, something I had not asked for. My sister and I went about our days. We got haircuts, we went to the opera. We ate cake. The smallest actions felt defiant, a middle finger to the aggressors trying to chip away at every joy. The front line felt far away, solid and unmoving, more wall than fire. There would be an occasional sound in the distance I couldn't recognize or account for—but for better or for worse, I believed I could control how close I came to the war, or how close it came to me. Don't we all share delusions like these, even (or especially) in peacetime? That death won't find us, not today?

Whoever comes to my grandfather's door, whether it's Nastia or myself and my sister, it doesn't matter. In the end, the wannabe rescuer will leave, and my grandfather will stay behind.

His books, his streets lined with acacia trees, his salted herring wrapped in newspaper, his shot glass—eternally, magically sterile—his trusted locks, his cattail marshes, his dacha or what will be left of it. His eighty-seven years. The years still ahead of him, I hope, years that are his and his alone to spend.

Of course he'll say, "I'm not going anywhere."

But I'm getting ahead of myself, already envisioning the parting.

His steel outer door and red-upholstered inner door will swing open. He'll have been expecting my sister and me. For a moment he'll simply stand there, beaming while his radio chatters on in the background. Then he'll spread his arms—

But I'm getting ahead of myself here, too. I may never see him again. My sister says she hopes that if he does leave us for good, it'll be quick and painless.

As I complete revisions on this book, it's Day 914 of the war. In Kherson, the few remaining residents traverse the streets under the cover of trees, constantly on alert for any buzzing. A grenade or mortar might drop from the sky at any moment. Russian drone operators stationed across the Dnipro are using the region as live target practice. These targets, many of whom are elderly or disabled and move slowly, must be easy prey.

I haven't made it back to Ukraine. At this point, I'm not sure when that will be.

Years ago, my grandfather invited me to come live with him

for three months so that we could spend our days talking. He'd tell me about his favorite writers, his favorite books, the ones he'd spent a lifetime collecting. He'd tell me more about his life under Soviet rule, more than what I'd already recorded during previous visits, which flew by, each a couple of weeks at most. No, this time we'd take our time. Every day we'd sit down for tea, or beer with salty fish. He likes to talk, can talk endlessly. Usually I get tired of it, start to squirm, ache to go outside and stretch my legs, but in this other scenario, this other fantasy, I won't. I'll sit and listen hour after hour as the sun arches over the kitchen window and the shadows circle, as the acacia leaves fall and regrow.

EPILOGUE: PASHA

Art Talks: Bridging Understanding with Paul Gurka

[Recorded by the Canadian Broadcasting Corporation on October 16, 2023]

INTERVIEWER: Today we have the distinct privilege of introducing you to a painter whose work has captivated audiences across the globe. He has become known as the chronicler of life in Kherson under military occupation, then liberation, then flooding, and now the continuing shelling by the Russian military. Please welcome Paul Gurka.

PAUL GURKA: Please, call me Pavlo.

INTERVIEWER: Pavlo, let's start at the beginning. You were born in Ukraine but lived in Canada for most of your life. How did you end up back in Ukraine, specifically in Kherson? In these times?

PAUL GURKA: I was on an organized tour, sightseeing. Then the war broke out.

INTERVIEWER: And so you found yourself in Kherson, the first major city to be occupied. What was that like?

PAUL GURKA: I have very few memories of the early days, to be honest. There's this quote by Constantine Tereshchenko, a local visual artist: "Culture is the thinnest layer of moss on the body of human existence. It was shaved off with a bulldozer, now there's an enormous wound."

INTERVIEWER: Did you try to get out?

PAUL GURKA: I knew immediately I had to stay. I figured I'd be more useful here than back in Canada. I joined the protests against the Russians. That's how I met my now wife, who didn't want to leave, either, because she'd finally finished an eleven-year house renovation. And I bought a house, myself. Fully detached, two bedroom, two bath, with a sundeck and a guesthouse.

INTERVIEWER: People are still renovating over there? Buying houses?

PAUL GURKA: When you stop hoping, you might as well lie down and die, no?

INTERVIEWER: Show us your first painting, Pavlo. Describe it for us.

PAUL GURKA: It's a bridge. Specifically, the Antonivs'kyi Bridge, which is a box girder bridge. It's supported by thirty-one pillars, thirty spans, and its total length is 1,366 meters, with a width of 25 meters and pedestrian sidewalks on both sides measuring about a meter and a half each.

INTERVIEWER: And why did you paint this bridge? What does it mean to you?

PAUL GURKA: Well, it's gone now, first damaged by the Ukrainian army to disrupt Russian supply lines, then blown up by the Russians as they retreated, to stop the Ukrainians from advancing. So I guess we should speak of the bridge in the past tense. It traversed the Dnipro, the river that cleaves Ukraine in half. One side's landmass connects to Russia, the other to Europe. The bridge was valuable, fought over, as I said. The site of unspeakable violence. So I painted the bridge as it must have looked before all that happened, when it was just a bridge.

INTERVIEWER: Next painting. Another bridge. A different bridge?

PAUL GURKA: The same one.

INTERVIEWER: And the figures on it, there? Ghostly, twisted.

PAUL GURKA: No, no, it's the bridge on a car-free day. So it's all these pedestrians just walking across it. My wife says it's nonsense, there's never been a car-free day here, but I had to imagine it.

INTERVIEWER: Next painting. Ah, this one's entirely black.

PAUL GURKA: Not entirely, if you look closer. It's the bridge at night. Monet was allowed to paint the same wheat stacks over and over, so I figure, why not.

INTERVIEWER: Your family in Canada must miss you very much. What do they say about your paintings, your success?

PAUL GURKA: My parents always wanted me to be an artist. Though they say my paintings are just getting shown for political reasons, like all art these days. What do you think of them?

INTERVIEWER: Of . . . ?

PAUL GURKA: My paintings.

INTERVIEWER: The bridges are, ah, very anatomically correct. Your background in engineering on full display.

PAUL GURKA: I was going for more than anatomical accuracy.

INTERVIEWER: Of course. Greater truth, all that.

PAUL GURKA: Which is?

INTERVIEWER: I'm sure our audiences would like to hear your answer rather than mine.

PAUL GURKA: Art exists in the liminal space between the giver and receiver. Go on, I'm all ears.

INTERVIEWER: All right, if I may, what I see is a bridge between Ukrainians and Russians, a coming together, of sorts. A yearning toward peace.

PAUL GURKA: Why don't you just say it?

INTERVIEWER: I beg your pardon?

PAUL GURKA: You hate the paintings. You can hate them, all right? I want you to. Art is supposed to provoke reaction. In fact, the worst thing you can tell me right now, if you don't love them, is that you don't even hate them.

INTERVIEWER: Next painting please, Mr. Gurka.

PAUL GURKA: Next painting.

INTERVIEWER: A bridge.

PAUL GURKA: Disappointed?

INTERVIEWER: I do not hate your paintings, Mr. Gurka.

PAUL GURKA: It's what you all do, in the free world. You waste your freedom and your clear skies on things that don't matter, like politeness and the perfect lawn. That's why I can't go back. I lived in a stupor and now, it's like, all the colors are saturated. Like someone took electrodes to my eye rods and jolted them. You become like a lizard, where there's no past or future, where everything's trained on the present.

INTERVIEWER: Of course. Everything is brighter to a visitor.

PAUL GURKA: Excuse me?

INTERVIEWER: You *could* leave, if you wanted to? You have somewhere else you can live.

PAUL GURKA: Where? Tell me, where can I afford to live anymore?

INTERVIEWER: Ah! A conversation to be continued—I'm afraid our time is running out. Any parting words for our audience?

PAUL GURKA: Did you hear that? Just now? Another blast.

INTERVIEWER: No, I didn't. Not from here. Thank you for your time, and best of luck.